Her most sweeping,
passionate novel
of love and glory
in the heart of Texas...

"YOU NEED ME AND YOU WANT ME,"

Grayson said. "You've been needing a good roll in the hay for a long time, but there wasn't a man left in the South strong enough to gentle you."

He kissed her again. When he pulled away, tears were bright in her eyes. "There is no passion for you in me, Yankee. There will never be. Now get out!" Maggie cried.

"I'll leave," he whispered against her hair, "for I want you when you're not angry or hurt. When you come to my bed with only me in your mind."

He paused and held her tight, knowing that his heart would break if he couldn't make her someday understand. He kissed her forehead and almost ran from the room, taking only time enough to grab his hat and guns before vanishing into the hallway.

Maggie stood watching the door, knowing that his words were true. She loved Grayson Kirkland. She had loved him since the day he'd saved her life. She'd fight him every step of the way, but she had the feeling he was man enough to finish any battle he started . . . and man enough to teach her how it felt to be a woman. . . .

Praise for *The Tender Texan* by Jodi Thomas:

"Excellent! . . . Have the tissues ready; this tender love story . . . will tug at your heart. Memorable reading."
—*Rendezvous*

Diamond Books by Jodi Thomas

THE TENDER TEXAN
PRAIRIE SONG

PRAIRIE SONG

JODI THOMAS

DIAMOND BOOKS, NEW YORK

PRAIRIE SONG

A Diamond Book / published by arrangement with
the author

PRINTING HISTORY
Diamond edition / February 1992

All rights reserved.
Copyright © 1992 by Jodi Koumalats.
This book may not be reproduced in whole or in part, by
mimeograph or any other means, without permission.
For information address: The Berkley Publishing Group,
200 Madison Avenue, New York, New York 10016.

ISBN: 1-55773-657-X

Diamond Books are published by The Berkley Publishing Group,
200 Madison Avenue, New York, New York 10016.
The name "DIAMOND" and its logo are trademarks
belonging to Charter Communications, Inc.

PRINTED IN THE UNITED STATES OF AMERICA

10 9 8 7 6 5 4 3 2 1

This book is dedicated to my writing buddy,

DeWanna Pace.

She helps me celebrate each victory,
she cries with me at each loss,
yet, her red pen never stops.

PRAIRIE SONG

1

Texas, 1866

Train tracks ribboned the West, tying mankind together as they cut the land into bite-sized slices for civilization to digest. With the Civil War over, this was a time for new beginnings, for both Texas and Cherish Wyatt. She'd seen enough suffering to last a lifetime, and now, at twenty, she planned to drink her fill of happiness. Cradled inside her Pullman sleeper, she closed her eyes and drifted into a sound slumber. The roll of the train and the smell of a coal-oil lamp outside her compartment lulled her into a sense of safety as the train raced through the night.

Before the moon had completed its path across the inky blackness, Cherish was jolted fully awake by the sudden weight of a body falling across her. Without warning, the odor of blood and dirt assaulted her senses even as the mass of muscle pushed her into the bed. Instinctively, she shoved against her intruder and clawed across the covers for her gun. Though slight in build, she could hold her own in a fair fight. This thief would draw a full measure of resistance for his attack.

A gloved hand clamped over her mouth with a slap that echoed the cracks of lightning outside. "Scream," a low voice whispered, "or make another move, lady, and it'll be your last."

Cold steel slid along her ribs, hesitating over each bone as if calculating the easiest point of entry. Cherish felt the point of a knife, sharp enough to run her through, and knew this would be no fair fight. With each rock of the train, the blade punctuated danger.

Cherish froze. The sleeper space that had only moments before cocooned her now closed in like a coffin of blackness.

"That's better." The stranger's low words brushed her ear. "I need some answers and fast. When I lift my hand, if your voice is above a whisper, you'll be screaming in pain. Do you understand?"

Nodding, she gulped for air as the leather glove moved an inch away from her mouth. Though her eyes strained against the darkness of the sleeper, she could define only the outline of the man above her. But she could feel his lean, powerful body and smell the rage that oozed from him like salty sweat from a whipped horse.

"Who are you, lady, and what are you doing here?"

Anger swept over her fear and, as always, her temper came to the defense of the weaker emotion. "I was sleeping. That's what people usually do in these new things." She ignored his first question.

"I thought this sleeper was empty." he countered.

A moment of relief washed over Cherish as she realized the dusty stranger hadn't come to rob or rape her. Her voice came in nervous gulps. "I booked a ticket at the last minute."

Suddenly the train slammed to a stop and Cherish felt the intruder's weight lower over her. She could sense how large he was, and as his long, tight muscles rested on her, fear climbed into her heart. She was strong for her size, but this man could snap her in half.

The stranger muttered an oath of pain as he lowered his head against the pillow by her ear. The knife at her side pulled back an inch, but his leather-clad fingers slid around her throat to assure her that he was still in control.

He seemed to need a moment to think, as he relaxed against Cherish, imprisoning her completely with his body. His chest pressed into hers and Cherish felt a warm, wet pool between her breasts. Blood! She could smell it, feel it dripping on her gown until the material clung to her skin. With each pounding of his heart against her, his blood pulsed out onto her.

Cherish twisted slightly and heard him swear again as she whispered, "You're bleeding on me." The disgust in her voice was apparent. The thought of another man dying brought bile to her throat as it had so many times during the war when there had been little medicine and men seemed to die by the hundreds around her. If she'd been ten nurses she couldn't have eased all their suffering.

With a grunt of effort, he pulled an inch away, molding his body between hers and the back of the berth. "Sorry for the inconvenience." Laughter mixed with the pain of his whisper. His gloved hand moved slowly down to the pool of blood between her breasts. "But if I must spill my life's blood I can think of no softer valley for it to fall in."

As his knuckles brushed the damp material in the space between her soft globes, Cherish was shocked by his words and movements. Never had anyone dared touch her so.

A thin light shone through from the passageway and the stranger's shadow materialized. The outline of a strong jaw and dark straight hair falling across his forehead were her only clues to his identity.

Footsteps shuffled at the far end of the car. Cherish heard the unmistakable sounds of gun hammers being pulled back to full cock.

"Search everywhere, men! That son of Satan couldn't have gone far with the bullet I planted in him." A man's voice shouted orders that rang through the car as hollow and frightening as a coyote's howl through a box canyon. "To hell with an arrest. We'll see him hang before dawn!"

The knife moved once more against Cherish's ribs. "I have no desire to hang . . . nor to harm you." His voice was only for her ears, but the emotion touched her. It seemed a plea, not for his life, but to permit him to spare hers.

Nodding, Cherish felt the stranger's breath let out slowly against her cheek. "Roll behind me," she ordered as she reached beneath her pillow, bypassing her Colt to retrieve her handkerchief. With shaky hands, she pressed the cotton against the center of his chest, only guessing where the wound might be. Warm blood seemed to be everywhere.

Gloved fingers stopped her progress. "What are you doing?"

"I'm trying to stop the bleeding!" She pulled her fingers from his and pressed the cloth once more against his chest.

For a moment he seemed unable to speak. "It's not deep," he finally whispered.

"Well, press this over the wound or you'll bleed all over my bed."

A low laugh rumbled in her ear as the sounds of footsteps warned of men approaching.

Vainly twisting her petite frame to try and cover his, she pushed him against the wall. The knife stayed at her ribs, less threateningly now, but his free hand circled her waist, pulling her into the outline of his body.

With trembling hands, Cherish slid the velvety curtain a few inches aside and blinked into the lantern light of the corridor. "What is it?" The terror in her voice was valid, but didn't seem unlike the shouts from all the other passengers.

A large man removed his hat to reveal a head as hairless as an onion. He leaned forward and the badge on his vest caught a glint from the lantern. "We're looking for a murderer. We thought he dropped in here, but he must have just passed through the car. He has to be here somewhere. But don't you worry, miss. Before we pull into Bryan, he'll be meetin' his Maker."

As Cherish hesitated, strong fingers pulled her back, making her drop the curtain. The hidden intruder's heartbeat pounded against her back as his hand drew the material of her gown into his fist. Cherish lay stone-still, afraid to breathe. The anger, the power of *this* man frightened her as none other could, not even a wild Comanche or a hell-bent Yankee.

"Well, good night, folks." The lawman's voice faded away as he and his men shuffled out of the car. "Sorry for the inconvenience."

Moments crawled by in silence as the stranger held Cherish to him. She could feel his breath near her ear. His fingers pressed her solidly against him each time she would have moved away. Slowly, as the other passengers settled back into sleep and the train jerked to a start, the knife against her side eased its vigil of threatened death.

Finally, she could stand the tension no longer. She pressed her cheek against his and whispered, "I didn't give you away. Now go."

The stranger shifted until he was once more above her, but he wasn't resting his full weight against her. "Thanks," he whispered. The single word seemed hard for him to say.

Anger heated her cheeks in the blackness, for Cherish suddenly only wanted him gone. "I want no thanks for keeping quiet and not getting a knife slashed through my insides. Who is it you've killed? Another reluctant berth partner?"

The stranger laughed. "I'll bet you're quite a woman in the light. If you look half as good as you feel and smell, I wouldn't mind sharing a bed with you again some time."

"Try, and I'll be the one who spills your blood." She resented his tone. He acted as though she were a loose woman of the streets who was in the habit of having men drop into her bed. "Don't mistake my silence for weakness. Knife or no knife, if I hadn't detested the thought of watching a bleeding man hang, I would have turned you in. So, go! Bleed to death somewhere else and save the use of a good rope."

Low laughter was his only reply as he shifted and bit off his glove. With a violent movement, he gripped her face in the darkness, his fingers moving in strong bold strokes across her cheek. "If I am going to die before sunup, let me do so with the taste of you as well as the feel."

Without hesitation, he lowered his mouth over hers, silencing any cries of protest. His lips were hard and demanding; his hand held her face, allowing no escape, as his kiss deepened into an outlaw passion she'd never known. No stolen kiss she'd allowed in the shadows had demanded and given so much at the same time. His need was like a liquid fire that raced through every inch of his body and spread over her, warming her from an undiscovered chill.

With a sudden moan he broke the kiss, as though it would have been too painful for him to continue. His breathing was ragged and with a shock Cherish realized his stolen kiss had affected him more than he'd planned.

The darkness might hide his face, but she didn't miss the slight tremble of his fingers as he touched her bottom lip for an instant, then pulled away. "Until we meet again—in the light," he whispered.

Jerking her head sideways, Cherish felt rage both for his advance and for her own reaction to his kiss. "When we do, I'll take great pleasure in slapping your face. I swear if you ever dare touch me again I'll see you dead."

The stranger lifted his body from hers. "It would almost be worth the price."

A moment later he was gone, pulling the knife through the curtain behind him. Just for a flicker, the oil light in the corridor shone on his right hand and the wide bowie knife held tightly in his powerful grip. In the time of a blink, Cherish saw a scar above his wrist and committed the mark to memory.

2

The constant clattering of the train muffled the patter of rain streaking the window, but did nothing to ease Cherish's mind. With a stamina born from years of nursing, she forced her tired muscles to move with slow, silent skill. Long ago she'd learned that fear was no excuse for neglecting what had to be done. She stripped the sheets from the bed, washed her bloody gown, and dressed, even though the hour was not far past midnight. There would be no more sleep tonight. The wounded stranger had put an end to any peace. Just knowing that he was probably somewhere on the train with blood still seeping from his chest and a posse of hanging-hungry men after him made the hair on the back of Cherish's neck stand up. It was the same feeling she used to get when a doctor cut into some soldier's leg and the sickly sweet smell of gangrene filled the air.

Her ears strained with every muffled sound for gunshots. He couldn't survive for long, and jumping from a train at this speed would surely rip the wound beyond healing.

After pulling her mass of blond hair beneath the hood of her navy blue cape, Cherish snapped her bag closed and silently walked the length of the sleeper. She opened the car door as quietly as possible and stepped onto the tiny platform. The wind whipped rain into her face as if taking desperate slaps at her in her moment of exposure. Cherish twisted the icy lever of the next car's door and hurried toward the light. She didn't want to be alone. Not tonight. Not after what had happened.

The interior of the passenger car she entered was lined with worn red seats occupied by those who couldn't afford a private berth. Cherish slid unnoticed into a seat across from two sleeping children and relaxed. For a few hours, the mismatched travelers were like a small city, kindred in their journey. Classes of people who would never think of conversing in other circumstances smiled and nodded as they passed one another in the tiny aisle. Earlier, she'd watched them unwrap food and share supper as well as cigars and war stories. Now, most were sleeping, but a few men still talked together as if unwilling to allow the others to see them disarmed in sleep. They told stories of the war that had ripped the nation and touched every life. A few even colored the dusty night air inside the car with tales of the hard times in Texas when the army was gone and Indians and cattle ran wild.

Cherish sat quietly, studying each member of the car. They were blended like marble among the seats: farmers still in their sod-reddened clothes, gamblers down on their luck, women in the black of mourning with children sleeping in their arms—all rambling across Texas toward new hopes and faded dreams. As always, she could feel a part of each one she met. Somehow, she'd been touched by all the people in her life but had been close to none. Her heart poured out to them, but never embraced a single one. It was as though everyone else in her life were part of a play and she alone hadn't been given a part. She seemed always at the footlights, watching as everyone else lived out their roles.

Squinching down in the seat, she frowned, thinking of how she loved people and wanted to help them, care for them, mother them, yet she seemed incapable of receiving love. For her there had never been a man to hold her, comfort her, love her.

"Margaret," Cherish whispered, remembering her aunt. Although Margaret was only eight years older, she'd dedicated her life to standing at Cherish's side, but that wasn't the same as the kind of love between a man and a woman. Even Margaret had had that kind of love once. He'd held her in his arms only one night before he'd ridden off to war and left her a widow, but the memory of that one night seemed to be enough to last her a lifetime, for Margaret had never remarried.

Cherish pulled her woolen cape closer around her and moved her head from side to side to release the tension. She'd been attacked an hour before by a man who had held her at knife-point and threatened her life. He'd touched her and kissed her as no one had ever dared; yet she sat silent. Even now she wondered why she didn't tell someone. Was it because her nurse's training went out to a dying man and she wanted no part of causing him more pain? Or was it because she'd have to admit to herself feelings she had never accepted? Had he jolted her from her observer's perch? For one moment had she been totally alive and not just watching others live?

Suddenly the train began to brake and people shifted like supplies in a wagon bed. As everyone settled back into place, an old man, looking like a bundle of rags, rushed into the car. He gulped to catch his breath and shoved his long, matted hair from his face.

"They caught the murderer!" he shouted. The old man slammed the door closed. "We're stoppin' ta take on water, an' they're gonna decide what ta do with him." He smiled a gum-lined grin. "Looks like we might have us a hangin' right off the water tank."

People scrambled to their feet as though free tickets had just been announced.

The barker smiled to himself. "I figured none of you'd want ta miss it. What a sight it's gonna be. A hangin' in the middle of nowhere. It'll be somethin' ta tell."

Cherish hugged herself as she fought the urge to vomit. The woman across the aisle awakened her children as joyously as if it were Christmas morning. A few of the men in back began to make bets on whether he'd jerk for a while or drop straight with his neck broke.

All at once the old man was an expert, passing among the crowd, talking and laughing and being thanked for spreading the news.

As he neared Cherish, he sank to one knee. "Ain't nothin' ta be afeared of, miss. He's just gettin' what he deserves. I hear tell he's sent many a man ta meet his Maker."

"I don't want to see him die," she managed to whisper.

The old man patted her shoulder as though he were her father. "I understand that. I felt much the same way the first time I saw a hangin'. Two black bucks, back 'fore the war, swung from the same branch. They was accused of attackin' a white girl. Town got so upset, they didn't even wait till sunup. Since then I've seen my share of hangin's and they do tend ta sober a man up."

He looked toward the woman across the aisle who was pushing her sleeping son's arms into a coat. "You let that boy see this, ma'am, I promise ya he'll never step outside the law. All it takes is one hangin' ta put the fear of the Lord in a boy." He patted her child on the head. "Don't stand too close, son. When they die, they lose all control of their vitals."

Cherish jumped up and ran from the car. She could stand no more of the old man's talk. Welcoming the cold air against her burning face, she leapt from the step as the train pulled to a stop. The night was cloudy but the rain had halted, and darkness spread like a black quilt over the earth. Either the train had frightened off any creatures of the night, or they too sensed the impending death in the air.

Staring into the shadows, she remembered how excited she'd been only hours before when she'd boarded with a telegram from Margaret. It read, "Tobin's will was found. He left me the house he told us about. Meet me as soon as possible where we planned."

Now, before the train would take her any closer to her new life, a man would die. Somehow the grand house in Fort Worth didn't seem so wonderful.

"Better hurry, miss," the old man yelled, "or you'll be too late."

"Too late!" Cherish lifted her skirts. She had to hurry, not to see this hanging, but to stop it. Somewhere among all these people must be a man of reason. There must be someone who realized a man's life was worth more than a midnight intermission on a train ride.

Pushing her way through the crowd, Cherish spotted the bald deputy standing on the first step of the last car, his rifle crossed over his chest and cradled into the bend of his arm as he guarded his captive.

Cherish calmed her breathing, knowing this man would respond to no words of reason about the value of life. His mind was probably set as firmly as the wrinkles across his forehead, but she had to try. "I'm a nurse. I understand the prisoner is wounded. If you'll take me to him I may be of some help."

Several men laughed with the bald man. "I reckon he is wounded, miss. It was my bullet that plugged him. That was probably what slowed him down. He's pale as a ghost from loss of blood. But I can't see no use in you fretting over his wound when he'll be dead in a few minutes from a rope."

"But I must see him; he's dying," Cherish pleaded. "I could patch him up and maybe he'd live to make it to the next town where he could have a trial."

Again all the men laughed. "Don't see no use in that. Wouldn't want to disappoint all these folks after waking them up. He's in pretty bad shape, but he'll make it a few feet more."

Cherish thought of trying to push her way past the man but he outweighed her threefold. Her Colt would be useless against so many.

"I insist on seeing him." She lowered her tone as if she could order him to stand aside. "It makes no sense to hang a dying man."

"Better he gets what's coming to him before he leaves this world. You'll see him, miss, when everyone else does. As soon as the priest finishes with him, we'll march him right over to that tower."

All eyes followed his pointed finger to the shadow of the water tower looming above the trees. Even now a man was climbing the wooden structure with a rope slung over his shoulder.

Moving closer to the step, Cherish demanded, "Who is in charge? I will speak to him before this insanity goes any further."

"The man in charge, miss"—his hot breath stung her cold cheeks—"was killed a few hours ago by the man you're trying to save. Maybe if someone had hung this bandit a long time ago, the sheriff would still be alive."

"But are you sure you have the right man?"

The deputy laughed. "I was sitting in the office when he came in. Sheriff Moore was in the back. This killer walked right past me. The next thing I know, there's gunfire and he's running out." The deputy raised his voice for all to hear. "We were on his trail in minutes. He rode till his horse was played out, then jumped the train. He was either damn lucky, or he knew the time of this train, the way he seemed to ride toward it."

He motioned to the half-dozen men around the car. "We all voted, just like a jury, to hang this killer tonight. If we wait till morning, he might get his strength back and like a snake brought in the house to warm, he'd turn on us and maybe kill again before we could stop him."

A priest stepped from the car and all hope of delay died. She felt as she had so many times during the war when men were killing one another faster than she could save them.

The deputy nodded in respect and stepped aside for the priest to pass. "Thanks for offering him last rites. I know it weren't easy for you, Father, after being there when the sheriff was killed. But we wouldn't want to do anything that wasn't on the up-and-up." He glanced at Cherish, smiling as if he'd won the argument.

The people rattled like paper tied to the tail of a dust devil. The priest stood on the last step of the car and pointed toward the rope now swinging in the wind. "God's will," he shouted as all except Cherish turned to watch the rope.

She only stared at the hooded brown robes hiding the man of God. How could he be party to this injustice? Surely he lived by some code. As she watched, he turned and slowly lowered himself to the ground. For a moment his robe's sleeves pulled almost to his elbows. Cherish saw his knuckles whiten as though the two-foot drop to the ground had been a great effort. She saw the dark stains of blood on his hands and knew the stranger inside the car must still be bleeding.

Then, in the light of a dozen torches, she saw the scars on the priest's right wrist: scars silently telling of a man past pain, scars betraying the true identity of the man beneath the robes.

Cherish almost shouted aloud at her discovery. Then she bit her lip, sealing her mouth against betrayal. She glanced at the deputy. He was picking which men would go into the car and bring out their prize. When she glanced back to see the man in priest's robes, he had vanished into the velvet night, his robes blending with the tree trunks and the tall brown grass.

Deputies marched up onto the platform, waving at the crowd as if they were performers in a sideshow. The bald man took a few moments to deliver a speech as though he were running for office. All the deputies crowded around, their guns lifted high in salute. The bald self-appointed leader raised his hand, playing his moment of glory to the hilt. "This is a time of justice!" he shouted. "Now let justice's hand rule."

He moved into the car, both guns drawn as if he were storming a well-armed fortress. All his men hurried after him. In the span of a hungry wolf's howl, shouts echoed from the car to the waiting crowd. The people held their breath as more men rushed into the car, ready to hail some unheard bugle's call to battle. Women clutched their children. Gamblers and farmers alike pulled guns from concealed places and took a step forward.

Cherish stepped back, unable to hide the smile on her face and not wanting the others to see her joy. The jackals would have no prey to pull apart tonight.

She caught the glimpse of a lone figure lifting himself up atop the car. His white shirt was milky in the night, and his black trousers clung like a second skin against his thin thighs. She studied the figure as he moved as silently as a shadow along the length of the car. No wounded man could have moved so, and the constant tilt of his head toward the car, where all the deputies were, told her he must be the priest who traded places with the bandit.

Soundlessly, like a cat, he jumped from one car's roof to another and disappeared into the sleeper. Silently, Cherish applauded the friar, for he had succeeded where she had failed. He'd saved a man's life when she'd only talked.

A few minutes later he jumped from the steps, adorned once more in robes. Cherish moved toward him and away from the angry voices still coming from the car.

"You changed places with the wounded man." Her words were spoken as fact, allowing no room for argument.

"With your help," the priest answered. "If you hadn't spent a few minutes arguing with the deputy I never would have had time."

Cherish looked up. "Are you saying I was a part of his escape?" The meaning of his words sank full into her mind. These men were so anxious to hang someone, they might hang the accomplices as well. "Are you threatening me to keep me quiet?"

"No." Again his words were direct. "I'm thanking you for your help and asking you for your continued silence." He raised his hand to her shoulder. "The man out there in the darkness is bleeding. I ask for your mercy. You have my word he doesn't deserve the death these men have planned. Your silence will be all the help we need. No one will suspect I squeezed through the window and hung on in the darkness until all the deputies rushed into the car. They will simply think he got away while they were giving speeches."

His hand warmed her shoulder as his words touched her heart. "You have the face of the Virgin Mary. Do you have her compassion?"

Studying his shadow-lined face, she guessed that he was not past his mid-twenties, but his eyes made him seem far older. He had cold gray eyes, frozen by seeing so much pain, perhaps. She wished she could talk with him more. If the priest had been present when the sheriff was shot, why would he now save the murderer's life? "I saw nothing," she whispered.

He nodded and pulled his hand away as the crowd washed around them in a flash flood of disappointed, tired voices.

In the moonlight she saw the priest's left hand, pale against the night. Along his wrist were tiny scars identical to those she'd seen on the wounded man's right arm. Confusion clouded her face as she looked up for an answer, but all he did was pull his robe sleeve lower to hide the tie that somehow bound him to a killer.

"Good night, Miss Wyatt," he whispered before he vanished, leaving Cherish to guess how he could possibly have known her name.

3

Grayson Kirkland watched Margaret Alexander storm across the street and enter the stable for the third time in as many days. He'd followed her ever since the sheriff told him about the telegram naming her as heir to Tobin Tyler's house. Grayson was a Union officer assigned to Texas after the Civil War. His job was to check on any leads, no matter how slim, that might help the government discover the identity of members of a secret organization. But in this case, the lead and the lady were both pretty slim.

As far as Grayson knew, the old man named Tobin Tyler had nothing to do with the gang calling themselves the Knights of the Golden Circle. The connection lay somewhere with the house that had fallen into Tobin's hands during a card game six months ago. When the old man died violently, unexpectedly leaving his house to Margaret Alexander, it was enough to raise a few eyebrows at headquarters and get Grayson assigned to the investigation.

Now, he laughed at the irony that had pulled him off the trail to this assignment, which his superior had referred to as light. This woman was twice as prickly as sagebrush and a hundred times more volatile. Margaret Alexander was a headstrong widow in her late twenties and far more dangerous than a pack of rustlers in the badlands. He'd watched her storm and stomp her way through every place in town and it seemed that the only battle she lost was at the stables. She was not the kind of woman anyone would harness the word pretty to. The black she wore did little to flatter her already pale features and thin lines. She'd need all her charm and wit to talk the Irishman Sam McMiller out of anything in the stable. And though Grayson had no doubt about her wit, he'd measure her shy of a full load of charm.

Strolling across the street, Grayson melted his large frame into the shadows of the stable. He already knew the argument he'd hear there, but he admired this woman's stubborn will.

Her voice rang clear in the musty air. "I must rent a wagon *this* morning. My niece will be arriving in a few hours and we have to get to Fort Worth."

Sam McMiller, the owner of the town's only stable, stood his full height but still didn't reach higher than Margaret's shoulder. "Aye, lady, I've told you for three days. I ain't givin' a wagon and team to two women headin' across open country. The Indians will see that as easy pickin's."

Margaret raised one pointed finger like a weapon. "You're not worried about our lives, only your wagon?"

Sam shrugged. "Maybe so, but if you can't find a driver, you best think about bookin' a seat on the stage."

Propping her fists on her hips, she lowered her voice, deadly earnest. "I was raised in this country, as was my niece. I assure you, sir, that we are perfectly capable of taking care of ourselves."

"Maybe." Sam rolled a wad of tobacco around in his mouth. He might need to spit, but he wasn't doing it in this lady's presence. "Get yourself a driver and we'll talk."

Margaret's voice sounded tired for the first time. "I've already checked everywhere. With the cattle drives starting up, there doesn't seem to be anyone."

"Did you check the shanties down by the track? I hear there's some men just in from Ireland. One might drive for you."

"I can hardly pay what the railroad is offering them. You may think I have money to burn, but I assure you, I'll not waste a cent. Not for a job I could very well do myself." Her voice was hard. "And I'll not leave my things at the station until someone decides he has enough time to haul them north."

"Well, might check down by the saloons. I hear there's a few . . ."

Before he could finish she was on him. "Are you suggesting I get some drunken lowlife out of one of those cribs of disease to drive me and my niece to Fort Worth?" With loving tenderness, she touched a brooch pinned at her bustline. "My dear Westley is probably rolling in his grave at the thought."

Sam McMiller had obviously had enough of her high-and-mighty argument. "Well, dig dear Westley up and let him ride shotgun."

Grayson almost laughed aloud from the shadows as Margaret's face paled and her eyes turned a murderous black. "It's a sad thing"—she pointed a slender finger into Sam's chest—"when men like my brave husband die and spineless weasels like you are left. Get the wagon ready. I'll be back in an hour with a driver even if I have to dress a pig in pants."

Storming out of the stable, Margaret headed toward the row of saloons without a backward glance. Grayson followed, chuckling to himself. He didn't understand why Sam wouldn't let her go alone. Any Indian would be skinned alive by her sharp tongue before he could get close enough to aim an arrow. If she'd gone to war instead of her precious husband, Westley, the South wouldn't have lost.

To his amazement, Margaret entered one saloon after another. Stepping just inside, she waited for everyone to turn and stare, then announced her need for a driver and her price.

He saw no disappointment in her carriage as she gathered her skirts and moved on to the next place. Grayson knew as well as she did that her price was a fair one, but she'd already been outbid by both the railroad and the cattle bosses. Yet, if pride and determination counted, she would win.

Near the end of the street, the road disappeared into a shantytown where the poor and newly arrived immigrants set up camp. The houses were little more than crates or tents connected by rutted paths. Those who stood around in the morning sun didn't look strong enough to eat breakfast, much less drive a team overland through Indian territory.

As Margaret hesitated at the sidewalk's end, three men, coated in mud and staggering with drink, approached her. Grayson moved in closer to listen. His finely honed sense of danger set off an alarm, making his gun hand itch as he forced himself not to interfere.

"Begging your pardon, ma'am." The smallest of the three men removed his slouch hat, but his voice lacked any flavoring respect. "We heard your offer back there and wanted to ask you a few questions about this job."

Margaret held her ground and stared directly down at the little man. "I have a job to offer one man, not three."

The short man jabbed at his partners' ribs and flashed a yellowed grin. "We understand that, but we all wanted to talk with you. If you'll just step over here out of the sun."

In the time it took Grayson to blink, the three men and Margaret had disappeared behind the building. His stomach twisted with a dread tight enough to wring out all caution. He crammed his hat low and hurried across the street.

But when he stepped into the shadows between the buildings, nothing but the rustle of trash greeted him. He moved down the littered pathway, knowing the lady he'd been following was in big trouble.

He rounded the corner to the alley, and relief washed over him as Margaret's voice rang out clear in the morning air. "I told you gentlemen, I only need one man."

The tallest of the three impatiently pushed the assigned spokesman aside. He was large-boned and wide-shouldered, but his hollow cheeks told of hard times. "We ain't interested in any more talk. We know you're carrying cash if you're hiring. We figure you'll pay the three of us right now."

"I will not!" Margaret slowly backed into a corner, her head held high, her voice showing no fear.

"You'll pay us now, or you ain't taking no trip, lady," the large man hissed while his short partner's head bobbed as if tied to a wagon spring on a rocky road.

"Yeah," the little man added. "You pay up, or else. You wouldn't be the first woman Pete's killed." He pointed his thumb at the middle man, who'd been silent. This one called Pete was dark with eyes that reflected a dead soul. Brown spit dribbled from the corner of his large bottom lip as his fingers opened and closed in anticipation.

All three men moved on her like hungry animals on a butcher's scrap. Grayson hesitated only a moment. He was under strict orders not to tip his hand, but he couldn't just stand by and allow a woman, even a southern one, to be robbed or killed. He stripped off his coat and hat and flung them in the weeds; then he unbuckled his Colts and shoved them safely into a crack between the buildings. Three against one was not odds he favored, but it was better than drawing the whole town's attention with gunfire.

Margaret was still trying to bluff her way out of her corner. "Touch me and I swear I'll see you dead in hell."

The man laughed, but none seemed to want to make the first move. They circled her, staying just out of reach. The small one chimed out, as if proving his manhood, "We ain't frightened by no helpless stick of a widow. You can give us the money easy or hard, doesn't make us no mind."

Stepping into the sunlight, Grayson glanced up at Margaret as if he'd just stumbled upon the scene. For a moment their eyes met and he forgot about the three men. There, in the middle of impending death, she stood without a hint of fear. Her gaze silently asked for his help, but didn't beg. For the first time in his life, Grayson looked at a woman and didn't see frailty and weakness. Margaret Alexander was no whimpering southern belle to be sheltered and protected. As the flash of her dark blue eyes studied him, he somehow knew that she could have gotten out of this without his help. But he was already there and already committed.

The short man took one look at Grayson's reddish brown hair and rolled-up shirtsleeves and yelled, "Get out of here, you foreigner. Go back to your shack and leave us to our business."

Grayson stepped nearer, unsure of how to respond. He could hardly say he'd been following Margaret for three days and knew that she would have no business with the likes of these bar rats. Also, though his accent was barely detectable, one of the men might pick up on the fact that he was a Yankee. This far south, in an alley with drunken rebs, he could still be in danger even though the war had been over for almost a year.

The taller man snorted. "He don't understand what you're saying. Look at him, all clean and fresh off the boat. Just another big, dumb Irishman. Don't know enough to even wear a hat in this country yet."

Grayson decided to play on their assumption. He smiled as if they'd just invited him to visit and moved nearer. His talent for assuming a role might just give him the moment's edge he needed.

"Get lost!" The little man shoved Grayson with his elbow. Before the drunk could recover his stance, Grayson's fist slammed into his gut, lifting him off the ground.

Dust flew as the little man withered into a ball, cursing and ordering his friends to kill the Irishman.

Grayson smiled as the two other men came at him. There was nothing he liked better than a good fight with men who needed to be taught a lesson. He felt awkward around most folks, but in a fight, no man was his match—in this case, no two.

Blow after blow flew through the air and hit flesh. Grayson's body was solid muscle and his years of living in the saddle made him powerful and strong. Within minutes, two robbers lay in the dirt, bleeding and beaten. As Grayson straightened in victory, he heard the click of a gun being cocked behind him. The sound was like a rattler's tick; once you hear it, you never forget it.

"Raise those hands, Irish, and turn around!" The little man's voice was shaky and high with fright. "I want to see your face when I plug you."

Grayson growled in dread as he turned toward the thief. A movement near the lady caught his eye as a gun fired. For an instant, he thought he'd been shot; then he saw blood splatter across the little man's chest. The thief stared, dead-eyed, at Grayson for a moment, then dove into a pool of his own blood.

Twisting around, Grayson caught sight of Margaret's slender leg as she slid a derringer back into a holster strapped to her thigh. *No,* he thought, *this is no helpless female.*

When she looked up, their eyes met once more, and for the first time he saw a hint of uncertainty in the blue depths. "I only did what had to be done." Her words were as straightforward as always, but he didn't miss the slight unsteadiness. "I . . ."

The sound of people running toward the alley rumbled in the distance. Within seconds men would be upon them, and Grayson and Margaret would have a great deal of explaining to do. Even though it was a clear case of attempted robbery, Margaret would be delayed several hours and Grayson's cover would be destroyed.

With the quickness of a mountain lion's leap, Grayson swept Margaret into his arms and lifted her over his head and onto a flat-roofed shack. Before she could protest, he swung himself up beside her and pushed her low against the wood.

They lay in silence as men ran into the alley, searching for the troublemaker who'd fired a gun inside the town limits. Grayson felt her tremble beside him as the men below shouted, but she didn't utter a sound. She pressed near him as though she could hide her slender form next to his huge bulk. Slowly, hesitantly, he lay his arm over her shoulder for comfort and felt her curl into his embrace. He marveled at the contradiction. He would have thought her all bone and iron, crusted by the hard times of war, but she came to him as soft as a child.

They waited as the two robbers recovered enough from their beatings to tell the crowd about how they had been attacked by a gang of young thugs. As questions were asked and the story retold, it took on more and more texture, with no thread of truth in the weave. Finally, the dead man was carried off and all the sightseers left the alley.

Grayson wasn't sure if it was the sun's warmth or the heat of holding a woman so close, but suddenly he could stand their hiding place no longer. He jumped down from the roof and raised his arms to her. As she slid into his hands, he was intensely aware of the soft curves beneath her harsh black dress. The feel of her was like being in the eye of a tornado. All seemed quiet, but a storm raged around him. He couldn't remember the last time he'd touched a woman when he hadn't had several drinks. He'd sworn off females at twenty and, except for a few saloon gals he'd met, there had been no exceptions these past ten years.

Grayson closed his eyes, not wanting to remember the nightmare of his past, not wanting to allow any hope of a future. But the fresh smell of her eroded his determination. He found himself longing to pull her against him, to break the oath he'd made to himself the day he'd buried his wife.

When she turned to look at him, her face and eyes were sculpted ice. "I thank you for your help and I wish I could repay you in some way." She shook her head and patted him on the shoulder as if he were a slow-witted child. "I wish you understood what I'm saying."

Grayson almost laughed aloud. Maybe he'd saved her from a lot of questions, but she'd saved his life with the shot she'd fired, and here she was thanking him. This was more woman than met the eye. He stared at her as she straightened her dress and moved away. How could such a tight-lipped, straitlaced lady make him feel such a need when he thought his feelings had long been dead?

She was almost out of the alley before he recovered enough to act. Shoving his feelings aside, he concentrated on his job. On impulse he ran toward her and touched her shoulder.

"Yes?" She looked directly at him without fear.

"Job." He made his voice thick with an Irish accent.

Her mouth dropped open. "You want a job?"

Slowly Grayson nodded as if unsure of her words. The less he said, the more likely she would believe the lie.

Margaret studied him for a moment, then smiled and linked her arm into his. "Well, why not. I know a stableman who can speak your dialect and he'll explain everything to you."

Grayson fell into step beside her and was happy to see his normally long stride matched hers as they walked. He had no idea what he'd just gotten himself into with the one word he'd said, but he figured this was one way to keep an eye on her and find out about the house she'd inherited. If he could play along and convince her that he couldn't speak English, maybe she'd feel free to talk with others around him and he'd be able to close this case promptly. He wanted out of the South. Although he wasn't ready to go home to Ohio, there must be somewhere he could travel and let the war die inside him.

He didn't want to think about any other reason he might want to be around Margaret Alexander.

Sam McMiller almost swallowed his plug of tobacco a few minutes later when he saw Margaret Alexander storming through the barn door with Grayson Kirkland in tow.

"Mr. McMiller," she ordered, "will you explain to this man what I will be needing in a driver? He is newly arrived from Ireland, I believe."

Sam looked at Grayson and almost laughed. He'd known the career officer for months and doubted if the man possessed a drop of Irish blood.

"And," Margaret added, "tell him I'll pay ten dollars for a week's work. Once we're in Fort Worth I may need him to help us move in. After that he can return your team."

Sam mumbled a few words and Grayson nodded as if accepting the arrangement.

"Good." Margaret smiled smugly. "Then it's all arranged. Tell him I'll meet him back here in one hour." She reached into her bag and handed Grayson a gold piece, but looked at Sam. "Tell him to buy himself a hat and a gun. An unarmed man is of no use to me."

Sam scratched his stubbled chin. "I know where I might find him one for a good price. A man about his size abandoned his gear here not long ago. I might even throw in a horse for this price."

Margaret said her good-byes and vanished.

Grayson watched her go, then flipped the coin she'd given him to Sam. "Mighty nice of you to offer to sell me my own gear and mount."

"Anytime, son, anytime." Sam chuckled. "But I don't know why you want ta go getting mixed up with the likes of that crow. I've seen widows like her before. She's all dried up and hard like petrified wood. It's obvious you don't have any Irish blood in you or you'd have more sense than to try lassoing a lightning bolt."

Grayson laughed. "Hitch up the wagon. I've got to go retrieve my hat and guns from the weeds. If she gets back before I do, tell her my name's Grayson McKirkland."

Sam snorted. "McKirkland, my eye. How long do you think you can fool her once she hears that damned Yankee accent of yours?"

"Long enough." Grayson winked. "Long enough."

As he walked away, Sam shook his head. The mountain lion and the lone wolf had just bedded down together for the night. As far as he was concerned, come morning there was going to be one hell of a fight.

4

The spring sun rose hot, sucking moisture from the earth in a thin veil of steam as the train pulled into the station at Bryan, Texas. Stepping from the train, Cherish saw the rows of blacks lining the platform as though the train to the promised land would arrive at any moment. She walked half the length of the platform before she saw her aunt. Margaret Alexander stood straight and tall, apart from the others, reminding Cherish of a queen among her subjects. Her ebony hair was pulled into its customary widow's bun, making Cherish smile at how ragged she would look in comparison to her prim and proper aunt.

"Maggie!" Cherish shouted, breaking into an unladylike run.

Margaret's hug was warm and tight as always, telling Cherish just how lonely and fragile this queen was beneath her dignified charade. Although Cherish was eight years younger and a head shorter than her aunt, she'd known since childhood that Margaret's need to be with her was greater than her need for Margaret. Her aunt had been like a little mother to her, then a sister, and now a friend. For most of their lives they'd been each other's only playmate. At times during childhood, their survival had depended on how tightly they'd clung together. Later, when Cherish had gone into nursing about the same time her aunt was widowed, Margaret had followed, not from any calling to heal, but so that she could stay beside Cherish. Even now, the month they'd been apart seemed like an eternity.

A huge man stepped onto the platform just behind Margaret. His hair was the color of red clay and his shoulders were granitelike with muscle. Not enough age lines marked his face to put him far out of his twenties, but hardness hung about him like a long-worn cape.

Cherish backed up, reaching for the gun inside her bag. The night's activity on the train had left her exhausted and jumpy, but she was still aware that a stranger stepping too close meant danger.

"Cherish"—Margaret read her niece's eyes—"don't let Grayson's size frighten you. This is the man who'll drive us to Fort Worth. He speaks little and he's quite harmless."

"But he's so big." She felt like little more than a child beside this man who looked as if he'd never in his life followed an order that didn't suit him. "Are you sure?"

"Believe me." Margaret laughed. "We've been through a great deal this morning and if he were a bad man, I think I'd know."

"Where did you meet him?" Cherish found it hard to believe that her aunt could so readily trust such a man. Margaret was the type who mistrusted all males until they proved themselves. And, unfortunately, most failed the test in her eyes.

"We kind of found one another." Margaret pointed to Cherish's luggage and Grayson shouldered the bags.

He followed them to a wagon, seemingly unaware that Cherish glanced backward several times to see if he'd absconded with her things. Cherish raised an eyebrow as her aunt allowed Grayson to lift her into the seat. Without a word of thanks, Margaret patted his shoulder, paying him no more notice than one would a beast of burden.

Shaking her head at his offered hand, Cherish climbed into the wagon without assistance. She was Texas born and bred. She believed in doing for herself. Until today she would have sworn Margaret felt the same, but her aunt seemed comfortable with this man. The idea of Margaret being less than full-starched around a man was almost as strange as what they were about to do. Cherish wouldn't have believed she would travel halfway across Texas to help Margaret set up housekeeping in a house that had once been reported as a gambling casino and trouble spot.

The sensible thing to have done would have been to return home to be among family, but she and Maggie had been on their own too long. They needed this house Maggie had inherited to recover from the war and to allow their minds to return to the everyday problems of living.

Excitement seemed as thick as humidity in the air. "How long will it take us to get to Fort Worth?" Cherish asked.

Margaret sat in the middle of the bench, holding the reins as Grayson climbed onto the seat beside her. Again Cherish saw her aunt pat him, this time on the leg, as she pointed down the road. She finally turned to answer Cherish's question. "We're leaving so late we may not make much time today, but I understand the roads are good."

Cherish didn't hear the last words, for the priest she'd met on the train crossed in front of their wagon. He was riding a horse far more spirited than any poor friar should have been able to afford. His lean frame sat the saddle as one born to it and his slender hands expertly caressed the reins. Polished black leather knee boots shone from beneath his robes.

The smile on his thin lips never reached his charcoal gray eyes. "Good day, Miss Wyatt." He pulled his mount alongside the wagon. In the daylight, Cherish could tell that he was younger than she'd thought, even though his black hair was touched with gray at the temples and his tanned forehead was deeply carved with worry lines.

She wondered again where he'd learned her name or why he'd bothered. "Good day, Father. I hope you enjoy your stay in town."

This time the twinkle of a smile touched his eyes. "Oh, I'm not staying. I'm heading on toward Fort Worth."

Margaret nodded toward the priest, volunteering information Cherish might have withheld. "So are we. You're welcome to ride along with us."

The priest looked at Margaret as if only just now seeing her. "Thank you, ma'am, but I have to wait for a friend." He hesitated a moment before fixing his gaze on Cherish. "If you need me once you reach Fort Worth, my church lies to the north of town. Just ask for Father Daniel."

"Thank you." Cherish wasn't sure what to add. Despite his kindness last night, she had the feeling she was looking more at a reflection of a man than at the man himself. There was something missing in him. If he hadn't been a priest, she might have guessed it to be his soul.

Margaret spoke like a mother correcting a child's manners. "And, Father, should you need us, we will be at a house called Hattie's Parlor on the south side. I understand it's near a part of town called Hell's Half-Acre."

Showing no surprise at their strange destination, the priest nodded, telling Cherish he knew more than just her name. Urging his horse forward, he disappeared into the street's commotion.

"Where did you meet him?" Margaret asked as she touched Grayson's arm and pointed forward.

"On the train," Cherish whispered halfheartedly. Her mind was trying to fit the pieces together of all she knew about this strange, thin priest. But, like parts of two puzzles, the pieces wouldn't go together.

They rattled through town and onto the muddy road leading to Fort Worth. Margaret talked of her plans for the house, the first real home she'd ever had that she could call her own. Both women needed a long rest. For four years they'd worked tirelessly to nurse the Confederate wounded. They'd thought they both would have to apply for work right away at some hospital, but thanks to an old man's gift they had a home to go to.

Sleep kept trying to overtake Cherish as the countryside slid slowly by. When they camped, she took only a few bites of dinner before she curled in her blankets beside the fire and fell asleep, the memory of the bandit's lips her last waking thought.

In the folds of her dreams, Cherish held the stranger in her arms once more, only now she was not afraid. He kissed her with passion as before but gentleness guided his actions.

Cherish awakened with the early dawn light touching her face and a longing in her heart. If the stranger had stayed around her, she told herself, he would have meant nothing to her, but the knowledge that this bandit was out of her reach made him the focus of her fantasy. Since she'd never seen his face, her imagination wove a daydream lover. She sat silently, remembering the dream and wondering what another meeting with him might be like.

Margaret talked of their future goals without needing more than a casual response from Cherish. Loving to organize and plan, Margaret didn't comment on her niece's silence until three days later.

Cherish satisfied her with excuses about being tired and unable to sleep. In reality it was her nightly dreams that each day filled her mind with the memory of passion and tender longings. Never, in all the years of the war, had a man she'd met troubled her thoughts so. She'd known his touch, and somehow he'd seeped deep inside her like a dye forever changing the color of her thoughts.

Her dreams continued until their last night on the road. Like the evening sky, her dream turned dark and brooding. The stranger reached for her, but they couldn't quite touch. His tender whispers were stolen by the wind before the sounds reached her ears. No matter where she moved, a shadow always hid his face from her.

Tortured hours of the nightmare continued until finally the rumble of thunder shook Cherish awake. She blinked, thankful to have escaped the haunting dream. Grayson was moving in the early light, stamping out the fire, tying down the wagonload. He and Margaret worked together wordlessly. The bond between this huge man and her aunt was almost a tangible tie. She'd never known Maggie to have anything to do with men after her Westley died. Her aunt had simply denied that there might be another man for her in the world. She'd always worked in hospital administration, only turning her hand to nursing when needed. For the most part she was never around any man a moment longer than necessary. Now, with Grayson, it was different. Although she treated him little better than she would a pet, she leaned on him as if he somehow had the strength she needed.

"Cherish!" Margaret shouted above the thunder. "Load up. We're going to try and outrun the storm; otherwise, I'm afraid we'll be trapped by mud."

Cherish helped hitch the horses, then climbed onto the seat as the first drops of rain splattered against her cheeks. Clutching her cape, she fought the whipping wind as Grayson slapped the horses into action.

They moved as fast as the road would allow, but within an hour the rain caught them full force. Without a word, Grayson handed Margaret the reins and climbed down. He walked to the horses' heads and began guiding them through the muddy river that once had been the road. Cherish's knuckles whitened around the seat as the rain grew worse.

Margaret finally passed the reins to Cherish. "I'm going to help Grayson!" she shouted over nature's wrath.

Cherish nodded. She'd been caught outside in storms before and knew they would certainly suffer more if they didn't keep the wagon moving in this open country. Fort Worth couldn't be much farther. With supplies low and only wet gunpowder, they were better off braving the storm than risking the danger of stopping.

Maggie's lean body twisted like an elm branch as she battled the wind and rain. She bent and pulled the back hem of her skirt between her legs as she and Cherish had done many times in their childhood. Then she tucked the hem into her belt, making her full skirt more like pants. Grabbing the bridle of one of the horses, she shouted at Grayson to move ahead.

Cherish's hands grew frigid and raw from holding the reins as she watched Maggie and Grayson plow through the knee-deep mud. The hours and the rain seemed like endless torture as they measured their progress from one hole in the road to another.

Again and again Cherish watched her aunt slip into the mud, and always Grayson's arm was there to pull her up.

The gray day had turned black by the time they reached the outskirts of Fort Worth. Stores and homes were boarded up against the storm, transforming the town into a near-abandoned settlement. The small city had obviously suffered during the war from lack of manpower. Now it was hard to tell if the town had been half-built, or lay in half-ruin.

They went past several houses before Margaret saw a man running from his barn to his house. She yelled out, asking directions to Hell's Half-Acre, but he only stared at her as if she were a devil and then turned to run inside. Margaret's harsh rebuke was not lost in the thunder.

Finally, they found a tattered pole of street signs. Grayson lifted Margaret's exhausted, muddy body onto the wagon. Cherish handed him the reins and snuggled into her hope- lessly wet cape as he climbed up beside her aunt. Wordlessly he took the reins in one hand and pulled Margaret beneath the protection of his free arm. He drove through the streets until finally they saw a large, two-story home set back from the road. An old sign was nailed to the gate: "Hattie's Parlor." It stood like an aging, defiant warrior atop a small, barren hill. Silently, it faced the wrath of the storm alone.

Staring through the curtain of rain, Cherish looked closely at her new home. The house dominated a rise with barns and chicken yards gathered around its skirt. With fallen shutters and broken porch steps it looked more like a beggar than the king of the mountain. A screen door flapped in the wind, seemingly pushing away all who might wish to enter. Grayson maneuvered the wagon around back and into an empty barn.

They were all too tired even to talk. The women knew that the horses must be attended to before any comfort could be sought. While Grayson unhitched the team, Maggie carried grain and water. Cherish found a worn blanket and began rubbing first Grayson's bay and then the team.

Finally, Grayson pulled the blanket from her hands and pointed toward the house. The women linked arms and made a run through the rain to the back porch.

Cherish left her soaked cape's protection as they reached the steps, then shoved the back door open with her last bit of energy. A single light blinked, blinding her for a moment.

As the room came into focus, she froze in fear. Exhaustion drained from her body like blood oozes from a shot man. Her fingers fumbled for her bag as her gaze concentrated on the end of a long rifle pointed directly at her heart.

"One more step and I drop ya!" a young voice yelled.

Margaret's arm tightened around Cherish's waist as she ordered, "Wait!"

The rifle barrel was shaking noticeably as a boy of not more than ten stepped into the light. "I got orders to kill anybody breakin' into this house. Don't remember bein' told any different if it were women."

"Put down that gun, boy," Margaret directed. "We're not breaking into the house. I'm Margaret Alexander and this is Cherish Wyatt. I own this place."

The boy lowered the gun a few inches. "You be the Maggie and Cherish that old Tobin talked about?"

Cherish laughed with relief. "Yes. Who might you be?"

"I'm Barfield Jefferson Parker. Bar for short." He lowered the gun to the table. "I live here with old Hattie. My ma was Miss Hattie's housekeeper, but Ma died last year. I stayed on so there'd be a man around the house. Miss Hattie kind of comes with the house and I kind of come with her."

Amid a round of thunder, Grayson's massive bulk shadowed the doorway. Bar jumped for his gun, but Cherish blocked his path. She laid her hand on the boy's shoulder, feeling the fear he wouldn't allow to show in his face. Patting him reassuringly, she whispered, "He kind of comes with us."

Bar straightened. His dark gypsy eyes looked up at Grayson. Only his bobbing Adam's apple gave away his nervousness.

Grayson removed his wet hat and slapped it against his thigh. He gave a nod toward Bar, and Cherish thought she saw the hint of a wink.

The boy stood his ground like a little rooster having his territory questioned. Cherish allowed her hand to glide lightly along his shoulder and felt the bone beneath his clothes. "If you'll take me to this Miss Hattie, I'd like to meet her. We've had a very hard day and would love to get into some dry clothes and perhaps eat supper, but we'll need your help."

"The boy can help you," came a voice from the shadows, as cold as the wind outside, "but all we got to eat is a pot of beans and some sweet-milk corn bread."

Everyone in the room turned toward the hallway as a woman entered. She was dark and ageless with bright scarves of red and gold tied around her hair and waist. "I'm Azile, the housekeeper. I'll tell Miss Hattie you're here, then bring food up to your rooms." Where the boy's complexion hinted of gypsy blood, Azile's left no doubt of it with her dark skin and eyes as black and shiny as sable. "I was Bar's mother's cousin so I came to help with the housework."

Cherish could feel the boy's shoulders tighten and decided either Azile was lying, or the boy wanted no part of being her relative.

Azile looked both of the women up and down and sighed as though she found neither of any interest. "We cleaned up the two-bedroom suite with a sitting room in the middle when we heard about old Tobin's will." She nodded toward the boy, silently commanding him to show them the way.

"That would be nice . . . ," Margaret began.

"Weren't expecting no man." Azile looked up at Grayson as though he'd just been left on the doorstep. "I ain't got a room ready for him. And I don't plan on doing no cleaning this time of night. He'll have to sleep in the barn."

Margaret straightened slightly. "He'll sleep in the sitting room. Bar, can you find him dry bedding?"

Bar watched Azile for a moment before nodding. No one missed the smile that spread across his face when Azile whirled her full skirt and disappeared as silently as she'd appeared.

Cherish felt a chill all the way to her bones as they moved down a mahogany-paneled hallway toward the front rooms. "This is a beautiful house," she whispered more to herself than to anyone else. She noticed several blank walls and empty spots where furniture should have been. Even run-down and dusty, this was one of the finest homes she'd ever been inside. Most houses in Texas were small— little more than dugouts—but this one was as grand as some she'd seen in New Orleans and Austin.

Bar carried the lantern before her. "I was born here. I know this place like a mole knows his hole. There're more rooms than you'd guess."

They passed one room after another filled with draped furniture. "Miss Hattie stays downstairs 'cause she's too sick to be moved much." He pointed to a closed door. "That's her room."

As he spoke, Azile stepped through the door. Unsmiling, she whispered, "Miss Hattie is already asleep. You'll have to talk to her tomorrow."

Cherish sighed. The dream of a hot bath was the only thing that kept her from curling up in the hall and falling asleep.

Bar turned toward the stairs. "Your rooms are up here where it's quiet."

Margaret opened her mouth to ask what he meant, but Azile spoke first. "We all hear things—ghosts screaming, spirits walking. This house has seen a great deal of evil and sometimes at night the walls cry in mourning."

Margaret huffed and motioned Bar forward. "I don't believe in ghosts. If folks could come back from the dead, I'm sure my Westley would have returned to me. He died in the war. Shot down in his youth by a damned Yankee bullet."

Cherish agreed with her aunt about the ghosts, but still caught herself turning her head to listen as they climbed the stairs.

An hour later all thoughts of ghosts were forgotten as she slid into the hot tub. She smiled as she heard Maggie talking to Grayson a doorway away in the sitting room. Her aunt was yelling as though the huge man were deaf to the language and not simply foreign to it.

"Take off those wet clothes!" Margaret shouted.

Grayson stood his ground, staring at her as if he had no idea what she was talking about even though his coat was dripping wet from his trips back and forth to the barn.

Margaret tightened the belt of her wool wrapper. "You need dry clothes. Take off those wet ones and I'll hang them by the fire."

Grayson fought back a smile and continued to stare. Only moments before, he'd thought he was too tired and cold to feel anything, but that was before Margaret walked through the door all fresh and blushing from her hot bath.

Margaret huffed impatiently and moved closer. "I don't understand how you sometimes read my mind and now can't seem to hear a word I'm saying." She touched the top button of his coat and loosened it as she spoke. "You'll catch your death if you don't get dry." Her fingers moved nervously yet with determination to the next button.

Fighting to control his breathing, Grayson let her continue. He could feel the hesitancy in her fingers as she slid her hand along the wall of his chest, opening his coat. For days he'd been near her, watching her move, listening to the softness in her voice when she talked with Cherish, feeling her every touch like a whip to the raw flesh of his memory. And even now, with his muscles too tired to ache, he still wanted to be near her. It had been so long, so very long, since he'd been around a lady. This strong, tall woman standing so close to him was driving him mad with her touch. He could almost feel the steam rising from his wet clothes as she pulled his coat away from his shoulders.

"I swear, Grayson. How can you just stand there dripping?" Her hand slid over his chambray shirt. "Even your shirt is wet."

Grayson stood like an oak against the storm of his need to touch her in return. Sam McMiller, back in Bryan, wouldn't have called her a cold crow if he could see her now in her royal blue dressing gown with her mass of hair damp and tumbling down her back like a midnight black waterfall. There was nothing hard or petrified about her once she'd removed her tight stays and laces, for Grayson had trouble keeping his eyes off her long, slender curves. The fire her nearness was stoking was almost consuming him as her fingers moved along to the last button of his shirt. He wasn't sure whether he wanted to crush her against him or turn and run.

"We'll hang your things by the fire." Margaret draped his coat over a ladder-back chair. "Grayson, you're acting like I'm trying to steal your clothes. I wish you could understand more of what I'm saying." She moved closer, tugging at his shirttail as though he were a child. "We have to get these off you."

Grayson's huge hand covered hers, stopping her progress. He imprisoned her fingers between his own and the muscle over his heart.

For the first time, she raised her eyes and looked into his stormy gaze. She could talk all she wanted to about him catching cold; she could even treat him like a child. Yet in that moment Grayson saw a hunger in her indigo blue depths, a hunger she wouldn't have admitted to him or to herself. A need basic to all men and women. A need she'd deny to her dying breath. But he saw it in her eyes for one long moment and her hidden desire touched his soul.

She looked away as if frightened, not by him, but by her own thoughts. "I asked Bar to bring a cot in here but I don't see one. You may have to sleep on the couch."

As she pulled her hand free from his grasp, he felt a gaping hole in his chest as though she'd pulled his heart out with her slender fingers. He closed his eyes and reminded himself that he was a Union officer with a job to do, not some lovesick cowhand who's been on the trail for three months. If this lady was involved with the Knights, he was obligated to see her behind bars and not anticipate her in his bed.

She moved near the fire, unaware of his longing. "There's no sense heating up the entire house." She pulled her robe together as though the fire gave her no warmth. "You can sleep here. I put no stake in ghost stories, but I'll sleep better knowing we're all close enough to hear one another."

Grayson watched her walk away, thinking he'd have to move his cot to the Oklahoma Territory to be able to sleep.

"Good night." Her whisper and the door's closing sounded in harmony.

Grayson stared at the closed door that barred him from the first woman he'd wanted since his wife died. *How many doors?* he thought. *How many doors in both our pasts will I have to break down to get to her?*

He yanked off his wet clothes and twisted inside the blanket Margaret had left on the long couch. "Get a grip on yourself," he whispered. "This woman is as hard as they come. Any man would be crazy to try and woo a widow away from her memory of the perfect husband. A husband killed, not by just a bullet, but a damned Yankee bullet."

It'd been ten years since he'd done more than hand over money to get a woman in his bed. He had a job to do and that job might just mean having to arrest Margaret and her niece. If they were connected to this house, they had to be somehow connected with the ring of outlaws who went by the noble name of Knights of the Golden Circle. Even if there was some argument among Grayson's superiors to let the Knights die away, Grayson wasn't ready to give up the fight. The war couldn't just end for him; it was all that had kept him alive. It couldn't be over—not yet.

But, by God, he'd seen her eyes and in them a need that matched his own. Yet he couldn't even tell her who he was or she'd hate him for the fool he'd played her. However, remaining silent was going to be as hard as standing still had been while she'd removed his shirt.

5

Cherish awoke with a start. The candle beside her bed flickered in a pool of wax and the tub's water was icy. A low creaking echoed through the high-ceilinged rooms as though the house were groaning in its sleep. She quickly dried off and slipped into her cotton nightgown. She had no idea how late it was, for the storm kept any hint of stars or moon from sight.

Crawling beneath the sheets, Cherish tried to get warm enough to sleep, but lightning jabbed at the blackness outside her window, making rest almost impossible. The constant roll of thunder reminded her of that night on the train. In the stillness of her room she could almost feel the stranger's presence. Any moment, he would fall on her with the smell of dust and blood and danger surrounding him. She closed her eyes and remembered how he'd kissed her with a hunger deeper than she'd ever known.

Cherish slammed her fist into the pillow beside her. "Forget him!" she whispered to the silent room. "Forget him and all the feelings."

Frustrated, Cherish climbed from her still cold bed. "I have no time for foolish dreams," she said to the silence, trying to convince herself. "No time at all." Lighting the lamp, she wished she could push away the chill as readily as she banned darkness into the corners of the room. She pulled a blanket from the bed, curled up beside the tiny fireplace, and rested her head on her knees. Firelight had always fascinated her, calming her troubled thoughts with its bright dance and warm breath. Her mind wandered to her family's farm. She thought of her childhood, when love filled her home to overflowing. The vision of her mother, angry and stoic as she waved good-bye the day Cherish and Maggie had left, played across her mind. How many times in the past four years had she wished she'd heeded her mother's advice and stayed home? Cherish tried to visualize one of the local boys kissing her the way the stranger had. But the vision wouldn't come. She would always love her parents, and visit them when possible, but she didn't think she could ever go home again.

Time passed slowly as her mind wandered, barely listening to the sounds around her . . . the storm, the crackle of the fire, the creaking of a door long unused.

Cherish stiffened. The sound came again: a door slowly opening, its hinges crying from age and neglect. Afraid to breathe, she turned her head from one entrance in her room to the other. The one leading to the hallway was locked, and the door opening into the sitting room was closed with the bolt still in its nest.

Her ears strained. Listening for the sound to come again, Cherish debated whether she wanted it to be real or whether it might be less frightening to question her sanity. What had the strange housekeeper, Azile, said? The dead walked the house and the walls cried. But Azile's eyes had the wild vacantness of someone who drifted from reality on the white smoke of opium.

The creaking came once more, an eerie noise of creeping terror. Waiting like an animal ready to spring for safety, she heard soft footsteps approaching her door. Cherish moved slowly across the room and, pulling her gun from her bag, she melted into the shadows between the bedpost and the wardrobe. She was not some frightened child to be caught unaware. The years of working in army camps near the front lines had taught her to prepare for the worst, even if praying for the best.

She watched as the doorknob on the hallway door turned. There was a long pause, then a knife's blade darted out like a snake's tongue between the door and the frame. With one jerk, the lock snapped back and the door moved inward.

Slowly, with deliberate pressure, the door opened wide. Cherish strained to see into the darkened hallway, but there seemed to be nothing but blackness.

"Who's there?" She made her voice calm, yet her hand trembled slightly as her finger caressed the trigger.

"You're awake?" a low voice whispered.

"And armed." She moved closer, trying to see into the hall, trying to place the voice in her memory.

A shadow moved, raising lean arms as if in surrender. "I mean you no harm, Miss Wyatt."

"Who are you?"

A thin man stepped from the blackness into the lamplight. "Father Daniel. We met on the train. I'm sorry to have frightened you, but I need your help."

Cherish almost collapsed with relief. The devils she'd imagined vanished from her mind. "But why break into my room? Why not just knock at the door?"

"This house has a few entrances other than the front door. I've known about them since I was a child. I need your help, and no one, not even the woman with you, must know."

"What kind of priest are you? You help murderers and use a knife like a key." Suddenly Cherish was not sure she should lower her weapon. She was not fool enough to think that only robes were needed to make a priest.

Father Daniel laughed. "Don't worry. I'm as real a priest as this town has known. It's just that sometimes the Lord and I must walk a little to the left side of the law."

Cherish remembered how he'd saved the man from hanging and knew somehow she owed this mysterious man a favor. "What can I do?"

The priest disappeared and returned a moment later, half-carrying, half-dragging the body of a man. "I thought I could help him, but we've ridden hard for two days. We've been out in the storm all night. When we finally got to town I couldn't just take him to the mission to die, and the town's doctor is seldom sober enough to be of any help." Father Daniel looked at her with helpless gray eyes, liquid with his plea. "He's lost a lot of blood and I'm afraid his wound is infected."

Turning up the lantern, Cherish watched the priest lower the wounded man onto her bed. He was covered with mud and blood, but she knew without asking that he was the same man who had almost been hanged that night on the water tower outside the train. "How did you find him?"

Father Daniel collapsed in the chair by her bed, his words barely a whisper. "He slept in my berth until we reached Bryan. Then I purchased two horses and met him outside town. He seemed to be fine the first few miles, but his bleeding made our traveling slow. We had to keep off the roads for fear of being spotted. Then the rain started and Brant grew weaker." As the clergyman talked, his words slowed and his body melted into the chair's comfort. "I thought he was going to die before I could get him here. There was nowhere else to turn. Hattie used to always have room to hide men who didn't want to be found and you'll nurse . . ." Without finishing, the priest fell asleep, his legs stretched out and his head against the back of the chair. He had laid his trouble at her door and now could rest.

"Hattie?" Cherish whispered, remembering the old invalid downstairs who had once been the owner of this house and now just seemed to go with it like furnishings passed from one person to another.

Placing a blanket over the priest, Cherish wondered if he'd slept at all in the past three nights. What drove this man of God to risk his life for a murderer? Didn't he know what he was doing was wrong? Or maybe he didn't care, for his reason was right. There had to be a bond between these two men, a bond linked somehow by the identical scars on their wrists.

Moving the lamp near the bed, she turned the wounded man's face toward the light. His skin was ghost-pale but warm to her touch, telling her that he was still alive and that the wound probably was infected. His jawline was hard and straight, his dark hair a touch too long, and his mouth pulled tight in pain.

She wasn't sure what she'd expected to see when she finally looked at the bandit, but even beneath the mud, his good looks shocked her. Why had she thought his face would be scarred, his nose broken, his mouth twisted in a permanent sneer? But here was the face of a young man with a long Roman nose and chestnut brown hair. She might need a shovel to remove all the mud from him, but Cherish aimed to see just what this man, who had dared kiss her as no other had, looked like.

Even now, as she touched him, she felt her heart race. For the first time in her life she wanted to touch him as a woman touches a man and not just as a nurse touches a patient. This outlaw covered with blood and mud was somehow the key to unlocking feelings she'd never allowed out.

Cherish slipped into her wrapper without taking her eyes off the man in her bed. She'd need hot water and bandages if she was to do him any good. Somehow she had to find help, but who? Grayson was the most logical choice. He'd hauled water for their baths and firewood. Maybe she could get him to bring up a few more loads. He'd be the least likely to talk because he hadn't more than nodded since she'd met him. Plus, if Maggie trusted him so completely, he must be worthy of trust.

Tiptoeing into the sitting room, Cherish stumbled over Grayson's discarded clothes. She could hear his heavy breathing coming from the couch and knew it would be no easy task to wake a man who had worked as hard as he had since before dawn.

With her usual passion for neatness, she straightened his damp clothes and folded them over a chair by the fire. A crumpled telegram fell from his pants pocket and curiosity made her take a moment to glance at it.

Cherish couldn't believe what she saw. She moved closer to the fire and read the message again. It was addressed to a Captain Grayson Kirkland and the short message left no doubt that he'd been assigned to a new job.

She read the last sentence three times. "More details with Friday train arrival." She'd been on the Friday train as had the priest and the wanted man. Since Grayson couldn't have possibly wanted her, he must be hunting one of the two men. Yet, why was he playing this game of not under-standing English? He obviously read it. Was he playing Maggie and her for fools, or was Maggie a part of this and, in her usual overprotective way, hiding the truth from Cherish?

Folding the paper, she replaced it in the pants pocket, then walked soundlessly out of the room. When she was safely back in her bedroom she bolted the door and whispered,

"Wonderful. Some rest I'm going to get. I know two facts for certain. Grayson is a Union officer probably looking for one of two men, and they're both less than ten feet away from him in my bedroom."

6

Dawn sifted through the thin curtains and ribboned the bed where the stranger lay. Cherish's hand trembled slightly as she dug once more for the bullet lodged in his chest. Tiny white lines formed around his mouth, but the man the priest had called Brant didn't cry out. He was awake and with her each step, though he didn't speak or open his eyes.

"There!" Cherish let out long-held breath. "It's out." Before, when she'd worked with a gunshot wound, she'd always tried to remove herself as much as possible from the person near death and think only of the bullet to be dislodged. But she found that difficult now. Even as she worked she thought of this stranger and how he'd touched her in the darkness of the train. His kiss had been unlike anything she'd ever dreamed a kiss could be. Just the memory warmed her blood as she watched his mouth tighten in pain.

His face was relaxed for the first time all night. *He's finally passed out from the pain,* she thought. Even though he hadn't said a word, she'd known he'd been with her, trusting her with his life. She felt him watching her work as he'd forced his body not to jerk when she cut into his infected flesh.

Quickly, she cleaned and closed the wound, marveling at his silence. When the wound was bandaged, Cherish wiped his pale face with a cool cloth. She had to admire this murderer for his courage. She'd seen men who endured a tenth of the pain she'd put him through scream for hours. Now, touching his face, she thought of how totally he'd placed himself in her hands. The sleeping priest beside the bed would have been no guard if she decided to run into the sitting room and tell Grayson a murderer lay near death in her room. The stranger had trusted her with his life.

She felt no fear of Brant now as she touched the dark brown whiskers along his jawline. His features were strong, but not hard. There was something boyish and reckless about him that made her want to know the person behind the tough man. She wanted to know what had molded a man so hard that no pain seemed to touch him.

"We're very much alike, you and I," she whispered. "We keep our pain within, never letting anyone see." She thought of how the loneliness she felt was like an invisible open wound over her heart. She pushed back from people, never allowing herself to get too close. The very trait that had made her a good nurse had also cheated her out of knowing how it felt to be in a lover's arms.

Closing her eyes, Cherish leaned against the headboard and tried not to think of anything but Brant surviving the next few hours. There was nothing to do but wait and see if infection set in. During the war, she'd had plenty of experience with gunshot wounds. More men died of the poisoning from the black powder than from the bullets. Brant might be one more notch on the black powder's handle of death.

Bar slipped into the room, carrying another bucket of water. His thin, half-grown shadow moved over the wall as silently as he moved about the house. She'd enlisted his help when she'd found him sleeping on the stairs and he'd helped her all night without once complaining. "You think you'll need any more water, Miss Cherish?"

"No, thanks," she whispered as she straightened. "You'd better get some sleep, and remember, in the morning you never saw this stranger."

Bar moved closer. "He ain't no stranger, miss. I've known him and Father Daniel all my life. Though I haven't seen Brant Coulter around here for a few years. Last time I saw him, he was downstairs arguin' with Miss Hattie about somethin'." Bar sat down by the fire as if thankful to have someone to talk to. "Miss Hattie told me later that Brant and Daniel was like me when they was kids, just kind of on their own. She said she didn't remember either of them ever havin' folks."

Cherish pushed a strand of blond hair back from her face. "I think I understand. The outlaw and the priest were child-hood friends. Then one turned out good and one bad."

Bar looked confused. "What do you mean?"

Cherish smiled at the child. "I mean one does good things and the other bad things."

Bar tilted his head as if letting this new thought wash around in his brain. "I don't know. I can't tell who's good and who's bad much any more. Like Miss Hattie. Folks say she ain't no good. Some won't even speak to her on the street. But she lets me live here when those folks that don't speak to her ain't offerin' me a home. Even last winter when Azile tried to throw me out 'cause she said feeding me was a waste of good food, Miss Hattie wouldn't hear of it. Not that she can't be meaner than the devil from time to time, but I owe her just as I guess Brant and Father Daniel do."

Cherish saw his point, but tried to make him understand about the two sleeping men. "Yes, but Father Daniel is helping save a life and this man killed another man."

Bar shrugged. "I've seen a few men that needed killing. I reckon if Brant Coulter kilt him, the guy musta provoked him mighty."

Father Daniel shifted in the chair, startling Bar. The boy crawled into the shadows like a half-wild barn cat when the barn door is suddenly opened. Cherish was shocked at the fear that danced into the boy's dark gypsy eyes.

"I gotta go," he whispered and vanished.

Father Daniel stretched and smiled shyly. "I'm sorry about falling asleep like that. How is our patient?"

"I think he'll live." Cherish studied the priest, trying to find some clue as to what had frightened Bar. There was only kindness in the priest's face. And mystery.

Father Daniel stood and faced the morning light. "I'll come back for him as soon as I can." He moved toward the door. "I thank you for your help. I'd best get to the mission before the whole town wakes up and knows I was here. There's a back trail behind the barn that leads right into the grounds of the mission."

Cherish watched him go, wondering why she hadn't told him about Grayson, or Grayson about both men. Who would she have betrayed in the telling? A priest who had done her no harm, or a Union officer who slept in the sitting room? She knew the law would see her as having helped a criminal, but her hatred for any Union soldier made her hesitate. The war could end easier on paper than in the heart. Hadn't the Union imprisoned a doctor only months ago for treating the man who had shot Lincoln? Grayson seemed a reasonable man, but the world was full of men who had been poisoned with four years of hatred.

A low moan from behind her drew Cherish back to the bedside. She knelt beside the bed, trying to hear what the wounded stranger was whispering.

Slowly he raised his hand and touched her cheek. "Be careful," he whispered. His eyes were feverish, yet penetrating with intensity.

"I will." Cherish leaned to within an inch of his face. "I know the truth about the man in the next room."

Brant slowly moved his head from side to side as if she hadn't heard him. "Be careful," he whispered, "of the priest."

Someone seemed to be calling Grayson Kirkland from far away. He could hear his name, but it was borne on the wind and he couldn't find its direction. He reached for the answer and touched the face of someone too real to be in a dream.

"Grayson! Wake up!" Margaret's no-nonsense voice brought him fully awake. "Grab your gun and follow me."

She didn't wait for him to answer, but disappeared into the hallway. Grayson's survival instincts had taught him long ago that the time between sleep and full awakening must be kept to a minimum if a soldier planned to stay alive. He grabbed his gun belt, flung it over his shoulder, and followed as he stepped into his pants.

The hallway was still in darkness, but he could hear Margaret's steps on the stairs. He soundlessly followed her as he slid one Colt from its holster.

She paused and waited for him at the bottom of the stairs. As he stood just behind her, she whispered, "I was dressing a few minutes ago and I swear I heard someone passing in the hall. When I glanced out to see if it was Bar, a tall shadow moved down the stairs."

Grayson slowly moved around her and entered the hallway that ran from the kitchen door to the foyer. He held his gun ready, for there was no frightened alarmist in Margaret Alexander. If she saw a shadow, then there had been a shadow. He crossed the empty hallway to the large front room that ran half of the length of the house.

The room was empty except for a few old chairs that had been abandoned, too useless to be sold and too heavy to be carried away. Grayson circled the room that looked like it might once have been a library.

There was nothing: no window had been opened recently; no exit door; not even a fireplace that a man could have disappeared into.

Grayson lowered his Colt and looked at Margaret. She was such a vision in her robe and bare feet. Her indigo eyes were wide with questions and the night had tossed her ebony hair to a mass of velvet. For a moment Grayson wished time would stop and he could just stand and look at her for eternity.

"I saw a shadow," she said resolutely as she crossed her arms in front of her. He could almost see the hardness entering her veins and flowing through her. With the light, the woman in the soft robe would disappear into the hard, straight widow with her hair hidden in a bun and her heart closed to all men.

"We all see shadows in this house." A voice from the hall startled Grayson and Margaret.

The housekeeper, Azile, filled the doorway with her colorful dress. The scarves about her head and waist caught the morning sun with rainbow colors. "Evil walks in this place. Take care."

Pulling her shoulders square, Margaret said, "The shadow I saw was not a ghost. I swear on the grave of my dear Westley that the shadow was that of a man."

"Maybe," Azile answered as she turned and disappeared as quickly as she had come.

Margaret tightened her robe belt. "I'll not be frightened by some crazy housekeeper who dresses like a prizewinning sow at the county fair."

Grayson laughed inwardly, wondering just what it would take to frighten this woman made of iron. He'd never encountered such a female. He wondered what kind of man this Westley Alexander must have been to win her and, once he'd won her, how he'd ever been able to leave her. She was not a woman to be bedded and left; she was the kind of woman a man could spend all his life loving and, when heaven called, regret that he didn't have one more night by her side.

"Aunt Maggie!" Cherish yelled as she ran down the stairs and into the room. "Are you all right? . . ."

Cherish almost collided with her aunt as she slid to a stop. Grayson quickly moved his Colt behind him. He knew without asking that Margaret wouldn't want Cherish frightened. He thought Margaret's protectiveness of Cherish was overgrown, but he found himself falling into the same pattern.

"Of course I'm all right." Maggie smiled as she patted Grayson's arm, silently thanking him for hiding the gun. "Grayson and I were just looking around. How did you sleep?"

Cherish glanced from one to the other, knowing her aunt was lying as she always did to protect her from any unpleasantness. The silent giant stood shirtless and barefooted, and her aunt hadn't taken the time to pull her hair up, something she always did before leaving her chambers.

Deciding not to argue, Cherish began her own lie. "I didn't sleep very well. Would you mind if I spend the morning resting?"

"Certainly not." Margaret patted Cherish's arm. "Grayson and I will inventory the house and then go shopping for what we need. I'd also like to call on the bank and see about the account Tobin left. I can't wait to get this house in order." She moved toward the stairs with her niece in tow. "I'll have Azile bring a lunch up to your room. You just rest and I'll check in on you when we return."

Grayson followed, wondering if Margaret realized Cherish was a woman in her twenties. She might be small in build, but he doubted she let anyone else treat her like a child. He'd been around Cherish long enough to know that she was bred of the same strong frontier stock as her aunt. There was a bond between these two women, if not of honesty, then of love. Somehow Margaret equated putting the house in order with putting their lives in order after living out of a suitcase for four years.

Margaret quickly finished dressing and began her inventory of the house while Grayson downed his breakfast. She wore a black dress with a thin line of lace at the collar and Westley's broach pinned over her heart. A butterfly, he thought, that had gone back into her cocoon of mourning. She wore her widow's weeds as proudly as a veteran does his medal of honor.

As Azile entered the kitchen, Margaret began her plan of attack for the day. "I will need your help today if you still wish to be employed here."

"Ain't got nowhere else I know of to go. If I had I would have quit six months ago." She tied on her apron. "You tell me what needs doing and I'll work till it starts getting dark. Then don't be calling on me for I'm not likely to come out of my room unless you're yellin' fire."

"First, I wish to meet Miss Hattie; then I plan to do some shopping, so you may wish to make a list of what you need."

Azile nodded. "I'll wake Bar and get him to write it all down after I take you to Miss Hattie." She started moving into the hall, assuming Margaret would follow. "Miss Hattie got the curse from her younger days and don't see too good.

Her mind flickers on and off like a single firefly on a lonely night."

Margaret, as a nurse, was schooled in the effects of syphilis, but still, as Azile opened the door, she was unprepared for the skeleton of a woman who lay in the middle of the huge bed. An ancient flint-lock rifle rested at her side, and her bony fingers patted the stock.

Miss Hattie must have been a woman of great beauty with her high cheekbones and flowing hair, but age had dried her into a brittle shell of what she once had been. Her faded eyes and pale skin made her look much more like one who walked with the spirits than like one of the living.

Margaret moved forward. "Miss Hattie, I'm Margaret Alexander."

Pale, watery eyes seemed to look right through Maggie. "Tobin talked of you." Miss Hattie's clear voice surprised Maggie. "He said you played a fine little mother to Cherish." She raised her head like a queen. "He said if anything happened to him, you'd see that no one bothered me until my daughter comes."

Margaret nodded. "I will do that, ma'am. Tobin was a true friend to my family and I will stand by his word."

Hattie laughed. "He was an old coot who talked almost as much as he drank, but you're right about him being a true friend. Ain't a man in a hundred worth the trusting and I guess I'd had my hundred before I found him."

Margaret reached for the gun on the bed. "Ma'am, would you like me to take that?"

"No!" Hattie screamed, her voice cracking with intensity. "I might need it. There are those who would want to take my treasure away from me."

Margaret noticed the large, shell-covered box on her nightstand. She doubted it contained anything of great value.

"You are safe now, Miss Hattie. I'll help you keep your treasure secure."

Moving closer, Margaret noticed that Hattie's bed was clean and her hair combed. "Is there anything I can do . . ."

"Who's that?" Hattie yelled again. "There in the doorway!"

Margaret could almost taste the sudden fear in the air. She looked back but saw only Grayson. "He's the man we hired to drive up here. I assure you, Miss Hattie, he will cause you no harm."

The wild fear didn't leave the old woman's eyes as she lifted the rifle from her bed. "I don't allow no men except Bar in my room. No men at all! Now, get out!"

Margaret glanced at Azile and the housekeeper nodded toward the door. "I'll calm Miss Hattie down. I got some tea that will settle her down," she said. "You go on and do the shopping. As far as what we need, I reckon you could say everything."

Backing out of the room, Margaret couldn't take her eyes off of Miss Hattie's face. The old woman had somehow turned the corner of insanity. There was no hint of rational thought in her voice as she yelled for everyone to keep away and for Azile to bring her medicine.

Margaret put her hand on Grayson's shoulder. "I need some air. I'm starting to wonder if this house was a blessing or a curse Tobin left me with."

An hour later, Grayson found himself following Margaret along the plank sidewalks of a town still in its adolescence. There were signs of a city, but the people acted like small-town folks as they stared at him and Margaret as if they were the morning's entertainment. Something told Grayson that no matter how many streets this town added or how fast these people bred, this place would always be a town and never a city like some he'd seen up north.

Margaret shoved package after package into his arms until he could barely see to follow her. He watched her calculate her money after each purchase as she budgeted out what was needed. He wasn't in the habit of shopping with a woman, but he could hardly tell her that. He simply followed and counted the number of stores to the barbershop pole that marked the end of Main Street.

"Careful, Grayson," Margaret whispered. He looked around the bags to see two Union soldiers coming toward him. They looked as though they'd spent the night heavy into drink and had been in foul moods since the sun rose.

Margaret guided Grayson into the street to avoid the men. The taller of the two soldiers noticed her action and stumbled into the street in direct collision with her path. "What's 'a matter, lady," he yelled. "Think you're too good to walk on the sidewalk with a Yankee?"

Margaret's back straightened slightly, but she didn't back down. She looked ahead as if the soldier wasn't there. "Come on, Grayson, we have more shopping to complete."

The Yankee again stepped directly in her path. "Don't like us, do you, Miss High-and-Mighty?" His words were slurred as he looked at his friend. "Here we saved the world for democracy and this is the thanks we get. This southern lady won't even speak to us."

Margaret's temper snapped. "I'll speak to you, you drunken swine. First, I'll have you know that Texas was a democracy before the war so you saved us from nothing. And second, I am too good to walk on the same sidewalk with drunken soldiers of any uniform so get out of my way before I'm forced to—"

"Forced to what?" The drunk was trying to regain some of his pride. Her tongue was too sharp for his muddy mind, but he didn't want to admit it. "I'm a Union soldier and I ain't afraid of no woman."

Grayson had had enough. He shuffled the packages and stepped around Margaret. He'd seen soldiers like this before. All the idealistic young men had gone back to their families when the war ended, leaving many losers to assume occupation duty in the southern states. They were men with no family or ambition who were addicted to trouble. During the war they'd found plenty to keep them busy, but now excitement was in short supply. Men like these made him ashamed to be from the North. Grayson could think of nothing he'd rather do than flatten both men into the dirt.

The soldier pulled his gun with lightning speed. "Take another step, reb, and you'll be dead. I've killed rebs bigger than you."

Grayson was torn between putting these men in their place and destroying his cover. He'd have liked nothing better than to tell them he was an officer and have them both reported, but then he would have wasted the past two weeks and Margaret would never speak to him again.

"Wait," Margaret yelled as she turned on the soldier like an angry hen on a stray dog. "Leave this man alone. He doesn't understand what you're saying and he wasn't even in the war."

The soldier lowered his gun. "Oh," he mumbled as his face reddened. He glanced at his friend, who was touching his head with one finger, indicating Grayson was absent a brain. The friend stepped off the walk and into the street next to his drinking buddy. "Yeah, Sam, ain't no sport in picking on the feebleminded. Come on, let's go get another drink."

Margaret opened her mouth, then closed it and took her chance to leave. She grabbed Grayson's shirtsleeve and pulled him forward. Grayson followed, swearing under his breath. The men had called him first a reb and then feebleminded. Nothing more humiliating could possibly happen today.

When they reached the end of the walk, he heaved a sigh of relief and turned to find Margaret marching into the barbershop like it was just the place she'd been looking for all morning.

He could do nothing but follow. When Grayson followed through the door with his packages, to his amazement, she was telling the barber how to cut his hair.

Anger sizzled in him like frost on a fresh-lit stove. Every man in the shop turned and stared at him like he was some huge retarded child who had to have his mother come in with him. Those who had seen the scene in the street a few minutes before were relating it to the others as all eyes stared at Grayson with pity.

Margaret paid no attention to their stares. "Go ahead and give him a shave after you cut his hair. I swear he looks like he hasn't seen a proper razor in a month."

"Yes, ma'am." The barber bowed. "I'll get to him right away; these other gentlemen won't mind waiting. If you'll come back in fifteen minutes, your man will be all fixed up."

Margaret nodded and whirled. "I'll be across at the bank." She patted Grayson's arm as she'd done since they'd met, only now the slight touch was a slap to his pride and not a comfort to him.

Without responding, Grayson dropped the bags on an empty chair and sat down in front of the barber. A second later, a warm towel slapped his face, soothing the burn of his anger and embarrassment. "Forget every kind word I ever thought about that woman," he swore to himself beneath the towel. "When I'm finished telling her what I think there won't be enough of her left to fill a snuffbox. Damned if she isn't the maddeningest creature God ever made on either side of the Mason-Dixon line."

He continued to swear to himself as the barber worked. After some time, Grayson calmed down enough to listen to the other men in the shop.

"I could never handle a woman like that, not even in a nightmare," an old man with a smoke-colored goatee was saying between puffs on his pipe. Each time he exhaled, his face became a blur for a moment.

"Now, Jack, don't go being so hard on her. You saw that broach she had on. It's called a widow's broach from Bull Run. My sister lost her first husband in that battle and she had one just like it. She gave it up to be melted down about the time she remarried, but it were the same kind. That woman lost her man in the first battle of the war and she's still mourning him. There's something to be said for that kind of strong woman. I'd give a lot to know a woman mourned me that long."

The barber stopped working and added to the conversation. "You're right. It was a hard war and the menfolk weren't the only ones who suffered."

Grayson tried to relax. In his thirty years of life he could never remember being so angry at a woman, or so attracted to one. When this job was over, he planned to pull her off her high-and-mighty pedestal and teach her she couldn't run over people. While he was at it, he might teach her a little about what it meant to be a woman. Not a widow, but a warm, flesh-and-blood woman.

The men in the shop changed the subject to the latest Indian raid, while Grayson silently planned his revenge on Mrs. Margaret Alexander.

7

The still warmth of late afternoon hung in the air like a thousand invisible spiders. Cherish could feel the heavy dampness brush her hot flesh, but she had no time to stop working. This spare room had to be cleaned before bedtime. Brant's fever had broken after three days and now he would be safe without a constant watch. Her plan was simple: she'd move him down the hall while the others were eating dinner. Somehow she had to get him farther away from the Union officer camping in the sitting room.

"Miss Cherish," Bar whispered from the doorway, "where you want this mattress?"

"In that corner." Cherish pointed with the handle of her mop. "Is my aunt back yet?"

"Yes and no. She came stormin' in, sayin' somethin' about how the bank still wouldn't release any of old Tobin's money. She grabbed the will and headed back toward the bank with that giant right behind her." Bar shrugged his bony shoulders. "She can storm and stomp all she wants but my guess is she won't be gettin' any money until she cuts them in or goes for the sheriff."

"If you ask me, everyone we've met in this town is out to see us gone." Cherish had only been out twice on short

65

errands, but she'd seen the frowns as people passed her on the street. No respectable women lived in Hell's Half-Acre, even on the hill. Between the townspeople's mistrust and the Yankee soldiers' looks, she'd about decided it might be safer to talk her aunt into selling the house and living somewhere else. Cherish doubted her aunt would pay a dime under the table and that seemed to be the only way anything worked in this place. It didn't surprise her that the banker would be corrupt, but she didn't know about the sheriff. "Bar," she asked as she finished cleaning, "what would the men in town do if they knew there was a northern spy around?"

"Don't rightly know." Bar scratched his dirty hair. "Back before the war there was a couple of Northerners that tried to stir up the slaves. White folks caught them by gettin' a loyal black to lie under the boards at church and listen to them talkin' of helpin' the slaves run away. Some of the men was mighty upset. They strung up the Northerners down at the hangin' tree and let their bodies swing till there wasn't nothin' left but the bones. But that was five years and a war ago."

Cherish nodded. *It was a lifetime ago,* she thought. Now, if she turned in Grayson she'd probably be the one hanged. One thing she knew for certain: if Grayson found Brant, the wounded outlaw would be the dead man. Her only alternative was to help Brant and pray that he got safely away before Grayson stumbled across him.

She shoved the cleaning bucket into the hallway. "Would you go downstairs and get a bowl of that soup Azile left warming? I'll check on Brant."

Bar disappeared down the stairs as Cherish unlocked the door to her room. Bulky shadows and thin ribbons of light made everything seem out of focus for a moment. She was several feet into the room before she saw that the bed was empty.

The door snapped closed with a pop. She fought back a scream as her worries blossomed into fears. Cherish whirled with the sudden instinct of a trapped animal and slammed into the bandaged chest of Brant Coulter.

Before she could step away, he pulled her against him, steadying himself as well as her with his actions. "I knew it was you taking care of me," he whispered. "When the pain was too great to even open my eyes, I could feel your hands moving across me. Each time I dreamed I was burning in hell, your cool fingers would touch me. Even when I turned my head into the pillow to fight back the screams I could smell your perfume in the linen."

Cherish didn't try to pull away. She told herself it was because she wasn't sure he could stand alone, but her heart knew it was far more. She wanted to see how tall this man who haunted her dreams was as he stood beside her. She wanted to look into his face and see how much of him was real and how much she'd made up from her need to have someone in her life.

When she didn't speak, he lifted her chin. "How long have I been here?"

Cherish was fascinated by his rust-brown eyes that flamed with anger and need. His chestnut hair covered his forehead and several days of stubble formed a short beard over his strong jawline. He was the most dangerous man she'd ever met. But somehow she felt no fear as he spread his hands out along her back and pulled her to him with a need pounding in his heart as primal as jungle drums.

"Three days." Her voice was lower than a whisper, but it only needed to travel a few inches to reach him. "I dug the bullet out of your chest the first night. The fever had already set in and didn't break until this morning."

"How could I not recover when the sight of you was waiting for me?" He brushed his thumb over her cheek to the corner of her mouth. "You're even more beautiful than you feel and smell."

Cherish smiled. "And you still have some fever. I've been afraid more than once that you wouldn't pull through."

"You saved my life," he whispered in more of a question than a statement. "That's the second time."

"It will all be wasted if you reopen the wound." She studied him and wondered if anyone had ever gotten him to follow orders in his life. There was a sadness that must have taken years to layer into his gaze. "You should stay in bed," she added, realizing that his fingers still touched her jaw.

A slow smile spread across his lips and laughter touched his dark eyes. "So should you, my lady, and I'm willing to share the accommodations."

Cherish's face reddened in shock as she raised her hand to slap his face. Her tiny palm hit his cheek full force, but he didn't flinch. "How dare you say such a thing to me! I should turn you over to the Yankees and let your body rot to the bone." Her passion might be untouched, but her temper had long reached full maturity.

Brant released her slowly as if only just understanding the danger she might bring with her perfect body and soft skin. "Why didn't you? You owe me nothing. I could have slipped away an hour ago, but I have to know why you helped me."

Putting as much distance between her and Brant Coulter as possible, she tried to think of the answer. She turned up the lamp and remained with her back to this stranger who seemed tied to her. "Maybe I think a man is innocent until proven guilty."

"I'm not." His voice was growing closer, but she didn't move. "I didn't kill that man down by Bryan but I've killed others." His words were as cold as granite, but his fingers were gentle as he brushed the hair at the back of her neck.

"The only thing I ever believed in was the South. I thought we'd win because we were right. Texas came into the Union freely and I believed we had a right to leave freely. The damn Yankees act like it was some holy war about slavery, but it was more than that. A lot of folks in Texas were against slavery too. Now I no longer have the South to believe in. I have nothing."

His fingers molded lightly over her shoulder. "I don't know why I'm telling you this, but I thought you should know. I appreciate you patching me up, but I'm a dead man anyway. It's only a matter of time before a bullet hits a few inches closer to my heart—assuming I still have one."

Cherish turned to face him, her eyes filled with sorrow. He was like so many rebels she'd seen in the past months. They were all sons of proud people, generations who had never lost a war, and now they were beaten, left with nothing, not even their pride. The war had drained it out of them one battle, one drop, at a time. They'd fought for their people, their land, and had come home to nothing, not even a hero's welcome.

"You can start a new life. Lots of men are heading for the West, where they can forget the war."

"No!" Brant's fingers caressed her throat. "For me there is no future. It's too late. Meeting you has given me substance for dreams until the end comes, and I thank you for that, lovely lady. For the past few years I thought there was nothing good left in this world and you've changed that. But I must leave before I bring you more trouble."

"But you can't go. You're too weak." For the first time in her life Cherish wanted to hold a man to her and never let go. Something more than pity bound her to this man. If she had shown him beauty, he had flooded her with feelings she thought herself incapable of having. All her life she'd heard women talk about caring for a man, caring more than reason would allow. Suddenly, she realized she cared for Brant. Somehow he'd broken the window through which she'd always watched the world. Somehow he mattered.

"I'm strong enough to walk, and Bar will help me get to a safe place." He leaned close and brushed his lips against her ear. "Before I go, tell me that I'll be in your dreams just as you will always fill mine."

"No!" Cherish looked into his chestnut eyes filled with a lifetime of longing. "It isn't safe for you to leave."

He moved his lips across her cheek until he was lightly brushing her mouth with his words. "Why did something as perfect as you have to fall in this world gone to hell?" Then he was kissing her, not hard and demanding as he had on the train, but soft and filled with need.

She melted into his arms, carefully placing her fingers over his bandaged chest. Being in his embrace was like dancing in a fire without getting burned. She felt the warmth spread into every pore of her body, but there was no pain. All her life she'd watched the firelight and been fascinated. Now the flames had become a flesh-and-blood man before her; and the fascination, passion.

His finger moved along the seams of her dress from her waist to her shoulder. "Dream of me," he whispered. "Dream of me, pretty lady."

"No," she answered, but her kiss testified to her lie.

Brant's low laughter tickled her ear. "I think you will, my love. I think you'll dream of me for a long, long time."

A sudden rattle at the door handle made them both jump. Brant stepped behind the door as Bar entered, carrying a tray of food. "Azile thinks you are the eatingest woman she's ever—" He froze as he looked up into Cherish's face. "What's wrong, Miss Cherish?"

Cherish tried to hide her emotions. "Brant is leaving."

Bar looked around and smiled as Brant stepped from behind the door and lifted his gun belt from the table. "You feelin' better, sir?"

"I been kicked worse and still got up to ride." Brant smiled at the boy. "You walk me out just in case I fall over?"

"Sure." Bar shoved the tray onto the table and dusted his pants like he had just been given an honor.

Brant looked over the boy's head to Cherish. "Bar, I've got a man's job for you when you get back. Would you keep a close eye on Miss Cherish and see that she stays out of trouble?" He winked boyishly. "She needs to know better than to doctor wanted men."

Bar stood an inch taller. "I'll keep an eye on her."

With a last look at Cherish, Brant disappeared out the door before she could say a word. Bar was right behind him like a shadow. For a moment Cherish stood in the center of her room, wondering how she could let this man slip once more out of her life without knowing if she ever was going to see him again.

A moment later, the slamming of the front door and her aunt's calling for her brought Cherish back to reality. She darted out of her room and down the stairs, knowing that Brant and Bar were on a collision course with her aunt and Grayson. But when she was halfway down the stairs, she realized that Bar and Brant had disappeared completely.

Aunt Maggie was storming in such a whirlwind of her own making that she probably wouldn't have noticed a buffalo herd heading down the stairs. But Grayson, just behind her, would have.

"I don't understand it!" Maggie yelled. "What do I have to do to get the money that Tobin left us? You'd think I was trying to rob the bank."

Cherish tried to be calm, but her voice broke slightly, making her sound like a child. "What's the problem?"

Maggie stormed up the stairs with Grayson, as always, only a step behind. "The banker says I have to wait until he thinks about it before he can clear the money. It appears a group of shady men were playing cards the night Tobin won the deed to this place. A local grocer had been given the debt by Hattie in exchange for past-due bills with the understanding he wouldn't take over the house until Hattie's daughter could come get her. The banker seems to think that the grocer was swindled, but that doesn't make any sense. The grocer shouldn't have played cards with the deed to this house. I'm beginning to think the losing hand might have inherited the place. After all, Tobin was killed not more than a week later."

Cherish was amazed. "Tobin was killed? Hattie has a daughter?" She laughed suddenly, thinking she sounded like a child who had been left out of an important discussion.

Maggie hesitated, pulling off her jacket and hanging it neatly on the chair as she directed Grayson to please bring up their dinner. He waited a moment, his eyes never leaving Maggie, making Cherish wonder if this giant of a man had ever taken orders from a woman. Slowly he turned and went to the kitchen.

Maggie leaned closer. "Don't you think Grayson much more presentable with a decent haircut? I mean, anyone can see the good Lord blessed him with size and not looks, but he does clean up nice."

"Less frightening, you mean." Cherish avoided the man as much as possible. "Now, finish telling me about Hattie and Tobin."

Maggie pulled off her black gloves and folded them neatly. "Tobin did die from a drowning as we were told, but when

I started asking around, no one wanted to talk about it. Finally, I found out that it was at a spot on the Trinity that hasn't been more than three feet deep since the town has been here. No matter how much Tobin had to drink, I find it hard to believe the old Indian fighter couldn't crawl out of three feet of water."

Cherish felt a cold chill cross her. "And Hattie?"

"She has a daughter she hasn't seen for more than twenty years. She told everyone she didn't mind losing the house because her daughter is coming to get her, but no one seems to know where the daughter is. Tobin agreed to let her stay on until the daughter comes. We sort of inherited the agreement."

"Can the lawyer help us?"

Maggie shook her head doubtfully. "My guess is he's more interested in starving us out than helping us, but I plan on going to see him again first thing tomorrow. They say he can be found most weekends at a saloon about a block away. Another strange thing is, he was at the poker game where Tobin won the house. He and a man named Spades were the two who found Tobin's body a week later."

"You're not going to see them alone, are you?"

Maggie shook her head. "Grayson will be with me. I have a feeling some of the people in this town wouldn't have even allowed me to talk to them if he hadn't been standing beside me."

Grayson entered almost at the sound of his name. He was carrying a tray of food with about as much grace as Bar. He held the tray as Maggie put the two bowls of soup on the table.

Maggie touched his arm lightly. "You should have brought three."

Cherish interrupted. "I had my soup brought to my room

a few minutes ago. If you will excuse me, I promised to help Bar in the kitchen." She could hardly add that she'd sent Bar off with a confessed killer and wanted to wait by the kitchen door for the boy's return. Bar had been no more afraid of Brant than she had been and Cherish found that comforting. Brant didn't quite fit the picture of a man with blood on his hands.

Maggie nodded to Cherish as she moved into the chair Grayson had pulled out for her. She accepted his kindness, as always, without comment.

They ate across from one another in complete silence. Maggie was lost in her plans to restore the house and Grayson was trying to figure out which one of the people he'd met today was connected to the group of men he was looking for known as Knights of the Golden Circle. Old Hattie probably knew but she wouldn't let him pass her door without screaming like he was trying to rob her of her few quilts. Even when she did talk to Margaret, Grayson could make no sense out of what she said. They'd been here three days and he was no closer to finding out anything than when he'd met the train in Bryan. He only knew that a crazy old woman sold the house to pay bills and now she was waiting for a daughter who hadn't shown up in over six months. If Tobin won the house by accident, he paid for his luck with his life. So far, almost every person they'd met looked like he was easily capable of drowning an old man for two bits, much less a house, or two women if they were in the way.

As they finished the meal, Margaret silently stood and placed her napkin beside her plate. "Good night, Grayson. I think I'll go to my room."

She was halfway across the sitting room when a scream shattered the evening air. Grayson grabbed his guns and was only a step behind her as they ran to the stairs. Margaret lifted her dress several inches as she descended the first step.

The wood gave suddenly with a creak of age and Margaret cried out as she tumbled headfirst down the steps. Grayson grabbed for her, but missed. As her body fell away from him, he froze in the dim light. For a moment he saw not Margaret's but his wife's body tumbling. How many thousands of times had he tried to block the nightmare from his mind? He'd had too much whiskey that night and the road was slippery with rain, but they were young and laughing as they took the last bend at full speed. In a moment's breath the wheel slid sideways and the carriage catapulted them out. Grayson landed in the mud at the edge of a twenty-foot ravine, but his wife had been thrown farther. Her body twisted over and over as she rolled. He'd heard her scream and then only the blood-chilling sound of bone slamming against rock. Over and over again.

"Maggie!" came Cherish's scream from the hallway. Grayson shook free of his nightmare.

He took the stairs three at a time but it seemed hours before he reached her body.

Cherish was on her knees next to her aunt. "Oh, dear God, Maggie! Maggie!" She looked up, her green eyes liquid with heartbreak. "Grayson, help her!"

Grayson knelt on the other side of Maggie, his years of logical thinking overpowering his fear and memories. "Don't move her," he whispered and the words somehow gave Cherish the direction she needed.

"Yes," she answered. "First we must check her for breaks." She leaned close to Maggie's face. "She's still breathing."

Bar appeared from the kitchen. He hadn't bothered to remove his jacket when he'd heard the screams.

"Bring a lamp," Cherish ordered as she set to work doing what she'd been trained to do.

Grayson stood like a sentinel, afraid that if he moved, he might snap right in half. Here was the only woman he'd cared about since his wife died, and he'd been no help to her either. For days he'd watched her, telling himself it was part of his job, but knowing that he was protecting her from harm.

Finally, Cherish raised her head to him. "I think the only thing broken may be her arm. Plus she's got a nasty bump on her forehead." Cherish pushed the ebony curls away from Maggie's face. "Grayson, would you carry her very carefully back up to the bed?"

Grayson nodded and cradled Maggie in his arms as though she were a sleeping child. He didn't hear Cherish shouting orders to both Azile and Bar. He no longer heard the insane screams of Hattie that had brought them all running in the first place. All he heard was Margaret's soft breathing against his ear and all he felt was her heart pounding against his chest.

As he neared the top of the stairs, he saw the cause of the accident. The top step had crumbled either from rot or from foul play. He'd gotten the feeling more than once in this town that they weren't welcome, but the thought that someone would try to kill the women to get to the house seemed drastic.

"Stay with her," Cherish ordered as she led the way to Maggie's room. "I'll get what I need to set the arm."

Grayson didn't need to answer; he had no intention of leaving her. He lowered her onto the pillows. For a moment, emotion overcame reason and he gently brushed her lips with his own.

"I swear, Margaret," he whispered. "I swear if this was no accident I'll kill whoever did this to you."

She moved her head slightly against the pillow. Her hand rose to the bruise already blackening her forehead. Grayson gently pulled her hand away from her face.

"Grayson," she whispered. "Help me."

He covered her slender fingers with his massive hand and silently swore his allegiance as a knight of old might have to his lady fair.

8

Cherish folded the cover under her aunt's bandaged arm and stepped to the door. She motioned for Grayson to follow. He unfolded his long body from the chair he'd been planted in for over three hours and crossed the room to the sitting room door.

"I know you want to stay with her, but I need to talk with you a moment," Cherish began. "She's resting nicely and won't miss you for a few minutes."

Grayson didn't try to act like he didn't understand. She'd heard him speak just after Margaret's fall and he would not play the fool now.

"Maggie's arm isn't broken, but her wrist is very badly sprained. The tea Azile gave her should help her sleep, but one of us should be near in case she awakens. Azile is ranting about the evil in the house. She claims accidents will keep happening until we leave." Cherish suddenly looked very tired. "I think it best that Maggie isn't left alone. You understand every word I'm saying, don't you?"

Grayson nodded, wondering if he should trust Cherish. From all he'd been able to find out, she'd grown up in a little settlement in Texas and had served as a nurse for four long years during the war. After the armistice, she'd stayed on until the last man either had been shipped home or had died. She'd lost one brother at Shiloh and had another crippled at Gettysburg, but other than that her family of eight siblings had all returned home except her. She was a Southerner born and bred but there was a chance she'd never even heard of the Knights of the Golden Circle.

"I know who you are," she whispered. She saw surprise register briefly on his face before he masked all expression.

His steel blue eyes turned hard and cold. Only a spy would know his identity, or a traitor. And if she knew and hadn't told anyone then she must want to bargain for something. Otherwise, why would she keep her information from Margaret? His suspicions were confirmed as she whispered, "I want to make a deal."

He nodded slowly, deciding to hear her out.

Cherish began with words that sounded very rehearsed to his ears. "I'll not tell Aunt Maggie who you are if you'll swear to me that you will in no way hurt her. She's a good and kind person and I'll not have her think she's been used as part of a plot by some Union officer."

For an instant the jumble of emotions cleared around Cherish and Maggie, and he saw that Cherish was the one who protected Maggie and not the other way around. Maggie might storm around making all the decisions and rules, but it was Cherish who cleared the road and locked the door against harm. He couldn't help but admire the little blond for her silent strength, though he doubted he'd ever trust her with the real reason he was here.

Grayson found his voice. "I have no intention of harming Margaret." No matter what else he had to do, something inside him would never allow him to hurt such a woman. With a shock to his system he realized he meant every word, even if he had to let her slip through his hands on this investigation. He'd never felt that way about anyone. His determined lack of emotion had made him an expert at undercover work and this was the only time he'd gotten involved.

"Then why are you here?" Cherish's voice was low, but strong.

Grayson's face grew hard and his eyes, like iron, brooked no compromise. "I also have no intention of telling you my assignment, Miss Wyatt."

Cherish was lost. If she told Maggie about Grayson, it would shatter Maggie's trust in the one man she'd been within ten feet of since Westley died. There was always the chance that Grayson's work didn't concern them at all. She drew herself up to her full height, but still she didn't come to his shoulder. "I need to think this over. But understand this, Officer Kirkland, if you hurt my aunt I swear I'll shoot you so full—"

Grayson wasn't a man to be threatened. "And if you, Miss Wyatt, step outside the law one time, I'll arrest you faster than you can pull a gun." He raised one bushy eyebrow. "And it's Captain Kirkland."

Cherish stormed out of the sitting room and into the hallway. Anger bubbled in her like an active volcano. She'd guessed one thing from Grayson: he didn't know about her helping Brant, for if he had, she'd be arrested right now. He was a hard, cold man whose only Achilles' heel seemed to be Maggie.

As she maneuvered around the broken stair, Azile called to her from the doorway of Hattie's room. Cherish hurried to find the old woman wide-eyed with fright.

Hattie's voice rushed past gulps of breath. "They've come to hurt us all." Her bony hand grabbed Cherish's arm. "They plan to kill us all, one at a time, and take my treasure."

Cherish cradled Hattie as if she were a child. "It's safe now. No one is going to hurt us."

The old woman stared up with glassy eyes. "They would have killed me already but I've got the names. They're never gonna get them or my treasure."

Azile handed Hattie a mug of drugged tea and whispered to Cherish. "There ain't no treasure or any papers for that matter. She's lost what little mind she had."

Hattie gulped the potion, then tossed the empty cup aside and clung to Cherish. "I need some more of that medicine the priest brings me. I'd go get it myself if I could. If I send Azile she keeps half of it for herself." She patted a box beside her as she leaned back and fell asleep, mumbling, "I'll never let them have my treasure or any old list. Never."

Hesitantly, Cherish reached and opened the shell-covered box. Inside was a cheap amber necklace. Cherish knew that quite a few of the old-timers kept amber as a way of warding off evil spirits. Beneath the necklace were a few letters addressed to Miss Hattie in a bold, childish hand.

"Her treasure." Azile sniffed. "The old bat is a few bricks shy of a load, if you get my meanin'. The tea should keep her quiet for tonight, but Lord help us tomorrow."

Without any thought of what time it was, Cherish grabbed her cape from the hook by the door and hurried out. There was only one person she could go to about both Grayson and Hattie's medicine and that was Father Daniel. If he knew the entire story, maybe he could help on both counts.

The wind was icy as she walked the street through a part of town folks had taken to calling Hell's Half-Acre. Since there were no cattle drives coming through, the streets were empty except for a few drunks sleeping it off near the saloon doors. She remembered the priest telling her about a back path to the mission grounds, but she didn't want to try it in the dark. Cherish moved as silently as an Apache over rocky land. The closer she got to the mission, the more Brant's words haunted her. The first night when they'd brought him in and he'd been so near death, he'd pulled her against him and whispered to be careful of the priest.

Cherish's hope of talking things out with Father Daniel soured in her mind. If she told him about Grayson and the priest was the wrong person to know that information . . . well, she could almost picture Grayson's body swinging from the hanging tree.

"Miss Cherish," a low voice whispered as a lean figure appeared from the shadows at the gate of the mission. "What are you doing here?"

Cherish touched the Colt in her pocket before recognizing Father Daniel's voice. "I came . . ." She tried to think. The priest wasn't dressed in his robes, but all in black with knee-high riding boots. He looked more like an outlaw than a man of the cloth. "I came to see if Brant made it here without reopening his wound and to ask about Miss Hattie's medicine that you bring her."

The priest's head rose slightly. "Brant didn't come here, Miss Cherish. But he will." The last words were a statement of undoubted fact.

Cherish felt the sudden cold of the moonless night and wished she hadn't come. "Do you know where he is?"

To her surprise, the priest shook his head.

"Will you step inside the mission? While you're here I'd like you to take a look at a little girl who was brought to us. She seems ill, but we can't find the cause."

Cherish followed the padre through the huge double doors to a mission that didn't live up to its exterior. Inside, the walls were unpainted and stark. Several children were sleeping on cots in the corners. A daughter of the church moved among them, placing thin blankets over each.

Father Daniel lifted a tiny girl of no more than two into his arms. He seemed awkward with the little one, as if he wasn't sure how to hold the creature.

The child began to cry, and turned huge, seeking eyes toward Cherish. Her eyes looked sore from being rubbed and her nose was red and caked from hours of dripping without being wiped. As Cherish lifted the child, she could feel the fever on her damp skin. She carried the tiny one to the light and looked closely at her before smiling.

"She has the measles, Father. It's a very common problem with children. As long as she's cared for and her fever doesn't go too high, she'll be fine."

The priest looked worried. "She's been sick since they brought her and two others in last week. They were the only survivors of a wagonload hit by Indians. The others are fine, but this one has been crying since she arrived." Father Daniel said the words as a complaint for he, as a priest, knew even less about babies than the average man. "The other little girl looks like she could be this one's sister, but I'd swear the baby boy is half-Indian. I thought her red marks were burns. I can't have all the children coming down with measles. The sisters have hardly enough time to feed them now, much less care for them sick, and I must leave in an hour." His face wrinkled in worry and Cherish couldn't help but wonder if it was for the other children or for himself.

Cherish had inherited a decisive instinct from her German mother. "I'll take the child."

Father Daniel looked at her in disbelief. "The Virgin Mary's giving spirit is in you, Miss Wyatt. I am in your debt once more. Is there anything I can do for you?"

Cherish wrapped her shawl around the child. "Yes. Let me know when Brant comes. I must see him. And please bring more medicine for Miss Hattie."

Without another word, Cherish cradled the child and headed back to Hattie's. She'd gone through measles with her brothers and sisters and knew there was much to be done to make the child comfortable. The tiny girl cried softly and clung to Cherish.

Grayson, Father Daniel, and even Brant would have to wait. All her problems didn't seem to matter as she thought of the child. As always, she had to help, she had to ease another's pain. It was sewn into the seams of her heart and there was no way she could turn away from her calling.

Grayson saw Cherish slip out the back gate and head down the road. He would have given a great deal to know where she was going, but there was no way he would leave Margaret. He'd taken one look at the step and known someone had cut it. There was no telling how many times they'd stepped on the wood before Margaret finally stepped in just the right place and the wood snapped. The light layer of sawdust on the second step told him the "accident" had to have been set up recently.

At least her fall had given him one answer: Margaret was not part of any of this, but he could not be sure of anyone else in the house, even Bar.

"Grayson." Margaret's voice sounded tired and sleepy from the cup of herb tea Azile had given her.

He moved to the side of her bed and marveled at how beautiful she looked lying there with her hair all around her and her dark robe pulled close for warmth.

"Will you help me out of my robe?"

The question was simple: an order no different than a hundred others she'd given him in the past week, but Grayson felt his mouth dry and his palms sweat at the thought of complying with her request.

Margaret leaned forward and lifted her bandaged arm. Grayson bent beside the bed and pulled her gently to her feet. He slowly pushed the robe from her shoulders and allowed it to slide along her back. As he did so, Margaret leaned toward him, resting her head on his chest. He lifted her and for a long moment held her in his arms, amazed at the pleasure it brought him to hold a sleeping woman again.

Her nightgown was plain white cotton worn smooth from years of wear. He could have guessed she would not be a woman to waste money on new nightclothes during a war. Her head moved slightly as she snuggled against his chest and he swore he could feel his heart turn over. Why couldn't she be like this all the time and not so stiff and starched? He knew the answer even before he finished the question. She couldn't have survived as a widow if her backbone hadn't been straight. She'd fought her way alone for four years and she was fighting every inch of the way now, as if this house and the little money Tobin left was all she had in the world. With a sudden realization, he knew. This was all she had. The memory of her Westley and her brooch were the only treasures she possessed.

Slowly he lowered her onto the bed and spread the covers over her. Then he returned to his chair by the window. He laid his Colts an inch from his hand and closed his eyes. No one, not even the ghosts of Hattie's Parlor, was going to bother her tonight.

An hour later, Grayson's peace was shattered by the cry of a baby. He jumped to his feet and had his gun in hand before he realized what the sound was. As he crossed the room he glanced at the still sleeping Margaret. The child's cry came again as he opened the door to the sitting room.

Cherish passed in front of the fire with the child cradled against her shoulder. "Close the door before you wake Maggie up," she ordered as if he were the one doing something out of the ordinary.

Grayson raised an eyebrow and studied her closely.

Cherish talked softly with the child as she continued to walk. Her voice didn't change but her words were for Grayson. "She's got the measles."

"And we're going to take care of her?" He couldn't believe with all their problems Cherish was taking on yet another one. What was this? A home for every stray sick child and orphan in town?

"No." She talked as if to the child. "*I'm* going to take care of this baby."

"But where? How?"

"As soon as my room warms, I'll take her in there."

Grayson ran his large hands through his cinnamon hair. "I . . ."

Loud pounding from downstairs silenced him. He glanced at Cherish and as their eyes met they both silently asked the same question. "Who could be visiting at this hour?"

"I'll get it." Grayson noticed a hint of fear in Cherish's eyes and wondered who she'd been expecting.

As the pounding came again, Grayson yanked open the front door. An old nun stood huddled against the night wind. She carried two wiggling bundles in her arms. As Grayson stepped to allow her inside, she shoved the bundles toward him and pushed away.

"Father said to take these two, for they got the spots also. And here is the directions to find Hattie's medicine. Give the paper only to Miss Cherish."

"But . . ." Grayson balanced the wiggling blankets in his arms as he blinked, and the old woman blended into the night even before he thought better of giving away his disguise by words of protest.

He carried his delivery upstairs. He'd meant only to dump them in Cherish's lap and return to his quiet vigil in Margaret's room but, even to his unskilled eyes, three sick children were more than one person could handle. He rolled up his sleeves and silently added his help, grumbling all the while about how he disliked children—especially ones with red spots.

By dawn he'd learned more about sick babies than he'd ever wanted to know. He was amazed that when they weren't crying, they were spitting up or coughing, or making a mess out the other end. A pile of towels and sheets large enough to keep a washwoman busy all day lay by the door and still the babies looked no better off than when they'd arrived. Bar lay exhausted on the floor by the fire as Grayson paced with the little girl Cherish had first brought home in one arm and a boy not yet old enough to walk tucked into the other. Cherish sat, sound asleep, in a corner of the couch with a sleeping baby beside her.

Margaret appeared in the doorway of her room and stood watching the scene before her. For several long moments she pieced the picture together. Finally, Grayson stopped his pacing and looked up at her with heavy, sleepless eyes. He didn't speak, but lay the infants down on their makeshift beds and walked toward her with a caring question in his blue-gray depths.

Margaret gently lay her hand on his muscular forearm. "I'm fine, Grayson. Don't look so worried." She could feel his arm tighten slightly, so she patted him gently.

Maggie's voice awakened Cherish. She rose up on one elbow. "Maggie," she whispered, hoping not to wake the children. "You look wonderful this morning."

"Which is more than I can say for the two of you," Maggie scolded gently. "Where on earth did these babies come from?"

Cherish laughed and explained. Maggie started shaking her head as she looked at the sleeping children.

"We can't keep them. There's hardly any money to buy food now and I have no idea how long it will take to get Tobin's money released." Even as she spoke, Maggie moved toward the children. Her slender hand reached up and covered a tiny shoulder. "We just can't," she whispered, but there was no need for Cherish to present any more argument. The children would stay until they were well.

"Miss Cherish." Bar pulled Cherish aside as she moved down the hallway.

"Yes?" She couldn't help but smile at the boy. He had a way of climbing into her heart with both feet.

"I was wonderin' if you make a habit of bringin' home every sick child or wounded man you find. 'Cause if you do, I might find myself worked to a nub before I can grow whiskers."

Cherish laughed. "I'm afraid I do, Bar. My father used to say I had a gift for healing. He told me once that my mother worked day and night to help her people when typhoid fever almost wiped out their town. Afterwards, folks said she had the gift. I guess I'm like her; I just can't stand to see folks suffer if I can help."

Bar nodded slowly. "I ain't never met folks like you and Miss Margaret."

"You'll get used to us." Cherish laughed.

"Oh, I don't mind helpin' out. Heck, I've hauled enough water in the past three days to fill twenty horse troughs. Bothers me some that Miss Margaret keeps expectin' me to use it on my own body. That woman gets an idea in her head and there ain't no way of reasonin' with her. Her Westley that she keeps talkin' about didn't by chance die of pneumonia from bathin' in the winter, did he?"

Cherish fought the urge to hug him. "No," she answered. "He died in the war just like a lot of other men."

"Oh." Bar shrugged and headed down the stairs just as old Hattie called him about hearing someone under her bed.

9

Brant Coulter leaned against the rough window frame and stared into the frosty night. He was thankful for the cold and rain. With no cattle drives camped nearby and the weather keeping all the local folks away, Hell's Half-Acre was as quiet as if it were respectable. He could still smell whiskey and filth seeping up from the bar below his room, but at least there was no noise. He lit the end of his thin cigar and studied the house on the hill at the end of Hell's Half-Acre.

He couldn't get his mind off of the beautiful woman who had saved his life. She had a way of seeping into every still moment and settling there, more than a memory, less than reality. Even though it had been almost a week since he'd seen her, his hunger for her hadn't diminished. But she was from another world and he couldn't live with himself if he soiled something as perfect as Cherish Wyatt.

A tap rattled him back from his longings. He tossed his cigar out the window and crossed the tiny room to his guns.

"Who is it?"

"It's me, honey. Holliday." A voice as husky as a miner's answered.

"Come in." Brant shoved his Colt back in its holster and relaxed. As the door opened a woman almost as wide as the frame waltzed in. She was like a day-old sweetshop with cinnamon hair, dark raisin eyes, and wheat-flour skin. Her huge breasts jostled like full-risen dough in her low-cut blouse and her walk seemed to advertise that anyone could buy her sweets for a bargain.

Holliday smiled with blood red lips that spanned her face. She was not many years older than Brant, but she'd lived her life in double time. "I know you said you wanted to be left alone, but I thought you might be wanting a girl to keep you company."

"No, thanks." The idea of one of Holliday's long-ridden girls almost turned his stomach, but he had to be polite. She was doing him quite a favor by letting him stay, even though he was paying well for it. "Your girls could probably use a night off before business picks up tomorrow."

Holliday chuckled and waved her porky little fingers in the air. "I wasn't thinking of one of my girls. I was referring to this wisp of a little thing that came in the back door with that boy Barfield. She told me she knew you were here and wasn't leaving until she'd seen you. I figure either you see her or I put her to work. After a few cowhands who leave their boots on, she'll lose some of that spotless clean look and probably start to enjoy my line of work."

The muscle across Brant's strong jawline twitched before he realized Holliday was kidding. She'd long ago replaced her heart with a change purse, but she wasn't an evil woman. Before she'd decided she could make more money on her back, she'd been one of Hattie's dealers at the poker games that used to run every weekend when he was a boy.

"Send her up," Brant ordered without giving her the pleasure of knowing that her joke had gotten under his skin. As she waddled out of the room, he looked around, suddenly seeing the filth of the place. Here, Cherish would be like a white rose dropped in the gutter. "Damn," he swore, wishing she hadn't found him.

Before he could move, she stormed into the room, a whirlwind of pure delight. Her voice was clear and a little high with anxiety. "Thank goodness I found you."

"What do you want?" He hadn't meant his words to sound harsh, but they did.

"I've come to rebandage that wound." She was using her most formal voice now, the kind she must have used on troublesome soldiers when she was at the army hospitals. "I don't want all my time to have been wasted because you haven't changed the dressing."

"I'm fine," Brant lied. The wound had kept him awake most of the nights. "I haven't even thought about it in days. So you can just turn around and go back home."

"No!"

"Get out." The sooner she learned to stay away from him the better. "Go on. The last thing I need is someone mothering me."

"I'm not mothering you." Cherish backed him into the wall with one pointed finger sighted on him like a gun. "Now take off that shirt and let me have a look at you."

Brant tried another way to get her to leave him alone. "I could ask the same of you. I've already felt what lies beneath that blouse of yours. Since you're trying to undress me, I wouldn't mind swapping the pleasure."

Cherish turned and opened her medicine bag. "It won't work. I'm not leaving until I've changed your bandage, even if I have to get your friend Holliday in here to sit on you while I do."

"She'd love that job."

"What job?" Holliday answered from the open doorway. "Here's the water you asked for, Miss Wyatt."

He didn't miss the smile of thanks Cherish flashed Holliday. It wasn't the patronizing smile of one who had given an order, but the thank-you of one who had asked a favor and had it granted. The huge woman swelled another size with pride and newfound self-respect. "You just ask for anything else you need." She glared at Brant. "And if this ruffian gives you any trouble you just yell and I'll come in and personally pull off one of his ears."

"I'll be fine." Cherish laughed. "But thanks for the offer."

As Holliday left, Brant studied Cherish, wondering if there was anyone who didn't love her on sight. "You win," he whispered, rubbing his endangered ear between his thumb and forefinger, "but do anything that needs doing now because I don't plan to be so easy to find again." Half the law in Texas was looking for him and this little lady didn't seem to have any trouble tracking him down.

As Brant pulled off his shirt, Cherish laid out what she needed. "Sit here," she ordered as she pulled a ladder-back chair in front of him and moved the lamp close to her side.

She worked, cutting away the bandage. She was careful to soak places where dried blood held the material to his skin. As she worked, Brant felt he would drown in her nearness. The light danced across her face, brightening her eyes with emerald fire and highlighting her hair to sunrise gold. Her hands moved over his chest, cleaning around the wound. He couldn't ever remember being touched with a light hand in his life. Even the few women he'd known had always been heavy-handed. No one had ever cared enough to try not to hurt him when they touched him. For a moment he wondered what it would be like to lie next to such a woman and make love to her. But it would never happen. The only way he'd ever keep such a woman near him was with fear, and somehow he couldn't bear to think of her afraid.

"Why did you come?" he whispered as she began wrapping the wound with a clean dressing.

"This has to be done." She didn't look up at him, but her hands gently spread the bandage in a caress along his ribs.

"But why?" He studied her. "I told you before I'm a walking dead man."

Cherish straightened and his eyes followed her as she put her medicines away. She was quiet for so long that he wasn't sure she was going to answer. "I've come to warn you that someone may be looking for you."

Brant laughed. "Half the lawmen in the state are looking for me."

"Then you must go!" Her gentle voice was pleading.

"I will." He tried to think of why he hadn't left already and realized suddenly that the answer was standing in front of him.

He pulled on his shirt, not bothering to button it. Suddenly, the walls of the room seemed to be moving inward. She was so tiny, so fragile. He was afraid to touch her. "Thanks for coming," he said between clenched teeth.

She played with the latch on the medicine bag. "I have to get back. We have children to take care of from the mission. All three are ill."

"I thought I told you to stay away from Father Daniel."

Curiosity twisted her beautifully shaped eyebrows. "Why? He's been nothing but kind to you. Perhaps you'd better tell me why I should stay away from the priest."

Brant was silent.

"I make up my own mind about people. I doubt that I need a man who's told me he's killed people to warn me against a man of the cloth. If he's done something, then tell me."

Only the tight muscle along Brant's jawline moved.

Cherish waited and grew impatient with his silence. What did she have to do to prove to this man that she could be trusted? "I must go," she finally whispered.

Brant didn't want her to leave, but he knew he had no right to stop her. She'd saved his life twice and the best thing he could do for her was stay out of her life. "Cherish." Her name was like a prayer on his lips. "Don't ask too many questions. There are a great many people in this town who have something to hide. And don't come looking for me again. It would only mean trouble."

She looked up and for a moment he thought he saw the sadness of a great loss in her eyes; then she blinked and the formal nurse returned. "Good-bye, Mr. Coulter. Take care of the wound until it's completely healed."

Before he could answer she hurried from the room. He moved to the window so he could watch her make the journey back to Hattie's Parlor at the end of the street. But Cherish didn't appear in the street leading to Hattie's. Only Bar's thin silhouette made the trip back toward the old house. It took Brant several seconds to realize something had to be wrong.

Even the air was thick with danger as Cherish walked deeper and deeper into the side streets. She knew she'd been smart to send Bar on home, but suddenly she wished she wasn't alone. The very shacks seemed to breathe as the cold air rattled them. She walked carefully in the center, between the buildings. No one bothered to clean the droppings from the road in this part of town, so the smell of horse manure blended in with the frosty air.

A shadow rolled from the steps of one of the shacks. "What ya want?"

Another shadow stretched and moved forward on all fours like an animal.

"I've come to see the owner of the house marked in green," she answered, trying to keep the fear from her face. She knew she was close, for the sickening sweet smell of opium spiced the air.

"Come to buy, did you?" The shadow stood and moved toward her.

Cherish didn't answer, but reached inside her purse for her gun.

The other shadow skirted the foggy moonlight and circled her.

"If she's come to buy, she's got money," a voice whispered from nowhere.

The shadows moved, circling her. They seemed more like rats than humans as they pulled their drug-sluggish bodies through the filth of the street. The ragged dark blotches along the walls of the other shacks began to come alive and move toward her. She realized, even if she could pull her gun and get one shot off, the rest would be on her before she could fire again. Years on the poppy had decayed their minds and morals until killing for a few coins seemed logical.

Cherish pulled her arms close around her and watched them moving closer and closer. She could smell their urine-soaked clothes and her skin shivered at the thought of one of them touching her.

The sudden report of gunfire shattered the inky air. For an instant the silver flash of twin Colts shone in the darkness. A low voice, thick with the promise of death, filled the street with a whisper. "Take another step toward the lady and it'll be your last."

Cherish ran toward the tall silhouette of Brant's lean form. She was in his arms before the smoke from his gun passed above his hat. With practiced skill, he slid one Colt into his belt. He pulled her close with his free hand while his other gripped the weapon that still pointed at the shadows that seemed to have evaporated back into the night.

"Walk slowly, but deliberately," he whispered. "If they're doped enough it may not take them long to try, no matter what the risk."

Cherish kept her arms tight around his waist and he led her back into the main street. "Relax," he groaned as his steps slowed into a stroll.

"I'm sorry," she whispered as she realized her grip might have been painful against his chest.

"I'm not complaining, but we want to look like we're just out for a walk in case someone should decide to investigate the shot. Which I doubt will happen in this part of town."

As they passed two men leaving a bar, Brant pulled her closer against him and leaned his head low. His hat covered her face from the men's view, but it brought their lips dangerously close together. For that moment, Cherish wished that he would kiss her as he had on the train so that she could know if the feelings she'd had the first time he touched her were real or just the result of fear and confusion. For now she felt no fear or confusion, only excitement.

They continued in silence until finally Cherish saw the light beaming from the second-story window of her house. As they neared, Brant turned so that they would come up to the back door. Soundlessly, they moved into the blackness beside the barn.

Cherish stumbled over the rough ground and Brant stepped in her path to steady her. She slammed into the wall of his chest before she realized what he was doing. Embarrassed, she jumped back, but his arms still held her securely. His lean, hard hands circled her shoulders as he imprisoned her. For a moment they stood together with only the low wind whispering around them; then he asked, "Why were you in that alley? Don't you realize what could have happened to you?"

Cherish resented him questioning her as though she were a child late for school. She pushed at the wall of his chest and answered, "If you must know, Hattie is in more pain each day. Father Daniel told me of the place where I'd find opium for her."

"That stuff is poison."

"I know, but she doesn't have long to live and if it will help the pain . . . sometimes she cries for hours."

"But why you? Why not Azile or Bar?"

Cherish looked up, realizing he was only a few inches from her. "I couldn't ask them to do what I would not."

Brant pulled her close. "But you have no tie to Hattie. She's just an old lady living in your house."

"She needs me," Cherish whispered as she paused in the shadows. "I had to help her if for no other reason."

"The way I needed you?" His breath was warm against her cheek, but his words were sharp. "What was I, last week's charity case? And Hattie is this week's?"

"No," she answered as his body suddenly pressed her against the barn wall. She could feel the anger in him as she tried to think of what to say. How could she ever explain to him how her need to help people filled a great void in her? With him, it was different. He gave as much as he took. When she helped him live, a part of her also sprang to life, a part she'd never allowed to surface.

"What am I to you?" His lips moved feather-light against her temple. "Maybe you're one of those women who loves to flirt with danger. First an outlaw, then an opium den."

"No. I care about you." All she could think about was

his nearness and the dreams she'd had of him since the night they'd met. Even now the memory of his kiss ignited a fire deep inside her. Could the reality of his arms be as wonderful as her fantasy? Would his lips stir her blood as they had once before?

Brant's warm hands pressed her shoulders against the damp wood. "Then show me how you feel." His fingers moved down her arms. "For I've thought I'd go mad from longing to hold you again. Show me that you feel the same about me."

Reason no longer mattered. She wanted to hold him once more beside her before she was forced never to see him again. He'd made it plain that their paths would not cross again. So this once she had to allow herself to feel. Raising her lips, she met his mouth with all the longing her dreams had kindled. She heard him groan as if he were in pain, but his kiss was demanding. Her fingers slid into his hair and she kissed him completely and wantonly, as she'd longed to do.

His hand lightly pressed against her back as if he were afraid to pull her near. Slowly, as her mouth opened to his kiss, his fingers slid beneath her cape and brushed across the material covering her breast. She molded within his hand as he swallowed her cry of surprise. His kiss pushed deeper into her mouth as his fingers pulled at the material covering her flesh. He didn't hear the material rip, or the buttons pop, for she was in his arms. A need to touch her consumed him, driving reason far into the corners of his mind.

For the first time, he wanted a woman totally, not just in his bed, but in his life. The realization that it was impossible only made this moment more treasured.

He turned a deaf ear to the voices inside his mind that told him it was wrong. He'd have given his life for this moment in time and he'd live a hundred lifetimes before he ever felt someone so wonderful again. With passion's starvation he shoved the material from her breast and freed her flesh to his rough, grasping touch.

She strained away, but he wouldn't release her mouth from his kiss. His ironlike arm tightened, forcing her closer. Though he knew his actions were unskilled and harsh for the lady in his arms, she'd settle into his way, for he knew no other.

Within a few heartbeats, she stopped struggling and he relaxed his grip.

Cherish jerked back violently, a cry caught in her throat. Shoving him away, she pulled her coat tight around her with trembling hands and stepped into the moonlight. Confusion and longing reflected in her forest green depths. She stood watching him as though the moon's light would somehow keep her safe from his touch—as though anything or anyone on earth could.

Brant made no move toward her, though he felt she'd ripped his heart out with her withdrawal. "Don't play games with me, Cherish."

"I wasn't."

Anger played in his voice as he turned to leave. There was only one person who could keep her from him . . . herself. Her withdrawal had been as deadly as cannon fire at close range. She hadn't needed to scream at him; her eyes had stabbed him deeply. "I understand," he whispered between his teeth.

Cherish looked at his back, suddenly angry at him for his forwardness and at herself for allowing it to happen. As always, her temper overruled caution. "You understand what?"

"I understand that I soil you with my touch." His words came hard and cold.

Tears stung her eyes as she heard the pain in his voice. She moved toward him and almost touched his arm before she thought better and withdrew. "You're wrong. I'm afraid of you, but not because of who you are. I'm afraid of the way you make me feel. No one has ever touched me the way you did just now."

Brant laughed, but there was no joy in his tone. "You mean you've made it to being a grown woman and no one has ever felt of you? Next you'll tell me you've never been kissed."

"I've been kissed," she answered directly, "and by men with far more gentleness than you."

Brant pulled his arm away from her reach. "I'm sorry I didn't learn the art of loving. I've been too busy fighting since I've been old enough to remember."

"Learn the art?" Cherish snapped. "With you it's a martial art. How dare you handle me as though I were some saloon girl handing out favors with drinks."

"How dare you invite me with your entire body and then pull away." His whisper was almost lost in the fog.

He stormed toward the back porch and waited for her to follow. When she was safely on the second step he removed his hat and leaned his head back. "I guess I should say I'm sorry for what happened back there, but a man once told me you're only truly sorry in life for what you didn't do, never for what you do. I didn't mean to frighten you."

Cherish placed her hands on his shoulders, trying to gain control of her emotions. Thanks to the steps, she was at eye level with him. "When I said you touch me, I meant deep down inside. I'm half-afraid of you and half-drawn to you. But no one, not even the gentle beaux I've had, has ever made me feel like you do."

His handsome face wrinkled and she leaned closer to whisper. "Seeing you, touching you, caring about you, is not a luxury or a pastime; it's a necessity. So stop telling me you're never going to see me again or that I think your hands dirty me. I'd like very much to see you again."

Brant was so shocked by her speech that he just looked at her and said nothing. Her dark green eyes were afire with mischief and delight.

"I have to go." Brant wanted to run. He couldn't bear to look at her and not pull her into his arms. And if she were in his arms at this moment he wasn't sure he could stop until he'd made love to her. "It will be dawn soon," he managed to mutter.

"When will I see you again?" Cherish knew she was being bold, but she couldn't go for days again without knowing where he was or if he felt anything like she did. She'd opened her soul to this man and all he'd said was that he had to go. Since she'd waited until she was twenty for her first taste of passion, she couldn't afford the luxury of dallying. She wanted Brant Coulter, but she wanted his love with his desire. She wanted the tenderness his eyes promised, not just the physical touching he offered. Suddenly, she realized she wanted it all from this man or nothing at all.

Brant looked up at the stars and tried not to think about her hands resting on his shoulders. "Tomorrow night," he whispered as he stepped away. "At midnight. I'll be in the barn if I can. But if you're wise, you'll stay away from me. And if I have any sense I'll never touch you again."

He walked away unsure he could leave her if he turned and saw her face again in the moonlight. God, how he wanted her. And yet she scared him more than a hundred posses. How could she pull away one minute and beg to see him again the next? She wasn't like the women he'd met. What she wanted might be the same, but she wanted it slow and deep, not fast and meaningless. Other women might want his money, or his body, but Cherish wanted him heart and soul. She was either as pure as she acted, or as crazy as old Hattie.

10

Margaret lifted one wet child and handed her to Grayson. While he dried the baby she stripped the next victim for "a good cleaning," as she called it.

"I'm glad Westley and I had no children." Margaret pushed a strand of ebony hair from her flushed face and continued, "I'm about to decide I'm not very maternal." She'd developed a habit of talking to Grayson without ever expecting an answer or caring that he didn't seem to understand a word she said. "I wouldn't have been able to go with Cherish if I'd had a child. There hasn't been more than a few weeks since she was born that I haven't been near her just in case she needed me."

Grayson really wasn't listening to her words. He was watching how her wet blouse clung to the rounded curve of her shoulders and loving the way she moved as she worked. Every day with her was a new level of hell for him. The more he burned for her, the more she talked about the angel of a man she'd married, her Westley. His memory was an invisible wall that kept Grayson away and made him realize that loving her would never happen except in his dreams. After all the years, he'd finally fallen for another woman, and she was married to a memory.

As he watched her, he smiled. He knew she was lying about not wanting children. All three little ones were better today and could have gone back to the mission, but Margaret had already told Father Daniel that she was keeping them for a few more days.

Grayson helped dress the children and bed them down. He smiled at what his supervisors would say in the office if they knew he was spending his time staring at a beautiful woman and rocking babies. He'd spent ten years convincing everyone how heartless he was when it came to criminals, and he'd never live it down if they saw him now. He'd had enough time to get away twice and send messages back to the office by way of an old stagecoach driver he'd used as delivery man before. He was beginning to believe that all the talk about a secret clan known as the Knights of the Golden Circle was just a tale cooked up to frighten blacks and skittish Northerners. Logic told him he was wasting his time with both the mission and the woman, but a few pieces didn't fit together around this place. And Grayson never left a job half-done. So, he'd asked to be assigned temporarily to the nearest post at Camp Wilson.

Leaning back in a chair, he thought of what he'd come up with so far: The accident hadn't been an accident at all. Cherish disappeared sometimes for hours. Old Hattie guarded her room like it was a bank depository. None of it made much sense. Even Azile's constant warnings about the house were starting to get on his nerves. The latest was her claim that she smelled death in the woodwork. But Maggie swore it was only the whiskey Azile mixed with her tea. Sometimes Grayson thought he could almost feel evil whispering through the hallways when everyone else was asleep.

"Grayson." Margaret grabbed his arm in panic. "Someone's out front."

Grayson started from his daydream. He moved to the window and watched as shadows drifted around just beyond the gate. There were several cottonwoods on the other side of the road that now darkened the spot where a dozen men met. Grayson watched in horror as he saw the men pull material over their heads as masks. He'd heard of this kind of trouble spreading through the South like a cancer, but this was the first proof he'd witnessed. He'd bet a year's pay that a few of these men were members of the Knights he'd been searching for.

The men were laughing, and judging from the volume, they'd been drinking. Several riders joined at the crossroads from town. A shot rang out as a call to ride, and the horses bolted into a full run. Shots echoed through the streets as others joined in the race out of town.

Grayson clutched Margaret against him and fell to the floor. His body rolled and covered hers as they waited a long, silent moment to make sure the firing had stopped. He was so aware of her as a woman that not even the danger penetrated his mind. He leaned his cheek against her hair and closed his eyes to dream for one moment that she was in his arms for another reason. He longed to tell her how she affected him, but one word would mean his betrayal, and she'd hate him for the rest of her life. How could she ever love a man who had fought against her beloved Westley? How could he ever compete against a ghost?

"Grayson." She whispered his name, and he fought the urge to press her into the floor with his entire weight. "I think they're gone." There was no passion, no hunger in her voice. The realization that she didn't feel the same about him was like an ice storm against his soul.

Slowly, he rose and helped her up. The pat she gave to his arm was an insult. He doubled his fists to keep from grabbing her and showing her he was a man and not a lapdog.

He turned to the windows and allowed the icy wind to cool his blood. He had a job to do, he reminded himself, and by God he'd do that job. Then he'd drink this woman out of his mind if it took six months.

As he stared into the night he saw one lone figure mount a horse and ride off to the west. There was no mistaking the slight build of the rider as he mentally cataloged this new evidence in his already growing file on Cherish Wyatt.

Cherish followed the gray dust trail of a dozen or more riders for almost a mile before she turned her horse and took a shortcut through rocky ground. She knew it was dangerous, but she had to reach the farm before the others, and this was her one chance.

As she rode, she tried to piece together all that had happened in the past hour. She'd waited for Brant in the barn long past the time they'd agreed on. Finally, voices drifted from the road. Silently moving around the house, she'd slipped unseen into the shadow of the cottonwoods. As more men arrived, their destination and purpose became clear. First, she'd listened to them argue about taking the short trail she was now on, but the vote had finally been that it was too risky at night. Then she'd heard parts of conversations about beating or hanging a few former slaves at Hank's place to teach them a lesson.

Even now, after miles of hard riding, their words still doubled her fists with anger. She had to reach Hank Stevens' farm first and warn everyone. She remembered a letter her mother had written early in the war about a family near Fredericksburg, Texas, who sided with the North's beliefs. Masked riders had raided their farm in the middle of the night. They'd demanded that the man and all his sons over twelve step out. When the peaceful farmer did as they'd asked, the masked men gunned them all down while the wife and smaller children watched. Cherish wouldn't let that happen now.

She spotted the large farmhouse in the distance and pushed the bay she'd borrowed from Grayson without asking into a full gallop. They must be given a chance to run or hide before the drunken mob of men reached them. If she had to, she'd stand alone while they had time to hide, but there was going to be no more killing.

"Stop!" someone shouted from the blackness. A man's shadow appeared from nowhere to stand thirty feet in front of her horse.

Without warning, the bay balked, throwing Cherish over his head and into freshly plowed dirt. She was almost on her feet when a strong arm clamped around her waist and pulled her across the ground. Before she could scream, the attacker dropped into a hole and pulled her down with him. He ran his hands along her sides, then, when seemingly satisfied she was not injured, he shoved her against the wall of the freshly built trench.

"Uncover a lamp and see who it is," someone snapped.

"No!" said her attacker in a voice that sounded familiar. "I know who she is. I'll see that she keeps her head down and stays out of trouble."

"I will not keep my head down." Cherish fought at the arm holding her as she glanced toward three men huddled in the trench. "There is a group of men on their way that are planning to beat, maybe even kill, some of the blacks on this farm. I'll not—"

A gloved hand covered her mouth, the touch oddly familiar. "You idiot," he whispered. "Quiet, or you'll let them know we're here waiting for them." His lips were only an inch from her ear and there was no mistaking the familiar aroma of danger that always seemed to surround Brant Coulter.

As he spoke, the sound of horses thundered through the air. Brant shoved Cherish against the dirt wall of the trench with his body. She could feel the earth move as the horses grew closer. A thousand questions jumped into her mind, but the nearness of his hand to her cheek kept her silent. She turned to watch.

When the riders were within thirty yards, the men in the trench uncovered lanterns and set them on the ground. All four, including Brant, raised their rifles and she heard one mighty click as they cocked their weapons.

The men on horseback stumbled to a stop, some losing their balance and falling off their horses.

A lone man stepped out of the trench and for a moment he seemed to face the hooded men alone. "I'm Hank Stevens and you're on my land." Three other shadows climbed up to join him.

Brant leaned close to Cherish as he climbed. "Stay here and don't move, or I swear this time I will break your pretty neck." Before she could ask any questions he'd jumped up to stand with the others.

A man on horseback, his face completely hidden in white cloth, yelled, "Get out of our way, Hank. We've come to teach your blacks a lesson! They've been giving some of the other darkies ideas."

Hank raised his gun. "The only lesson to be learned here tonight is that folks should keep off other folks' property if they want to stay healthy." His words were punctuated by the raised weapons of his friends. "I'll figure you got lost since you can't see very well out of those masks. So either take them off or turn around and go back to hell where you belong for all I care."

"But, Hank!" someone shouted from the back of the horse-men. "You ain't sidin' against us and for those darkies?"

Hank's rifle turned toward the voice. "Any slave I had on this place is free now, and the way I see it every one of them is more man than the whole pack of you."

The masked men were angry. They'd ridden all this way and done a great deal of talking and drinking, and now they had no intention of returning to town without a fight. One man slid from his horse. "There ain't but four of them. We're almost twenty. Hank wouldn't shoot a fellow Confederate over a few slaves."

Hank pointed his gun at the man now standing on the ground. "I see no Confederate soldiers before me, only cowards. In all the years of fighting I never had to hide my face as you do now."

The hooded man moved forward. "I'm bettin' you're fed up with killin', Hank." He kept advancing. "I'm thinkin' it would take more than this to get you to kill again."

He'd guessed right. Hank hesitated a long moment, then turned the gun barrel skyward. He couldn't kill anymore. But he couldn't stand by and allow his former slaves to be beaten either. The law might have taken them out of his hands of ownership, but he still felt responsible for them. In one mighty jerk of anger Hank raised his gun butt and slammed it into the hooded man's head. The gun fired harmlessly in the air, but all hell broke loose on the ground. Horses reared. Guns fired. A few riders kicked their mounts and ran, but most scrambled to the ground and joined in the fight.

Cherish blinked in amazement. All had been still one moment and now men were fighting all around her. In an instant she realized how outnumbered the four men were. Gathering up her skirts, she climbed the embankment and joined the fight. She grabbed one of Brant's discarded Colts and began using it as a club, swinging at every cloth-covered head she saw.

A few times the victims turned, then froze as they saw their tiny attacker. Before they had a chance to react, she landed another blow, sending them into a peaceful sleep. Dust billowed up to her neck but still she fought. The smell of blood and anger assaulted the night air as the pounding of blow after blow against flesh echoed around her. One by one, the men fell until finally only Brant and Hank remained standing. Hank shook his head, taking no pleasure in what he'd done. Brant gripped his shoulder in pain.

Hank wiped the blood from his nose and pointed toward her with his head. "Thanks, little lady. You're not bigger than a chigger, but you pack a mean bite."

Brant whirled to face her and she saw murder in his auburn eyes. He was bleeding from several cuts on his hands and face, but none seemed to give him near the pain as looking at Cherish.

Hank pulled one of his men up. "You all right, Phil?"

The man mumbled as he wiped both blood and sweat from his face. "Take more than the likes of them cowards to kill me. Why, I've gotten hurt worse fightin' nightmares."

Hank bellowed several names and a line of black men appeared from the side of the house. For the most part they were old men, long past their prime, or boys wild-eyed with fear from what they'd seen. Hank pointed as he issued orders for the hooded men to be tied to their saddles and sent home. He lifted one of his friends in his arms and turned toward the house. "Brant," he added over his shoulder, "bring that little filly of yours in the house. I'd like to meet her."

Brant stood where he was until Hank was several feet away. "I'd like to kill her with my own hands for not following orders," he whispered only for her ears. "Don't you know what you've done?"

"I've helped." Cherish's anger matched his own. She'd ridden out to warn them, she'd fought like the others, and now she was being yelled at like she was a child. "I have just as much right to be here and stop this injustice as you do. How could I have stayed in town when I overheard that those men planned to hurt innocent people?"

As she talked, she moved closer until now they were only a hand's width apart. His rust-colored eyes turned a deep brown as passion replaced anger. Instinctively, she wiped a drop of blood from the corner of his mouth. His head turned slightly to follow her touch.

"I did what I had to do," she whispered as the longing for his arms became a great ache within her. Her instinct about him had been right. He wasn't evil. He'd stood with Hank to fight for what was right. She'd never wanted to hold anyone in her life as much as she wanted to hold Brant Coulter right now.

But he closed his eyes and leaned his head back. When his words finally came they were slow and filled with agony. "Don't you see? They've seen you. You've signed your own death warrant."

11

Dawn broke without any peace at Hattie's Parlor. The children had been taking turns crying as if conspiring to keep the adults up all night. Hattie was yelling for her pain medicine. Azile, half-drunk, swore she'd seen a raven fly by her window before breakfast. Although she wasn't sure what it meant, she was sure it was something bad. Stacked on top of everything was Margaret's growing panic that Cherish was missing.

Grayson had his own theories, but he remained silent as she stormed and worried through the hours of darkness. If the girl hadn't taken his horse he might have left Maggie with the children and tried to follow Cherish.

By noon Maggie could stand the wait no longer. She had to see if she could find her niece. She dressed in her most proper clothes and went to the sheriff's office with Grayson following a step behind.

The deputy was the only one in the office when they arrived. He was a nervous man in his mid-thirties. He proved to be of no help, and foolishly suggested that young girls sometimes run away with their fellows. He was quickly and sharply corrected by Margaret, who assured him that Cherish would do no such thing without talking it over with her. Finally, more out of self-defense than interest, the deputy promised to file a full report, but Margaret doubted he could sharpen his own pencil, much less use it.

A sheriff, looking like he'd been in a bar fight, wandered in while they were talking and slumped into his chair. After he listened to Margaret's description, he raised one eyebrow, paid close attention, and even asked a few questions about Cherish.

Margaret glanced in his direction. "You've seen her, haven't you?"

The sheriff shook his head vigorously, then cradled it as though deeply regretting the action. Finally he answered. "I saw her once at the back door of Holliday's saloon."

The deputy quickly agreed and offered to go over to Holliday's and ask a few questions.

Margaret badgered the sheriff for several more minutes but gained no more information. She refused to believe that any possibility existed that Cherish might have visited a saloon.

As they marched back home, Grayson debated whether to tell her about Cherish leaving or not. She was guessing all kinds of things that could have happened to Cherish, but Grayson knew one fact. The girl left of her own free will and there wasn't much the law or Margaret could do about that.

All evening Margaret paced. She searched the house completely just in case Cherish had fallen somewhere and was lying unconscious. As evening veiled the day, Father Daniel came to call. He looked tired and Grayson didn't miss the bandage on his hand or the bruise along his hairline. The priest explained them both away as a spill from his spirited horse, but Grayson somehow doubted his story.

The clergyman did have a calming effect on Margaret, however. He listened intently to her story and patted her hand gently as he told her he'd do whatever he could to help. His pale gray eyes held a world of sorrow in their depths and somehow Margaret felt better at having laid her problems at his door. When he finally left, he gave her a brotherly hug and told her he'd pray for Cherish's safe return.

Grayson watched him walk away and wondered if Father Daniel was any closer to God's ear than anyone else. Somehow he doubted it. Something about the priest made Grayson nervous. He couldn't put his finger on what didn't fit together, but he always had the feeling that he needed to wash his hands after touching the man. Grayson felt that somewhere beneath the layers of concern and love was a kind of filth so deep that no amount of lye soap would ever wash it away. He'd spent ten years bringing in murderers, thieves, and traitors, but none gave him the bad taste in his mouth that the priest did. It was no more than a hunch, but Grayson had stayed alive because of his hunches.

Hours later, when Margaret called him, he felt like he'd only just closed his eyes. She was dressed and proper as ever, except for the lines of sleeplessness around her eyes. "We're going to talk to this woman named Holliday. I have nowhere else to turn."

While he dressed, she stepped into Cherish's room and checked on the babies, then rattled off instructions for Azile and Bar. Azile was only half-listening, but Bar nodded his understanding. When she returned, Grayson noticed she'd slipped her derringer into her pocket instead of putting it in the strap holster on her leg.

Margaret was all starch and vinegar as she marched down the street to the core of the area known as Hell's Half-Acre. She didn't seem to see the stares or hear the whispers as she continued until she reached the saloon owned by the woman named Holliday.

Without a moment's hesitation, she pushed the door aside and stepped into the filthy establishment. The initial stench that met Margaret and Grayson was almost overwhelming. Margaret stood for a minute at the entrance to allow her eyes to adjust to the dimness. Grayson's senses went on immediate alert. He had seen too many of these places not to know that trouble was just waiting for an excuse to explode. The walls of the saloon were a dull gray and black from a mixture of smoke and whiskey, and the floor was so dirty that straw had been thrown down to absorb some of the spilled liquor and spit. Grayson had heard it said once that if a man died in a bar like this, it might be two days before anyone would pick him up off the floor. Not till his body finally outsmelled the grime did they lift him up and toss him into the street.

"I wish to speak to a woman named Holliday," Margaret said to a sleepy-eyed bartender after getting her bearings and determining that no one was going to ask her if she needed help.

Grayson carefully watched the few people left in the bar from the night before. They were long into their liquor and posed no threat.

"I'm Holliday." A huge woman stepped through a side door from where voices were coming. "I'm a little busy right now with this big poker game going on. Could you come back later, lady?"

Margaret turned her full attention to the almost topless woman. For a moment Margaret's mouth dropped open slightly at the size of the big-breasted woman whose blouse had slipped to the point that nipples the blood red color of her lipstick were showing just above the worn lace.

"I'm Margaret Alexander." Margaret extended her hand. She might be a proud woman full of her own sense of right and wrong, but she was not fast to judge people, no matter how they dressed or where they came from.

Holliday's smile showed her approval. There wasn't one lady in a hundred who would look her in the eye, much less shake her hand. This thin widow had just made a friend without doing a thing besides offering her hand. As she took Margaret's hand and pumped it, Margaret introduced her to Grayson.

One painted eyebrow bounced up. "Your man?"

Margaret straightened. "No. My employee."

Holliday wasted no time moving the few feet to Grayson. "Hi ya, honey. How come I ain't never seen you in here before? A body could use a strong man like you." She heaved her huge breasts against his arm as she added, "I'll bet you'd give a girl a hell of a ride."

Grayson tried to keep from laughing, not at Holliday, for she was plying her trade quite well, but at Margaret's reaction. His lady was about to scratch this whore's eyes out and he loved seeing the fire in Margaret's face. He crossed his arms, only giving the overpainted woman more arm to rub against.

She moved her body back and forth across his forearms and licked her scarlet lips. "Don't forget to come a-looking for me, darling," she whispered. "My door's always open to a fine strapping man like yourself."

Margaret found her tongue. "He doesn't understand what you're saying."

Holliday laughed and stepped away. As she did so, she heaved her chest once more, pulling the material even lower for Grayson's benefit. "Oh, he understands. There ain't a man alive who doesn't understand me."

Her wink was bold and inviting. Some other time Grayson might have enjoyed a night with such a woman, but lately all he'd been hungry for was Margaret, and he knew no other woman would satisfy him.

Holliday walked back to Margaret and put one fist on her wide hip. "What can I do for you, ma'am?"

"I'm looking for my niece, Cherish Wyatt. Have you seen her?"

Holliday motioned for the bartender to pour her one, and studied Margaret carefully while he made the drink of half-whiskey and half-rye. Finally, with drink in hand, she answered. "I may be a lot of things, Mrs. Alexander, but a liar ain't one of them. I don't think I'd be doing no one any harm by telling you your niece came to my door once. She doctored a man staying upstairs and left." Holliday's eyes narrowed as she read Margaret's expression. "There weren't no harm that come to her that night, you have my word."

"And the man's name?" Margaret asked, knowing that the woman spoke the truth. Cherish would go anywhere, even into a place like this, if she thought someone was suffering.

Holliday's eyes narrowed. "I make a habit of forgetting names as soon as they pay. All you need to know is that she left here without coming to any harm."

Margaret nodded, knowing she'd get no more information out of this woman. "Thank you for your help."

Holliday lifted a tray of beer and headed to the back room. "I better get this refreshment to those fools who've been playing all night before they break the place down."

As she opened the door wide to accommodate both herself and the tray, Margaret looked into the smoke-filled room.

Grayson had already turned and was halfway to the door when he realized Margaret wasn't at his side. He glanced over his shoulder and saw her face drain of all blood. Before he could stop her, she moved to the door Holliday had left open and whispered, "Westley?"

Her one word was like a death toll on the entire room. Every man froze and turned toward her as she stood in the doorway. "Westley," she whispered again as if confronting a ghost.

A tall, heavyset man stood up behind the table. His chest and stomach were wide with years of drink and his shoulders permanently rounded from playing a lifetime of poker. His hair was pulled back from a hawklike nose and his face was saloon pale.

"Margaret!" He looked at her directly with eyes the color of well water. "I always knew someday you'd find me. You were too stubborn to allow me to remain a dead hero."

Margaret's world was shattering. "But, Westley, you died."

The huge man laughed, inspiring the laughter of his comrades. "Gentlemen"—he made a wide sweep with his hand—"my wife. I've been dead more than four years and she still mourns me."

"But"—Margaret ignored the comments of the others—"you didn't come home."

"To what?" Westley's drunken mind resented her. "To a farm where I'd die a slower death than in battle? To you, my barren wife, who was so cold in bed I'd rather sleep with whores. At least they are warm for my money."

Margaret's hand began to shake and she moved it inside her pocket. "You're nothing but a lying traitor, both to me and to your country."

"Better a traitor than your husband. How many times do you think I'd allow you to turn me away? I should have whipped you senseless that last night when you wouldn't let me touch you again. You should have taken my seed until you swelled. I wanted to leave with my brat growing in your belly so you'd soften and not be the hard woman you've become."

"Stop!" Margaret shouted.

"Why, Maggie, you know it's the truth." He turned to his friends. "Look at her, gentlemen. A man would freeze to death in her bed. Would you believe my last night before I left for battle she tried to lock me out of our bedroom."

"Stop!"

Westley didn't listen. "Why? I knew the South's cause was hopeless early on and got out. Our marriage was just a convenience. Everyone was getting married before they left. It took me a few months to have my fill of army life, but it only took me one night to have all I wanted of you, woman."

"I said stop!" Margaret raised the gun from her pocket and fired. "I'll make myself a true widow."

All the men at the table hit the floor in a heartbeat. Grayson could hear them cussing as they wallowed in the tobacco they'd been spitting all night. Westley darted for the door, but Margaret fired again. He stumbled. Her third bullet hit him in the leg.

Margaret's world was falling apart. Her hands were shaking badly, but she closed her eyes and fired again, sending splinters from the door Westley had just limped through.

Grayson didn't know how to stop her. In a moment, she would have a half-dozen men firing at her. He leaned and grabbed her around the waist. His sudden jerk made her drop the gun. Before she could bend to reach it, he threw her over his shoulder and ran from the saloon with her screaming and kicking like a wounded mountain lion.

Folks on the Acre were used to all kinds of wild happenings, but they stopped and stared, open-mouthed, as Grayson stormed down the street with Margaret over his shoulder.

When he reached the house, he carried her up the stairs past Azile, who didn't act as if anything was out of the ordinary. When he was finally in her room, he slammed the door and set her on her feet.

As he'd expected, she came at him like a madwoman, kicking, hitting, and screaming. For a while, he let her pound against his chest, knowing that her pain hurt her far more than her fists could ever hurt him. He watched in silence as her hair tumbled around her face and wondered how even a fool such as Westley could be so blind.

"I hate you!" she screamed. "I hate all men! Why didn't you let me kill him?"

Finally, she collapsed in tears at his feet, crying and drawing herself inward like a child too hurt to turn to anyone for help. The one man she'd ever tried to love had betrayed her, had lied to her, had made her a joke to his friends.

Grayson could stand her screaming. He could even take her fighting and swearing, but he could not endure his Margaret crumbled to the floor like some soiled garment someone had thrown away.

He bent and lifted her into his arms and carried her to the old overstuffed chair by the window. She clung to him like a child now, stiff and broken. All her dammed-up emotions poured out in her tears. A lifetime wall against pain crumbled around her.

For a while he let her cry against his wide shoulder as he stroked her hair and comforted her. But slowly, as her cries turned to whimpers, his comfort turned to caresses. He moved his massive hands along her back, molding her close against his chest. He pulled her legs against his hip, so her thigh rested over the center of his need. With slow, loving movement, he buried his face in her hair and drank in the wonderful smell of her. He kissed her forehead and neck. He tasted the soft curve of her ear. Dear God, he was growing drunk on her, and she still wasn't aware of his advances.

She was lost in a crumbling world. All these years she'd built a life around the fact that she was a hero's widow, and now she was only a coward's wife. Her heart was exploding in pain and only Grayson's soft stroking kept her from going over the edge to insanity. Each time she felt the pain build, his hands would move along her back, or he'd pull her close as if pleading with her not to grieve too hard.

Willingly she accepted his comfort as she cried. His hands felt strong, his lips warm against her burning skin as he kissed first her cheeks and then her eyes. She relaxed in his strong arms as her mind drifted to all the horror of what had happened. Over and over she heard Westley's words and the laughter of the other men in the room.

Grayson kissed the salty tears from her cheeks and brushed her mouth with his lips. When she didn't pull away, he grew bolder. Her mouth was open as she sobbed against his shoulder. He turned her head slightly and kissed her long and tenderly.

For a moment she seemed to awaken as if she'd been asleep. She pushed at his chest and tried to move off his lap, but his arms held her fast as his kiss continued. His one hand twisted into her hair, holding her head, while his other arm lay across her, imprisoning her. After a few heartbeats, she stopped struggling and returned his kiss. Her mouth opened wider and his tongue explored the honey taste of her kiss.

Finally, when he pulled away to kiss her neck, she whispered, "We can't be doing this. It isn't . . ."

He silenced her with another kiss and she accepted his mouth willingly. The right or wrong didn't matter to her. She needed to believe for one moment that she was alive, that she was desirable.

When he freed her lips once more, she voiced no protest. She leaned her head back against the arm of the chair and closed her eyes, allowing the pleasure of his kiss to wash away the wounds on her heart. His touch was like a warm liquid moving through her body, relaxing, warming, and welcome.

As she relaxed, Grayson slowly unbuttoned her blouse and pushed it aside to reveal the tight stays she always wore. Slowly he pulled the bow on the first ribbon. As it released, he saw the swell of her breasts so tightly bound inside. The second ribbon enlarged the swell, exciting him far more than any woman had. The third ribbon freed the top of her breasts to push above the last binding. A thin lace camisole was all that kept them in bounds. Grayson pulled the last ribbon and shoved the offending garment aside. How could anyone bind up such great beauty?

Without hesitation he ran his huge hand over the thin lace of the camisole. Cupping her ripe breast in his palm, he couldn't hold back a smile of pure pleasure. Her flesh fit the cup of his palm to perfection. As she gasped in surprise, he ran his thumb over her hard peak and pulled her mouth to his. She was ready for his kiss now, hungry for the taste of passion. Each time he pushed into her mouth he tightened his hold on her breast slightly. There was no need for words; he could feel her pleasure in his hand.

After several minutes, he released her mouth and allowed her to lean back and stretch. She no longer pulled away, but smiled as he moved his hands beneath the camisole to touch the warmth of her flesh.

Her hair was tumbling over the arm of the chair. He reached and pulled it forward, loving the ebony silk as it formed a thin veil over her creamy breasts.

He allowed her to move, determining where he kissed her. She closed her eyes as he touched her face, then leaned her head back while he tasted the warm flesh of her neck and below. The low sounds coming from deep in her throat drove him mad with need for her. And always, as his mouth moved against hers, his hands caressed her skin.

He led her into a long swim in this new passion before he slid one hand beneath her skirts and moved his fingers over the silkiness of her thighs.

Again she struggled in his arms, but his hand remained firm while his mouth demanded her full attention. Slowly, she relaxed and he began to move his hand over her legs, dipping deeper into the folds of her skirt with each caress. Her cries were of pleasure as she curled her fingers into his hair and begged for him to deepen his kiss. His lips obeyed as his hands continued to explore.

She leaned her head over his arm as he lifted her breasts to his mouth. While he tasted her, she whispered, "It isn't right. I shouldn't be doing this."

Grayson forgot all but the woman in his arms. "Then tell me to stop, Maggie. Tell me to stop, because I'm planning to make love to you. I want to love you as a woman as fine as you should be loved."

Reason touched her passion-drugged brain. "You can talk? You understood every word I've said?"

Grayson pulled her lips to his but he didn't kiss her. "That doesn't matter. What matters is I want you. I've wanted you since I first touched you and now I know you want me. Your body was made for my touch. No woman has ever felt so wonderful in my arms. No woman but you, Maggie."

Margaret tried to pull away, but he kissed her hard and long, bruising her lips with his desire. His arms pulled her body against him, but he could feel her withdrawal.

"No!" she screamed when she was finally able to break the kiss.

"We'll talk about it later. I'll tell you everything, but right now, I'm bedding you."

"I can't love a man who has lied." Suddenly her passion had grown cold. "And I'll never again bed a man I don't love.

What other lies do you have to confess? You've allowed me to make a fool of myself for days."

Grayson bit his bottom lip until it bled and still his anger threatened to explode. He lifted her off his lap and tossed her none too gently on the bed. "I want to love you, woman, and by God I know you want it also. So stop acting like some virgin just out of school and admit you need me as much as I need you." He rolled beside her, flattening her into the feather bed with his weight.

"I do not need you. I don't need any man."

Grayson ignored her protest and ran his hand over her body as his leg pinned her down. "You need me and you want me. You've been needing a good roll in the hay for a long time, but there wasn't a man left in the South strong enough to gentle you."

He kissed her again, but there was no answer in her lips. When he lifted his face to study her, tears were bright in her eyes. "Would you take me against my will, Yankee, and add rape as well as lying to your name?"

Grayson fought the urge to hit her. *Damn*. He knew if he said more than three words she'd know he wasn't from Texas. He'd never hit a woman in his life, and the mere thought that it was in his mind sobered his passion. "I've never raped a woman." He shoved himself off the bed. "God, woman, you can be cold when you're of a mind."

She pulled her blouse together and sat up. "I think I've already been told that once today."

He saw the pain in her eyes and knew he could add no more sorrow to those indigo depths, no matter how much she'd hurt him. "Your husband is not only a traitor and liar, but he's an idiot as well. There is a great fire in you. You're a woman worth paying a lifetime to have. You can sit there with your nose in the air, but it doesn't change a thing. When I kissed you, I felt the passion. When I touched those beautiful breasts of yours, they hardened with need. And when I pushed my hand up your thigh . . ." He smiled as her cheeks burned. Just the memory fired his blood. "Forget what that fool Westley said. You're a woman, warm and wild in my arms, and I plan to someday satisfy that passion in you. You're the kind of woman a man searches a lifetime to find and no little misunderstanding will stand between us. I'm going to love you until you cry out my name in joy and forget what part of the country I'm from."

"Never!" she answered, for despite her embarrassment, he'd given her back her dignity. "I'll shoot you dead if you ever step foot on this property again. So, get out!"

She jumped from the bed and opened the door. "Get out and don't ever come back! There is no passion for you in me. There will never be. Look to Holliday for your bedding, not me."

As Grayson passed her, he pulled her hard against him and kissed her once more. He'd expected her to fight, but she didn't. His tongue forced her mouth open as his hands shoved her blouse from her shoulders. His fingers roamed freely as she swayed toward him. His kiss continued until he felt her respond and she clung to him for support. He moved his hands to her sides and lifted her arms around his neck. She was perfection—the first woman who ever fit in his arms. Now, she was leaning against him, smelling of need and tasting of desire, and he couldn't resist touching her.

Finally, when they were both dizzy, he broke the kiss. "Now who is the liar?" He cupped her breast in his palm and felt the hard peak beneath his fingers. "I'll leave," he whispered against her hair, "for I want you when you're not angry or hurt. I want you when you come to my bed with only me on your mind. I want you when there are no lies between us." He paused and held her tight, knowing that his heart would break if he couldn't make her someday understand why he'd lied. She'd know the reasons and accept them, just as she'd accept that they belonged together. "Understand this, Maggie: no matter what the law or anyone says, you're mine and there is no one that will keep you from me."

He kissed her forehead and almost ran from the room, taking only time enough to grab his hat and guns before vanishing into the hallway.

Margaret stood watching the door where he'd gone and knowing that his last words were the truth. She loved Grayson Kirkland. She had loved him since the day he'd saved her from being robbed. She'd fight him every step of the way, but she had a feeling he was man enough to finish any battle he started . . . and man enough to teach her how it felt to be a woman.

12

Evening brought a howling north wind that whistled through the passageways of Hattie's Parlor. It rattled the panes in the windows like loose keys on an old upright piano. Margaret made herself keep busy as the hours passed. She'd cared for the children, cleaned every room in use, and spent over an hour trying to make sense of Hattie's ramblings. Yet, with the night, her troubles and fears mounted. She had no idea where to look for Cherish, and the longer her niece was gone, the more time Margaret had to imagine what might have happened to her.

Azile complained about seeing a raven fly by her window again just before dawn, so Margaret did what she'd seen many German families do to ward off evil. She took a pair of scissors and placed them on a nail beside each door. Even though she had no faith in the superstition, it seemed to help Azile, as she carefully opened each pair into the shape of a cross and explained that they would cut any evil that entered. Azile whispered that she believed nothing would stop the evil from coming to the house.

Well after midnight, Margaret climbed the stairs to her room. She was exhausted, yet her worry over Cherish held sleep at bay. Finally, she closed her eyes tight and thought of the way Grayson had held her. She remembered each of the times they'd touched and how his chest had felt as solid as wood. She needed his arms desperately tonight, but her pride would never allow her to go to him. Finally, she fell asleep, wondering if a man like Grayson would ever need a woman, for she knew she'd never fully love a man who didn't love her as well as want her.

The next morning, Margaret found herself peeping through the curtains like a child at a thin weasel of a man standing on her front porch. It was not yet past nine, but he already had a sweat ring around his collar and he clenched his case as though it were priceless.

"You think we oughta let him in?" Bar stood beside her as if he'd decided that without Grayson around and after Cherish's disappearance, he had to protect Margaret.

Margaret rested her hand on the boy's shoulder, needing him far more than she wanted to admit. "Who do you think he is, Barfield?"

"One of them lawyer guys that seem to crawl into town after every good rain. They hang around long enough to figure out there ain't much money in a cow town, then they up and leave for Dallas. Ain't no tellin' what he wants this early in the mornin', but my ma used to say ain't nobody but bill collectors and undertakers that do business before noon."

Trying to believe the best while fearing the worst, Margaret nodded for Bar to open the door. "We'll never know until we let him in, will we?"

The lawyer hadn't even fully removed his hat before he was talking. He smiled a nervous little insincere smile and bobbed his head as he talked, making the volume of his words go up and down. "Morning, Mrs. Alexander. I'm Mr. Ira Wallman. I'll hope you'll excuse the early call, but I have some very important business to discuss with you. I also hope you don't mind my dropping by, but Mr. Alexander assures me you're an early riser."

Margaret refrained from asking how Mr. Alexander would know anything about her sleeping habits. They were only married two nights before he left, and both mornings he'd been too hung over to notice what time she'd risen. She simply asked, "How is Mr. Alexander? Dying of my bullet wound, I should hope."

The little man jumped back a few inches as if he were suddenly very much aware of how deadly she could be. He briefly looked her up and down in what looked like a twitch, but displayed no emotion. "Your husband was limping, but I believe he will recover. If you'll allow me, I have some papers that must have your attention. When Tobin died, he owed me money for legal matters. I was about ready to assume the house when you showed up."

"Papers?" Margaret didn't move from the hallway or invite the little man to step in farther. She stood by the door and watched him balance his case on his knee as he tried to get out everything he needed.

"Yes." He waved the papers in front of him as if the written word was the only truth in the world. "It seems that since you inherited this place while still legally married, your husband has control of the house as well as half of the funds."

Margaret shoved her hands deep into her pockets and almost laughed aloud as the lawyer's face paled. "Mr. Alexander has no claim to me or to this house." Her voice was deadly calm as she backed Mr. Wallman out the door. "In fact, as far as I'm concerned, I'm still a widow. And if Mr. Alexander doesn't see it that way, all he needs to do is step within my gun sights and we'll have a short talk."

"But, Mrs. Alexander, the law . . ."

Margaret raised her chin. "I'd rather hang as a murderer, than deal with the coward who calls himself my husband. And, Mr. Ira Wallman, if I'm going to hang for one murder, the rope will pull no tighter for two."

The man ran almost full speed off the porch backward. When he had reached the relative safety of the road, he yelled, "He could have you arrested for attempted murder! I could have you arrested for threatening me. He'll be coming by to claim what's his and there isn't anything you can do about it. He told me to tell you that you'll be sorry for the day you ever met him."

"I already am!" Margaret slammed the door and yelled for Bar. He appeared before she could complete his name, telling her he'd been listening to every word. "Go ask Father Daniel if the children can come back to the mission—and you stay with them. This house may not be safe when that snake of a lawyer delivers my message."

Bar stepped forward, a flicker of steel in his dark gypsy eyes. "I'll see that the kids are safe, but I'm standin' with you if trouble comes."

Margaret realized she was looking at a boy who was more of a man than most ever would be. She wouldn't dishonor him by arguing. "Thank you," she answered, knowing she'd find a way of getting him to safety before Westley arrived. Her husband was lower than a coyote and she had a feeling he wouldn't come alone. His kind always traveled in packs.

A sudden pounding on the door made Margaret and Bar jump. Margaret's first thought was that the lawyer had returned, but the shadow framed against the door's curtains was far too broad. The visitor's stance was not that of a frightened man, but of a proud soldier at full attention.

Slowly, bracing herself for another battle, she opened the door, not noticing that Bar stepped just out of sight and lifted his ancient rifle.

Blinking away the morning sun, Margaret stared at the spotless dark blue uniform of a Union officer. His boots and buttons were polished and his hat was low, shading his face. His shoulders were wide and powerful. He bowed slightly as she looked up. For a moment, the old hatred of his uniform returned and she almost touched her brooch; then she remembered that her husband hadn't died at the hands of the Yankees.

"May I come in?" a rich baritone voice asked as the officer removed his hat to reveal neatly combed cinnamon hair.

Margaret looked into blue-gray eyes and suddenly forgot how to breathe. Only pure willpower prevented her from fainting as she stared at Captain Grayson Kirkland.

A slow smile spread across his weather-tanned face, telling her his careful tailoring had had the effect he'd planned.

"I told you I never wanted to see you again." Her words lacked the conviction they'd had two nights ago. She realized she was repeating the same words to every man she encountered.

"I had to come." He ran his hand over the sharp crease of his felt hat. His eyes told her there was much more he wanted to say, but he seemed at a loss for words. His gaze seemed to hunger for the sight of her as if it had been months since he'd seen her and not two days. He'd spent a great deal of time and effort to impress her and now he couldn't find his tongue.

Margaret pushed the door, afraid of what she might do if she looked too long into those wonderful stormy-day eyes. "Good day, Captain Kirkland."

Grayson shoved his boot between the door and the frame just before she completed her withdrawal. His words came slow, but direct. "I'm not leaving until I've had my say, Maggie."

Anger and pride blended in Margaret's words. She resented him using the family nickname as if he were a longtime friend, as if he were her lover. "I'll not listen to a blue-legged liar!"

Grayson didn't budge, but pushed the door firmly with one hand. He could have easily won in a battle of strength, but it would never be his way with Maggie. "You'll listen to me because Cherish's life may depend on it."

Margaret froze. He'd said the one thing that would get him inside. In her anger she'd thought she was the reason he came, not Cherish. Of course she had to listen even if it meant accepting a Yankee officer into her home. Cherish, as always, came first in her life. She stepped back and motioned for him to enter.

Grayson walked past her and laid his gloves and hat on the entryway table as if he'd done so a hundred times. "Barfield!" he snapped, knowing the boy would be within hearing distance. There seemed little left of the silent Grayson except the familiar wink he gave the boy as Bar bolted out from behind the door.

With childish haste, he fired a thousand questions at once. "Where did you get that uniform, Grayson? Lordy, do you look grand. Where did you go two nights ago? We could have really used you here this mornin' when a lawyer came to take the house from Miss Maggie. When did you start talkin' so much? I thought you only talked to Miss Cherish."

Smiling at the boy, Grayson tried to answer his questions, but his explanation was meant for Margaret's ears. "I had to come into town without letting anyone know I was with the army. There are some evil men in this place, and I think Miss Cherish has accidentally gotten mixed up with them. I never intended to harm anyone with my silence. In fact, Miss Cherish and I talked about it several nights ago. As for these clothes, I rode over to Camp Wilson and picked them up last night along with what information I could about Miss Cherish."

Bar was walking around Grayson. "You sure do look different. I wouldn't have recognized you and that's a fact. Mind if I take a look at that Colt? It's the new Union issue to officers, ain't it?"

Grayson emptied the bullets into his large palm and handed the weapon to Bar. While the boy examined the gun, he studied Margaret. She was standing quietly by the window, her arms folded tightly over her chest. She was a fragile queen, one blow away from being broken. He wanted to comfort her, to put his arms around her and tell her that nothing would ever frighten her again. But he knew she wanted no part of him. The knowledge ripped at his heart like a dull blade. All his life he'd been an honorable man and the one woman he wanted it to matter to believed that he was only a liar.

"I was with the army long before the war. My job stayed pretty much the same when the war broke out. I track down convicted men and see they serve their time. Sometimes I investigate groups that think they can organize and work outside the law." There was so much more he wanted to tell her but he didn't know where to start. "I'd worked in Texas before the war broke out. I have a homestead up in Ohio I haven't seen since I buried my wife there almost ten years ago. At first I took the job so I could wander, but later I was good at it and the army needed me." He wasn't sure she was hearing a word he was saying. "Maggie?"

"Do you know where Cherish is?" Margaret asked without looking at him.

"No," Grayson answered, wishing he could see her eyes, "but I read a report stating that there was a small-framed woman at a farm three nights ago where a group of men were planning to harass ex-slaves."

"Cherish would have no part of that!" Margaret's eyes were black with anger as she finally looked at him.

"I know," Grayson answered. "She was fighting against them."

"Was she hurt?" Margaret moved a few steps toward him.

"The report didn't say." He wished he could have told her differently. "The men who helped the farmer out, and the woman with them, have gone into hiding. I fear the men searching for Cherish are the same men I'm looking for. They were a group who called themselves the Knights of the Golden Circle back before the war, which was just a fancy name for a group of radicals who wanted to traffic in slave trade. If she fought against them, she's made herself some powerful, faceless enemies."

Fear touched Margaret's eyes before her backbone straightened slightly. "What can we do?"

"I can find Cherish before they do," Grayson answered. "The army will do all it can to protect her. Until last night when I read the report, I believed that she might be in league with the Knights. They supposedly sometimes met in Hattie's Parlor before the war, but the law was never able to catch them."

"That's why you came with me to this house."

Grayson nodded. "When we started, I didn't know how much you knew about the Knights."

"Maybe I know all about them. Maybe I know all about this house."

Grayson smiled. "Maybe, but I'd bet this uniform I just paid a month's pay for that you don't. You hide a lot of things, but your nature isn't one of them."

Margaret could no longer hold his stare. She turned slightly. "So, where do we began to look for Cherish?"

"We?" Grayson raised an eyebrow. "I'm not taking a woman into the frontier."

"I'm going with you and nothing you can say will stop me," Margaret answered.

He had the feeling she was going or he'd have another fight on his hands. And fighting with her was the last thing he had on his mind. He wasn't sure that she wouldn't be safer with him, riding through Indian territory, than here with a husband hating her and a house that seemed laid with traps.

"Be ready to ride in an hour." Grayson walked over and picked up his hat. "You'll have no use for anything but necessities. Where we're going won't be easy."

"Nothing in my life to this point has ever been easy," she answered. Again he fought the need to hold her.

An hour later Grayson returned with horses and two uniformed men. He stationed the two soldiers at the front door with orders to shoot any man who tried to enter the house.

Margaret appeared wearing riding pants and a white cotton shirt. She looked very young with her hair in a long ebony braid to her waist. Grayson had always admired her lean figure, but to his shock he found her even more alluring in pants. As he lifted her into the saddle, he allowed his hand to rest on her leg a moment longer than necessary.

When she didn't pull away or cut him to the quick with her sharp tongue, he knew the answer to a question that had haunted him since their fight. She wanted him just as deeply as he wanted her.

He turned away, wishing he could think of the right words to win her, but words had never flowed easily and now they were dammed up inside of him. She wasn't some saloon girl to grab and show her what he wanted; she was a lady who had to be talked to, and Grayson hoped that there would be time later.

13

Brant Coulter shifted his rifle on his arm and leaned back against the gully wall. The night was as black as the inside of a Franklin stove. Dark, rumbling clouds formed a ceiling so low he felt like he could have touched them if he'd tried. Normally, he'd never have built a fire, but when he'd lifted her down from her horse, Cherish was soaked to the bone from a mixture of the hard ride and the humidity. She'd catch pneumonia before he could get her home safely if he wasn't careful. The gully offered the only protection from both the wind and the searching eyes of anyone who might be following them. Its walls hid the fire, and hopefully the gray of the smoke would mix with the low clouds.

Watching her as she slept, Brant wondered what kind of woman continually risked everything for others without ever thinking of herself. Even in the long hours they'd ridden, the only worry she'd voiced was to hope that the others had made it safely away. She was so loving, yet a part of her always seemed out of reach. Sometimes when she looked at him he could see the loneliness in her eyes. She reminded him of a sister in the mission where he'd stayed as a boy. The nun was always caring for others, but in the end she died alone without anyone at her side.

There was something so impoverished about Cherish. Protecting her was as natural to him as breathing, as if somewhere, before they'd been born, the angels had assigned him this one task in life. But this time the angels had messed up, for all the trouble she was in now was his fault.

He wanted to say he was sorry, but he couldn't lie to himself or to her. Trouble had followed him for as long as he could remember. Even as a boy, he'd broken the law to survive. But this time he hadn't meant to get someone like her involved. Curling beside her on the bedroll, he realized that finding her was the one thing that ever happened in his life that he didn't feel was wrong. He laid his arm protectively over her shoulder and fell asleep for the first time in over forty-eight hours. A feeling of being home filled his senses as he held her tightly against his heart.

In his dreams waited his only peace: no war, no Union prison, no hatred. As the hours passed, Brant dreamed of all that might have been if not for the war taking his youthful years and leaving him hollow inside. He'd lived outside the law most of his life, but when he'd tried to fight for Texas, it had been a Union prison that taught him the horror of jail. It didn't matter what he'd done or hadn't done: he swore that he'd never spend another day in a dark cell.

A steady rain fell, but he slept on, wrapped in hope, for he no longer believed in reality.

Slowly, he was pulled from sleep by thunder that sounded like it came from within the earth. The ground rumbled as if a thousand horses were coming toward him. Lightning flashed, making a moment of day in the blackness. Brant jerked suddenly, realizing she was no longer in his arms.

"Run!" Cherish screamed as she pulled at his arm. "Run!"

Brant shook his head to clear it. He grabbed his rifle and they ran up the gully embankment only seconds before a wall of water crashed down upon their campfire. Where dry land once had been, now a fast-moving river flowed.

Pulling Cherish close, Brant watched the water rush past. Her arm went around him as she shook with fear. The rain was cool on his face, unlike her body, which was so warm against his. Instinctively, he drew her to him.

He hadn't planned to kiss her. She was in enough trouble without having to fight off his advances, but suddenly there was no thought, no need within him, except to feel her in his arms.

Her lips were warm and sweet and tasted of fresh rain-water. His kiss was long and tender, and desire built with each moment of pleasure. To his shock, she didn't pull away, but ran her hands inside his coat and spread her fingers over his wet shirt. When he would have ended the kiss, she held tight and drew him to her as if she needed more.

The realization that he might have to protect her from himself shook Brant worse than if the flash flood had hit him full force.

"Cherish," he whispered into her wet hair when finally he pulled his lips from her, "I can't be doing this." He'd promised himself he'd not touch her again and face the withdrawal she'd shown him before. "We have to get out of this rain."

She nodded, kissing the corners of his lips lightly before pulling away, as if she'd allowed herself all the emotions she could at one time. He took her hand and they began running toward higher ground.

After several minutes, exhausted and covered with mud, Brant saw the flicker of a campfire among the shallow caves of a low ridge. In this country it was a sure bet that the open fire would not be a friendly one, but, faced with catching pneumonia, he had to give it a try. The rain was flowing in a steady sheet now, with no sign of easing. He knew he'd never find the horses, so his only hope shone above them in the dancing flames.

Finally, breathless and freezing, Cherish and Brant stepped from the curtain of rain beneath the protective ledge of a cliff. They blinked at the firelight for a moment before they saw the figures huddled around it.

Women. Indian women and children, all staring wide-eyed at the ghosts who appeared from nowhere. Brant could taste their fear, as thick as the rain in the air. No one moved to show how they felt. He lowered his rifle and held his hands away from his body, showing them that he meant them no harm.

As his eyes adjusted, he saw that they weren't looking at him at all. They seemed only to see Cherish. She'd pulled her long, blond hair from her coat and was moving slowly toward the fire. All the dark eyes of the Indian women were on her as they held their children close.

Cherish warmed her hands and whispered, "What's the matter with them?"

Brant studied them carefully. "I think they're not sure if you're real or a spirit."

"Can you tell them that I mean them no harm?"

Brant moved closer to the fire. The women didn't take their stares off Cherish. He looked at the rich blues and reds of the clothes and blankets. "They're Apache," he whispered. "Something is wrong. Apache men don't leave their women unarmed in caves. Even an Apache woman would fight to protect her children, but I see no weapons."

Cherish could sense something was wrong even before Brant pointed out the lack of weapons. She counted six women, each with one or two children huddled in blankets around her. The youngest woman, maybe fourteen, held a tiny baby wrapped in her arms. She watched Cherish with huge eyes filled with sorrow and fear.

"Move very slowly," Brant whispered as he pulled off his coat and spread it on a rock to dry.

The heat from the fire made the shallow cave feel as warm as a summer night. Cherish stripped off as many layers of clothing as she dared, then sat by the fire as though she'd been invited.

After an endless silence, one of the babies began to cry and a woman lifted the child in her arms. When she pulled its face to her breast, Cherish saw the child beneath the blankets.

"Brant." She moved closer to the nursing child. The woman didn't protest as Cherish pulled the blankets from the baby's face. "This child has just had measles."

Brant knelt beside Cherish. "That explains why these women are here alone. They've been isolated from the tribe."

Cherish touched the woman's shoulder and smiled as she nodded toward the baby. "What can we do to help?" she asked him without looking away from the woman.

"We can get the hell out of here the minute the rain stops." Her endless need to help people was starting to get on his nerves. "You can bet someone is bringing them food and firewood. These are Apache. They'll cut out your liver and feed it to their dogs. Didn't you hear about the raid last week?"

"They are mothers whose children are ill."

Brant stood and faced the rain. "Will you stop trying to save the world and start thinking about your own neck for once?"

Cherish wasn't listening to him. She was moving from one mother to the other, her eyes asking permission to look at each child. Hesitantly the mothers unwrapped their children and Cherish smiled and nodded. "Some still have a little fever, but as long as they're kept dry and warm they should be fine."

Brant paced in the cave opening. "Which is more than I can say for us if the tribe comes back." He watched the water, willing it to stop, but the rain took no more notice of his problem than Cherish did.

When she moved to the youngest mother, the woman didn't want to show her the child cradled in her arms. She held the baby tightly against her chest and shook her head. Cherish gently touched the blanket, then fought to keep from making any sound that might show her horror. She stood and joined Brant by the door.

"Brant," she whispered, "the child of the young mother is already cold and stiff."

The mother might not have understood the words Cherish said, but she pulled the baby close and rocked it softly in her arms.

Tears welled in Cherish's eyes. "I wish I could help her."

Brant watched Cherish and thought he'd never wanted to hold anyone as much in his life as he wanted to hold her now, but he didn't want to be another one of her charity cases. Even her passion seemed doled out in spoonfuls.

Finally he touched her shoulder and said, "Apache, for all their blood lust, have a fear of death. I've heard that they sometimes burn all the belongings of the deceased and refuse to touch anything of his."

Cherish moved silently to the young mother. She held out her arms for the child. All the other women pulled their children and blankets tight around them.

The mother of the dead child stared up at Cherish for a long moment, then slowly lifted her baby's body.

Cherish took the child and moved close to the fire. With great dignity she unwrapped the baby and bathed its already darkened body. Then she ripped a long strip of cloth from her underskirt and wrapped the infant.

Every woman watched as the strange woman dressed the child for his last journey. Brant at first didn't understand what Cherish was doing, then finally he whispered, "White, the color of the clouds. You pay the baby honor."

Cherish folded the blankets. "If only I had yellow for the sun."

Brant slowly pulled his knife from his boot. He lifted a lock of her golden hair and raised his eyebrow in question. When Cherish nodded, he cut the curl free.

Cherish made a circle with her hair on the baby's chest, then folded the final blanket over him. When she looked up at the young mother, she didn't miss the pride in the woman's face. Cherish's father had told her how important color was to these people: black for night, brown for earth, yellow for warmth. Now the child was in white, forever in light, and the sun would warm him always.

Raising her head, Cherish smiled at Brant. He returned her smile with a nod. She handed the baby back to its mother, and looked back to Brant just before a round weapon materialized from the sheets of rain and struck him against the back of his head.

She screamed in horror, watching him crumble like a boneless body. Two Apache warriors stepped on either side of him, filling the opening to the cave with their dark bodies striped in red and black paint: red, the color of blood. The color of violent death.

14

Cherish watched as the two Indians dragged Brant across the floor of the cave and strapped him to a rock. One pulled his shirt open while the other forced his head back to make sure Brant was unconscious. Then, to her horror, they walked to the cave opening and drew arrows from a leather case.

She had no intention of watching while they used his body for target practice. They were young and this would probably be their first kill. While they shouted and shoved one another for the first shot, she ran to stand in front of Brant.

As she faced the two young braves they looked at her in surprise, as if she was more of an irritation than a barrier. They talked as if debating which one would shoot her to get her out of their game. The taller of the two raised his bow, strung the arrow, and pointed it directly at her heart.

Cherish closed her eyes and waited for the arrow to pierce her. Silently, life pounded in her ears, screaming to continue, but she didn't move. The blow didn't come. She took a deep breath and braced herself once more. But still the expected blow didn't come. Slowly, she opened her eyes, and to her shock, the young Indian mother was standing between her and the two braves.

Cherish couldn't understand what they were saying, but the girl kept pointing to the dead baby. The braves looked like two children cheated out of their fun. With a sudden order, the men moved back into the rain. Silently, the woman followed.

Cherish wanted to stop them, but she knew they thought it was time to get back to the tribe and they couldn't understand anything she would say to them. The young woman picked up her dead baby and carried it proudly before her. Cherish had a feeling that she'd tell her grandchildren someday about the way her baby had been honored in death. As she passed Cherish, she removed a blanket from her shoulder and handed it to Cherish. Then, in a moment's passing, they were gone as if they'd been smoke and not real.

Rushing to Brant, Cherish cut him loose. A huge knot protruded from his head and blood oozed from a small cut. Cherish cleaned the wound as best as she could, then wrapped the blanket around them both. She held tightly, allowing the sound of the rain to finally calm her into sleep.

"Thank God I've found you!" A voice entered Cherish's dreams. She felt Brant move beside her, but for a moment she didn't want to open her eyes and leave sleep's warmth.

"Hank?" Brant rubbed his hair and felt the knot on one side of his head. He looked at Cherish for an answer, but she only yawned.

Hank was stamping out their fire. "I followed the smoke in from the east. I remembered you saying you were heading north. I had to try and warn you not to go any farther or you'd run into Apache. If the rain hadn't slowed you down, I'd have never caught you." He looked at the blanket they were sleeping under and raised an eyebrow. When neither of them volunteered an explanation, he continued, "I've got a plan that should keep Cherish safe."

Brant stood and straightened his clothes. He glanced at Cherish. She either had some answers he needed, or he'd had one hell of a dream. But maybe it would be best to wait until they were out of Hank's hearing. The man had a way of telling everything he heard to anyone who would listen. "What's your plan?" Brant asked.

"I came from town yesterday and I found out that the army's got men stationed on the front porch of Hattie's Parlor. Talk is, they're protecting it from some gambler who's making a claim on the place. The army is just there to see no one comes in or out until the court can settle things. I figure we can sneak her in and she can hide out right there in the house. Then we don't have to wait for her to be shot somewhere out in open country."

Brant shook his head. "Too many people know about the way into Hattie's."

But Hank was sure about this. "No. I've been thinking. We could board up the passage from the inside, so we could get out if needed, but no one could ever get in. The passage hasn't been used by the Knights since before the war and these new hooded warriors ain't bright enough to figure the passage out. There's probably not a handful of men in the country who even remember it."

"What gambler? What passage?" Cherish felt like her head was full of cotton and she couldn't understand a word they were saying.

Brant picked up his rifle. "Come on, I'll show you." He walked into the sunny morning and saw their horses tied to Hank's saddle. "While we ride I'd like to have a little talk with you about last night."

Cherish pulled her hair up under her hat. "Oh, nothing much happened. I just saved your life again."

Brant laughed. "I thought I told you my life's not worth your time."

Cherish glanced to make sure Hank was out of earshot. "Your life is worth a great deal to me. If you had been dead, you'd have been no warmth beneath the blanket."

Brant's handsome face twisted with new pain. "The thought that I slept beside you all night without touching you pains me more than this damn headache."

Cherish loved having the upper hand with him. She folded the Indian blanket and ran her fingers slowly along the bright colors. "Too bad I couldn't say the same, Mr. Coulter."

It took Brant a moment to understand what she'd implied. By the time he reached for her, she was already out of the shelter of the cave and heading toward the horses.

As he lifted her onto her horse, he whispered, "Tonight."

There was a challenge in his rusty depths that made her heart pound even harder. "Perhaps . . . if you can stay conscious."

Hank yelled for them to ride and there was no more time for conversation. As they covered the miles, Cherish pieced together her feelings for Brant. There was a rough exterior about him that frightened her, but inside she felt a bond with him as if their souls were linked. He was the first man who had had the power to shake her from her observer's post of watching life, and she wanted to take a few steps into this new emotional world while she had the chance.

As they traveled, Brant told her of growing up in the streets of Fort Worth. He talked of how he and Daniel, who was two years older, had become friends. His folks had been killed by Indians and Daniel's by an angry slave who worked their farm. He'd planned to kill the whole family, but Daniel's parents had hidden him in the food cellar. Daniel had huddled in the total blackness, frightened, listening to his parents scream as they suffered a violent death.

Hattie's Parlor was a big gambling place back then and she paid the boys to run errands, so Brant and Daniel had met and become friends. When the war came, Brant was seventeen and in a hurry to fight. Daniel wanted no part of it, so he joined the church.

Cherish listened quietly, wanting to ask a hundred questions. One kept turning over and over in her mind but he never mentioned the scars on both their wrists. When he talked of the young Daniel, he did so with a softness in his voice that wasn't there when he mentioned Father Daniel.

Just past nightfall, they were on the outskirts of Fort Worth. They circled the back of Hattie's barn and went around to the dark side where Brant had once kissed her. There, to her amazement, beneath a layer of dirt, was a trapdoor.

Hank held the door. "I'll stay here and keep watch. You get Cherish to her room safely. When you return, we've got a meeting to go to."

Brant took one step into the passageway and looked back at Hank. "Problem?"

Hank nodded but said no more. Brant took Cherish's hand and led her into the total darkness.

The air was cool and damp against her skin. She could smell the earth around her, but the passage was tall enough for her to walk through.

Brant talked softly as though to calm her fears. "Hattie says her English mother would have called this a 'priest hole.' Back a long time ago, when priests were often being hunted in Europe, they built all the abbeys with secret ways to get out."

"Why did Hattie build this?" Cherish drew closer to him as they continued through the blackness.

"When she first constructed the place she had a few gentlemen friends who came to call and didn't want anyone knowing that they had visited her. When the Knights met here before the war, a few of them might have known about this passage, but most came through the front door of Hattie's. Back then they were proud to be members of the group. Talk was, even old Rip Ford, who had been head of the Texas Rangers, was one of the organizers."

Cherish had heard of "Rest In Peace" Ford all her life. He'd been everything from a senator to a newspaper editor. If he'd been involved, this group of Knights must have been a powerful organization.

Brant pulled her on through the darkness. "As far as I know, only Daniel, Hank, and me know about it now. And Barfield, of course. I showed it to him the other night when I left. Hattie locked the inside door years ago and told everyone to keep out."

"How much farther?" Cherish tried to keep the fear out of her voice but the tunnel was closing in around her and she could feel thin lines of spider webs brushing her face. She moved closer to Brant.

"We're almost there." Brant slowed and pulled her even with him in the slender tunnel. "But before we go into the house I've got a few questions about last night."

Cherish laughed, loving the way she'd teased him. They were close, brushing one another in the darkness, but he didn't touch her. She could feel his breath against her hair and smell the blending of leather and danger that always followed him.

"What happened last night?" His voice was hard, demanding information.

Cherish raised her hands to his chest and spread her fingers out over his shirt. "You don't remember?"

She heard his sudden intake of breath as she boldly pushed his jacket aside and leaned her cheek against his heart. Laughter and excitement bubbled inside her, but she kept her voice low. "I know you told me to stay away from you, but last night you voiced no objection . . ."

"Cherish, what happened?" His voice was tight, coming from between clenched teeth. "I told you once to stop playing games with me."

"I'm not playing a game." She moved her lips to touch his throat as she talked. "I loved being in your arms last night."

His body was as hard as stone. He knew the kiss in the rain had been a mistake. She was so soft, so tiny, so fragile. His love would crush her and destroy them both. She belonged with a gentle man who ran a mercantile and came home every night at six, not an outlaw whose days were numbered.

"I want you to hold me like you did in your sleep last night," she whispered against his throat. "I want to know that what I feel for you is returned."

Her hands moved into his hair as her body leaned into his. "Please hold me, Brant."

Like an oak in a violent storm, he snapped from the blow of her pleading. His arms went round her and crushed her against him as his lips found hers. For a moment his kiss was hard and fierce with need. She molded against him willingly, melting into his very soul.

Slowly, his kiss softened. He loosened his hold on her. She responded by brushing his hair with her fingers. Her hands moved hesitantly to feel the hard wall of his chest and trace the lines of his shoulders.

As the kiss continued, he realized that this was what she wanted and needed: not the wild passion of sexual arousal, but a gentle loving. He forced himself to relax and touch her softly, lightly. His kisses turned tender. His mind was whirling like a dust devil. The few times he'd had sex, it had always been wild and almost brutal, with a whore who earned her money in numbers. But with Cherish the world had shifted and changed and, to his surprise, he found the slow loving far more satisfying. If he didn't slow down, he'd frighten her as he had a few nights ago beside the barn.

He loved the feel of her warm, soft body against his. He loved the way her small hands touched him, like he was a treasure she'd found and had to explore. And most of all he loved the way she made him feel inside, as if he were worth a great deal to her, more than anyone else in the world. She wasn't a woman of the streets turning tricks for money. She was a priceless angel. He secretly wondered if she would ever need him as much as he needed her.

Cherish broke the kiss and cuddled into his arms. "Thank you," she whispered.

Brant kissed the top of her head. "For what?"

"For holding me," she added. "There is no gentler place than your arms."

Brant laughed, for he doubted anyone in the world would agree with her. But, because she thought it, it somehow became true. He found himself moving his hand over her shoulder and holding her securely in his embrace.

"I'm afraid sometimes," she whispered. "Afraid that there is no part of me left. During the war I hurt so badly for the wounded that I finally had no feeling remaining. But with you it's as though you found the tiny little feeling left in me and pulled it forward."

"You care about everyone. I was just one of the hundred you fought to save." Brant didn't want to admit it, but he'd seen her put everyone ahead of herself.

"No!" Cherish rubbed her head against his chin. "I need to help people but I *feel* a need for you."

Brant wasn't sure what she was asking. "What do you want of me, Cherish?"

"This is a good start."

"And if I touch you again, will you pull away?"

"Maybe," she answered. "And if I ask to be held again, will you hold me?"

"Always," he answered as he pulled her against him. "As long as there is breath left in my body."

Minutes later, Cherish passed through the passage to the basement of Hattie's Parlor. She stepped into a large room without windows. Only the light from the open stairway door gave her direction. When she started up the steps, Brant didn't follow.

"Good night," he whispered as his hand released hers.

She turned to hold him one last time, but his shadow had melted completely into the blackness. She wanted to ask when she'd see him again, but she knew there was no answer to her question.

As she reached the top of the stairs, Bar appeared. His thin face broke into a bright smile. "So you're the latest ghost who's been hauntin' this place."

Cherish laughed.

Bar danced by her side, not knowing how to show her just how pleased he was about having her home. "Everybody was real worried about you, but when I heard you might be with Brant, I figured you were all right."

Cherish caught the flittering boy and hugged him. He stepped back, embarrassed by the unaccustomed display of affection. "Miss Maggie's gone with Grayson to look for you."

Guiding him into the kitchen, Cherish ordered, "Fill me in while I fix something to eat." She glanced over her shoulder. "You hungry?"

"Always," he answered as he jumped onto the counter and started talking as fast as he could. By the time she'd fixed some food and they'd eaten, Cherish knew everything that had happened since she'd left.

Although she resented Grayson's interference in her life, she was thankful for the guards at the front door. She was sure that whoever this man was, who was claiming to be Westley, he would be unable to get into the house. She excused herself and went upstairs, anxious to close her eyes and dream of being in Brant's arms.

15

Grayson decided that riding next to Margaret ranked somewhere between being tortured by Indians and trailing a
buffalo herd. When she wasn't questioning his judgment
in direction, she was referring to him as a "damn Yankee."
By late afternoon the sky had turned dark and brooding and
so had his mood.

"We'll make camp there." He pointed to a cluster of
cottonwoods.

Margaret followed but asked, "Don't you think we need
to make more miles? After all, they have quite a start on
us and, assuming we're going in the right direction, we'll
never catch them at this rate."

Grayson gritted his teeth and swung from his horse. He
was beginning to see why he'd enjoyed his job for so many
years. For the most part he'd been alone.

She didn't wait for him to help her down, but jumped to
the ground and began unloading supplies. As she worked,
she speculated on how he ever caught any outlaws if he
always stopped so early.

When he set up camp she followed behind him, arranging
everything in different order and explaining the practicality
of each adjustment.

Grayson took his anger out on the slab of bacon in his pack. He cut into the salted meat with a vengeance, but didn't utter a word.

As he gathered firewood, she questioned how wise a campfire would be in this open country. Wouldn't everyone for miles see the flame at night? With each remark, Grayson threw another log on the campfire until it blazed high enough to roast a full-grown mule deer until it was well-done. He had no fear of an Indian or outlaw attack. It might be a pleasant diversion to being henpecked all day. He laughed suddenly to himself. If he were attacked by savages, they'd better kill Margaret outright, or she'd be telling them what to do and rearranging their camps as well.

The sun was setting somewhere behind gray clouds when they ate. She complained about the pork being too salty and the coffee far too strong to be healthy.

Grayson ate his meal in silence, then rolled onto his bedroll and pulled his hat low, ending, he hoped, her lecture for one night. To his relief, he heard her moving across the fire to her own bedroll with only the sound of the flames and the wind to touch his ears. He'd decided somewhere in the last ten miles that she was the most frustrating female in Texas, if not North America. He was beginning to wonder if she'd come with him to find Cherish or just to make his life a living hell.

Finally, her movements stopped and her breathing grew regular with sleep. He smiled to himself, knowing that the only prayer he'd have tonight was that she didn't talk in her sleep. He let out a long breath and relaxed.

Hours later, raindrops splattered on Grayson's hands, waking him instantly. He lifted his hat and studied the sky. With the instincts born of one who had lived most of his life without a roof over his head, Grayson grabbed his gear and headed for the shelter of the trees where he'd tied the horses.

By the time he'd returned, the splatters had become a drizzle. He stood for a moment over Maggie, debating whether to awaken her or allow the rain to do so. If she woke in a river, she'd have plenty to complain about. At least this was one thing today she couldn't blame him for. Courtesy won over judgment as he nudged her softly with the toe of his boot.

She came alive like an angry bear, grabbing her blankets and running for the trees. By the time he'd collected her gear and followed, she was already huddled in the shelter of a huge cottonwood.

"Why didn't you awaken me earlier? I could have helped you move everything. Won't this erase any tracks we might find? We should have left yesterday." She continued, but he'd stopped listening. A person can hear only so much before his mind just shuts off. He knew she was angry with him about lying to her and she'd taken the best vengeance— not with a clean wound to the chest but with a thousand tiny marks. Her badgering was pricking him an inch at a time, killing him drop by drop. Before they'd finished this search, he'd either be dead or a murderer—her murderer.

"Grayson, are you listening to me?" She pulled at his arm.

"No!" He looked down at her in the darkness. He could only see her outline, but he knew the shine of her ebony hair and the glow of her indigo eyes by heart. Her hair was free now and floating around her like a shadowy cloud. If he could just look at her with her mouth closed, he'd love her the rest of his life.

"I've had it!" She suddenly pushed at him. "Stop standing there like an innocent statue. If you're trying to make my life miserable, you've succeeded."

Like a flash of lightning across his mind he realized what he'd done. All day he'd taken the roughest trails, ridden harder than he would have pushed any other man or woman, and even blackened the coffee as if daring her to complain. Nothing made sense to him anymore. He understood why she was angry at him, but why had he tried to push her? He wanted her to accept him, to love him, yet all he'd done was make her dislike him more.

"And another thing, Captain Kirkland. Don't you ever wake me with the toe of your boot again, or I swear you'll be walking with a limp."

Grayson's sudden laughter angered her more. He realized how foolish a game he'd been playing. He'd had his pride hurt. All day he'd been pushing her, baiting her, so that he'd learn to hate her and be able to forget the hunger always burning inside of him.

"Stop that laughing!" She shoved him away from the shelter of the cottonwood and into the rain.

Grayson turned his face to the storm and roared. He'd been such a fool. She was never going to allow him to get away with an inch. And he was never going to allow her to get away from him no matter how many faults she discovered in him.

"You've gone mad!" she yelled above the rain. "First you don't listen and now that mud-coffee must have polluted your brain." She poked at him with her finger. "You've lost what little mind God gives Yankees."

Grayson pulled her to him. "Quiet!" he shouted. She tried to jerk away, but he held her fast. The rain was falling on them both with shelter only inches away, but still he held her close. He loved watching the water splash against her cheeks and run down her face. The cold wind cooled his anger but whetted his passion.

He lifted her suddenly into his arms and returned to the safety of the tree. She shook the rain from her hair and turned her back to him.

"Everything you've said today has been right." He knew he was talking more to himself than to her. "I thought if I could irritate you enough, you'd grow angry and I'd grow angry and maybe, just maybe, I wouldn't want you in my bed or in my life."

Maggie spun around and shoved him. "Well, you've done a fine job, for I don't want you at all. I want you as far out of my life as you can get. And as for in your bed, Captain Kirkland, it'll be a cold day in . . ."

"Liar!" He pinned her gently against the aging tree trunk and ignored the jabs and kicks she so freely gave him. "You want me, Maggie. You can fight and kick and call me every name you know, but you want me as much as I want you."

"I'll have you know, I never . . ." She didn't finish. His mouth came down on hers with all the force of the spring storm. He leaned back and lifted her off the ground into his arms, and she clung to him as she floated inches above the earth. Passion thundered in their ears as the white lightning of their love shook both of their bodies with desire.

When she would have turned away and broken the kiss, his lips demanded her compliance. Her fingers dug into his hair and all the world fell away except his arms. Her body made her the liar he'd called her, for every part of her wanted him and had since he'd first touched her. She could deny it to her grave, but there was no denying the way she fit alongside him. Her body moved against him, answering the years of need and longing in them both.

Slowly, he turned and lowered himself to the ground. He leaned his back against the tree and pulled her into his lap. His kisses had grown tender, satisfying a longing so deep inside her she was afraid to move for fear she might starve in a moment without him.

As his mouth finally moved from her lips to her neck, she whispered, "I hate you."

His lips didn't stop their journey, but continued along her throat. "Do you?" he whispered, biting lightly at her ear. "Do you hate the way I kiss you, or is it the way my hands move over you?" As he whispered to her, he moved his fingers along her legs and arms, branding her with his touch, forever charging the banks of her passion with his constant flow of desire.

His arms were no longer imprisoning her, but she didn't pull away. He moved one finger down the opening of her blouse and pulled the first button free. "I think I inspire more than one emotion in you."

Maggie gasped in shock as he boldly stroked her breasts with his hand. His laughter was warm and playful. "Tell me what direction to take now, Margaret. Tell me what trail to follow to make you happy."

Margaret tried to push away. "Don't make fun of me!"

He grabbed her hair in his huge hand. "Never," he whispered, wondering what he'd done wrong.

She shoved away and stood, then realized she could go only a few feet without getting drenched by the rain. She folded her arms over her chest and tried to stop the blood from running at double time through her body.

Grayson stood behind her, wishing he could think of the right thing to say. He wanted her so badly that every part of his body ached, but he didn't know what words were the key or what he'd done to cause her sudden coldness.

As he stood watching her, hating himself for not taking the time to understand how to make a woman happy, he heard her sobs—soft, deep sobs.

"Maggie," he whispered. But she stayed turned away.

He forced her to look at him, but the shadows hid her face. "Maggie?" Suddenly all the hardness of the woman he'd spent the day with passed away and only softness remained. She crumbled before him. Her sobs tore into him like thorns.

He pulled her silently to him and she came willingly into his arms. "What's wrong with me?" she whispered, and her words of pain stung him far more than her words of anger. "All my life I've heard men's comments. I've heard them laugh at me and say I'm cold and bloodless. Even Westley told me he expected no feeling from me on our wedding night."

She pulled at his shirt as her words ripped him apart. "He came to me all loud and drunk. I froze up, afraid to move for fear it might hurt more. Something is terribly, terribly wrong with me! Tell me what I'm missing that all the world seems to have."

"Nothing," he answered. "Nothing at all. You're all the woman a man could ever dream of."

There was no need for more words. He held her until she was warm and relaxed in his embrace. Gently, he kissed her salty tears away.

For the first time in his life he wished his hands were softer as they moved over her silky face. He tried to touch her as lightly as possible, for he didn't want to scratch her with his callused hands. When his finger passed her lips, she opened her mouth to their touch and he could no longer resist the invitation to kiss her. His tongue slid into her mouth, brushing the sharpness of her teeth as he tasted her.

This time he wasn't demanding a kiss, but giving, and she accepted willingly. He sat beneath the tree and pulled her down once more, only now he placed her knees on either side of him so that she faced him completely. He kissed her until she was sure she'd die from the beauty of it. Her head felt light and she clung to him to keep from falling backward. He was awakening something deep inside her that no one had ever tried to find.

Gently, his hands moved over her back, stroking her from shoulder to waist. Hesitantly, as his kiss deepened, his hands pushed lower until his long fingers covered her hips and pulled her gently against the center of his need.

Maggie jerked away, suddenly unsure, suddenly afraid. She'd had a man inside her before and it was not a thing she wished to repeat. She wished she could see Grayson's dark eyes, but his face was only a plain of shadows.

He seemed to understand her fears, for his caress moved back to her spine and along the sides of her blouse. His kiss taught her of a joy and a pleasure she'd never tasted. With remembered skill, he drew her into his love play.

When she was floating in pleasure, he moved his hands to her waist and pulled her against his chest. "Open your blouse, my love," he whispered into her hair. "Allow me to feel your softness in my hand."

Maggie straightened her back and moved her fingers slowly to the buttons of her blouse. Hesitantly, she unbuttoned the long line of pearl buttons to her belt. As she worked, his thumbs circled at her waist.

Lightly brushing her camisole, Grayson moved his hand from her waist to her throat. The silk was soft in his hands but didn't bring him the pleasure her flesh would. He pulled her once again to him. "Completely open," he gently ordered.

Again she straightened, her hands trembling. She pulled the ribbons fastening her camisole until it fell open in a thin V to her waist. Her breath was coming in rapid, short gulps and she was thankful for the night. Her cheeks were hot from her own actions. Never had she been so bold. Never had she undressed for a man. Never had she felt so desirable. Grayson was a huge, silent man who was strong enough to hold her in his arms, and she wanted to please him. She wanted for one moment in her life just to be a woman in the arms of a man who needed only her.

Grayson's other hand remained at her waist as he leaned to kiss her. She could taste the hunger in him, yet he didn't touch her. With her shirt undone, she felt free. Timidly, she leaned against him, flattening her breasts against his chest. Again he kissed her until the world became only his arms. Slowly, his hands moved down once more to cup her hips and pull her to him. This time she pushed against him, unafraid, knowing that her action made his heart pound faster and his kiss deepen.

When she leaned away her breath was ragged. Only his hand about her waist kept her from falling. He pulled her to him once more and whispered, "Maggie, open your blouse to me." She wasn't a wild horse to be broken, but an equal to be met. She had to give, for he would never take from his proud Maggie.

Silently, she pulled her blouse and camisole wide until the material slipped from her shoulders. Hesitantly, his fingers circled her throat and moved downward, stopping only a moment to touch each breast. The feel of his light touch was a liquid fire that burned across her, and she leaned back, allowing him full range over her flesh. He raised a knee to brace her back.

"Tell me you want more," he whispered softly. His huge palm covered her breast and circled. At first the action was light, but when she didn't answer, the pressure and her pleasure increased. "Tell me!" His fingers tightened slightly and she arched in passion.

"More!" Maggie gasped as his other hand slid along her waist and unbuckled her belt. With one shove, he pushed the material low on her hips so his hands could caress the curve of her waist.

She moaned with pleasure as he buried his face between her breasts. He moved from side to side, tasting her flesh. A fire raged deep inside her. Never had she felt such pleasure and she twisted her fingers into his hair and pulled him closer.

He took his time, leisurely feasting on her soft skin. When he raised his head, he whispered, "Don't lace and hide any part of your beauty from me." He lightly bit at her flesh. "Say my name, Maggie."

"Grayson," she whispered in her soft southern accent.

"Again," he mumbled as he continued to kiss her.

"Grayson!" she cried.

With pleasure, he returned to kiss her while his fingers tugged at her breasts, now pointed and full.

When finally she lay back in his arms, she whispered, "I've never felt . . . I've never known . . ."

"Shh," he answered. "I know." He didn't have to be told she'd never been awakened. He knew he was pulling her into deeper water than her emotions had ever treaded. A part of him cursed her husband Westley for not taking the time to please her and a part of him thanked the man for allowing him the great pleasure.

He lay her next to him and felt her tense. "Easy, Maggie. I'm not going to hurt you. I'll never hurt you."

He kissed her until her body relaxed and moved with the rhythm of his hands. He moved his fingers over her, loving the passion that mounted with his touch. His mouth covered her breast as his hand slid her riding pants from her hips. With loving care he moved his fingers between her legs. The material of her undergarments did little to hide the feel of her warmth. He could hear her crying his name softly as he moved to the other breast and pressed harder with his hand. She cried his name again as he tugged at her hard peak.

Slowly, his other hand replaced his mouth and his lips returned to claim her kiss. He wanted to taste her cries of passion. She was moving now, pushing against his hand, twisting as he stroked her, straining for more of his touch.

He fought for control of his own need. For this night he would make her aware that she was a desirable woman. Tomorrow he would make her his.

His kiss became wild with the fire inside her. He could taste passion in the lining of her mouth and feel it in the pressure against his hand. Her arms fell back beside her head as pleasure consumed her body.

Suddenly, she pulled her mouth from his and moved her head back and forth, crying his name as he'd dreamed she would someday.

"Don't stop!" she pleaded. "Please, Grayson!"

He smiled as she jerked and cried out in pure pleasure. Her body moved once more against him, then she relaxed into his arms. Holding to him as though she might be swept away, she whispered his name once more. He cradled her gently and pulled her blouse around her. This was the way he wanted her, beside him, all soft and satisfied. He moved his hand over her hair, loving the way she rested her hand on his chest.

When her breathing had returned to normal, he whispered into her damp hair. "There's more."

Maggie laughed. "I'm not sure I can take more."

"Oh, you'll take more, my love, and ask for it as you did tonight by crying my name"—he kissed her forehead— "next time we travel the road together, and then there will never be another man's name on your lips when you cry out in passion."

He pulled her closer and found she was asleep. Smiling to himself, he realized he'd taught her about the need of passion. Tomorrow, maybe he'd teach her of love. He ran his hand along the side of her body and she curled closer to him. "You're mine, Maggie. Mine forever, whether you know it or not."

16

Grayson had already built a fire and started breakfast by the time Margaret awoke. She tossed her mass of ebony hair over her head and watched a slow, steady smile spread across his rough face. He looked younger when he smiled and she realized how little he allowed himself to do so.

"Coffee's ready." He stood and brought her a cup.

Margaret found she couldn't meet his eyes. "I must look a mess."

"You look beautiful," he corrected; then he pulled his hat low, shading his eyes as if embarrassed at his boldness in the daylight.

She downed the hot coffee and smiled. "This tastes wonderful."

For a moment she saw his eyes look down at her blouse and she knew he was thinking of the storm and the way he'd touched her. All night she'd slept in his arms and she knew the feel of him at her side would never leave her memory. Even now, when he would talk of nothing but the trail and the weather, she knew they'd both be thinking of the way his hands had moved over her body.

He returned to the campfire. "The rain washed out any prayer of our trailing Cherish. There's not much choice but to turn back and wait for another clue."

"Do you think she's all right?" Maggie was suddenly filled with worry.

"I think she's fine. She's with men who know the country and when she returns to the house, she'll be safe with my men on duty."

Maggie stood and helped break camp. They said nothing else to one another, but she felt his eyes following her as she moved about. As they rode back toward Fort Worth, she thought of the way he'd held her and how he'd made her feel. No man had ever taken the time to show her love. Somewhere inside this quiet man was a blindness for her shortcomings. He didn't seem to see what all the others did and she loved him for it.

The day was hot with last evening's rain, making the air thick and heavy. They traveled fast and hard, but she didn't complain, and over and over again she saw him slow to make sure she was doing all right. When the sun was straight overhead, he stopped after crossing a stream and asked if she'd like to rest for an hour.

Maggie nodded as she watched him swing from his saddle and turn to help her down. He lowered her slowly to the ground, allowing her body to slide along his. When her feet touched the ground, she looked up into his stormy eyes and smiled, knowing what was on his mind.

She thought he might kiss her, but he merely said, "I'll build a fire and see if I can't catch a few fish for lunch."

"Do you think we're close enough to town for it to be safe?"

His hands were on her waist. "I think we're too close to town." His thumbs rubbed against her ribs and she understood his meaning.

As he fished, she unrolled her bedroll and stretched out on it. The warm sun was her blanket and the grass her pillow as she fell asleep, aware that his eyes were constantly watching her.

When she awoke, the shadows were long and the sun was already out of sight behind the trees. Maggie sat up with a start. "We have to hurry. I must have slept too long. It's getting late."

Grayson rose from his position by the fire and walked toward her. "Want some fish?"

"But it will be full dark when we get back."

"No," Grayson said slowly, "it will be morning."

"But . . ."

He knelt beside her on one knee. "Maggie, give me one night before we have to go back to be all that we are."

She understood. In town she would have to be so many things, but here she could be only herself without all the stays and laces. She looked away, unable to hold the hunger in his eyes. "Is there coffee to go with the fish?" Her question was all the answer he needed.

Grayson poured her a cup. As he handed it to her, their fingers touched and Maggie almost dropped the coffee. She watched him leisurely walk back and squat by the fire to refill his mug. When he stood, his fingers moved over the hot metal cup, but it was her skin that suddenly burned. He stood watching her as if there were no place and no one in the world except her.

Evening covered the earth. The fire danced across their faces and in their eyes. The gray smoke from the flames rose slowly as fireflies began to twinkle in the dusk of the prairie. When she'd finished eating, she went to the stream to wash and sat by the water for a long while, listening to it gurgle. She knew Grayson was waiting for her but somehow the waiting made it sweeter. She'd lived a long time with no dream of love in the future. Now she wanted to enjoy the dream for a moment before it became reality.

She undressed and lay her clothes neatly over a log. Then she washed each part of her body and wrapped herself in a thin army-issue blanket. Combing her hair until it fell soft and full to her waist, Maggie walked back to the fireside.

Grayson had moved their bedrolls over under the shadows of the trees. There was the soft scent of spring in the cool air. She smiled, knowing they'd need no fire to keep them warm tonight. He was stretched out with his hat over his eyes and his legs crossed at the ankle, but she knew he wasn't asleep. His Union jacket and gun belt lay within reach of his hand.

As silently as possible she moved toward him. When she stood beside him, the campfire to her back, she whispered, "Grayson."

He lifted his hat and she laughed at the surprise in his eyes as he saw her standing before him wrapped only in a blanket. Without hesitation, she lowered the wool covering her. She saw the joy and passion in his blue-gray depths as he beheld her. She was beautiful to him; she could see it in his eyes. Never in her life had she been treasured by any man and now she was. The knowledge washed over her, warming her from deep inside.

She sank to her knees and he sat up. "God, woman, you are a sight!" He finally stumbled over the words.

Reaching, he brushed the curtain of hair from her full breasts. There were a thousand things he wished he could tell her, volumes of words it would take to tell her of her beauty. But all he could do was stare. Her form was his measure of perfection from her full breasts to her slender waist and hips.

Suddenly Maggie grew nervous. She didn't know what to do. She looked down and grew embarrassed at her boldness. Never would she have thought she'd ever stand nude in front of a man. Lifting the blanket she covered herself and whispered, "I . . ." Her mind would think of no words.

Then Grayson's hand was on the blanket, pulling her to him. He drew her into his arms and kissed her until she forgot all about being embarrassed. He lay her down on the blankets and spread his powerful body over hers for warmth. For an endless time he kissed her tenderly and explored every part of her body with his gentle hands.

There was no withdrawal, no hesitation in her. She moved in response to his touch as though she'd known it all her life. She kissed him with the same passion that he showed her.

Again the feeling of being loved washed over Maggie and she cried out softly with pleasure. Only tonight, she wanted to give him pleasure as well. She moved her hand over his skin and when she felt his muscles tighten, she repeated her actions. Silently, he was teaching her, and she was loving every lesson.

She pushed his clothes from his body and loved the hard feel of his flesh. His chest was covered with fine brown hair that tickled her skin as he moved over her. She'd never touched a man so boldly and as she realized the power she had over him she laughed.

Grayson relaxed by her side. "What's so funny?" He tickled her ear with his words.

"You," she teased. "You're so hairy and your skin is so hard. I can make your muscles tighten just by brushing my hand over your chest."

Grayson groaned as she proved her point. "But your skin is so soft and hairless." He laughed. "And I can make you move simply by moving my hand." He slid his fingers across the peak of her breast and watched her arch to his touch as though her entire body were begging for more—which was exactly what he planned to deliver.

They continued to touch one another until both were hot with desire. Maggie moved mindlessly to his embrace and her breathing was shallow and quick.

Grayson rolled above her, bracing himself with his hands on either side of her head. He sank until his chest pressed lightly against her breasts. "Please, Maggie."

Maggie shook her head. "No. I'm afraid. It hurt so badly before." She felt panic climb up her spine like poison ivy, destroying all the pleasure she'd felt. The memory of her wedding night came back full force. She'd cried in pain then, but Westley had told her it was every wife's duty. When he'd finished, he'd left her bleeding and alone while he'd gone back to continue drinking.

Maggie couldn't face the pain again. "Please, Grayson, don't. Can't we just do what we've been doing?" He suddenly looked dark and frightening above her and she realized she'd gone too far to only play at lovemaking with him now.

His lips brushed soft kisses over her face as he whispered, "My Maggie afraid? You're the strongest woman I've ever known. There isn't a man alive or dead I respect more than you." She looked into his dark eyes as he continued, "I didn't hurt you last night did I?"

"No," she whispered as she allowed his hands to stroke her hair and calm her.

His kisses were lightly brushing her lips. "I want only to bring you pleasure. Maggie, you have to start trusting me sometime. Trust me now. Please, my love."

She had no one else to trust. She'd seen all the good in him, but Westley had been all bright with speeches about bravery when she'd met him. Somehow, deep inside, she knew that Grayson was different. Maybe it was the way he always cherished her. Or maybe it was the way he'd pleased her last night without asking anything in return. She had to trust Grayson or wither and die. Slowly she did as he'd asked. She moved her legs and felt him push inside her. As he entered, for a moment she pushed at his chest, trying to escape. Then he began to move in an easy rhythm. As his body pressed her gently against the earth, she joined in the dance. Together they moved as one across passion's threshold.

He lowered himself onto her and she accepted his weight gladly. His mouth found hers and she tasted wild passion on his lips. For once in her life there was no holding back. She gave herself, body and soul, to this man and he answered with his love.

He pushed further and further into her, losing himself in his need. Now that he knew she was with him, he would not dishonor her with a light lovemaking. All the years of loneliness and longing melted away as he made love to the one woman strong enough to be his. Even when he'd married all those years ago, he'd always held back, afraid of being too passionate, but as he held this wildcat in his arms he knew there was no such thing with Maggie. Each time he gave, she demanded more. She wanted all his passion, all his love.

With an explosion of pleasure inside them both, Grayson tightened his arms around Maggie and rolled to his back. For several minutes he could only hold her and wonder at the miracle that had happened. Her body was warm and damp on top of him. Her hair was half-covering his face. He could feel her breathing against his neck and her heart pounding against his heart. Never had he imagined loving a woman could be like this. There were no bars on his love. He'd die for her, or kill for her, but he'd never let her go.

Kissing her head, he whispered, "Are you all right, my love?"

"No!" she answered as she flung her hair back. "I'm angry." She rose off him, her fists knotted against her sides. Her dark blue eyes were midnight with the fire still smoldering inside her.

Grayson watched her closely, praying that he hadn't hurt her and silently calling himself a fool for not taking more care. She was more beautiful now, all red and damp from loving, than she'd ever been before.

She hit his chest. "Why didn't you show me this sooner? Think of all the nights we've wasted with you only a few feet from me."

Grayson laughed and pulled her back down onto the blanket. He'd have to content himself with kissing her until he could make love to her again—which he did again and again until they both fell asleep, too exhausted to even put their clothes back on.

As dawn touched the sky, Grayson reached to pull Margaret into his arms, but her warmth was no longer at his side. He sat upright, searching until his gaze fell on her by the stream. She was dressed and her hair was already braided down her back. For a moment he felt a great sadness, for their night together had come to an end. With the light he knew they wouldn't talk of passion. He'd drank long and deep of her last night and still he felt he was dying of thirst for one more swallow.

Margaret straightened and walked toward him, carrying the coffee pot. "I thought I'd make breakfast while you shaved."

Grayson rubbed his rough jaw. He never shaved more than once a week when he was on the trail, but he took the hint. He stood, carefully covering himself as he grabbed his clothes. Margaret wasn't the kind of lady that would want to be shocked by a man's nude body at dawn. She was the kind that would never allow a man to eat a meal in his undershirt, or take his coat off in church no matter how hot the day. She was also the kind of woman who filled every man's dreams of desire and passion, but he wasn't about to tell anyone.

By the time he returned from the stream she had breakfast made. He carefully waited for her to sit before folding his huge bulk beside her. They sat in silence as they ate. He watched her as if he'd been starved far too long for the sight of her. She avoided looking at him. The pattern continued until they were saddled and ready to move out.

As he lifted her onto her horse, he held her in midair for a moment. He had to ask the one question on his mind that would not wait. "Maggie, are you sorry?"

Now she looked at him with her dark, endless, indigo eyes. "No," she whispered. "Never."

Suddenly he didn't care that it was broad daylight and they were standing in the open where anyone for miles around could see them. He kissed her long and hard. She was his and no man on God's earth would keep her from him.

When she finally lifted her head, her cheeks were fevered with passion. There was nothing else that needed to be said. He lifted her onto her saddle and they rode toward Fort Worth, both lost in their own thoughts.

When he'd seen her politely to her door, he talked with his men on duty. Once assured her house was safe, he excused himself. He wanted to pull her in his arms and say good-bye, but he would not disgrace a respectable lady that way. She was not the kind to be made light of by gossip. He would see her later. Now they both needed sleep.

But sleep wouldn't come for Grayson as he lay in the only hotel in town. He finally climbed from his bed and rode back down to Hell's Half-Acre. He'd thought about his problem all day and the first thing he had to do was get rid of Westley. A man could hardly court a woman with her husband living in the same town. He'd thought about calling the gambler out, but knew there would be an investigation if an officer shot a civilian. So he took the only logical course of action and prayed to God that Margaret didn't find out about it.

17

Maggie was bombarded with hugs from Cherish and Barfield as soon as she entered the house. They had a hundred questions for her and she tried to answer theirs as she asked her own questions about Cherish. Maggie laughed and hugged her niece, feeling a joy surround her that she had never known before. Everything in her life was brighter— as if someone had cleaned the smoke-caked lantern that surrounded her eyes.

Cherish told Margaret of the raid on Hank's place and of the Indians she met, but she left out Brant Coulter's name altogether. She didn't want her aunt to worry about him.

Bar explained how the lawyer had been by twice and how the guards had sent him packing both times. The afternoon settled into a party atmosphere. Even old Hattie seemed glad to see the young ladies back, though she didn't remember their names. So many people had come and gone from her house over the years that she viewed everyone as transient.

Maggie made a fabulous supper, silently hoping Grayson might come by.

Azile was of little help to anyone, for she was upset by the past days' events. She seemed like a flesh-covered ghost

walking from room to room. She'd drank herself to sleep
for so many nights that dawn no longer cleared her eyes.

Cherish gave Azile time off to go into town and visit
a woman who knew about signs and who might be able
to tell her the meaning of the raven at her window every
morning. In truth, the women were glad when Azile left;
her fears darkened their reunion.

As evening passed, a peace fell over the house. When
Grayson didn't come, Margaret politely offered both the
guards a meal. They seemed hesitant at first, obviously
having heard about her shooting at Holliday's; by the time
she served dessert, however, they were dishing up mighty
compliments in their funny northern voices.

Margaret would never allow herself to flirt, yet she
couldn't help but notice the way they looked at her: not
like she was some dried up widow, but like she was a lady.
They were as respectful and kind as if they'd been with
a friend's mother or sister. Even when she went inside,
she heard no harsh remarks when they thought she wasn't
listening.

Maggie smiled to herself. Grayson had changed her, not
just on the inside, but somehow on the outside as well.
His unshaken belief that she was desirable had softened
the edges of her personality.

Bar fell asleep on the floor while Maggie and Cherish
did the dishes. Cherish excused herself to check on the
horses Brant had left in their barn. Maggie climbed the
stairs exhausted. Both women seemed to need a moment
alone with their thoughts and dreams.

"I'll be perfectly safe," Margaret insisted as she shoved
the last bit of breakfast into her mouth and dusted the crumbs
from her hands. "Bar will be with me and I'll have a gun in
my pocket."

"Ain't anyone goin' to mess with Miss Margaret," Barfield chimed in as he lifted his plate toward Cherish for a third refill. "Especially not after what she did at Holliday's place. I heard one man say that if he were her husband he'd be in the Oklahoma Territory by now."

Cherish frowned at him, fearing he might have hurt Maggie's feelings, but Maggie only laughed and nodded as if Bar had proved her point.

"I'll be back in an hour. I only need a few things," she added casually as she stood. "I thought I'd stop by the dry goods store and see if I can find any material for a new dress."

Cherish tried to hide her shock. In twenty years of knowing Margaret she'd never heard her say such a thing. Oh, she bought bolts of cloth when necessary, but always with little or no interest. Even for her wedding, she'd insisted that there hadn't been time to buy anything new. Now, with them almost penniless and having their lives threatened, she'd decided to look at fabric.

Silently resolving to watch Margaret more closely, Cherish wondered if the fall from the stairs hadn't somehow injured more than her wrist. Her aunt was different. She couldn't quite put her finger on how, but Margaret was different.

Margaret didn't seem to notice Cherish's gaze following her. She lifted her bag and marched out of the room as if there were nothing in the world more to worry about than the weather. Bar grabbed the last buttermilk biscuit and ran to catch up.

Sunshine warmed Margaret's face as she stepped out into the bright afternoon. The streets were busy with supply wagons from several small cattle drives that were stocking up for the long days across unbroken plains to markets. Fort Worth was fast becoming the last place to stop at the beginning of the long trail and the first place to return to when the cattle were sold. The stores sold supplies to the chuck wagons and the saloons provided a place for the returning cowhands to lighten their money pouches.

Margaret held her head high as she marched toward the dry goods store. Today her dress was dove gray and the brooch was missing from her jacket. She hadn't told Cherish, but Bar had taken her once treasured brooch to the goldsmith and she'd gotten enough to buy supplies for a month, with some left over for a few yards of material.

The store was crowded with Monday afternoon shoppers. The customers were mostly women who had nothing better to do than browse while their husbands visited the blacksmith or had a drink before heading back to their farms.

Without a word, Margaret moved to the dry goods and began looking through the bolts of cloth. She heard the shopkeeper whisper, "That's her," but she paid no notice. In a town this size, one could hardly shoot one's husband in a bar without being talked about.

A plump woman, dressed from toe to crown in pink, whispered back, "Well, I'll be. I never would have thought her that kind."

"Can't never tell," answered another woman. She and her friend were alike enough to almost be a matched set. Both women's faces turned sour as they looked toward Margaret. They crossed their short arms over their plump bodies and bobbed their double chins.

Margaret kept fumbling with the material.

The shopkeeper paused while wrapping a package. "Weren't bad enough that she shot her husband. Then, last night, she was named as stakes in a poker game. Like she could just be passed around to the winner."

Margaret's head shot up, her new dress completely forgotten. The plump ladies looked away, but the shopkeeper met her stare.

"Sir, you must be mistaken." Margaret walked toward him. She would ignore just so much talk about her before she confronted a liar.

One plump woman nodded her head as if her neck had suddenly been replaced with a wagon spring. The other wagged a stubby little finger. "I think she's right, Charlie. Look at her. She isn't the kind of woman who would be gambled over in a saloon."

The former shook her head. "Can't ever tell, I told you. Money doesn't make a lady any more than respectable clothes can change a whore."

Margaret's dark eyes stared at the two women, silencing them both. She needed no supporters, she could champion her own cause.

The storekeeper suddenly looked embarrassed, more from the fear of losing a sale than from anything he'd said. "I'm sorry, ma'am. I'm just repeating what I heard. Some huge man sat down with the regulars last night at Holliday's place. He gambled most of the night until it was down to just him and your husband. The final pot"—he swallowed loudly—"your name was thrown in to cover the bet. The man that won the pot got to keep you."

The pink lady whispered something to her friend and they moved farther down the counter.

Maggie's eyes were funeral black and her body so stiff it might have snapped like overbaked peanut brittle if she'd been touched. In all her life, of all the comments and jokes she'd heard about herself, never, never, had anything been as bad as this. She had no need to ask who the huge man was and she wasn't sure she wanted to know who won the last pot.

Without another word she marched out of the store and headed down the street. People jumped out of her way as she walked in long strides toward Hell's Half-Acre. Conversation halted in midsentence, whittlers' front chair legs hit the floor, and mothers pulled their children inside. Margaret couldn't have drawn more attention if she'd been Lady Godiva herself coming down the street.

When she reached the door of Holliday's, Margaret turned and ordered Bar home. The boy backed away, but he didn't turn around.

Margaret marched into the saloon with the same determination she'd had when she'd gone looking for Cherish days ago; only this time her rage would steady her gun hand.

As she stepped inside, Holliday turned from the bar. The saloon owner smiled as Maggie entered. "Afternoon." She raised her drink. Maggie's gunplay had done more for business than a rainy weekend after roundup, so Holliday owed the lady a salute. Every man within twenty miles had been in to have a drink and talk about the Confederate widow who tried to kill her deserter husband.

Margaret nodded. "Miss Holliday, where is he?"

"If you're asking about your husband, I never know where husbands are. This once, I might make an exception—if I knew. I've had a few like him that weren't worth the bullets to kill them, so I reckon I'd tell you if I could."

"I'm referring to Grayson Kirkland." Maggie didn't miss the frown that narrowed Holliday's eyes. She looked as though she'd really regret losing Grayson.

"He left here about two last night. I offered him a bed"— she didn't bother to look embarrassed—"but he said he had one at the hotel." Holliday might have added more, but she felt a growing respect for this skinny woman who never backed down.

Margaret thanked her and turned toward the door. As she stepped into the sun, she collided with Bar. Bar jumped back in fear, then looked ashamed for his weakness and forced himself to stand in range of a blow.

His silent strength brought reason to Maggie's mind. She placed her arm around the boy and said, "Thank you for waiting. You may see me home." Her tone was crisp, but her touch was gentle.

Bar straightened with pride and walked through the crowd of people who had gathered. Margaret didn't look at their faces. She'd reached a point where she no longer cared what people thought. She was silent all the way back home, but her mind was working . . . planning.

Cherish stepped into the evening air and took a deep breath. She'd spent the afternoon hearing all about what Maggie planned to do with Grayson when she saw him again. After all the ranting and raving, one thing was clear to Cherish: her aunt was in love with Grayson Kirkland. If she didn't kill him over what he'd done, she'd probably be very happy with the huge man.

It had been hard for Cherish not to talk about Brant with Maggie, for he was in her thoughts. She walked to the barn, wondering when she'd see him again. They hadn't discussed meeting, but she knew she could get a message to him through Hank or Father Daniel.

Bar tumbled out the back door trying to eat a slice of pie without spilling any of the juicy bites of apple. "I'll see to the horses tonight, Miss Cherish."

Cherish waved him toward her. "I'll help." When they were well free of the house, she added, "We both could use the peace and quiet."

Bar rolled his eyes upward. "I've heard stories of what Indians do when they torture white folks, but it ain't nothin' compared to what Miss Maggie's goin' to do to Grayson. If I was him, I'd pay the undertaker before I came to call at this house."

Cherish laughed and prayed the Yankee was up to the challenge of loving her aunt.

They walked toward the barn together, but Bar stepped on ahead to light the lamp while Cherish took a moment to look at the stars.

She loved the evening most of all in this land. She loved the way the sun blazed out slowly in a long moment of glory before it fell. Then the stars would span the night sky. As a child, Cherish used to sleep out on a wide porch and watch for falling stars to wish on.

She glanced over to the barn and noticed that Bar hadn't lit the lantern. Like a wisp of wind that comes up suddenly before a storm, she heard a thud just inside the barn. Bar must have tripped over something and fallen. She ran to help him.

Stepping into the darkened interior, she reached for the lantern. The odor of hay and horses blended with a foreign smell to the area . . . whiskey.

Cherish groped again in the darkness for the lantern. It wasn't on the hook. She stepped back suddenly, feeling that she wasn't alone. "Bar?"

The toe of her boot struck something. Cherish knelt in the blackness, feeling her way along Bar's unconscious body. "Bar!" Panic froze her spine. She could hear the slow breath of someone behind her in the shadows.

"Brant?" she whispered.

Something moved through the blackness, rustling the straw on the ground between her and the door. Fear rippled in tiny waves along her skin.

"Who's there?" she said louder. Brant wouldn't frighten her so and she couldn't believe he'd ever hurt a child. Maybe a drunk had crawled in to sleep and now only wanted an escape. The smell of whiskey assaulted her nose as she stood and moved toward the door.

Heavy footsteps ventured closer . . . stalking.

Cherish fumbled behind her, grabbing in the blackness for something, anything, to use as a weapon. "Identify yourself," she said with all the volume she could shove past her contracting throat, "or I'll scream!"

Large, beefy hands jetted from the shadows and encircled her arms. They jerked her violently backward against a wide expanse of stomach. The odor of cheap cigars blended with whiskey as sweaty hands closed around her like a greased bear trap.

Cherish tried to scream, but a rag was shoved into her mouth with enough force to choke her. She gagged and stumbled forward as her attacker pulled her arms high against her back. Her knee crashed against the corner of a stall. She heard the wood rip through material and flesh. Pain seemed everywhere on her body.

"Is that any way to greet your uncle?" A low voice sounded in her ear, laughing as she struggled. "I haven't seen you for five years, Cherish, but I'd know that spitfire attitude of yours anywhere. You Wyatts were all alike, always thinking you were high-and-mighty. Always giving us the feeling you thought you were better than the rest of us hill-country farmers."

Cherish twisted, but he held her tight. She pulled with all her strength. Her efforts were answered with the back of a hand across the side of her head. He slapped her again with no more concern than one might show a stubborn horse.

"You grew up real fine, girl. Not as tall as your aunt, but ain't many women are." He turned her to face him and pulled her into the thin beam of moonlight by the barn door. "You're a hell of a lot prettier, though."

The man before her bore little resemblance to the wild, recklessly handsome Westley she'd remembered. The years of self-abuse had scarred him, knotting normal features into an evil mask. His body, once hard and tanned from working outdoors, was now soft and pale.

His fingers bit into her flesh. "Yes, you remember me, don't you?"

He slapped her again and she was terrified at the pleasure his action seemed to give him.

"Do you have any idea how much I always hated your family? My dad never stopped reminding me how much smarter all your brothers were, and how much harder they worked than I did. But I fooled them all. I married their Maggie. Dear Maggie. You all loved her and made her one of your family, but I offered her something all you Wyatts couldn't. I promised her a house of her own, where she wouldn't be the orphan little sister or the old-maid aunt. She jumped at the offer without taking a close look at the man behind it."

Cherish fought to spit the rag from her mouth, but he shoved it in further, bloodying her nose with his force. Cherish was so angry she could have killed him easily. Westley Alexander was never one of the family. He'd only been married to Maggie a few days when he'd left, and Cherish had only seen him a few times before the marriage. She remembered her mother crying the night Maggie married, fearing the girl had made a mistake. But Maggie had insisted it was what she wanted. She was over twenty and it was time she had a house of her own. She'd planned to live with Cherish until Westley returned and they could start farming. But Westley had never returned . . . until now.

"That's better," Westley hissed as Cherish finally stopped struggling. "I only want to talk to you, little girl. You don't

have to get high-and-mighty with me like your aunt did."
He laughed and his foul breath stung her eyes. "She wasn't
so uppity when I left her. I knew she was still a virgin and
she bleeds red like the rest of us. I brought her down a few
notches that first night but I knew she wouldn't say anything.
A woman like her would take a lot without admitting to the
world anything about her private life. The next night she
tried to lock me out. By the time I beat some sense into her
I was too tired to bed her."

He pulled Cherish closer. "You still a virgin, girl?"

Cherish kicked at him with all her might, not caring that
each kick cost her dearly as he twisted her arms.

"Stop that!" He shook her so hard that Cherish felt like
she might faint. "I just want you to deliver a message to
my dear wife." He blackened her arms with his grip. "Tell
her to sign those damn papers the lawyer's got or I'll be
coming to visit and reclaiming my husband's rights." He
pushed Cherish hard.

Losing her balance, she stumbled to the ground, almost
freeing herself from his grip. "I don't want her. I want this
house, and nothing she can do will stop me from having
it. There isn't any law that will come between a man and
his wife."

Fear welled inside Cherish. She pushed violently toward
him, hoping to throw him off balance. He stumbled backward
a few steps, dragging her with him. When he recovered his
footing, rage oozed from him. He turned her to face him and
slammed his fist against her jaw. "Before you go getting
any ideas"—his fist slammed again—"don't tell anyone but
Maggie the message or you'll be sorry. A few Yankees at
the door ain't going to stop me from getting that treasure.
I'll find another way in."

His anger had made him reckless. He dropped one of her
arms and laughed. "I've always thought it would be fun to

bring another one of you Wyatts down to size." He shook her as if she were a rag doll. "I should probably just kill the both of you and take the house. It was supposed to go to me that night in the poker game, but I let old Tobin sit in, just to see if he remembered me."

Cherish spit the rag out while he was increasing his hold on her arms. She pulled away from his grip and screamed— a long, loud, eardrum-busting scream of outrage and pain.

Westley hesitated in panic, then dropped her arms and ran. A moment later the two guards appeared. One took a shot at the shadow running down the hill while the other caught Cherish as she fainted.

Hours later, Bar lay sound asleep on a cot in the sitting room, his head bandaged. Cherish had been safely tucked into bed with her bruised arms wrapped in cool cloths and her knee bandaged. Maggie whispered one word: "Who?"

Cherish tried to answer but no words passed her swollen lips. She formed a name in a half-whistle, half-hiss, but it was enough of a word to make Maggie nod.

Cherish closed her eyes to the pain and to the world.

Maggie covered her niece and knelt beside the bed, crying softly. Somehow, all this had been her fault. She'd foolishly married Westley, believing that after he'd had his wild days for fighting he'd come home and settle down. But he'd lied— she'd known her mistake even on their wedding night—and now he'd hurt Cherish for no reason.

As Maggie buried her head into the covers beside Cherish, she didn't see a shadow move from behind the door and slip silently down the hall to the stairs leading to the basement and the tunnel.

18

Grayson Kirkland crossed the crowded, dusty street and headed for his hotel room. He thought about when the war started and recruits came in from the farms so dumb they didn't know their right foot from their left. Some sergeant tied straw to one boot and hay to the other and made them march to "hayfoot, strawfoot, hayfoot, strawfoot." The nickname of "strawfoot" began to be used for anyone so muddled he didn't know his right from his left.

Tonight, Grayson thought he was probably the biggest strawfoot in the South. Why had gambling with Westley ever seemed like a good idea? He knew there would be hell to pay when Margaret found out, but he figured he had a few days to tell her. Maybe by then Westley would be long gone. But now it seemed everyone in town saw her go into Holliday's this morning . . . everyone except him.

Crossing the tiny lobby, Grayson picked up his key from the desk and headed up the stairs. He was almost to the landing before he changed his mind and decided he needed a few drinks before dreaming of Maggie's anger.

He walked to the small restaurant that doubled as a bar at night and sat down in the corner. The place was almost empty. All the cowhands sought more lively saloons with girls and music. Only the serious drinkers would pick a little place like this with only a bartender and a few drunks to keep him company.

He was thankful for the dim lighting that hid the questionable cleanliness of the place. Even his glass felt grimy, but at least the floor looked like it was swept monthly, which was more than he could say about most of the places in Hell's Half-Acre. Fort Worth would probably be better off if they burned the whole Acre to the ground.

The bartender brought him a bottle and wandered off without comment. Grayson laid his hat on the table and unbuttoned his uniform. He'd worked all day at getting some legal action taken against Westley Alexander. He'd tried everything, including badgering everyone he knew to step in on Margaret's behalf. But the law was clear. A husband had a right to all property the wife obtained during the course of their marriage.

A shadow moved across the table. When Grayson looked up, the stranger was only a silhouette in front of the light.

"You Grayson Kirkland?" the man asked.

Grayson touched the butt of his Colt and nodded.

The stranger moved closer and straddled the chair across from Grayson. His wide-brimmed brown hat covered his face, but his dress and nervousness told Grayson a great deal. He'd guess this boy to be one of those who grew up in the war. He was too old to be afraid of death and too young to have lived.

"I understand you're looking for a group of men that met before the war known as the Knights of the Golden Circle."

Raising his glass, Grayson tried to see the man's face as he continued.

"I've got a warning for you. Stop looking if you want to remain healthy."

"And if I don't?" Grayson asked.

"I was just told to deliver the message." The man stood and backed away. "Somebody's been killing off all the Knights, one by one. If they find out it's you, your life won't be worth a Confederate bill."

"What makes you think I'm behind the killings?"

"You've been hanging around the house."

"So have several women and a boy."

The man stood. "Yeah, but we figured the Alexander woman was the only one with enough backbone to shoot anyone, and after seeing her firing over at Holliday's we eliminated her as a suspect."

"Who is 'we'?"

The man touched his hat in a hint of a salute and turned without answering.

Grayson watched him go, then leaned back in his chair and mulled over the words the young man had delivered. He wondered who could possibly be killing the Knights. If someone hated them so much, wouldn't it be easier to just turn them in? If they were still raising hell, the Union army would take care of them. Rumor was that they'd collected quite a sum of money to start a slave state down in Cuba before the war. If the money was still lying around, who knew? Maybe the Knights of the Golden Circle were killing one another.

Suddenly, the whiskey tasted sour. He disliked the idea that there might be civilians involved in his work. Whenever there were, they always managed to get themselves hurt or killed.

Grayson dropped a gold piece on the table and headed for his room. He'd better get a good night's sleep before he faced Margaret's wrath in the morning. He smiled, remembering how black her eyes always turned when she was angry. *Well,* he thought to himself, *tomorrow morning they're going to be as black as a moonless road at midnight.*

Ten minutes later, he was lying on his bed trying to piece together all the senseless facts he knew about the Knights when the door flew open. A woman draped in a long gray cape entered and slammed the door behind her so hard that the hinges rattled.

He didn't have to ask who it was.

"Maggie." Grayson rose to his feet and waited for her attack.

She lowered her cape and looked straight at him with those indigo eyes that always made him feel like someone had poured hot coals into the pit of his stomach. She didn't speak; she only looked at him.

Grayson was prepared for a fight. He'd even agree that he deserved her anger, but the silence was unnerving. "Maggie, I thought . . ."

He took a long breath. What did it matter what he thought? He'd done a stupid thing to try and gamble for her. He should have known Westley wouldn't leave just because of some card game, but it was the only thing he could think of besides killing the rat. "Maggie, give me a chance to explain."

Margaret's back straightened slightly in the way it always did when she had heard enough. Her words came direct and without emotion. "I need your help."

"What?" A bullet through his chest wouldn't have surprised him more than her request.

Studying her closely, he saw it then: the pain and fear that rested in the corners of her mouth and the moistness of her eyes. She whispered the words but they could have had no more impact if they'd been a call to arms. "Cherish has been hurt."

Grayson grabbed his gun belt from the bedpost. He crammed on his hat and walked toward her. "Lead the way," he said, and they left without another word. She might be mad as hell at him, but it could wait if Cherish was in trouble. Grayson knew that Margaret would never have to ask for his help twice.

They walked down the stairs, ignoring the looks boldly turned their way. He figured they made quite a sight: a huge Union officer and a tall Confederate widow. Only, judging from the looks on everyone's faces, they knew she wasn't a widow through no fault of her own.

Grayson offered his arm and Margaret took it without any hesitation. He pulled her close as they maneuvered through the Saturday night crowd. Most were young men filled with the dreams of the spring's cattle drive. These were their last few days in town before months in the saddle; they wandered around in packs, wanting to see and taste everything all at once. Only Grayson's size and the Colt strapped to his side kept them at arm's length tonight.

"Why didn't you send Bar or even Azile?" he asked as they neared the house. "A lady should never be out on a night like this."

"Azile left and hasn't returned. I fear she's drunk somewhere or, worse, has found more drugs. We think most of Hattie's furniture disappeared to buy Azile's liquor and drugs. Bar was hurt, also." Margaret's voice was calm, but her fingers trembled slightly on his arm.

Grayson pulled her closer and stepped up his pace. They moved through the foggy night like wisps of blue and gray smoke on a windy day.

When he reached the porch, both soldiers stood at attention. "I'll want a full report," he snapped at one without stopping, "as soon as I've seen Cherish."

He climbed the stairs three at a time and was already in Cherish's room before Margaret reached the door. Carefully he studied her, noting the bruises along her arms and the cut lip and cheek. One of her eyes was almost swollen closed and the other had dark rings of purple around it. She looked so tiny and helpless as she curled in sleep amid the covers.

Margaret whispered by his side, "Your men found her and Barfield in the barn. He'd been knocked unconscious."

Grayson glanced from Cherish to a cot that had been set up by the fire in the sitting room. Bar was curled on it, asleep, his dark hair fanning across his bandaged forehead. "Do you have any idea who did this?"

Margaret stood in the doorway, as stiff as if she were sculpted from ice. "I think Westley must have."

Grayson shook his head. "He told me he was leaving town at dawn and I made it clear he'd better not dally."

Margaret stepped back into the sitting room and Grayson followed. Her voice was tightly controlled. "You believe a man who faked his own death and became a traitor?"

Grayson removed his Union jacket, suddenly not wanting any reminder of the war coming between them. "No." Lord, why did she always have to make him feel like a wet-behind-the-ears pup? "I guess I was just hoping he'd leave before I had to kill him."

"But why?" Again her voice was so cold he thought it might crack the window glass at any moment. "Don't you Yankees like traitors? After all, that was one less you had to fight."

"Margaret, don't."

"Don't what?" She moved a few steps closer to him. "Don't state the facts. Don't make a fool of myself. Don't fall for a lying Yankee who embarrasses me before everyone in town."

"I thought it might work. I thought he'd leave." Now the idea seemed dim-witted even to Grayson, but last night it had seemed so logical.

She stood less than an arm's length from him and she might as well have been across the Mississippi. "When we find him, I'll kill him myself. I only need your help in locating him." She pointed one slender finger at his chest. "And then, Captain Kirkland, I never want to see you again as long as I live."

Grayson knew it was senseless to argue with her now. She was primed for a fight and that wasn't at all what he wanted from her. "If you want it that way," he answered, thinking of other things they'd done together besides argue.

"I not only want it that way, I plan to have it that way."

"Agreed!" He didn't miss her surprise. Without waiting for her to answer, he threw his jacket over the chair and unstrapped his gunbelt.

Her eyes grew wide. "What are you doing?"

"I'm sleeping here tonight. Whoever hurt them might just try to get to you. They got past the guards to Cherish, but they'll have to kill me to get to you."

"But you can't sleep here."

"Why not? I have many nights before." He sat on the couch and began pulling off his boots.

"But that was before I knew you could talk."

Grayson laughed. "Among other things."

"But it wouldn't be proper."

"You asked for my help." He knew she had no one else to turn to or she wouldn't have come to him. It was starting to look like everyone in this town wanted Cherish and Maggie out of this house.

He unbuttoned his shirt. "If I help, I stay." He didn't want to tell her, but he'd had to pull all the rank he could to get the army to loan him even two men from Camp Wilson. They'd be going back at dawn unless he had more proof about the Knights.

Maggie's gaze fell to his chest for a moment and her face softened a fraction, but then she remembered how he'd lied and humiliated her. There was no room in her life for another man she couldn't trust. What had happened two nights ago could never be erased but she would make sure it was never repeated. From this point on, her lovemaking with Grayson would only be in her dreams, never again in reality.

"You can stay on the sofa." Her chin rose slightly. "But I swear I'll kill you if you force yourself on me."

"I didn't before, and I never will," he answered as he relaxed against the couch. "You'll come to me, Maggie."

"Never!" she screamed a moment before she slammed her bedroom door.

Bar rolled on his cot, opened one eye to stare at Grayson a moment, then, fighting to keep down a smile that tickled his lips, he fell back asleep.

Fog thickened over the town. Shouts of drunken cowhands from the saloons had quieted by the time Brant Coulter opened the door of the mission and slipped inside.

Silently he headed toward the flicker of light in the back of the mission. If Father Daniel was there, he'd be in the light; he had hated the darkness since he'd been locked in a cellar while a murderer slaughtered his parents.

Near the back of the mission, Brant spotted Daniel kneeling by the altar. At first Brant thought the priest was praying, but as he neared, he saw several guns and knives spread out beneath the altar.

Brant walked up behind the priest. In one flicker of the candle, Brant grabbed Father Daniel and pulled him to his feet.

"I have a few questions. We have to talk."

The priest showed no surprise at seeing Brant, or fear at his sudden assault. He twisted Brant's fingers from his shoulders and motioned with his head toward the back door.

They walked out of the church without a word. Both men were so similar in height and weight that their shadows mirrored one another.

When they stepped into the night air, Daniel leaned his head back and took a long breath, as if he knew what was to come. Brant leaned against the wall of the church and lit a thin cigar.

"I want to know who hurt Cherish," Brant said as he exhaled a cloud of smoke.

Father Daniel shrugged. "It wasn't one of the group. They wouldn't hurt a white woman. Frighten, maybe, but hurt, no."

"Then who? Daniel, I have to know."

"It was Margaret's husband. He's been asking too many questions around town. Our guess is that he believes the old story about the Knights leaving a stash of money with Hattie. He's tried every legal way to get the house but that giant keeps getting in his way. He's been snooping around far too much for him to stay healthy."

Brant dropped his cigar and ground it into the dirt. "Daniel, you'd better be telling the truth for once. We owe Cherish one."

"Agreed. I wouldn't lie about this. Remember what we used to say: 'closer than brothers.' "

Despite himself and all else between them, Brant smiled and raised his hand. As their fingers clasped he echoed, "Closer than brothers."

The priest turned his gentle gray eyes toward Brant. "Want me or one of the boys to kill Westley?"

"No," Brant answered. "I do my own dirty work."

It was almost dawn when Westley Alexander stumbled out of Holliday's back door. The beating he'd given Cherish had flamed his loins and he'd taken more than his money's worth from one of Holliday's girls. He laughed thinking about how he'd picked a petite young woman with blond hair to climb the stairs with. She hadn't fought as hard as Cherish had in the barn, and the whore had taken his blows without screaming. Her eyes were the wrong color and for that Westley had made her pay. When he'd left her, she was whimpering in a corner like some little animal, her offensive eyes swollen shut from the wrath of his blows and her white limbs darkening with bruises. He laughed, now remembering how he'd run his hands over her nude body one last time just to see her shiver in fear. The sight had been almost enough to make him want to mount her again.

Dried weeds moved in the alley as though a breeze had been trapped in one corner.

"Who's there!" Westley shouted. He clutched his pocket where he'd hidden the brooch Maggie always wore. He'd seen the boy sell it and found it a simple task an hour later to go into the store and lift it from the case. In a few days he planned to shove it in her face and have a great laugh about how she'd played his widow all these years.

Something stirred the trash and Westley laid his other hand on the small derringer in his belt.

The early fog was still as thick as flour gravy. Westley heard a light tapping to his right. He swung around, ready to battle any robber.

A long, wide hunting blade slashed across his gut in one quick pull, then disappeared back into the fog.

Westley grabbed his stomach and fell to his knees. His gun fired uselessly into the fog. Blood trickled between his fingers and ran down his pant legs as he fell forward in the dirt and litter of the alley.

19

At the sound of someone talking, Grayson rolled from his makeshift bed on the sofa. He could see the dawn light filtering through the windows, but he knew he hadn't slept more than a few hours. Each time Margaret had passed the sitting room to check on Cherish, his senses had become fully awakened. Most of the times, he'd forced his eyes not to open. He didn't want to see her in nightclothes with her hair trailing down her back like a black velvet waterfall. Even the shadow of her form would remind him of the slender curves that molded so perfectly to his touch.

He heard the voice again and realized that Cherish's mumbling had once more awakened him. Pulling his pants on, he went to her room. She was talking in her sleep as she had most of the night. The words could scarcely escape past her swollen lips. "Brant," she uttered over and over like a frightened child calling the one person she trusted to help her.

Grayson could make no sense of the name. In the weeks he'd known these women, he'd never heard Cherish mention anyone whose name sounded even similar. He glanced over to Bar's cot. The boy was missing. A moment of worry raised his eyebrow, then Bar appeared in the doorway of the sitting room.

"Mornin', Grayson," he said as he tried to pull the bandage from his head.

"Where have you been?" Grayson didn't miss that the boy was fully dressed.

Bar dropped to the cot. "I went out to the privy. When I woke I thought I felt fine, but the walk out there and back wore me out. If you don't mind, I think I'll lie back down."

He tumbled back into his cot and fell asleep before Grayson could think to question him further. The huge man bent and straightened the boy's covers. Grayson scratched his rough stubble and wondered if he'd have to tie Bar down to get him to rest as Margaret had ordered.

Stretching his muscles, Grayson folded himself into the chair next to Cherish. He'd be just as comfortable sitting up and, if she talked again, he wanted to hear every word.

But Cherish quieted into a peaceful sleep and Grayson closed his eyes. Somewhere in his sleep, he thought he felt Maggie touch his hair lightly. Yet, moments later, when he pulled himself awake enough to open his eyes, she was nowhere in the room. He tried to go back to sleep but the memory of her in his arms allowed him no peace.

An hour later, with a pounding on the front door, full daylight bombarded Hattie's Parlor in regiment force. Grayson was up and halfway down the stairs before he realized he'd forgotten his jacket. Maggie was right behind him, already fully dressed with her hair pulled back in a neat bun. For a moment he fought the urge to grab her and kiss her until her face was warm with love and her lips wet with passion. The woman just looked too damn proper in the morning. But he knew if he touched her, the fire he saw wouldn't be passion.

She stepped past him and flung the door open to the sight of the sheriff standing between two deputies. The weasel of a lawyer danced behind them as if he'd been tied like a noisy can to the sheriff's tail.

Margaret completely ignored the lawyer's chimes and looked at the sheriff. "If you've come to question Cherish, you'll have to wait until she's able to talk."

"No." The sheriff looked down at his hat as if someone had mentioned something he should have done, but hadn't thought about. "I'd like to ask you to come down to the office with me, Mrs. Alexander."

"I'm sorry." Margaret shook her head. "That is out of the question. I have two injured people to take care of upstairs."

No one paid any notice as the lawyer shouted, "Resisting arrest! I told you to watch out for her, Sheriff. She doesn't do what she's told, even when I tell her it's the law."

The sheriff snorted like a wild animal trying to clear the scent of the little man from his nose. "I'll have to insist, Mrs. Alexander." He glanced up at Grayson. "You see, I have an injured man."

"Shouldn't you call the doctor? I'm only a nurse."

"Oh, I called the doctor, but I'm afraid I'll have to take you in. You see, Mrs. Alexander, it's your husband who's been stabbed. He was in an alley a few blocks from here and didn't see who came at him. Right now all the clues we got point to you being the one who assaulted him. I'm afraid you'll have to come with me for questioning."

Only Margaret's years of rigid behavior kept her from crumbling like a frightened child. Without thinking, she glanced at Grayson for support.

He stepped around her to address the sheriff. "There must have been some mistake. Mrs. Alexander couldn't have stabbed anyone. She's been upstairs with her niece all night."

The sheriff looked doubtful. "You were awake all night? No one could have passed out the door without your noticing?"

Grayson thought of Bar leaving for the outhouse. He hadn't even noticed the boy. Even if his mind would logically assume she could have left without his knowledge, his heart would never allow him to believe Maggie would stab someone.

"The guards you had posted had to report back to their camp at dawn, so anyone in the house could have walked the few blocks to the alley where Westley was stabbed."

"But no one did."

The sheriff didn't miss Grayson's hesitation. "We found her brooch in Westley's hand and Mr. Wallman is ready to swear he heard her threaten to kill her husband."

"That's right," Wallman chimed.

Grayson briefly thought of fighting the sheriff and his two half-awake deputies. But someone—Maggie—might get hurt. He tried to make his tired mind think. "It had to have been someone else. Even I told Westley if he wasn't out of town by dawn yesterday that I'd kill him. I have no more alibi than she and plenty of reason."

The sheriff rubbed his chin in thought. His gaze slowly moved across Grayson's lack of dress. "Appears you might have had reason also, Captain Kirkland. Maybe you'd better come along with me as well."

"No," Bar yelled from the top of the stairs. He held to the railing as he descended. "They didn't kill Westley. I did. He knocked me on the head and hurt Miss Cherish. I had to teach him. Ain't no man goin' to do that to me and get away with it." Bar's last bit of strength drained with his words. He would have crumbled down the last few stairs, too dizzy to stand, but Grayson caught him.

"Damn if this doesn't beat all. The man ain't even dead yet and you folks are lining up to confess. Well, I don't believe no half-grown boy stabbed him, or no Union officer. As for Mrs. Alexander, she strikes me as the most likely. She's already tried once and what with a lover living right in her house, she might be in a hurry to get rid of an extra husband."

He grabbed Margaret by the arm and pulled her onto the porch as both his deputies raised their weapons to Grayson.

The huge man was already kneeling to lay Bar down and give them one hell of a fight, but Maggie stopped him.

"No, Grayson," she called from the steps. "I'll straighten this out at the sheriff's office. Right now you have to take care of Bar and Cherish, at least until Azile returns." She pulled the sheriff along with her as if knowing she had to leave fast before Grayson did something dangerous. "I'll be back in an hour."

Grayson wanted nothing more than to charge the guns and take Maggie away with him. He'd never been left minding the nest in his life and he didn't like the trapped feeling it gave him now. But he knew she was right. Someone had to stay with Bar and Cherish. He watched her go, her head high, her back straight. The sheriff and the lawyer were hurrying to keep up with her.

Without a word, Grayson lifted Bar and carried the boy back up the stairs. He might not know much about nursing, but he could at least keep them safe until Maggie returned.

Margaret told the same story to everyone at the sheriff's office. She knew nothing of Westley's stabbing so her answers were short. By noon, she had the feeling that the sheriff wouldn't even have investigated the assault except for all the gossip. One deputy, who everyone called Wart, kept filling the sheriff's mind with what something like this might lead to if he didn't take action now. So the sheriff continued to hold her for questioning as, one by one, everyone in town stopped by to watch.

As the day passed she grew impatient with the deputy named Wart. He reminded her of a molting chicken. Big blotches of skin could be seen beneath thin hair. He strutted around, nervously toying with every object in the room. His clumsiness seemed the only constant in his personality, for he'd be all talk one moment, then silent the next.

Finally, the sheriff could endure no more of her complaining or of Wart's dropping things. The sheriff obviously thought it would be no great chore to break a woman's story—any woman's—but then he'd never met Margaret. "Lock her up," he finally ordered as he grabbed his hat and headed toward the door. "She's to talk to no one until I've checked her story. And, Wart, get her anything a woman would need."

"Where you going?" The deputy looked even more nervous at the thought of being left alone with Margaret. She had taken several opportunities to correct him on his behavior. The idea of spending an evening with her reminding him not to slurp his coffee or put his feet on the desk seemed no less than a death sentence.

"I'm going over to the hotel to see how Alexander's doing. If he dies, we got a murder. If he lives, all we're messing with is a wife who cut her husband. I can hardly haul in every husband or wife who tries to make themselves single. If he's not dead by nightfall, I might as well let her go home."

The deputy nodded. He started to take Margaret's arm, but hesitated. As the sheriff closed the front door, he opened the jail's only cell and waited, as if expecting her to jump at him at any moment.

Margaret stepped inside. "I will need"—she began with a frankness that allowed no discussion—"clean blankets and sheets, a bucket of hot water, a broom, a mop, lye soap, and ammonia. I'll not spend the evening in such filth."

The deputy hesitated only a moment before running to get all she'd requested. Then he stood and watched in amazement as Margaret cleaned the cell completely.

When she was finished, she rolled her sleeves back down and looked directly at the deputy. "Please bring that table and chair. I don't intend to sit on a freshly made bunk."

As he moved to obey, she asked, "Where on earth did you get a name like Wart?"

"It's my initials." He answered as if being called on by his teacher. "Washington Andrew Randolph Tucker."

"Well, your folks should have been ashamed of themselves for calling you such a name, Mr. Tucker. Every single name of yours is a fine one, but the initials will never do."

Wart nodded his agreement and asked if she'd like an extra chair brought into her cell.

As Margaret nodded, the office door opened with a pop. Holliday's large bulk waddled in carrying a tray of food.

The deputy rushed to hold the door. "What's all this?" he asked, almost knocking the tray from her hands as he tried to look under the cloth.

"The lady's supper," Holliday answered with a shake of her head to indicate she'd just wasted words saying the obvious.

"She can't have any visitors." The deputy tried to sound as if he had some degree of authority, but Holliday walked right past him.

"Well, the food ain't company. Open that cell door so I can set her tray down." Holliday looked at Margaret. "Now don't you worry none, miss. This ain't my cooking. I got it over at the hotel." The old sporting lady set the tray on the table.

Margaret's carriage was high and proud, and her voice sincere. "Thank you. It was very kind of you."

Holliday looked embarrassed. "Weren't nothing. I just wanted to tell you I don't think you did it. Even if you had, it were your right after what he did to you. After I seen what he did to my girl this morning I wished I'd been the one to gut him."

The deputy cleared his throat. He knew either of these women could cut him into bite-sized pieces. They might walk on different sides of the street, but their strength formed a bond.

Holliday turned toward Wart. Her face melted into a lover's softness beneath all the paint. "Now, Wart, honey, you know I ain't gonna pass any big secrets to Miss Alexander with you standing right there looking so handsome an' doing your duty." She patted his arm lovingly.

Wart's chest swelled, along with other parts of his body. He looked like a man who had an itch that had gone too long since scratching, but one glance at Maggie kept him from voicing any future plans he had for Holliday. He nodded and moved to his desk, allowing the two women a degree of privacy.

Holliday spread the place setting and withdrew from the cell, but paused close to the bars as the deputy locked the door. "I don't think what the sheriff is doing is right, holding you like this when everyone in town can think of a dozen folks that would like to have kilt Westley Alexander." She pinched up her lips as if thinking she might have said too much in front of the deputy, then added slowly, "Is there anything else I can do? I heard about Miss Cherish's trouble last night."

Margaret's hand reached through the bars and rested lightly on Holliday's arm. "Will you check on my niece? There is no one else I'd trust with such a request." Their eyes met and they both knew that Holliday had doctored her share of bruises the size of a man's fist.

Holliday's ample bosom swelled larger and her chin rose. "I'd be honored," she answered. She felt like she owed Margaret a great deal simply because the woman always treated her as an equal. Miss Margaret might be a lady, but she wasn't a snob.

"And I will be in your debt," Margaret answered. She had no time to add more, for Holliday almost ran from the room.

Margaret lifted the covering on the food. "Mr. Tucker, if you'll wash your hands, you may join me for supper."

Wart glanced around to make sure she was talking to him and then ran to scrub his hands.

Grayson couldn't have been more shocked when, just before sunset, Holliday appeared at the front door. There she was in all her painted glory with her fists on her hips and a mission in her eyes.

When he opened the door she marched in like Sherman's army crossing Georgia. She removed her hat and jacket and hung them on the hall rack as if she'd done so every day of her life. "Where's that useless housekeeper, Azile?"

Too stunned to protest, Grayson answered, "She never came back last night."

"That means she's drunk down around the shanties. She was never no good, but who else is going to want to live with a dying old woman." Holliday marched up the stairs. "How's old Hattie, anyway? It's been a month of Sundays since I've seen her."

"She's been yelling all day, but if I even go near her door she threatens to shoot me with that cannon she keeps on her bed."

Holliday nodded. "The old bag hasn't changed much. I'll see to her as soon as I look in on Cherish and the boy. Have they had supper?"

Grayson nodded, remembering how feeding Cherish had been harder than herding a hundred head of longhorns over the open country in a thunderstorm.

Within ten minutes, Holliday had checked on everyone and was reorganizing everything. If there was one thing she knew, it was how to run a house. Grayson had struggled all day to make Cherish comfortable and keep Bar from moving around too much, but he'd succeeded mostly in spilling soup on her bed and frightening old Hattie farther into insanity.

Now, with Holliday to help, it all seemed so simple. He lifted Cherish in his arms as the old woman changed her sheets. She was so small, like a child. He was almost afraid he might break her. When he laid her back on the bed he was sweating worse than if he'd lifted a ton and not a hundred-pound woman.

When he finally remembered to feed the barn animals it was dark. He hadn't bothered to carry a lantern when he returned to the house. He knew his way across the yard and through the house without any need for light. As he passed each room, checking doors and windows, out of the corner of his eye he caught a shadow in the trees near the front road. It flickered and was gone.

Grayson climbed the stairs silently. "Holliday!" he whispered. "Stay with Cherish and Bar. We got company out front."

He didn't wait for an answer, but crossed the dark sitting room for his rifle. As he reached for the weapon, a hand shot out to grip it just above his fingers.

"Don't be alarmed." A voice shattered the silence. "I'm here to help."

Grayson pulled at the rifle and the man released his grip. "How did you get in here and who are you?" He moved so that the firelight shone on a tall, slender man in black, who wore his guns like an expert. For a moment Grayson was reminded of Father Daniel, but this man was harder, more powerful.

"Neither of those questions is important," the stranger answered. "What is, is that I have the same goal as you and that is to keep the folks of this house safe."

Grayson knew the man could have shot him from the darkness, but hadn't. If he'd made it this far into the house he could have crossed the sitting room and frightened the others—or worse—while Grayson was in the barn. But he hadn't, and for that one reason Grayson trusted him. "Let's go. We've got company coming downstairs."

"I know," the stranger added, "and from the mixture of whiskey and gunpowder it could be deadly."

Both men took the stairs at a run. From the wide hallway foyer, they could see both the front door and the kitchen entrance, but there were too many windows to cover.

Grayson watched the road while the unknown man never removed his gaze from the kitchen entrance. "Mind telling me your name? I'm not in the habit of turning my back to a stranger."

"If you knew my name, you'd probably be less inclined to trust me." The stranger laughed. "But believe this: I'd protect Cherish with my life."

Glancing at Hattie's door, Grayson added, "There's an old woman . . ."

"I know," the stranger interupted. "She's safe enough. Besides, she'd probably kill both of us if we tried to move her upstairs."

Agreeing, Grayson glared over his shoulder at the man. Whoever he was, he knew this house and its occupants and, strangely, that information made him more an ally than an enemy.

Grayson opened his mouth to ask a few questions, but the sound of shattering glass stopped him. Suddenly the trees across the road were alive with men.

"They think Cherish and the boy are alone," the stranger whispered. "They've been drinking and building up the courage to come after the treasure some folks believe is buried in here."

"Do you believe the rumor?"

The stranger's face twisted into a mask of a man much older than his time on earth reflected. "I gave up believing in anything years ago."

"Fire above their heads and maybe we'll frighten them off." Grayson watched as the drunken figures seemed to stretch across the road.

"I don't believe in wasting bullets," the stranger answered.

There was no time to argue. Men stormed the house in a flash flood of bullets and shouts. Grayson felt the stranger lean his back against his and they both began to fire. Suddenly, the night was bright with flashes and smoky with panic. The attackers yelled and scattered in cowards' retreat. They had been all ready to charge at once but now none would take the lead. Before the gunfire stopped, several were limping or being helped back into the trees.

Grayson and the stranger reloaded silently and prepared for the next assault. It came with less fanfare, for the jackals had become snakes, sneaking up to the house in the shadows. Grayson ran out of ammunition first and knelt to reload.

With one violent shove, the stranger pushed Grayson backward and stepped over him. With lightning swiftness, he aimed and fired. A man jumped back out of the window, his gun firing harmlessly at the stars. The attacker's screams could be heard as one of his friends helped him crawl back into the blackness.

The realization that the stranger had saved his life shocked Grayson far more than the screams of pain. He shoved the remaining bullets into his Colt and stood beside the slender man. "Thanks. Stepping in front of me, you could have taken a shot meant for me." Grayson thought he knew men, bad and good, but this one had him baffled. "Why take that kind of a chance?"

The stranger reloaded his rifle and answered, "I saw the way you lifted Cherish while Holliday changed her bed. You treated her like you cared."

That was all he said—all he needed to say. Grayson knew what he needed to know about this man. He leaned his powerful shoulders against the stranger's back and they waited for trouble to knock once more.

But not a sound came for several minutes. Then, a loud thud rumbled on the side of the porch like someone had thrown something heavy against the house. All was silent. The shadows of men disappeared. Drunks returned to the bottle for their comfort and dreams.

The two men in the hallway waited, shoulder to shoulder, for several long heartbeats. Finally, the sound of a horse galloping toward the house tightened their nerves.

"Kirkland!" the rider yelled. "Kirkland. It's the sheriff."

Grayson moved to the door and watched the sheriff climb the steps. He knelt beside the bundle that had been thrown on the porch.

"I heard the gunfire and . . ." The sheriff pulled at a blanket covering the bundle. His gasp seemed to suck the air from the night. "Hell's thunder! You better get a light."

Moments later, when Grayson returned with the lantern, he felt his stomach turn at the sight at the sheriff's feet.

The body of a woman lay completely covered in blood as if she'd died an inch at a time. Her skin was swollen and bruised with cuts crisscrossing her flesh. The only clothing she wore was a brightly colored scarf of red and gold knotted about her neck. Her limbs were tangled where bones had been broken.

Grayson turned to talk to the stranger, but his partner in battle was gone.

The sheriff lifted a note that had been pinned to the blanket. He glanced at it and handed it to Grayson.

Grayson looked down at the message. His eyes turned to steel in the lantern light as he read the words written in a clear, sober hand:

> "THE TWO WOMEN MUST LEAVE
> OR THEY WILL BE NEXT!"

20

Brant slid his arm beneath Cherish's legs and lifted her. "Come with me, baby," he whispered into her golden hair.

Holliday laid a blanket over Cherish. "She'll be safer with you than here. I'll take Bar with me. The girls will keep an eye on him."

Cherish opened her still-blackened eyes. "Brant?" There was no fear in her tone, only relief.

"I'm here, darling. I'm going to take you somewhere safe."

The door creaked slightly and Grayson's bulk suddenly blocked the path. "You're not taking her anywhere, Brant Coulter. You must be mad to think she'd be safer with you."

The corner of Brant's lip twisted up, but the rest of his face was stone-hard. "I see you figured out who I am, Captain Kirkland."

"You planning to add kidnapping to your list of hanging crimes? How many men have you gunned down in cold blood now, Brant, six . . . seven?"

"Enough that one more won't matter much."

"I never heard of you hurting a woman. But I guess one crime builds on another." Grayson didn't bother to pull his gun. He knew he could never get a clean shot with Cherish in Brant's arms. Plus, from what he'd heard about Brant Coulter, he knew he wasn't the type of man to use a woman as a shield. Coulter had been causing trouble in Texas for years, but oddly enough it had been directed at southern leaders or other outlaws and never toward the Union.

"I'm not kidnapping anyone. I think Cherish would be safer with me than in this house. She saved my life once and I owe her this one."

"She'd be safer with one of the most wanted men in Texas? Where would you take her, into Indian territory? Or maybe to a hideout with other outlaws?" Grayson moved closer. He believed that Brant had only her welfare in mind and that one tool had to be his weapon.

"This house was built to withstand Indian raids. Between the two of us we can protect it. But if you take her out in the open, she might end up like the housekeeper."

Holliday's eyes widened. "What happened to the house-keeper?"

"Her body got dropped on the porch a few minutes ago. Whoever killed her must have been out of his mind from the looks of what was done to the body—even after she was dead."

"Oh, Lordy, Lordy, save us!" Holliday had a way of getting religious when she felt the Grim Reaper knocking.

"That settles it." Brant moved toward the door. "I'm taking Cherish with me. Those men tonight only wanted the house. They'd heard the rumors like everyone else in town that there was a stash of gold hidden in here. Times are hard for some of the men. They lost everything in the war and they're looking for a quick gold mine. Desperate men do desperate things."

Grayson crossed his arms and didn't move. "Maybe they were the Knights of the Golden Circle looking to find some old records on their organization? Uncle Sam would give a great deal to see such a list."

Both Brant and Holliday laughed. Holliday waved her hands in the air as if erasing his words. "Those boys haven't been around in years. They were all talk and brag anyway. They spent hours talking their noble talk, then they spent all their money down at my place on drink and girls."

Grayson's sharp eyes didn't miss Brant's silence. He'd bet a month's pay that Brant knew a great deal more about the Knights. Who knew, maybe he even was one. If Grayson could find one man, it would be all he needed to find out who the others were and if they were still active. But right now they had two women's lives at stake and that list of men, if it existed, would have to wait.

Brant finally broke the silence. "I'm taking Cherish, be it around or over your body, Yank."

Grayson wasn't in the habit of killing a man who had just saved his life. There was no mistaking the way Cherish clung to him that she wanted to be with Brant. *Hell,* Grayson thought, *she whispered his name half the night.* Grayson stepped aside. "Give me a week to clear this mess up, then bring her back. You're a man every lawman in Texas would like to get his gun sights on. She won't be safe with you for long."

"One week." Brant maneuvered through the door. His dark eyes left no doubt that he'd planned to fight and was surprised at Grayson's agreement. "Don't worry, Captain, I'll take care of her."

Grayson laughed. "Oh, if you even frighten her, I'm not the only one you'll have to deal with. Wait till you face Maggie."

Margaret Alexander was pacing the cell floor faster than a Baptist preacher paces the hallway during a "love offering."

She'd give Wart just enough time to settle back in his chair before snapping at him. The deputy was growing more nervous every minute. He'd resorted to the habit of running his fingers through his thinning hair. Margaret was sure she could see more scalp with each passing.

"You've got to let me out of here, this minute." She jabbed her finger at him. "Do you really believe I'm safer in here, where anyone in town could walk in and shoot me, than I would be in my own house?"

Wart almost dropped the gun he was cleaning. "Sheriff said to keep you here until they investigate the murder of your housekeeper."

Margaret softened her voice. "Look, I've been with you all day so it's a sure bet that I didn't kill her. I should be the one person in town *out* of jail, Mr. Tucker."

Wart thought that over. Her logic made sense and when she called him Mr. Tucker, like no one in his life ever had, he wanted to believe everything she said. She was a hard handful of a woman, but she sort of grew on a person.

The sheriff saved him from having to answer by coming through the door with his usual haste. Two men carrying a cot came just behind him. The sheriff opened the door to Margaret's cell and waved the men inside. They dropped their charge, none too gently, on the cot in her cell and hurried out.

Margaret stared in shock at the pale face of Westley Alexander. "What is the meaning of this!" she screamed.

The sheriff stepped past the barred door and locked it behind him. "Doc said your husband ain't going to make it unless he's got somebody to look after him through this fever. I took him over to Holliday's but her girls wouldn't touch him. A couple even said they wished they'd been the ones who put the knife into him. Father Daniel at the mission said he had his hands full."

The sheriff smiled as if he'd just solved a great mystery. "So, I figure, you're a nurse and you got a stake in his living."

"But I'm in jail because you believe I'm the one who attacked him!" Male logic had often eluded Margaret but this time it flabbergasted her.

The sheriff scratched his chin and considered the point. "I couldn't think of no one else to nurse him. I was hoping maybe you had a taste of jail and would be willing to help him live."

"I'd rather watch him die!"

"If he does, you'll be hung before the week's out."

Wart jumped from his desk chair and added, "Look at it this way, Miss Margaret. If he lives you'll have another chance to try and kill him."

To Margaret's amazement, the sheriff nodded as if Wart's suggestion was rational. The whole world was on a train to insanity and these two philosophers were the engineers.

She forced herself to look at Westley. Whoever had doctored him hadn't even bothered to button his shirt and vest when he'd finished. The bandage that had been laid over him now drooped to the side as if the doctor had considered it a waste of time to secure it properly. He was, in truth, near death. His fever was high and the wound was seeping. The area around the stitches was already showing signs of being infected.

Standing back a foot, she stared down at this man she hardly knew. She had carried his name proudly all through the war and he had dishonored her. If that had not been enough to make her hate him, he'd beaten Cherish. Margaret wished him dead from the very depths of her soul, but if she was ever going to get out of jail and help protect Cherish from the terror going on at Hattie's Parlor, she had to save Westley's life.

"Mr. Tucker! Fetch my bag from the house and put on a pot of water to boil. I'll need whiskey, soap, and plenty of clean bandages."

The sheriff smiled. He knew most folks didn't like Westley Alexander and could care less who killed him, but Westley and the sheriff had downed an ocean of drinks together and he reckoned he owed him one. He watched as Margaret worked and laughed to himself. Wouldn't they have a joke telling old Westley that his wife was the one that saved his life? After talking to her five minutes, he'd known she wasn't the one who'd stabbed Westley. But a man had to take some action when he was sheriff, before the town started thinking about how he might need replacing.

Wart returned with the bag. Margaret worked fast, not wanting to touch Westley any more than she had to. In a matter of minutes she'd cleaned the wound and applied a smelly black salve. As her hands slid along his flabby abdomen, she thought of how she'd touched Grayson the night they'd spent together under the stars. His stomach had been hard and tight.

Margaret forced herself to continue. She drew strength from Wart's logic. Westley had to recover so that she could make him pay for what he'd done to Cherish.

With the skill of a professional, she wrapped the wound. Her actions were ordered by reflex as her mind tried not to think. Finally, she placed a cool towel across his forehead and asked to be excused from the cell.

The sheriff motioned for Wart to follow her outside and keep an eye on her, but the deputy allowed her privacy once they were out back.

Margaret walked to the washstand several feet away and began pouring water into a tin basin. As the water splashed silver in the moonlight, her hands began to shake. Water spilled everywhere and she had no control. Suddenly her entire body was shaking. Her fingers released the tin pitcher and it clattered noisily to the ground. She gripped the side of the stand for support, for the world was turning, flying upside down.

"Margaret!" A voice shouted from what seemed like a long way away. "Margaret!"

The earth was moving like a swing through the air. All she could see before her was Cherish's face all bruised and bloody. The description of Azile's body materialized in her mind. The feel of Westley's flesh crawled across her skin as the smell of his wound filled her lungs. They blended with all the bodies she'd seen over the four years of war . . . all the blood . . . all the pain.

"Margaret!"

Someone was pulling her to him . . . pulling her into the strong wall of his chest . . . pulling her back to reality.

Maggie held tightly, afraid that if she let go she'd release all the sanity left in her mind. She clung to him with the last hope in her life, burying her face against his chest so she could no longer smell the blood.

Grayson pulled her against him. He'd known something was wrong the moment he'd seen her. "Margaret," he kept whispering as his hands pressed her closer to him. He wanted his warmth to flow into her. He'd seen strong men snap after battle and knew he had to get through to her without delay. She had to find her axis before she was thrown off center forever.

Slowly, he felt her strength returning. He made no effort to kiss her, for now was not the time. She needed his friendship, not his passion. She needed an anchor to hold to for a moment.

When her hand was steady on his shoulder and her breathing had slowed, she pulled away from him. He let her go and dropped his arms, knowing that she wouldn't want to be reminded of her weak moment. He didn't ask if she was all right, for he knew the concern would not be appreciated.

Without a word, Margaret walked to the back door of the jail. When she reached the steps, she turned and asked in a voice as cold and calm as ever, "Why aren't you watching Cherish?"

"She's safe." He wasn't about to tell her that he'd sent Cherish off with one of the most wanted outlaws in Texas. If she found out, there would be hell to pay. Brant Coulter would probably turn himself in just to avoid her wrath.

"And what about Bar and Hattie?"

Grayson opened the door for her, hoping to end the discussion. "Bar's with Holliday and she sent a couple of her girls over to sit with Hattie."

Her next question hit him square between the eyes. "Then why are you here?"

"I . . ." Grayson wasn't sure how much she knew about Azile's killing. If she didn't know about it, he wasn't about to be the one to frighten her. "I thought I'd check on you and see if you needed anything."

Margaret marched through the door ahead of him into the office. "If I needed anything, I would have asked Mr. Tucker."

Grayson glanced around but all he saw in the room was the sheriff and Deputy Wart. "Well, maybe I thought I'd stay around and make sure you're safe."

Margaret didn't look at Grayson. "Mr. Tucker will make sure of that. He's even volunteered to walk Holliday up to the house to check on Hattie."

"Hattie will never know. She's too far gone," Grayson mumbled as he glanced around the room for some guard he hadn't seen, but again all he saw was the aging sheriff and the dim-witted deputy. "Maggie, you don't know what kind of trouble is out there. I'm sleeping here tonight to keep an eye on you."

Margaret turned her back to the men. "I trust Mr. Tucker will be willing to do that."

Grayson lost all control of his already loud voice. "Who in the hell is Mr. Tucker?"

The clatter of a chair falling backward and a box of bullets flying all over the floor answered his question.

An hour later, Grayson propped his own chair against the wall by the door and leaned back, trying to get his huge body in some position where he could sleep. He heard Margaret moving about the cell taking care of Westley, but she never acknowledged his presence. If she needed anything, she politely asked Mr. Tucker.

Grayson cursed under his breath. The damn woman didn't know when a man was trying to save her hide. He was bone-weary and madder than hell at the way she treated him, but the need for her still kept him from ever finding a comfortable position.

About midnight, the sheriff got tired of hanging around waiting for something to happen and decided to go over and try his luck at poker. Being a sheriff was his part-time job, with gambling being his true occupation. But one career helped out the other, and in a town this wild there weren't too many men standing in line to wear a badge. Being the sheriff usually kept the game he was in honest, and being a gambler taught him how to read a man.

" 'Night, Sheriff," Wart said as the sheriff grunted and left. The moment the door closed, Wart lay down on a cot in the back and started snoring.

Grayson swore again. Why was it that people who snored always managed to fall asleep first? He raised the brim of his hat enough to watch Maggie. She covered Westley and moved to the corner of the cell where her belongings had been placed on a small table. Slowly, with weary hands, she pulled the pins from her hair and shook the curls free.

Grayson fought the urge to go to her. He didn't want another scene. Even though she'd allowed him to hold her in the dark out back, he knew she was still angry with him.

With long, graceful strokes she began combing her hair. The black mass waved past her hips as she turned her back to him. As the brush moved through the silky strands, Grayson could almost feel his fingers touching it. He remembered the night they'd spent by the stream. He remembered how she'd come to him all fresh and washed with her hair tumbling free. He could almost taste her mouth and feel the fullness of her breasts pressing against him. He wanted her a hundred times more than he'd ever wanted a woman but there were more than bars that stood between them.

Margaret's mind might lock him out, but he knew he'd already shattered the walls surrounding her heart. Grayson smiled to himself. She was a strong woman, but in the end she'd surrender. After all, that was the way it was meant to be, and one of these days—soon—he planned to convince Maggie of that fact.

21

Brant carried Cherish through the tunnel with great care. He couldn't believe that he was taking her with him. Holliday had assured him that she had no broken bones and that in a few days her wounds would heal. But Brant had never been responsible for anyone in his life except himself and the responsibility frightened him more than a hanging.

He'd traveled the back streets of Fort Worth all his life and knew how to slip from shadow to shadow without anyone aware of his passing. He moved as swiftly as he could without endangering his precious cargo. She was so light in his arms, more pleasure than burden. Yet each time he looked down at her brought pain, for he knew that eventually he'd have to leave her forever. What kind of love, or even friendship, could exist between an outlaw and a lady?

Somehow fate had allowed them to be together once again and he planned to enjoy the only slice of heaven he'd probably ever know. For one week she was his. All he had to do was keep them alive.

As he reached the mission, he saw Father Daniel crossing the yard with another man. The two men were arguing in low, snapping whispers. Brant melted into the shadows before they saw him. The last thing he wanted was another run-in with Daniel.

The priest's voice carried through the night. "But what about the housekeeper?"

The man with him threw his arms up in disgust. "I told you, we found her dead near the opium huts. All we did was wrap her body up and throw it on the porch while the drunks were storming the house. You didn't think we'd resort to killing women, did you? All we're after is the list. As soon as we find it, then all that Alexander woman will have to worry about is the drunks and her husband."

"I've told you before, if there were a list, I'd have found it by now." Father Daniel was getting madder by the minute and Brant knew it would be only a matter of time before he lost control. But there was nothing Brant could do about it with Cherish in his arms.

The other man tried reasoning with the priest. "We have to get rid of that Union officer for a few days. With every drunk in town thinking there's a treasure hidden in that house, there will be hell to pay if anyone finds that list besides us."

"Fat chance of that. My guess is the thing never existed. As for Captain Kirkland, talk to Wallman, not me. He'll think of something. So far, the only one he hasn't been able to twist to his plan is Margaret Alexander."

The men moved out of Brant's hearing and into the mission. As silently as a cloud crosses the moon, Brant crossed the open area of the mission and entered the barn. He laid Cherish gently on the hay and saddled his horse.

Cherish made a little sound like an injured child as he lifted her into the saddle and climbed up behind her. He hesitated, not knowing where he could touch her without hurting her.

Tenderly, Brant pulled her against his chest and wrapped the blanket tightly around her. "It's all right, baby," he whispered.

She cuddled against him as they rode down the back trail of the mission and out of town. The moon was a huge gold piece in the sky, guiding their path eastward. She fell into a deeper sleep and didn't wake until it was almost dawn.

As she stirred against Brant's warm chest, he whispered, "We're here." He could have covered the distance in a few hours, but he hadn't wanted to jar her, so he'd walked his horse and held her until his arms ached from cramping.

Lifting her to the ground, he carried her into an old dugout almost buried in the side of a hill. "I found this place by accident a few months ago. It's shielded from view on three sides by ridges, and the cottonwoods have grown up so high by the creek you can't see it from the front unless you know what to look for."

Laying Cherish on a straw bed, he turned and lit a candle. "I figure this must have been someone's homestead ten or more years ago and the Indians ran them out. Or maybe they just got tired of living out here alone and moved to Dallas."

Cherish looked around the tiny, one-room shelter as Brant moved about. Three of the walls were dug out from the earth with the top and front made of logs. Even though the sun was coming up, the little home was still dark and cool. Cherish lay back on the small bed and smiled. The room reminded her of the homestead where she'd been born: cool and earthy. A dugout always had a way of welcoming folks—warm in the winter, cool in the summer. When she'd been a child she'd often taken her naps in the cool darkness of the dugout behind her home. Now, she stretched beneath the blanket and closed her eyes.

Brant settled them into the place while she dozed. He stabled his horse in the trees by the stream and split enough wood to keep them warm should the night turn cold. Then he cooked the handful of beans from his saddlebag until they were a thick, brown soup.

"Cherish," Brant whispered as he stood at the foot of the bed. "You want something to eat?"

She looked up at him and smiled with the trust of a child. He could tell she was feeling better. The bruises on her face were fading and for the first time since the beating she was hungry.

They ate in silence. He wasn't sure what they should talk about. He'd seen people, men and women, sit down to a meal together and talk quietly, but he'd never given much thought to what they would actually say. Finally, when she'd finished her second bowl of soup, he lifted a medicine pouch from his saddlebag. "I think I'd better change the bandage on your knee."

"It's not that bad." Cherish looked embarrassed. "I'm not used to anyone taking care of me except for Margaret. I can change it myself later."

Brant knelt beside her bed. "No. Holliday would have my neck if she thought I wasn't taking the best care of you possible. That old woman makes up her mind about a person the minute she sees them, and if she likes you she considers you blood kin from then on. You lie back. I've changed a few dressings before."

Nervously, Cherish leaned back in the bed and remained still as he lifted back the covers on her legs. More to calm her nerves than out of interest, she asked, "You've known Holliday long?" A smile lifted the corner of Brant's mouth. "I've known her most of my life. She's not as old as most folks think, but she's danced to a few too many fiddles."

"You like her?"

"Sure. She's helped me out of a few tight spots, but her heart and friendship aren't for sale." Brant laid all the bandages beside Cherish. "I think she'd like to find a man to take her out of the business, but so far the only one who's offered is the half-witted deputy in town." Cherish leaned back and closed her eyes as Brant rolled his sleeves to his elbows and began.

Slowly, as if he were afraid he might hurt her, he pushed her nightgown up over her bandaged knee. She smiled as he gently unwrapped the wound.

"It looks like it's healing nicely." Brant's voice sounded tense as he worked. "I'll put some more salve on your leg and wrap it with a fresh bandage."

Cherish watched him closely. "You're acting as though you've never doctored a wound. I'm not breakable."

Brant didn't smile, but concentrated on what he was doing. She thought about how he'd kissed her with such fire the first time they'd met, and how now he seemed afraid to touch her.

He finished wrapping her knee and carefully pulled her nightgown back over her legs. "You need to rest."

Cherish allowed him to pamper her by tucking the covers around her. "Thank you," she whispered. "You've a very gentle touch."

Brant knelt on one knee beside her bed. "Cherish, I don't. Most of the time I'm around you I feel like I'm going to hurt you. You've got to tell me if I should do something and don't. I've never spent much time around a lady like you."

She didn't hear him, for as soon as her eyes closed she was asleep. He looked down at her, thinking she was the most beautiful woman he'd ever seen. She was so perfect; she had no place in his life. Maybe, if they'd met back before the war, but not now. He'd killed too many men for the law to listen to his reasons.

Grabbing his bedroll, Brant moved out of the dugout. He spread his blanket by the door and lay down, welcoming the hard earth beneath him. What kind of hell had he gotten himself into this time? The most perfect woman he'd ever known in his life was sleeping a few feet away from him

and he couldn't touch her. If he did, he'd be all the evil
names folks had always called him. He was an outlaw who'd
stolen pretty near everything, from food when he was hungry
to gold when he was broke, but he couldn't steal her heart
and he had no chance of winning it. Something inside him
wouldn't allow him to touch her against her will. The stolen
kiss on the train had cost him dearly in days of longing. He'd
never be able to live with himself if he took from her what
she did not offer.

Brant swore under his breath. For once he had to be the
good guy. He had to take care of her and see to her needs,
and keep his passion locked up tight. When he'd touched
her on the train, he'd frightened her. When he'd opened her
blouse behind the barn, she'd pulled away from him like he
was something evil and dirty. Well, he wasn't going to see
that look in her eyes again. He was going to live this week
out without jumping on her like some love-starved cowhand
who'd been lost on the range for a year. She wasn't like the
women he'd met before. She was the kind of woman he'd
seen walking her children to church on Sunday, the kind
who'd never even speak to him.

Laughing to himself, he tried to relax. Folks back in town
would never believe Brant Coulter could be a gentleman for
a week. He'd prove them all wrong even if no one knew but
himself. He'd lived through months in a prison camp once.
Well, he could sure as hell live through a week of looking
at a beautiful woman.

Morning came before he was sure he'd fallen sound
asleep. His body felt as if a buffalo stampede had trampled
over it during the night. He rose and checked to see that
Cherish was still sound asleep, then walked the fifty yards
to the cottonwoods where a creek rattled over rocks.

Recent rain had made the water deep enough to come
to his shoulders and Brant enjoyed swimming in the icy

stream. The water cooled his blood enough to allow him
to think about Cherish without wanting her body pressed
beneath his own.

In the days that followed, Brant began to think that he
was about the cleanest human that ever lived. As she got
better and began to move around, the tiny, one-room house
seemed to shrink. Every time he turned around he was
bumping into her, or feeling her hair touch his shoulder,
or standing so close that he could smell the wonder of her.
Sometimes, when he was out in the open, he could feel the
warmth of her body standing behind him even before he
turned to look.

Everything she did made her more desirable. Because he'd
forgotten to bring her any clothes, she'd taken to wearing a
pair of his slacks and his shirt. The rope belt he'd tied about
her waist made the outline of her breasts and hips more pro-
nounced. In the evenings she liked to sit outside and brush her
hair dry in the last rays of the sun. Brant would always stand
several feet away and wonder if he would eventually die
from longing to run his fingers through the golden strands.
For surely it was as necessary as breathing or eating.

But the worst thing she did was a small gesture that most
folks wouldn't even notice, yet it drove Brant wild. Each
night, after he'd watched Cherish all day and thought he
could stand no more of her without having her, she'd come
close to him and kiss him softly on the cheek. He'd ram his
hands in his pockets and refuse to even move, as he felt her
silky lips against his face and her tiny hand on his chest when
she stretched to kiss him. She'd whisper, "Good night," and
turn into the dugout. He'd head for the stream like a man
full of demons to be cast out.

On the fifth day they spent together, the wind was hot
from the south and the air was dry. He could hear the leaves

rustling in the cottonwoods like whispers on a warm day. In those five days, Brant hadn't seen another living soul except for Cherish, and that had been a hell of a heaven. Every time he turned around she was closer to him than he realized. With the whole state of Texas to walk around in, he swore to himself, you'd think that they could go an hour without bumping into one another, or reaching for the coffee pot at the same time, or starting through the door at the exact same moment. Even when they'd eaten supper at the tiny table in the dugout, her knee had accidentally touched his and remained against his leg. She probably thought his leg was the table leg but Brant was very much aware of her touch.

Finally, the sun set, and Brant excused himself for the night. Just as he reached the cabin door, Cherish stopped him. She leaned into him and kissed him as she had every night and, as he had every night, he tried to ignore her touch.

He hit the water a few minutes later like a man who had been in the desert for days. The icy bubbles rose over him as he crossed the stream again and again, trying to use up some of the energy inside him. *Hell,* he thought, *if I keep this up— not eating, not sleeping, and swimming—I'll look like one of those dried apple dolls little girls make in the fall.*

Exhausted, Brant climbed to the bank and pulled his pants over his wet legs. With the languor of a resting mountain lion, he stretched in the grass and allowed the wind to dry his chest. It felt good to press into the earth and become a part of nature around him.

He was almost asleep when he heard something move in the brush beside him. Before he could react, a sudden weight hit his stomach and a knife pointed against his side.

"One move and it'll be your last!" a soft voice whispered into his ear.

"Cherish?" Brant froze. He could have easily fought off an attacker, but all his senses halted any action. He could smell the sweet, fresh smell of her and feel her long hair brushing against his bare chest as she thought she was holding him down. Her breath was warm against the hollow in his neck and her touch was light as she slid her palm along the damp hairs of his chest.

He relaxed as he tried to understand her game.

"I said, don't move!" She tickled his ribs with the knife as she spread her weight over him. "I don't want to have to kill you, but I will."

He felt her breasts flatten against his chest as her free hand moved into his wet hair. She pulled his face close against hers and whispered, "I need some answers and I need them now."

Brant laughed, suddenly loving her game. He decided she'd either gone mad or found his bottle of whiskey, but either way the feel of her on top of him was wonderful.

"I'm not in the habit of answering questions at knife-point."

"Well, you'll answer these, or you'll scream in pain."

Brant smiled in the darkness, for there was no hint of believability in her threat. "You'd make a terrible bandit," he whispered.

She moved the cool blade along his ribs as if her slight action would in any way threaten him. "I'm tired of waiting. I was taking care of the wounded when most girls were learning to flirt. I don't know what else to do to make you want me the way a man wants a woman."

"So you attack me at knife-point?" Brant was trying to keep from laughing aloud.

"It was the last thing I could think of that might work. I'm tired of not feeling. I want to be treated like a woman.

I want to be kissed like you kissed me on the train when you hadn't even seen my face."

"And if I refuse?"

"Then I'll just have to kill you. I can't leave any witness around who saw me make such a fool of myself."

Brant laughed and rolled over suddenly. The knife fell from her grip as he pinned her in the grass. He spread his hands out to hold her arms and rested his leg across her legs. "So you want to be kissed, do you? That's the ransom for my life?"

She turned her face to him and he felt her reply in the softness of her lips against his cheek.

"I'm not sure I can stop with a kiss," he whispered. "Once before you ran from me when I went farther." His lips lightly brushed her cheek. "How could you think you'd have to threaten me to get me to kiss you? I've been living through hell trying not to touch you all week. I'm not sure I can give you what you ask without giving you a great deal more."

Cherish strained beneath him, fighting to free her arms. For a moment, he couldn't let go. He wanted her so badly; still, he had to tell her the truth before he started. She might be just playing a game, but he'd already bet his heart on the outcome. Reluctantly, he released her hands and raised himself off her.

But instead of rolling away, Cherish pulled him back down. Before he could stop her, she dug her fingers into his hair and pressed her mouth to his.

The touch of her lips exploded in his brain like a cannon fired at point-blank range. He tasted her lips and reason no longer mattered. He felt her arms holding him against her as her mouth opened to his.

Brant rolled to his side and drew her close. His hands moved down her back and he pressed her to him, unable to hide his need for her any longer. He explored her mouth as he felt her hands combing through his hair. He was lost in the wonder of her as his kiss deepened to a passion unlike any he'd ever felt. A thousand swims in icy water wouldn't cool the fire that burned inside of him.

His hands could no longer remain still. He yanked the shirt free from her belt and ran his palms over the flesh beneath the oversized shirt. A fire within him made him want to hurry, yet a part of him wanted this moment to last forever.

Suddenly, he broke the kiss and sat up. It took every ounce of strength he had not to touch her, but he ran his knuckles across his mouth and asked, "Cherish, are you sure?"

Slowly, she moved beside him, her hair tumbled around her face, her cheeks red with emotion. Hypnotized, he watched as she unbuttoned the shirt and slid it off her shoulders. Her skin was pale in the moonlight. Her breasts were high and pointed with desire. She was like a statue of perfection and for a moment all he could do was stare. When she raised her eyes to his, her green depths were full of passion and mischief. "Do I have to find the knife," she whispered, "to make you love me?"

Brant pulled her to him without any further hesitation. Half the lawmen in Texas could have been in the trees taking aim at him and he wouldn't have noticed. Cherish was in his arms.

He made love to her with a need as wild as the state they lived in. Never in his life had he dreamed passion could be so all-consuming. He'd had women before, but being with them had been nothing like being with Cherish. The more he gave, the more she wanted. She needed to feel every level with him, completely, as if she'd been starved of feelings all her life and he was her only teacher.

He tried to go slowly, but the need for her was too great. When he moved atop her, and entered her, he felt her stiffen in pain, but her fingers dug into his shoulders and pulled him to her. For a moment he tried to withdraw, afraid he had hurt her, but she held him tightly and whispered his name.

When he exploded inside her, he thought his heart would stop beating. All the pain and longing in his life was swept away in one moment of paradise. He lay for a moment beside her on the ground and wondered how he'd been able to touch the stars without leaving the earth.

She curled her nude body against his and lazily kissed the side of his neck. "Thank you," she whispered as if she didn't realize she'd just given him the greatest gift in the world.

Brant couldn't have talked if his life depended on it. He lifted her into his arms and carried her back to the dugout. In the warm darkness of the cabin he made love to her again, slowly and gently. He had only dreamed of loving someone this way, for never had he had the time or the desire to so completely possess a woman. Her body was a wonder to his touch, just as he'd known it would be. He took his time, moving over every part, loving the way she cried his name softly when he pleased her. Never in his life had a woman cared for him, and this one cried his name as if her need for him came from deep within.

Gently he brought her again and again to the edge of heavenly bliss and made her wait until she could stand it no longer and pulled him to her wantonly. When he moved inside her, he felt a lock twist around his heart and he knew he'd love her until the day he died.

When his passion was drained once more and Brant lay beside her too exhausted to speak, she rolled against his damp body. "Thank you," she whispered again.

There were a thousand things he wanted to tell her, but his mind could no longer sort them out. He ran his fingers along her back until his hand rested on her hip. Kissing the wet hair away from her face, he leaned his chin against her forehead and fell asleep, sure that he'd died and gone to heaven.

Cherish rested her head on his chest and smiled as she listened to his slow, steady breathing. Her heart was full of love for this tender man and nothing could remove the memory of her night of passion. If he disappeared tomorrow, she'd had this night, this time, this love. She knew what it was to be totally alive and, for all of eternity, all time would be measured from this moment on.

22

"I'm going to let you out now, Mrs. Alexander," the sheriff said while he moved a match from one side of his mouth to the other. "Your husband looks like he's going to recover, thanks to your care for the past three days. I hope you understand I was just doing my job." He looked a little nervous as he unlocked the cell door.

Margaret didn't bother to acknowledge that the sheriff was talking to her. She lifted her medicine bag and jacket and walked out of his office without a backward glance.

Wart and Grayson were standing outside talking when she stepped into the sunlight. Wart removed his hat. "Good day, Mrs. Alexander."

Margaret smiled at him. "Good day, Mr. Tucker."

Wart fell into step with her, leaving Grayson to follow. "If you have any more trouble around your place, don't hesitate to call on me to help. The sheriff thinks it was just a group of boys that got liquored up and decided to go on a treasure hunt. But if they give you any more grief, just call me. Holliday usually knows were I am."

Grayson watched her thank Wart and cross the street toward home. She walked past him with no more notice than one might pay a hitching post. The woman could hold a grudge longer than a tadpole could tread water. She marched up the hill toward Hattie's Parlor without even a glance back to see if he was following. He led his horse and walked behind her. He couldn't remember closing his eyes for three nights. The simple act of combing her hair each evening had fired his imagination and pushed sleep behind other needs. Now he didn't even want to talk to her. He knew she'd see the lines in his face and, knowing Maggie, she was probably making his life a hell on purpose.

When they reached the front porch, she turned around to face him. "I wish to thank you for helping with Cherish. It was kind of you." Her face was its usual barrier of stone. The sheriff's words about keeping a lover in her house had hurt her proper sense of values and Grayson's failure to deny the charge wounded her even more. Never in her life had she questioned what was right and proper to do until she met this huge man who never seemed to have more than a few words to say.

She faced him now with icy blue eyes. "The sheriff tells me that Bar has been taking care of Hattie and that he'll be back today to help me. I think you can go back now to your duties in the army, whatever they are. Judging from the number of times they contacted you at the jail, you are needed more by them than by me."

Grayson thought he deserved a little more than a thank-you on the porch for almost getting himself killed. His tired muscles were slowly twisting with anger.

"Now, if you'll just tell me where Cherish is, I'm sure I'll be fine."

"She's safe." Grayson tied his horse to the hitching post. He wasn't about to tell Margaret that her niece was with an outlaw.

"Where?"

"With a friend," Grayson said for a lack of a better term. "She'll be safe and back in a week."

"A friend of yours?" She raised her voice on the last word.

Grayson fought the urge to yell what he knew she was thinking: *Yes, another lying Yankee like me.* Instead, he said, "No, a friend of Cherish and Father Daniel, I believe."

Margaret nodded as if realizing she would get no more out of him. "Thank you. I'm sure she's safe if the woman is a friend of Father Daniel's. Good day, Captain Kirkland." Without a backward look, she turned and walked into the house.

Grayson was right behind her. He fought the urge to tell her that Cherish wasn't with a woman friend, but decided he didn't want to fight that battle on top of the one that was blowing full gale right now. "Good day!" he shouted. "Are you dismissing me? First you ask for my help and now you dismiss me like I'm little more than a day hand around the place. You do try a man's patient nature."

Margaret moved to the kitchen. "I asked for your help because of Cherish and I had nowhere else to turn. If what you say is true and she's safe, then I no longer have need of your services. I thanked you. What do you want . . . pay?"

Grayson fought the urge to belt her across the room. He'd never hit a woman, but he might have to break his own arm to keep from it if she kept up this cold manner. He'd shoot a horse for being half as stubborn as her.

"Hell no, I don't want pay!" He took a step toward her, but she moved away. "Maggie, you've come right back to this house. Don't you understand? Someone is trying to run you out. Damn it to hell, half the town seems to want you out of here. Cherish is safe, but you're not."

"Stop swearing in my home, Captain Kirkland, and stop talking to me as if I'm a slow-minded child."

"Stop acting like one."

"I can take care of myself." Her chin rose slightly. "I always have."

"That's right. No one's ever taken care of Margaret. She can take care of herself. She doesn't need anyone, does she?"

Margaret's eyes were black with anger. "That is correct. I have no use for a traitor husband or a lying Yankee."

"Well, I'm staying here to see that nothing else happens." Grayson couldn't remember folks ever saying that being stubborn was one of his top traits, but he was sure planning to cultivate it now. Damn, the woman was bringing out bad habits he'd lived thirty years without noticing.

"You are not staying here!" Her voice lost an ounce of control. "You've embarrassed me in front of the whole town. You've lied about who you were and then you've dragged my name through a gambling hall. I've lived my entire life without anyone ever gossiping about me. If you stay here with me now, everyone will talk."

Grayson saw her point. He didn't give a damn about what anyone said, but she did. All she'd had to live on was a paper-thin pretense of respectability, and she clung to the shreds even now. "Then come with me," he said. "I'll get you a room at Camp Wilson. You'll be safe there."

"No. Someone has to stay with Hattie. She's too weak to be moved," she answered. "This is my house, my only-ever house, and I'm not leaving it."

He'd never wanted to hold her as badly as he did right now with her standing in the kitchen looking like she'd like to sharpen the knives on his bones. But she had her only house ever. Just about everything had been stripped away from her, but she still had her pride and he loved her all the more for it.

"Then I'll sleep in the barn until Cherish gets back, but I'm not leaving you alone."

For a long moment he looked at her, not seeing the stubborn woman before him, but only the little girl who'd never possessed a home of her own. If he could, he'd give her his family's homestead back in Ohio, for it mattered little to him. This house, even with its curse, was all she had to call hers.

Hattie's sudden shouts made them both jump. Margaret looked at him with stormy, dark eyes and said, "I have to take care of her now. She's been here all alone for a while and is probably frightened. When I come back, I want you gone—off my property, and out of my life forever."

"But . . ."

"I'll not take in another liar." For a moment she dropped her guard. He saw the pain her statement cost her, but she wouldn't back down.

Before he had time to argue, she turned and disappeared into Hattie's room. Grayson slammed his fist onto the tabletop and said every swearword he knew loud enough to be heard in every room of *her* house. The damn woman was determined to get herself killed. Oh, she could come to him to ask for help for Cherish but not for herself. She knew as well as he did that she wasn't free to see him out in the open, proper-like, and she wouldn't allow herself to be the kind of woman who would accept a favor from a friend for herself.

Grayson headed for the barn. He'd take care of the animals, then board up the downstairs windows so she wouldn't have any unexpected company. If he had to, he'd sleep on the porch, but he wasn't leaving Maggie alone with a crazy old dying woman and a boy. She may have always gotten her way in the past by bullying everyone around her, but he wasn't giving in to her no matter how far she stuck out that proud chin of hers. She was the first thing in life he'd found worth living for and he planned to be with her, even if it killed him.

He walked across the yard, not noticing the gray clouds gathering above him. His mood was darker than any Texas storm and twice as deadly. Why did the first damn woman he'd fallen for since his wife died have to be so stubborn? All he wanted to do was take care of her and she acted like that was some crime he should be horsewhipped for. Someone should have explained to her that this was the way it was supposed to be and it looked like that someone was going to have to be him.

Three hours later she appeared at the barn door. She stared at him as he paused from sawing a board, and her voice rose above the wind and thunder. "Why haven't you gone?" The day had turned ugly, with black clouds boiling along the horizon. The wind whipped at her gray dress in angry blasts of hot air.

Grayson laid down his saw but he didn't bother to put on his shirt. "I'm not leaving you, Maggie. You know what's between us is something too deep to cut out and I don't give a damn what anyone says. You belong to me. You're mine as completely as God ever made a woman to be and no promise you made years ago to a no-good stranger will change that."

"I don't want you or need you. I can manage for myself."

He moved closer to her. She wasn't seeing it the way she should at all. "I know you can take care of yourself," he admitted to both her and himself, "but I'm not leaving." He tried to sound direct and sure, but when facing a woman who always thought she was right, it was hard not to question his own logic now and then. "I will not leave you, Maggie. You mean too much to me."

For the first time, Margaret looked like she was losing control. "There can't be anything between us, Grayson. Don't you see? It can't be."

"It was and it is." He moved nearer. "I can't stop feeling the way I do about you just because your dead husband shows up. Or because someone was wise enough to stab him."

Her eyes widened slightly. "Were you the one?"

Grayson laughed. "No, but I wish I had been. I'd have pushed the blade a little deeper. Was it you?"

"You know I couldn't have done it. I was here with Cherish."

Grayson looked her up and down as if assessing her. "Even if you had, you'd be no less beautiful." He watched a strand of hair pull free of her bun and float in the wind about her face. He moved closer and ground his hands into fists at his sides to keep from touching her. "And my need for you would be no less."

She was grasping for straws. "That's another thing. You have this blind spot when you look at me. I'm not young, or beautiful, or desirable. I've never been and I never will . . ."

He grabbed her by the waist and pulled her against his bare chest. He stepped backward into the shadowy darkness of the barn where the wind could no longer tease her hair. "That subject is not open to discussion," Grayson whispered. He would take almost anything from this woman, but not her questioning of how he felt toward her. Before she could pull away he drew her to him. His mouth covered hers with a fire that burned him to his core.

Ten years of loving no one had left him starved. He'd been little more than a boy when he'd buried his wife. He'd loved her, but not the way he loved Maggie. Her death had shattered his ideal of young love, but Maggie's withdrawal was pulling his heart out by the roots.

His kiss was savage with need and hungry with desire. He locked her in his arms and demanded her response. Vaguely, he felt her try to pull away, but he twisted one hand into her hair and held tight. If he had a blind spot toward her, it was a breach large enough to engulf them both and swallow them for eternity. No one had ever been as important to him. She was not a luxury but a staple he couldn't live without.

Trying to remind her of another time, when he'd thrust inside her with passion's longing, he pressed her full length against his hard body. As she molded to his demand, his grip lightened. This was how he wanted her, all soft and waiting for his touch. He moved his open palm along her back, loving the way her body fit so perfectly against him. His hands spread over her hips and pulled her against his need.

Finally, the woman is coming to her senses, he thought as his kiss deepened and his hands moved around her waist to cup her breasts.

With one violent shove, she was free of his arms. She stepped into the barnyard not even noticing the wind that whirled around her. Her indigo eyes were black with anger and liquid with pain. She clenched her fists against her sides and shouted at him as though he were half a mile away and not a few feet. "No! I'll not let it happen again. I made one mistake in loving the wrong man and it cost me dearly, plus it almost cost Cherish her life. I'll not allow myself to feel anything, ever again."

A part of Grayson wanted to strangle her. She blamed herself for something no one could have stopped. Now she'd sentenced herself to a life alone because she was afraid. He wanted to pull her near and hold her, for he suddenly realized his brave Margaret was afraid to love— more afraid of loving than she was of facing the years ahead alone. Loneliness was a prison she'd lived in most of her life. Its walls were bare and its boundaries narrow, but it was the one place where she knew she could survive.

He stood at the barn door and watched her cross the yard. He'd fight the world for her, but he wasn't sure he could fight her and win. He couldn't hurt her anymore, even if he knew leaving would rip his heart out.

"Maggie!" he yelled as she reached the porch.

She turned and pushed the strands of ebony hair from her face, but didn't speak.

"I'll go," he shouted, "as soon as Cherish gets back, if that's what you want."

Maggie nodded once as if a second time might break her in half.

Every powerful muscle in Grayson's body tightened. He wanted to run to her and hold her so tightly she'd never break his grip. But force or shouting wasn't the way to win her. He wasn't sure what it was, but he'd find it if he had to try for the rest of his life. He'd lived in that same prison of loneliness and, unlike her, he never wanted to go back.

He worked in the barn until it was dark. As he crossed to the house he was still no closer to figuring out what to do. When he stepped into the kitchen, Bar, not Maggie, greeted him.

"Miss Maggie said for us to go ahead and eat. She wanted to sit with Hattie for a while longer. The old girl ain't doin' so well. Her arms and feet are starting to curl up like she's going back to bein' a newborn baby."

Grayson washed his hands and sat down across from the boy. "Is Hattie in pain? I heard her yelling earlier."

"She was, but she got a letter from her little girl. It settled her down some. The doctor we had out here once said the old lady would never live to see spring. That was two years ago."

"You were here then?"

"Sure. My ma was alive then. She used to take care of Hattie before Azile. When Ma died, Azile came, but she was different. Always asking questions that no one had the answer to and sometimes sneaking off to town and staying for days."

Grayson put his hand on the boy's shoulder. "You know she's dead, son."

Dark gypsy eyes looked up at Grayson. "Yeah, I know. Can't say I'm sorry. A fella can't go around gettin' too attached to people. They all just die or run out on you when you least expect it."

"Barfield?" Maggie's voice caught them both by surprise.

Bar stood. "Yes, ma'am."

Maggie handed him an envelope. "Is this the letter that came for Hattie today?"

Bar suddenly looked nervous. "Yes."

"You know she treasures the letters. She keeps them hidden under her bed in a box."

"Yes, ma'am."

"And you know the daughter who lives up north is never coming."

"Yes, ma'am."

Grayson looked confused. "Why not, if she keeps writing? She might just show up any day. Who is to say that she's not on her way right now? Maybe she just couldn't come because of the war."

Both the others looked at him with the sadness of no hope in their eyes.

Maggie placed an arm around the boy's shoulders and hugged him to her. "The daughter's not coming because the envelopes have no postage."

Grayson flipped the paper over and saw that there was nothing except Hattie's name written there. He looked up at Maggie and raised one eyebrow.

She touched Bar's hair with her fingers. "How long have you been writing them?"

Bar owned up to his crime. "Ever since she got sick. Three, maybe four years. She started losin' her mind from the present back. She could remember some guy that was here six years ago, but she couldn't think what she'd eaten for breakfast. One day she forgot that her daughter had died years ago. She started worryin' about why she hadn't gotten a letter. So I just wrote one and that made her real happy for a long time. It was somethin' she could hold onto when her mind flooded with fear."

He turned wide, dark eyes up at Maggie. "I didn't mean no harm. Everybody said she only had a few months to live, so why shouldn't she have some hope? It's better to have a daughter that might come than no one at all."

Grayson studied Maggie's face, but she held herself too tightly in control to allow the tears brimming in her eyes to fall.

She patted the boy's head. "What you did was wrong, but maybe for the right reason." Hugging him close she whispered, "Bar, no matter what happens I want you to know you have a home here with me. I promise I'm not going to die or run out on you. I know what it feels like when you wonder where you'll be sleeping from week to week. I don't want you to worry. My home will always be your home."

For the first time since they'd known him, the little boy showed beneath the little man. He wrapped his arms around Maggie and cried. He held to her as if she'd just announced his greatest fear and in so doing wiped it from his mind forever.

Grayson watched the scene between them. He wanted to scream, *What about me? How long do I have to wander before someone welcomes me home?* Deep down inside him, he made a promise that he'd win Maggie back. Then the three of them would be together. At their age, they might never have children, but they'd have Bar to raise. He stood suddenly and stormed out to the barn. He needed time to think. If he didn't figure out how to get Maggie back soon, Bar would be grown.

And it had better be something better than gambling for her, or she'd probably deal him a dead-man's hand herself this time.

23

Before he was fully awake Brant pulled Cherish to him. The predawn blackness mixed with the world of his dreams. She felt so wonderful in his arms: fresh as the first touch of spring rain and warm as the last ray of sunshine on a long summer day. He buried his face against her neck and lightly kissed her skin. *Damn,* his groggy mind thought, *this is too good to be a dream.*

Cherish turned her face to him and kissed his full bottom lip. When he didn't respond, she tugged at it lightly with her teeth. "Kiss me back," she demanded.

Brant would have awakened from death to answer her request. He kissed her slowly and tenderly. He could never remember being gentle in his life, but he was gentle with her now. To him, bringing her pleasure was a sweet torture he'd gladly die from.

He raised himself on one elbow. As his tongue tasted the inside of her mouth, he lowered his chest over her and heard her moan with pleasure as his hard muscles pressed against her softness. Loving Cherish would have to be slow and easy, he reminded himself. For loving her was the only pure heaven he'd ever known. He moved above her and suddenly living became more beautiful than any dream.

Hours later, when he awoke again, Cherish was gone from his side. Brant had looked into death's cold eyes many times, but never had he felt the fear that slammed against his chest now. Somehow, she'd vanished like a dream at dawn.

He rose and looked around the shadows of the dugout. Only emptiness stared back. Dressing quickly, he went outside where she always sat to comb her hair. The day was as still as a tomb and the air was heavy, like it always gets just before a storm. All night, when he'd been loving her, he hadn't thought about what it would be like when she was not with him. Now he realized that for every moment of pleasure, he'd suffer a day of pain when this week ended.

The sound of her humming drifted to him from between the cottonwoods. He ran toward the stream, willingly sacrificing all the days he had left to live for a few more moments with her.

Cherish was standing waist-deep in the water, washing. Her body was bare to the morning sun and glistening with droplets. When he approached, she whirled and lowered herself into the water.

Brant could only watch her. She was like a painting too wonderful to describe. The thought that such a woman so freely gave herself to him was beyond the realm of possibility. He'd lived so long with nothing that the sudden feast of her was too much.

"I've decided," she said as she rubbed soap over her arms, "that I shall never do again what I did to you last night."

Brant felt his throat tighten in pain. He wasn't sure he wanted to hear more. How many times in his life had he heard people change their minds about caring for him? How many folks had taken him in, promising him a home and love, only to turn him out when times got hard and he was just another mouth to feed?

"I'm ashamed of being so bold." Cherish looked up and saw him lower his hat to hide his eyes. His stance was defensive, like he was waiting for a blow from nowhere to strike him. If she hadn't been able to still feel the gentleness of his touch, she would have sworn that this man was incapable of such tenderness. He looked stone-hard and unyielding.

Slowly, she moved toward him, letting the water splash just below her breasts as she moved. "I promise I'll never force you to love me at knife-point again. You'll have to come freely or not at all. I'll take no more. I could have accidentally harmed you."

With a sudden splash, Brant was in the water. It didn't matter that he was fully clothed; he swam toward her in long, powerful strokes. He pulled her into his arms and lifted her high in the cool morning air.

Cherish's laughter mixed with the gurgling of the stream as he carried her to shore.

"I thought you were sorry about last night," he whispered as he hugged her so tightly he feared he might break one of her ribs.

"No." For the first time she saw a touch of the frightened little boy in this outlaw. "I'll never be sorry about last night."

His lips found hers and their kiss warmed her body. When he reached the shore, he lowered her legs so that both his hands could caress her cool flesh.

When he finally raised his head, she whispered, "I love you."

"No." Brant pulled away and the sadness in his chestnut eyes was now for her. "Don't love me. I have no life to offer you, no future."

Cherish held his arm fast in her fingers. "You love me too, whether you say the words or not. How could I not love you after what you've given me? I thought something was wrong with me. I was dead inside. You taught me to feel. I'll always thank you for what you did."

"What I've given you?" He cupped her chin in his palm and lifted her face until their eyes met. "Don't you know what you've given me? I've never had anyone care about me. I've never had anyone crawl under my skin the way you do. I'd kill myself before I'd hurt you, so stop thanking me. And stop loving me. I'm not worth it."

Anger flashed across Cherish's face like a brushfire through dry kindling. "How dare you, sir, say such a thing about the man I love." Her fist was flying through the air before either of them realized it. With all the force in her, she clipped him on the chin and sent his head jerking backward.

Brant lost his balance on the wet bank and stumbled several feet into the shallow water. He rubbed his jaw and looked at the woman before him. She was nude and dripping wet with her fists doubled for battle. He'd never backed down from a fight in his life, but he lost this one in one blow. He'd stand there and let her hit him all day without ever thinking of fighting back.

"You might as well admit you love me." She turned and headed toward the house. "For I'm not going to speak to you until you do."

He caught up to her as she reached the branch where she'd left her nightgown. "I don't mind you not talking to me as long as you'll sleep with me," he teased.

Quickly he dodged another blow. As she swung, he caught her around the waist and pulled her close. "All right, before you beat me near to death, I'll say the words. I love you. God, I love you, woman, more than I've ever loved anything or anyone in my life."

Hours later, when they lay close together in the late afternoon sun, Brant whispered, "If only I could give you a future."

Cherish rolled close and held to him as if she knew even now that she must start the process of letting go. "I have you now and now will have to be enough."

He lifted her hand and kissed each one of her fingers. He thought of telling her why he'd killed the men he had. A part of him wanted her to know his reasons, even if she might not understand. But he'd have to tell her the ugly parts of his life, the parts no one except Daniel and he had seen. Then he'd have to tell her why the last man he'd probably have to kill was Daniel.

Suddenly, he knew he couldn't share that part of his life with her. She'd never know the reason for the scars on his wrist, or the reason he was hunted for murders he never committed. She'd never know the bond between him and Daniel that kept him alive and that would someday be the reason both men would die.

Cherish spread her hand over his chest and felt his heart pounding beneath her fingers. She fought the urge to thank him once more for all he'd given her. Even if they were parted and were never allowed another time together, they'd had last night and today. She'd learned to feel, to care beyond reason. Never again would she feel like she'd just watched everyone else living life, for now she had a memory, a memory of living and loving. He'd touched her with magic and made her feel. She'd treasure the loving and endure the pain of good-bye, knowing that after today she'd never be quite the same.

They didn't make love that night, but held each other and talked of things lovers confide only to one another. All the barriers had been shattered between them. There was nothing but honesty and love left. Neither mentioned the future, when their days together would only be memories. For the night was a time of whispered dreams and gently woven memories.

At dawn, Brant saddled his horse while Cherish dressed. When he returned to the dugout, he found she'd straightened the place as though they'd be coming back to it again. She'd even picked wildflowers and placed them on the table.

Brant lifted a sunflower in his hand and crushed it suddenly in his fist. "They'll only die," he whispered between clenched teeth.

"No!" Cherish answered as she forced his fingers open and took the flower from his hand. "I'll always remember them here like this. They'll always be alive to me."

Suddenly, Brant snapped like the stem of the flower had. He pulled her into his arms and held her.

"I won't let the world take you back." He buried his face in her golden hair. "You're all the beauty I've ever known."

Tears rolled unchecked down Cherish's face. "I know," she whispered as she stroked his hair. "I know how you feel, but I must go back."

Brant knew they couldn't stay there forever. It would only be a matter of weeks, maybe days, before someone stumbled onto the place. For a moment he envisioned her standing at the door of the dugout watching some bounty hunter gun him down. Maybe she'd run toward him and get caught in the crossfire. He knew some men would think nothing of shooting her if they thought she was his woman—or, worse, murdering her just to get to him. His only hope of keeping them both out of danger was to keep moving. He had to travel fast and he had to travel alone. And no one must ever know she meant anything to him, or her life would be in jeopardy.

"I'll love you every moment I live," he whispered against the warmth of her neck. "I know we can never be together, but that can't stop the way I feel."

She pushed his hair from his eyes so she could look once more into his handsome face. "And I'll love you," she whispered, "every hour of every day for the rest of my life."

Brant lifted her hands to his lips and kissed each palm, closing her fingers as if she could somehow hold onto his kiss to use in all the lonely nights to come. Then, hand in hand, they stepped into the sunlight.

They left the dugout without looking back. He wasn't sure he could. He lifted her up into the saddle and swung up behind her. They rode fast across the open country, both knowing it was best not to postpone what had to be.

As the miles thundered beneath the horse, the sky blackened with impending rain, and lightning flashed along the horizon. Brant encircled her in his arms, protecting her from the wind. He wished he could ride far enough and fast enough to outrun his past, but there was nowhere they would be safe to just love one another.

When they reached Fort Worth, he rode up the back road to Hattie's Parlor until he could see the barn. He swung from the horse and reached up for Cherish.

She slid into his embrace and held tight. "I love you," she whispered. "I love you more than life." Tears blended with the rain on her face.

"I know," he whispered as he tasted the salty tears on her cheeks.

He tied his horse and walked to the barn. He didn't dare go any farther, for even now he was putting her in danger.

"I'll find a way to see you again," Brant promised. "You'll be safe with Grayson and Margaret."

"I'd rather be with you than safe."

"I know, but I can't risk your life." He smiled down at her with a depth of love that surrounded her. "I've never said 'I love you' to another person in my life, but I love you. Right now, I have to love you enough to say good-bye."

With a sudden force he pushed her from him and stepped into the blackness. He was gone before she could say anything to get him to stay just a minute longer. His last words rang in her ears as she crossed the yard and entered the house.

Brant watched her go, feeling as if all the good in the world had just stepped out of his arms. He leaned against the barn wall and closed his eyes. All his life he'd watched folks who cared about each other. He'd seen them walking arm in arm, or helping one another in a thousand little ways. But he never dreamed he'd care for someone that way. He would have sworn it wasn't ever in him to do so, but then came Cherish with her belief that he was gentle and kind. The frightening thing was that when he was near her, her belief made it somehow true.

Voices drifted through the cracks in the barn wall. Brant forced his eyes open and listened.

Grayson's low tone sounded first. "I need a few more days here before I take any other assignment."

Another voice, higher, younger, and flavored with nervousness, came through the cracks. "I'm sorry, Captain, but the orders asked for you. Word is only one man at a time could get close to where these men hide out. If we sent a patrol they'd know we were coming for miles and pick us off from the cliffs above. But you're an expert at hunting down men who don't want to be found, and we might never get this good a lead again. This may be our one chance to find out who these men are who call themselves the Knights."

"And if I refuse?" Grayson couldn't endure the thought of leaving Margaret, even though it had been quiet for a week now. At this point, he wasn't sure he cared if the young second lieutenant said they'd court-martial him for not following orders.

The young man's answer came low and slow. "If you don't do this, more innocent people will die. The group over at Hank Stevens' place was just the beginning of more promised bloodshed. You've got to get in and stop the leader from getting another midnight ride organized. We can guess who all the followers are, but the leader is a mystery we've got to get solved fast. He's the kind of man who does the planning then lets the others do the work . . . the kind who orders people killed, but doesn't dirty his own hands unless he has to."

Grayson's voice sounded tired. "By 'stop,' you mean 'kill.' "

"If that's what it takes. We have to stop this leader before he gets an organization going that should have died and been buried before the war."

Grayson sighed. "All right. Give me a few minutes to make up some story to tell Maggie and I'll meet you out front."

"No," the officer snapped. "I'll ride out now. No one is to know where you are going, and if you're caught— or killed—you have had no orders from us."

Suddenly, Grayson laughed. "Sounds like just my kind of assignment. If I don't come back, let my cousin up in Philadelphia know what a fool of a relative he had who went and got himself killed after the war. As far as I know, we're the only two Kirklands alive and I keep trying to cut the population in half."

"And Miss Margaret?" the younger man asked.

"I'll tell her all I can right now. I'm not leaving without having a talk with her."

Both men moved from the barn without hearing Brant slip away.

24

Margaret was running down the stairs as Grayson rounded the corner leading from the kitchen. She almost collided with him in the shadows, but his warm, steady hand reached out in the darkness to steady her.

For a moment she didn't speak, but only stood, so close and yet beyond his reach. Finally, she found her voice. "Cherish is home and she looks wonderful."

"Is her friend with her?" Grayson fought the urge to pull Maggie into his arms. He could feel her light breath against his shoulder and smell the fresh, starched air that always seemed to surround her. He was surprised his voice could even sound normal when all his thoughts were of her.

"No." Maggie lowered her head and moved past him. "There was no one with her."

Grayson wondered if his nearness brought the same sweet agony to her as her closeness did to him. He tried to make his body think of something, anything, besides the way she'd felt when he'd held her all night in his arms. "If you have no objections, I'd like to have a few words with her before I go."

Maggie nodded without looking up at him, then disappeared into the kitchen.

He climbed the stairs two at a time and knocked at Cherish's door. The girl was a puzzle to him, but he had to talk with her. Brant had proven a man of his word, both when he'd fought at Grayson's side and when he'd promised to get Cherish back in a week. Perhaps she was also to be trusted.

When he opened the door, he saw her sitting by the fire watching the flames as though they held some secret she was looking for.

"I hate to disturb you, but I need to ask a few questions."

Cherish flashed him a kind smile and motioned toward the room's only other chair.

Grayson stepped over to the fireplace, not wanting to be half the length of the room away from her when he asked his questions. "You look much better than you did a week ago when Brant Coulter carried you out of here."

She shrugged. "I'm feeling fine, but I'd guess my health is not the reason you came up, Captain."

Grayson didn't try to deceive her. "I've worried all week about whether I made the right decision to let him take you. I should have arrested him when I had the chance. How could a lady like yourself have even met such a man as Brant Coulter?"

"You did the right thing, Captain. I've known Brant since I patched him up once . . ." She hesitated, not wanting to tell Grayson what a short time ago that had been. "He's a kind, gentle man. I couldn't have been safer or in better hands."

Grayson had to laugh. He doubted anyone else in the state would feel that way about Brant Coulter but her. But if Maggie could turn him into a madman, maybe Cherish could turn an outlaw into a saint.

"Do you think you're well enough to press charges against Westley?"

"No. I can't." He could tell by her voice that her mind was made up. "No matter what else he is, he's Maggie's husband and it wouldn't be right. But if he ever touches me again, I'll kill him."

"Someone already tried."

"So I've heard." Cherish looked into the fire. "Do they have any idea who it was?"

"No, not a clue," Grayson answered. "The only person in this town we know for sure didn't knife him was you. You were in no shape to move that night." He knelt down beside her chair and whispered, "I have to leave and I'm not sure I'll make it back. I can't tell you anything about where I'm going, but if you don't see me in a few months, would you tell Maggie something for me?"

Cherish's chin rose slightly, reminding him that she was from the same proud bloodline as Maggie. "Tell her yourself, Grayson," she said in her soft voice, but as an order just the same. "You've spent too much time staring at her and not talking to her."

Grayson rubbed at his chin. "I've tried, but she is the hardest woman to talk to when she's angry." He unstrapped his Colt and handed it to Cherish. "Keep this handy while I'm gone. Maggie's not as indestructible as she thinks she is and an extra gun around might help. I can get another one at Camp Wilson."

Cherish leaned over and kissed Grayson on the cheek. "I'll keep an eye on her. I've been doing it most of my life." She winked, telling Grayson she wanted to keep her statement just between them. "Don't worry about us. We were raised in Texas. Those men might have caught us unaware once, but not again. Take care of yourself. She loves you, you know."

Grayson smiled. "She's got one hell of a way of showing it. If she loved me any more I'd be staked over a fire out in the front yard."

They were both laughing when Maggie opened the door. She stepped inside and glared at them both as though they had lost their minds.

Grayson stood and crossed the room. "I have to talk with you, Maggie."

"We've said all that needs to be said."

He waited for her at the door.

She ignored him for several minutes before letting out a quick irritated sigh and stepping into the hall. "All right, what is it? I can't have you standing in the door all night even though we have nothing left to say. Tell me and be gone."

"We still have a great deal to say," he answered. "I have to leave on an assignment for the army. I don't know when I'll be back. But I want you to know that I'm coming back."

Maggie raised her chin ever so slightly. "I'll not wait."

Suddenly, he could stand her coldness no longer. He pulled her into his arms and kissed her soundly. When her cheeks were burning with fire and her lips were swollen from his kiss, he raised his head and looked down into her wonderful indigo eyes. "You'll wait." He winked. "Because, like it or not, you love me. I plan on making you see it no matter who I have to fight, including you."

Before she could deny his claim, he was gone, leaving only silence in the hall.

Maggie touched her lips with trembling fingers. She wanted to run to him and tell him that he was right. Nothing else in the world mattered except being in his arms. But years of restraint weren't broken with a kiss. She wouldn't allow her life to turn on a heartbeat.

Tears spilled from her dark blue eyes and she whispered, "Fight for me once more, my love. Please, fight for me once more."

*   *   *

Grayson crisscrossed the country north of Fort Worth for two weeks before he found the rock formation that marked the entrance to a place known as Hollow Horn Canyon. A dark, reddish brown beard covered his face, making him look more like a mountain man than a Union officer. He'd traded his uniform for buckskins and his boots for knee moccasins. One of the reasons Grayson was so good at his job was his ability to change the way he looked. Anyone seeing him now would have sworn he'd never worn a uniform for any army, and that might keep him from getting shot from a distance as he entered the canyon.

Spring had finally settled into the land and everything around him was turning green. Early storms had mellowed into a few soft showers and the sky was an endless blue. Everything was fresh and light except for his mood. He'd worked too long in the field not to know when something wasn't right, and this job smelled worse than week-old fish heads left in the sun.

It didn't seem logical that, even if there were a few Knights of the Golden Circle left, they'd meet out in the open country this far into Indian territory. The longer he rode, the more resigned to one fact he became. Someone wanted him out this far for only one purpose and that was to kill him. Somehow, he'd stumbled on some truth about the Knights and they wanted him out of the way.

Grayson kept riding toward what he suspected was a trap. He knew he was teasing a rattlesnake, but he had to play along and see just how fast the snake would strike. They'd find he wasn't as easy to kill as they thought, and he might just find out who was behind the gang.

Another problem kept nagging at the back of his mind. It could be possible that they wanted him away from Maggie. He swore under his breath that if anyone harmed her while he was gone, he'd kill every man involved. He'd decided at dawn that if he didn't find some signs of the hideout today he'd turn back toward Fort Worth.

Grayson tried to wipe the worry over Maggie from his mind as he stretched in the saddle and looked toward the late afternoon sun. He could smell trouble the way cattle smell a storm. The canyon walls were high and rocky. Even a half-wit like that deputy, Wart, would have been able to figure out that this was a perfect place for an ambush.

Suddenly, a silver light flashed, dancing off something metal along the canyon's rim. The sun winked again along the ridge, silently hinting at trouble.

Survival instincts snapped Grayson into action as he jerked his rifle from its sheath and swung from the saddle. As his foot touched the ground, fire exploded in his shoulder and liquid pain flooded his brain. Before the sound of the first shots had died, another round bounced on the canyon walls and pain struck his leg, doubling him over in agony.

The world darkened—first to deep shades, then to evening black. Grayson stumbled forward, dragging his almost useless leg into the cover of rocks. He threw his body over a three-foot wall of granite. More shots followed, but they were only tiny explosions of rock above him. He closed his eyes and forced the pain from his mind. *Think.* He pushed away the blinding heat in his shoulder. He had to be ready to act or he'd be a dead man.

With sweat pouring from his face, Grayson ground his teeth together and pulled the bandanna from his neck. He tied a knot over the leg wound. The blood from his shoulder seemed to be everywhere, dripping hot over his chest like tears.

He heard horses riding toward him. Then gunfire seemed all around him, bouncing like thunder in the hollow canyon. He pulled his rifle up and forced his head to clear enough to look over his rock fortress. Three men were climbing toward him, but someone hidden across the canyon was firing on them each time they advanced.

Grayson leaned back and tried to make sense of the battle. Being shot at didn't seem so insane, but someone fighting to save him didn't fit into his logic at all. He always traveled alone. That was part of the job. He'd learned a long time ago never to depend on anyone but himself. But someone was out there, attempting to keep his attackers from reaching him and finishing the job they'd started.

The firing continued until dark; then Grayson heard the sound of horses riding further back into the canyon. He relaxed against the rock, knowing they'd given up until daybreak. A low rumble rattled from his chest as he laughed, finding it somehow funny that he'd cheat them by dying before they could return to kill him.

Suddenly a body swung over the wall of his tiny fortress and slammed into Grayson. Before Grayson could raise his rifle to fire, the weapon was kicked from his grip. He reached for his pistol only to have it follow the path of his rifle.

"Stop trying to shoot me, damn it!" snapped a voice filled with anger. "I didn't spend all evening keeping the vultures off you to have you shoot me in gratitude, Yank."

Grayson's gaze narrowed, barely discerning the face of the thin shadow of a man before him. "Brant?"

The stranger grunted. "I've been trailing you for a week. You leave tracks a blind squaw could follow."

"I hadn't thought anyone would be looking for me." Grayson watched the outlaw closely. "So, why were you?"

"I knew you'd get yourself killed if I didn't." Brant knelt down beside Grayson and touched the blood covering the huge man's shoulder. "Damn near succeeded. Don't get me wrong, Kirkland, I could care less if you live or die, but Cherish thinks a lot of you."

"You rode all the way out here just because Cherish wanted you to keep an eye on me?"

Brant laughed. "I'm crazy, but not that crazy. Maybe I just don't happen to like the men who tried to gun you down. Some folks give us outlaws a bad name. I recognized them. The leader, now with a plug of lead in his leg, looked like a weasel of a man who practices law back in Fort Worth. I heard he was real disappointed when Margaret showed up to claim the house. He thought it would be his by spring. The other two were just hired guns, and not very good ones at that."

The pain in Grayson's shoulder was clouding his thoughts but he unclenched his teeth long enough to ask why.

Brant leaned against the rock beside the Union officer as if they had nothing better to do but chat in the darkness. "They should have killed you with one shot. That was very sloppy. Then, when I showed up, they ran. But they'll come crawling back about daybreak. We'll have to wait until the moon's high before we move. Fortunately, it'll be a rustler's moon tonight so the light won't be very bright." Brant moved swiftly in the darkness. "I'll tie up your wounds as best I can and then we'll get the hell out of here."

As Brant worked, Grayson questioned him again about his interest in whoever hired these men to kill him.

For the first time in his life, Brant told the true story. "Back before the start of the war, I got involved with a group of men known as the Knights. Most were good, God-fearing men who went a little crazy with panic thinking about how the blacks were going to rise up and kill all the whites. The Knights got some money together and loaded it and all the slaves they could buy or steal into a boat leaving Galveston one night. The plan was to start a slave state in South America."

His voice lowered as he remembered. "I was only a little older than Barfield. Daniel was two years older than me. We were about three days out when cholera broke out. The slaves went loco, all moaning and crying about dying. There were seven men in charge; Daniel and I were just along for the ride. The men got together and decided what they were going to do. There was only enough room in the one longboat for seven men and the gold. They chained Daniel and me together so we wouldn't cause any trouble. They said it was part of a code agreed upon by all the men. We thought they were just going to leave us afloat. Then they opened fire on the slaves."

Brant was silent for so long that Grayson wasn't sure he would, or could, continue. Finally, he cleared his throat. "I still hear those folks screaming. It was that high, hollow scream that comes when anyone knows he's going to die. Most of the male slaves were chained and there was nowhere for them to run. One woman, blood covering her face, fell into me and Daniel. I tumbled to the deck, dragging him with me. I guess the men thought they'd shot us. With her blood spilled all over us they didn't check too closely. They loaded the gold in the longboat, threw a lantern against the galley door, and disappeared over the side.

"I was unconscious, but Daniel pulled me to the edge of the deck. We hit the water about the time the whole ship caught fire. The slaves who hadn't died during the shooting were screaming as they burned. It was years before I could get that smell out of my lungs; and still I wake myself up sometimes, thinking I've heard them scream again."

Grayson finally saw where the story was leading. "So you decided to hunt down the seven Knights and kill them one by one."

Brant laughed without humor. "No. Daniel did. While I went off to scout for the Confederacy, he took it as some kind of crusade. Only we looked so much alike, folks guessed it was always me. Before I knew it I had quite a name as a gunman, and every hotheaded kid in the state wanted to call me out. I wasn't living a saint's life, so the handle fit. Murder became like a drug to Daniel. He'd wear the robes till he found one of the men, then he'd take great pleasure in killing him. With each murder, his mind slips a little more and I get a grander reputation, which I couldn't disclaim without endangering him."

"Why are you telling me this?" Grayson's pain-riddled mind couldn't make any connection between Brant's story and his attackers except that both were somehow tied to the Knights.

"I don't know, Yank. Maybe I figure you'll be dead by morning so you're a safe person to tell. Maybe I've lived with the secret too long. In my own way, I'm probably as crazy as Daniel. I even tried to stop him on the last murder and Lord knows that bastard deserved to die. But when we both ran from the scene, guess who got the blame? Hell, if they find your body I'll probably get stuck with your death, too. I've killed enough men to hang ten times, so what difference does it make?"

Grayson tried to stand. "I have no intention of dying and causing you more problems, Coulter."

He would have fallen if Brant hadn't caught him. With one mighty heave, Brant lifted Kirkland onto his back and started down the rocks. "Well, if you're not going to die, I might as well get you out of this canyon."

Grayson was blinded by the pain. He felt like his arm was being ripped from his shoulder and his leg felt deadly cool, but he didn't cry out. He ground his teeth together and listened to Brant's cursing.

"Next time I save a damn Yankee's life, I'll pick a smaller one." He let out a string of obscenities as he kept walking toward his horse. "I can't believe how much you blue-legs bleed from a couple of little holes." Swinging Grayson none too gently over his saddle, he added, "The guys shooting at you took your horse with them. I've got to get you hid out before dawn; then I'll see if I can't steal your mount back. Maybe if I'm lucky I'll find the body of that lawyer."

Brant grabbed the reins of his horse and started walking toward the cliffs. "Yank, it would sure help if you'd stop bleeding. You're leaving an easy trail. Hell, if you ain't the easiest man to follow in Texas."

Grayson's last thought was that he'd like to kill Brant Coulter. He remembered all the wonderful things Cherish said about the outlaw and decided she must have him mixed up with someone else. Grayson was sure if there was any good in this man it would have to be picked out of him with tweezers.

Brant didn't slow down until they'd climbed for an hour. He knew Grayson had passed out from loss of blood and only hoped the man would stay that way until he could get them to someplace they could defend. Finally, he spotted a crack in the wall wide enough for a horse to go through. He led his mount through it to the other side of the canyon wall and then backtracked to cover the entrance with brush.

He took the time to wrap Grayson's wounds in hopes of stopping any more bleeding. He slowly led the horse down the back side of the cliff and into a wooded area thick with hundred-year-old cottonwoods and elms.

Just after dawn, the pain pulled Grayson from his dreams. He opened his eyes to see Brant leaning over him with a knife in his hand. Brant's face was twisted in concentration as he pointed the knife at Grayson's shoulder.

"I'm not finished yet," Brant whispered moments before his fist slammed into Grayson's jaw, sending the injured man back into unconsciousness.

Grayson didn't open his eyes again until late afternoon. Now, not only his shoulder and leg were throbbing, but his jaw felt like it had been stung by a hundred bees. He noticed Brant several feet away and wondered if he'd already died and this was his hell. He'd always figured hell would be full of rebs.

Brant frowned at Grayson as he tried to move. "I patched you up best as I could. I sure wish Maggie or Cherish were here."

Grayson moved his unharmed arm and rubbed his jaw. "So do I. Your bedside manner leaves a little to be desired."

Brant shrugged. "Sorry, but I couldn't have you yelling to high heaven while I cut the bullet out."

"I'm not in the habit of yelling because of a little pain." Grayson's blue-gray eyes studied him closely, wondering if this man had come to save him or kill him.

Brant propped one of his long legs up on the rock beside him. "Yeah, I figured that. But by then, you were already out cold."

Grayson cradled his bandaged arm. "I don't know whether to thank you or call you out."

"You owe me nothing. What I did, I did for Cherish—not you, Yankee. If I hadn't seen your kindness toward her, I'd have left you as breakfast for the buzzards."

Grayson smiled. "You care a lot for that little gal, don't you?"

Brant shrugged, trying to make his reply casual, but he didn't fool Grayson. "I want her to be happy. She could never be with me. There'd always be some kid coming up looking to claim my bounty money or make a name for himself by killing me. I sometimes have nightmares that she'll see me gunned down. No matter how much I want her, I can't have her. So I'm going to take you back and let you watch over both women. You might say saving your life is my good-bye gift to her."

"Aren't you forgetting something?"

"What?"

"Maggie doesn't want me within a hundred miles of her."

Brant laughed as he stood. "Now that, my friend, is your problem. I'd sooner face a regiment of seasoned Yankee guerrillas than that woman, and I've only heard about her."

"I'll figure out a way." Grayson closed his eyes and tried to make his head stop throbbing. "If I live through your doctoring."

25

Margaret tucked the blankets tightly around Hattie's bed. The old woman was little more than a flesh-covered skeleton. Her mind rarely touched reality now, and Death waited only a step away to walk with her. The only comfort for her seemed to be the box she kept tightly clenched in her arms: her treasure of letters. Father Daniel had been to see her almost every day in the month that Grayson had been gone. Several times he'd asked that the room be cleared so that he could hear her last confession, but each time her screams brought Maggie back to comfort her and the priest was forced to leave.

"I'll sit with her awhile today," Bar said as he sank into the chair by her bed and propped his boots on the footboard. "When Grayson comes back he said we'd have work to do outside, what with pulling all the boards off the windows and everything."

Maggie straightened her shoulders. "Grayson isn't coming back. It's been more than a month and to hope now would only be foolish. If he were coming, he'd be here by now." Her tone was as emotionless as her face. Only the tight grip she held on the bed frame gave away the depth of her pain.

Bar tilted his head and studied her. Her prim and proper manner didn't deceive him. "You want him to come back, don't you." He said the words as fact.

It was too simple a statement to be denied. She wanted him back with every fiber of her being, but she'd learned a long time ago that wanting something and getting it were different things.

She was saved from answering by a pounding at the door. Maggie hurried to see who it was even though she'd learned over the past month that the caller was usually unwanted.

Much to her displeasure, Mr. Wallman was standing on her porch with yet another paper in his hand. His face looked pale and his eyes were puffy and red.

" 'Morning, Mrs. Alexander." He had an irritating habit of starting to remove his hat then placing it back on his head with a quick tap. "I've been talking with your husband and he's . . ."

"My husband is dead." She fought the urge to snatch the hat from his head and give him a quick lesson on how to greet a lady.

"Now, Mrs. Alexander, don't start that again. We both know full well your husband is alive and recovering over at the hotel. Fact is, I'm thinking he'll be good as new in a few days. He's eating regular and healthy enough to walk down to the bar every night for a drink."

"He'll be dead if he sets foot on my property."

The lawyer shuffled as though his shoes had suddenly become too big and he was trying to keep them on. "That's another point of fact you seem to ignore. By law this house is half his. He has as much right to be in this place as you do and now that that giant of a hired man has left, there is little you can do but accept the facts. I'm sure if you two spent some time together, you'd work things out like most folks do."

Margaret took a step toward him and the little man stumbled backward. "Now don't go yelling at me, Mrs. Alexander. Your husband would have already been by to claim his rights if it weren't for his untimely injury and the fact that we seem to have a little trouble getting the sheriff's cooperation these days. But Westley wanted me to let you know that he'll be here tomorrow to claim his rightful place as lord of the house, and there isn't a legal thing you can do about it."

Margaret was so angry she had to bite her tongue to keep from yelling. After several breaths she said, in what she thought was a low voice, though it shook the panes on the windows behind her, "If he comes, please ask him to wear whatever clothes he wishes to be buried in."

The little lawyer was too shocked to reply. He stood, like a lazy frog, with his mouth wide open.

"Good day, Mr. Wallman."

The lawyer looked skyward as if giving up a hopeless fight and turned to limp away. Maggie thought of asking about his injury, but decided she couldn't stand him on her property any longer than necessary.

She remained on her porch until he was down the hill. With the carriage of a queen, she turned and went inside, then collapsed behind the door and whispered one word as though it were a prayer: "Grayson."

Then, slowly, she straightened her back and walked to the kitchen to fetch her rifle. She might go to jail for what she planned to do if Westley came tomorrow, but she'd go to jail as a widow. There was no room in her heart, or in her house, for him.

That night no one in the house could sleep. They all knew that tomorrow would bring trouble. Maggie paced her room, trying to think of something, anything, she could do besides gun Westley down when he stepped on the porch. Bar positioned himself at the front door with his old rifle and refused to budge. His theory was simple. Anyone wanting to get to Maggie or Cherish would have to pass through him first and he didn't plan to make that easy.

Cherish checked each door and window downstairs. Grayson had boarded up the house so completely that it was like a fortress ready for attack.

About midnight they all tried to settle down and sleep, but the wind whistled through the boards on the windows, making a long *woo* sound and the old walls on the second floor creaked as though they were crying in agony. An evil crept through the empty hallways on feet as light as spiderwebs, silently shaking any feeling of safety from everyone's mind.

Cherish tried to ignore the sounds of the wind, but gradually a *tap-tapping* picked its way through the other noises to bother her. Without rhythm, the tapping began to knock against her worried mind. Pulling on her wrapper, she picked up Grayson's Colt and tiptoed down the stairs.

At the foot of the stairs, where the door leading into the basement was hidden in the shadows of the hallway, she heard the *tap-tapping* louder—a cry now, not a whisper. For a moment she just stood staring into the shadows as if waiting for the blackness suddenly to take form.

"What you think it is?" Bar asked, making Cherish jump and almost drop the Colt.

She glanced to her side and found him only an inch behind her. The look of fear in his dark eyes held back any angry words she might have blasted him with for sneaking up on her. She lifted the gun carefully into her pocket and tried not to allow her voice to show her fear.

"I'm not sure. I don't think it's someone behind the lock, for the tapping seems too random."

The tapping came again, making them both step back. The irregular patterns somehow were far more frightening than any rhythm might be.

Bar straightened as if proving he wasn't afraid. "It could be them ghosts Azile used to tell us about. She said they walked these halls because so much wrongdoin' has gone on in this place. Maybe when we locked the door a month ago, we trapped one of them down there in that cellar."

Cherish smiled, hoping he couldn't see her face in the darkness. "Bar, there are no ghosts. And if there were, they could pass through things like a door. A lock wouldn't stop them. Also, ghosts like dark places. They wouldn't be afraid of the cellar. It would be a great place for them."

Bar shrugged his bony shoulders. "It don't comfort me none when folks always start off tellin' me there ain't no such thing as ghosts and then proceed to list their habits. How come everyone knows all about them if there ain't no such thing?"

Cherish saw his point, but wanted to ease his fears. "Maybe it's wind traveling through the tunnel and making the tapping sound."

Bar nodded, accepting that as a possibility. "Well, if the door by the barn is open a little, I'll go out back and close it."

"No, that could be dangerous. Remember, we both encountered Westley out by the barn." She tried to make her voice sound like the problem was only minor. "I'll go through the tunnel and close the outside door. I can find my way in the dark without any problem."

Bar looked worried. "You're not goin' down there alone. I'm comin' along."

Cherish didn't argue. She touched her fingers to the Colt in her pocket and unlocked the door before her courage dwindled. Both froze for a moment and leaned backward slightly, as if bracing themselves for something when she opened the door. But only the cold blackness of the basement greeted them.

They were as close as Siamese twins when they passed onto the landing and closed the door behind them. Bar took the lead, feeling his path from step to step as they inched their way down the dusty stairs. Cherish lost her ability to judge how far apart the steps were. If it hadn't been for Bar's guiding hand on her arm, she would have felt lost in the blackness. They crawled down the stairs on their hands and knees, like two-year-olds afraid to risk stepping from one step to the other.

Cherish tried to remember how many steps it had been across the room, for she knew the entrance to the tunnel was on the opposite wall, hidden in the shadows between two rows of shelves. Once at the tunnel entrance, they'd only have to cross maybe thirty feet and they'd reach the outside. She silently decided she'd risk the run back to the house across the courtyard, then remembered that the house would be locked against her.

As they neared the end of the steps, Bar suddenly shoved her down, covering her shoulder with his thin arm. His breath brushed against her face as he whispered, "Quiet! I hear somethin'."

Cherish turned her head toward where she knew the tunnel was and listened. For a moment, her blood throbbed so loud against her temple that she couldn't hear anything. Then sound crept to her from somewhere in the darkness. Someone was feeling his way along the wall of the underground passage. They could hear his feet shuffling and his fingers sliding along the uneven corridor. His breath was labored and his footsteps clumsy.

A match was struck and for an instant the passageway glowed as orange as a harvest moon on a frosty horizon.

Then all was black again and a voice swore, "Damn, that was my last match."

Cherish bumped heads with Bar as they both moved toward each other. He whispered the name already forming on her lips: "Westley!"

Somehow, Westley had found the entrance to the tunnel. Her mind thought back to the night in the barn. Maybe that was what he'd been looking for when she'd stumbled upon him. Fear twisted in her spine as she thought of what might have happened if he'd found the tunnel and the door unlocked while they'd been asleep upstairs.

Bar started inching his way up. Cherish followed suit. They had to get to the top and lock the door before Westley made it out of the tunnel. And they had to do it without a sound.

Halfway up the steps, Cherish stopped. She could hear Westley's breathing. He'd reached the end of the passage and was stepping out into the large, empty space. The air was already thick with the smell of his sweat. She inched her way up another step, afraid now to open her eyes, even though she knew she wouldn't even be able to see her hands in front of her. It would only be a matter of minutes before he found the stairs.

Like dawn's first glow, a light radiated from somewhere deep in the tunnel. Within seconds it filled the entrance with an unnatural yellow-orange radiance. Bar once more covered her as completely as he could with his arm. They were far enough up the stairs to look down on the light, but if someone looked up, he couldn't help but see them, even in the shadows.

"Who is it?" Westley shouted as if someone were entering his land unlawfully.

A thin man in black stepped through the tunnel with the skill of one who'd walked it many times. "I wondered how long it would take you to find this entrance." The stranger's face was still a mystery, but his voice was low and familiar. The light reflected off his highly polished knee boots.

"The others told me about it at the poker game, but they didn't bother with details," Westley answered. "This house and everything in it is mine, so don't start bothering me. I rigged the game to win it, but the banker started to get suspicious. So I passed the winning hand and the deed to the old man. I figured I could buy it back if I got him drunk enough, but I finally had to kill old Tobin when he wouldn't see reason. I know there's a treasure in this old place and I aim to find it."

"There's no treasure. The men at the game just wanted to up the pot that night. They knew you wouldn't be interested in this place without the lure of the treasure. Only problem was you believed it—enough to kill for it. So you can stop looking. The only treasure lies in a dying woman's insane hopes and dreams."

Westley huffed up like a toad swelling to sing. "If there isn't any treasure, how come you and the other Knights are so anxious to get your hands on this house? You're the ones trying everything to frighten the women away. I'd be mighty happy to let the women live here once I get the treasure."

The stranger set the lantern down. "Sure, you'd let them live here. Tell me, Westley, how many times do you plan to catch Cherish in the barn and beat her, until she dies from one of the assaults like the girl at Holliday's almost did?"

Westley snorted. "Hell, I can think of other things than a beating I plan to give that uppity girl. She didn't ever press charges, so I figure I can do whatever I want to. When I get tired of riding my bony wife, I might just give Cherish a time or two. It'll be quite a setup: two women to keep me happy and all that gold Hattie hid before the war."

The stranger moved so fast it seemed like it all happened in only a blink of the lantern. A long, silver blade flashed as he pulled it from his boot. A moment later, Cherish heard the unmistakable sound of metal being thrust into flesh . . . Westley's flesh.

The overweight man dropped to his knees, blood flashing in the light as it dripped through his fingers onto the already damp floor. His eyes were wide with shock and unrestrained fear.

The blade struck again from behind. Cherish covered her ears as the metal hit his spine. When Westley slumped forward, a gloved hand gripped his hair and held his head back. Without hesitation, his killer slid the knife across his throat, plowing a deep row of crimson from ear to ear. Westley's eyes screamed of pain, but sound could no longer pass his throat. As blood flowed like a waterfall, his eyes froze open in a death stare.

With a flick, the stranger wiped his knife on Westley's shirt and replaced it in his boot. "I should have aimed for your throat the other night instead of your gut."

For a moment his wrist flashed in the low lamplight. The scars of the boy betrayed the man.

Cherish stared at the scars crossing his wrist and fought back a cry that started so deep inside her it would have pulled out her heart if she released it.

With powerful grace and speed, the stranger was gone, taking the light with him. Cherish opened her mouth to scream, but Bar's fingers closed over her lips in a firm grip. His hand was shaking with fear, but he held tight. "Don't scream, Miss Cherish. Don't scream or he'll come back and kill us too."

It was several minutes before they could make their limbs work to climb the rest of the stairs. They slipped through the door and locked it. Then they slid to the floor as if their backs would keep out the horror they'd witnessed.

Bar let out a long sigh. "I reckon he killed Westley."

Cherish nodded, not trusting herself to speak. There was no reason to check the body. She'd seen men look into death's face too many times for her not to know the stare from which no man ever blinked.

"You think if he'd found us, he'd have killed us too?"

She closed her eyes, not wanting to even imagine what would have happened it he'd seen them. With a jerk, she nodded, and suddenly they were hugging like two children sharing the same nightmare.

Bar finally whispered, "You know who it was, don't you?"

Cherish looked at the boy and thought he looked older than he had at supper a few hours ago. "Yes." She fought back the tears. "I know."

26

It took Brant almost two weeks to get Grayson back to Fort Worth. The huge man was as hard to haul as a grizzly across a waterfall. He never complained about the pain he was in, but he yelled about everything else. Brant thought several times about slugging him again, but he knew part of the problem was simply that they were two loners accustomed to picking their own trail at their own speed.

When he finally succeeded in reaching the outskirts of Fort Worth, Brant said a silent prayer of thanks and decided that no matter what he'd heard about Maggie, she didn't deserve a bear of a man like Grayson Kirkland. Brant vowed if he ever came upon the Yankee wounded again, he'd shoot Grayson and save himself a lot of misery.

Since there was no way Brant could get Grayson to Hattie's place in broad daylight without being seen, he took the Yank to Holliday's. He trusted Grayson as far as he trusted about any man, but not enough to show him the tunnel into Hattie's.

Holliday welcomed them with her usual warm hospitality and open palm. It took her several minutes to get a room emptied out. With the men from a cattle drive in town, she was having to double up on every room's activity. Brant could tell by the noise coming from below that they would be safe as long as he had money.

While Holliday got Grayson settled into a room, she sent word for Cherish to come. In less than an hour, Cherish was tapping on Holliday's back door.

As she entered, Cherish smiled an honest greeting to the older woman. " 'Morning, Miss Holliday. How are you today?"

Holliday crossed her arms over her chest. "I'm as busy as a three-dollar whore during a half-price sale and now I got a man up there who's been telling me there ain't no woman that will suit his fancy but you."

Cherish tilted her head. She'd known Holliday long enough to realize when she was kidding.

"He come riding in here telling me that it had been over a month since he'd seen the likes of you and he wanted to see his lady."

"Brant?" Cherish shouted.

"And . . ." Holliday didn't finish, for Cherish was already up the stairs.

She ran to the last room on the landing. When she flung the door open, she saw her outlaw standing by the window, watching the street. His hair was longer and in need of a trim and his clothes looked as if they had a pound of soil layered into them. When he turned to look at her, his eyes were hungry with need.

For a moment the nightmare from the night before flashed in Cherish's mind. She saw the knife and the wrist with scars on it. Had it been the right or left hand? Brant or Daniel? Her fear and the horror of what she saw made her uncertain.

But when she looked into Brant's warm brown eyes there could be no doubt of one thing, and that was her love for him. No matter who he was, or what he'd done, she loved him. She loved him totally, without reason. Right or wrong, good or bad, couldn't color that fact. For the first time Cherish couldn't stand watching, but had to feel.

Dropping her bag, she ran into his waiting arms. For one moment the world stopped and there was only Brant. All the nights of lying awake thinking of him disappeared as she clung to him. He'd opened the door to all her locked-up feelings, and with the pleasure had also come the pain of missing him. There were many fears and questions in her mind, but doubt that he loved her was not one of them.

He lifted her tiny body off the floor and swung her around, loving the way she came to him. Never had anyone opened her arms and heart to him. She'd been on his mind every minute of every day since he'd been gone. He pressed his lips against her ear and whispered, "I love you, baby. God help us both, I love you."

She seemed to be laughing and crying at the same time as she held his face in her hands and kissed him. "I'm so glad you came back to me," she whispered. "I was so afraid."

"Afraid?" Brant laughed. "Not the girl who threatened to kill me if I didn't make love to her."

Cherish wrapped her arms around his neck. "I was afraid you wouldn't come back to me."

Brant's words were lost in their kiss. He knew that someday he wouldn't return, but for now she was in his arms. For now, he'd live the dream of happiness, if only for a moment.

A loud baritone voice shook the couple back to earth. "I hate to interrupt this homecoming, but I'm dying over here."

Brant didn't release Cherish as he looked toward Grayson. "Hell, he's too mean to die."

Cherish pushed away from Brant, her cheeks red with embarrassment that someone had witnessed her show of emotion. She grabbed her bag and hurried to Grayson's bedside. He had more dried blood and dirt on him than she'd ever seen on a man.

Holliday entered with a huge tub of water. She sat it down on one of the chairs and propped her bulk on another as if getting comfortable for the show she knew was going to take place.

Cherish checked his wounds and agreed with Brant that he was in little danger of dying. Both his leg and his shoulder needed to be cleaned and bandaged again, but neither showed any sign of infection. He had no fever and his color was good despite the loss of blood. She closed her bag and stepped back from the bed.

Grayson looked confused. "Aren't you going to do something? I've had to put up with this madman's doctoring for two weeks."

"You put up with me!" Brant yelled. "I'd as soon bunk with a buffalo than spend any more time with you. You're about the most ungrateful . . ."

"A blind, three-legged dog could pick a better trail than you," Grayson interrupted. "We must have ridden over every ridge and through every tree line between here and Canada."

"Well, at least I pick a trail and not just leave one. You had the thoughtlessness to bleed for ten miles."

Suddenly both Brant and Grayson were laughing, a rich, full laughter that filled the room. They realized that they sounded like two children complaining to their mother. Cherish looked from one to the other and wondered if madness might be contagious. She wasn't sure whether they were friends or bitter enemies.

Grayson finally stopped laughing and looked at her. "Can you get these makeshift bandages off? I think Brant used the horse blanket, the way they itch."

Grateful that Grayson could take her mind away from her disturbing thoughts of Brant, mischief danced in Cherish's green eyes. "Why should I, when you have a perfectly good nurse in Maggie to take care of you?"

Grayson rubbed his beard. "I don't want Maggie nursing me. She's so mad at me she'd probably cut a pound of hide right off me."

Cherish folded her arms. "Well, I'm not nursing you, so that only leaves Brant or Maggie."

Grayson growled like a bear. He'd already had all he wanted of Brant's none-too-light touch. In fact, he'd had all he wanted of everyone and everything in Texas. General Sheridan was right when he'd said that if he owned Texas and all of hell, he'd rent out Texas and live in hell.

Before Grayson could finish telling everyone exactly what he thought, Holliday yelled out the door for two of the many drunks who always seemed to be at her place.

"These boys will deliver him right to the door of Hattie's Parlor for a free drink."

"Like hell!" the Yankee yelled.

With one mighty twist, Holliday covered Grayson in the quilt and motioned for the men to haul him off. They could hear Grayson cursing and threatening revenge as the drunks carried him down the stairs, bumping into about every third rail.

Holliday stepped to the doorway. "I'll see that no one bothers you for a while. You two look like you might have a lot to visit about."

Cherish started to say something, but the door closed before she could get a word out. A heartbeat later she was in Brant's arms. His need for her was a liquid fire that flowed through his lips and into her veins. With him she was alive, completely alive. But her heart was slowly dying, inch by inch, as she tried to remember any detail that would make Westley's killer Daniel and not Brant. The voice was Daniel's, she kept repeating to herself as

Brant held her, but logic told her that the whisper could have come from either man.

When he broke the kiss, she could see the need in his eyes. He knew nothing of her questions. "I want to love you," he whispered against her mouth, "but not here. Not in this place."

Cherish shook her head. "It doesn't matter." She knew she couldn't stop loving him, even if he had been the one who killed Westley.

Brant pulled her arms away. "It matters to me. I need to clean up. The thought of lying with you in a bed that has been warmed by half the cowhands on the Chisholm Trail is not to my liking. I'll come to you tonight, through the tunnel."

He could feel her tense in his arms. "Not through the tunnel," she whispered.

"Don't worry. I've walked it a hundred times without a light. I know it by heart."

Brant placed his hands on her shoulders and lowered her to sit on the bed. He knelt in front of her and took her hands. "What is it? What's happened?"

Cherish fought back the tears. Then, like opening a window, something clicked in her mind. "What did you say?" She pushed the tears away with her palm.

"I said I know the tunnel by heart."

"No. About the light."

Brant looked confused. "I never use a light. Daniel is the one that always has to carry a lantern through the tunnel. He can't stand to be in the dark."

Now her tears were falling with relief.

"What is it?" Brant demanded.

"Last night . . ."

The door suddenly flew open and Holliday hurried in. "Sorry to have to cut this short, but Wart just found Westley Alexander's body down by the river." She smiled as if she'd just delivered grand news. "Someone said they saw you, Brant, dragging it there early this morning and everyone's looking for you. You'd better get while you can. I don't want no more bullet holes in my walls."

Brant pulled Cherish to her feet. "I didn't . . ."

"I know," she answered, suddenly realizing she could never have loved a man who could have killed someone so callously. Tears ran down her face as she looked up at him, knowing that this might be the last time she saw him. "Take care, my love."

Brant ran, more because he couldn't face seeing the pain in her eyes than because of any posse chasing him. He knew she was afraid for him, but he'd also seen the trust. Somehow she'd known he hadn't killed Westley.

Maggie sat on the porch with her gun across her lap. She'd decided Cherish and Bar had gone insane. They knew today was the day Westley had said he was coming, yet they acted as if it was just any ordinary day. Cherish had even trotted off to Holliday's to help some poor injured drunk without even taking her gun. Bar had wandered off to the barn, even after they'd agreed yesterday not to go anywhere unless someone was with them.

Well, she wouldn't let down her guard. She'd be ready when he came.

Maggie let out a long sigh and watched the sun touch the roofs of Hell's Half-Acre. One good thing about today: Westley hadn't shown his face. All her worry and dread would have to wait for another day. She had slept very little the night before and Cherish and Bar looked like they hadn't slept at all. Now they'd face another night without sleep, dreading what the morrow would bring.

Maggie rested her rifle against the door frame. For a little while, she'd thought she'd travel down the hill and confront

Westley before dark. She wanted to have it out once and for all and be done with him. But she wasn't sure what she'd find down there. It was better to wait for him to show up here.

The quiet evening was shattered suddenly by two men heavy into drink. They lurched up toward her, carrying a load in a blanket. Maggie stood and watched them as they approached. She could only guess what kind of wild animal they carried in the quilt stretched between them.

Hearing a moan from beneath the blanket, Maggie quickly lifted her rifle and slid her finger over the trigger. This might be some kind of trick Westley was using to get near the house without being shot.

Grayson remained still for fear they'd drop him again. He'd decided he'd died and been left in hell with two of Holliday's drunks. They'd twisted the blanket so tight he could hardly breathe, then they'd accidentally bumped into every post between Holliday's and Hattie's. Twice, the imbecile carrying Grayson's feet dropped him, causing great pain to his wounded leg. By the time they pitched him onto the porch, Grayson was promising to murder them both slowly.

Neither man waited for him to untwist from the blanket, but ran as soon as he hit the wooden porch.

Grayson threw the quilt aside and tried to stand, wondering what he'd ever done to Holliday to make her hate him so much. Now, to add to the bullet wounds in his shoulder and leg, he had a bruise over one eye from where he guessed his head had collided with a hitching post, and a cut in his side where he'd scraped against something when one of the drunks stumbled.

When he turned toward Margaret, the murder in his eyes would have struck most women dead on sight. But Maggie simply stared at him as if disapproving of the fact that he was getting blood on her porch. She didn't even bother to lower her gun, which was pointed at his middle. At this point, Grayson doubted if one more wound would add any more pain to what he was already feeling.

"You look like death warmed over in a dirty pot."

He smiled despite the pain. "Hell, woman, you think I look bad on the outside. You should see what you've done to my heart since I've known you."

When she didn't run to him, like he'd hoped she would, he pulled himself up and swore over the pain in his leg. She should be hugging him just about now, he thought. Hell, what did the outlaw have that made Cherish run into his arms? Grayson looked at Maggie, knowing that if he wanted her he'd have to go and get her himself, for she didn't look like she was going to budge an inch.

He tried a step, but when he put his weight on his leg, pain jabbed into his consciousness and everything faded to black.

Maggie broke his fall with her body, but she couldn't hold his weight. She crumbled to the ground with him in her arms. For a few minutes she just held him, feeling his pain and thanking God that even wounded he'd come back to her. Then, Bar and Cherish were there, helping her get her man into the house.

It was completely dark when Grayson opened his eyes again. He was lying on a bed in the front room of Maggie's house with both women staring at him. Cherish looked as though she'd been crying and Maggie looked as beautiful and angry as ever. Several lanterns were lit around him and the smell of lye soap was thick in the air.

"We decided it would be easier to bring the bed down than to try to get you up those stairs," Margaret said in her matter-of-fact way. "I've seen men die with half the injuries you've suffered."

Grayson smiled. For the first time since he'd been shot he felt wonderful. His wounds were expertly cleaned and bandaged and Maggie was softly touching his arms even as she scolded him.

"I don't plan on dying." He stared at her.

"I should hope not!" Bar yelled from the hallway. "I'd have hated to waste all that time haulin' water for a man that just up and died on me."

Grayson laughed and forced himself to look away from Maggie. "I appreciate it, son."

Bar smiled. "Don't mention it."

A pounding at the door made everyone jump.

"Stay with him," Maggie ordered Cherish and Bar as she grabbed her gun.

Like a mini-army, they all took their battle positions. Cherish moved to Grayson's side and handed him back the Colt he'd loaned her. They both relaxed at the sound of Wart's nervous voice at the door.

"I'm mighty sorry to bother you so late," he began.

"Nonsense, Mr. Tucker. Come in."

Wart stepped just inside and removed his hat. While he mutilated the brim, Maggie waited. She didn't bother to set her gun aside, since his nervousness told her the news he carried was not good.

Finally, he took a deep breath and blurted out, "I'm sorry to have to be the one to tell you this, but they found your husband dead a few hours ago. Holliday wouldn't even let me have a drink until I came up to tell you just in case no one else had."

Grayson couldn't help but notice that no one in the room looked shocked except Maggie. He breathed a deep sigh, for he'd already decided he'd have to kill one worthless husband before he married Maggie. Someone had saved him the trouble.

"Now, don't worry, ma'am. We know who did it." Wart ran his hand through his thinning hair. "An outlaw by the name of Brant Coulter. Two men identified him as the one dragging the body toward the river."

Cherish looked at Grayson and whispered, "He didn't do it."

"I know," Grayson answered with a wink. "He was too busy making my life hell to try and kill anyone else."

"Mrs. Alexander, if you'll step out on the porch, there's some men needing answers about what to do with the body."

Margaret nodded as Wart continued, "The murder weren't robbery 'cause he had this in his pocket." Wart handed her a fistful of bills.

Accepting the money, Maggie stepped outside without saying a word or showing any feeling beyond the first shock of learning of Westley's murder.

As soon as the door was closed, Grayson leaned on one elbow and frowned at Cherish and the boy. "All right. Let's have the story about how he died."

They both started talking at once as if thankful to finally lay what they'd seen onto someone else's shoulders. They had to trust someone with their story. If they told the sheriff, he'd think it was proof that Brant was the killer and never would have believed it could be Father Daniel. Although Cherish and Bar knew it was him, neither had seen his face.

When Maggie returned, no tears were in her eyes. "I've made arrangements for him to be laid out at the hotel. He'll be buried at dawn. I'll not wear black," she stated simply; then she disappeared into the kitchen to cook the evening meal. She'd done all the grieving for that man she planned to do. Now there were folks to feed.

Cherish remained with Grayson a few moments. "I'm not sorry he's dead, but I wish Brant wasn't the one hunted for his murder."

"Brant can take care of himself. If he's smart, he's fifty miles away from here by now."

Cherish didn't reply. She only looked out the window and remembered what Brant had whispered to her about coming to her room tonight. If he came, it could mean his death. If he didn't, she felt that her heart might break from longing for him.

Maggie returned with a supper of soup and hot bread. She insisted on feeding Grayson, finally threatening to break his good arm if he didn't allow her to take care of him.

Bar disappeared into his room upstairs, looking exhausted, and Cherish followed minutes later, more to leave Grayson and Maggie alone than because she thought she could sleep.

Maggie cleared the dishes and pulled her chair close to Grayson's bed.

"What are you doing?" Grayson raised one bushy eyebrow at her.

"I'm going to sit up with you tonight," Maggie answered simply.

"I don't need anyone coddling me like I was a child. I think if I survived the past two weeks in the open, I can last the night with a roof over my head."

Margaret stood and began to tuck his covers around him. "Stop shouting at me. I'm right here and I'm going to stay right here in case you need me during the night."

Grayson's unharmed arm shot out from the covers and grabbed her by the shoulder. He pulled her to him with one mighty jerk. When his lips were touching her cheek, he whispered, "I need you during every night, Maggie, but not as a nurse." His mouth moved over her face, lightly tasting her skin.

She tried to pull away, but he held her fast.

"When I'm able to get out of this bed, I plan to get right back into it with you."

Anger flamed in her indigo eyes. "Turn loose of my neck, you mammoth brute, or I'll shoot your other leg and you'll never walk out of this parlor."

Grayson studied her closely before slowly releasing his fingers from around her shoulder. He expected her to pull away, but her face remained a breath away from his.

"Don't ever threaten me again, Grayson Kirkland," she whispered. "And don't ever use force on me. You may be as strong as an ox and about as bright, but my aim is true. I'll not be manhandled by you or any other."

He suddenly wished he'd tightened his grip around her neck a moment before when he'd had the chance, but he didn't touch her now. When she was all angry and afire she was even more beautiful to him. He'd realized other men couldn't see her beauty and he only felt sorry for them. For when she was like this, she reminded him of a storm, all flash and thunder and raw beauty.

Her bottom lip brushed his jaw as she continued, "You'll not get me in your bed with threats or by bullying me. When I come to you, it will be of my own will and for no other reason."

She moved an inch closer and suddenly her lips found his. Her kiss was slow and filled with the passion he loved to taste. He lifted his arm and lay it gently across her back, then pulled her next to him. Careful of his wounds, she leaned into him until he could feel the light rise and fall of her breasts against his chest. Her back was still as slender as ever, but her breasts seemed fuller, more inviting.

He moved his fingers over the front of her blouse and pulled the buttons free, smothering her protest as he kissed her. When he shoved the material from her breast, her mouth opened wide to him. While his tongue tasted the soft lining of her mouth, his hand covered her ripe flesh. For a moment he spread his palm over its peak and circled, loving the way she arched to his touch. He kept his palm only barely touching as her flesh strained for his embrace. Slowly, he lowered his hand over her full breast. As his fingers tightened around his find, he heard her moan low in the back of her throat.

"Maggie." He whispered the name of his world as she returned his kiss. Her hands were moving mindlessly in his hair, pulling, stroking, loving.

Reluctantly, his hand left her breast. He gently knotted the mass of her hair into his fist. "You'll come to me, my Maggie," he whispered as his lips moved over her face, loving the way her mouth remained slightly open and waiting for his return. "And when you do, I want your hair down and free." With her hair still between his fingers he returned his hand to her breast. His mouth claimed hers as he moved the silk of her hair over the velvet of her skin.

He wanted all of her at once. She was his woman, the woman no one knew existed except him. His kisses grew hungry, bruising her lips with need while his huge hand closed over her breast, claiming ownership.

Finally, when he could live without the taste of her soft globe no longer, he broke their kiss. With a swift action, he slid his hand down her back and shoved her up so that his mouth could reach its goal. She pushed at him gently in a halfhearted effort to escape, but her cries were only of pleasure. Her breath came fast and ragged as he took his fill of her softness. Her hands gripped the headboard above her as she willingly accepted his loving attack. He brushed his hand along her arm to her shoulder and down. As he stroked her side, she moved closer, filling his mouth with her flesh. When he moved his fingers lower to her long, slender thigh, she began to cry his name in pleasure. He took his time, loving the way she moved against him as his tongue circled her softness. He was mindless with the pleasure of her and the knowledge that she was his alone.

Suddenly, she grabbed his hair and pulled his mouth back to her lips. Now the inside of her mouth was hot with need and wanton with desire. His kisses turned gentle.

When she leaned away, her eyes were filled with a fire not started by anger. "When I come to you," she whispered, "you'll have to do more than kiss me."

Grayson smiled, knowing exactly what his Maggie wanted and needed. "I'd best mend fast or a night with you in my bed might kill me."

"It very well might, Yankee." Maggie laughed.

They were too wrapped up in one another to notice the thin black shadow that opened the kitchen door and slipped past them to the stairs leading to Cherish's room.

27

Cherish was curled by the warm fire, almost asleep, when she heard her door slowly open. She'd gone two nights without sleep and her mind drifted between dreams and reality. For a moment she listened to the creaking and didn't move; she'd known he'd risk everything to keep his promise. Somehow, no matter the danger, Brant had come to her tonight.

"Brant," she whispered as the thin black shadow moved into her room.

Abruptly, the shadowy figure brought back all the evil she'd seen the night before. She could smell Westley's blood once more and feel the depravity as thick in the air as humidity. The stranger was not her lover, but the devil she'd seen murder a man with no more care than if he were slaughtering an animal.

Jumping to her feet, Cherish ran toward the gun at her bedside table. Her only chance was to shoot before he pulled the knife from his boot. The memory of the night on the train when it had been Brant's hand that held a knife flooded back to her. Daniel and Brant blended in her tired mind until they became one. The scars were not on one's left and the other's right arm, but on both arms of one man.

As she touched the weapon, gloved fingers covered her

hand. With only the firelight to see by, the darkened figure above her seemed huge and frightening. The leather of his glove was cool against her hand as his fingers pried the gun free of her grip.

Cherish jerked away, fighting wildly. Terror fed upon her wildest nightmares and grew in her mind. She would not die, helpless, on her knees, as Westley had, but fighting.

He twisted her violently toward him and covered her mouth with his free hand.

"Cherish," he whispered. "Baby, it's me."

Cherish froze, trying to understand his words. She looked up, but his face was in shadows.

"Don't be afraid of me," he whispered and the sorrow in his voice touched her heart.

She melted into Brant's arms. The horror of her nightmare vanished as the memory of his love surrounded her. Suddenly she was crying and laughing at the same time. "I thought you were . . . ," she whispered as he kissed her tears. "I was so afraid."

Brant cupped her face in his hands. "You thought I was who?"

Cherish closed her eyes, not wanting to tell Brant the truth about his friend. "The priest," she finally answered in a voice so low it could have been a thought that passed between them.

"Has Daniel harmed you?" His fingers were rough in his need to know. "Has he done something to you?"

"No," she answered, realizing how important her reply was to him. "Bar and I saw him kill Westley last night. He looked so much like you did just now, that for a moment I thought it was Father Daniel in my room."

Brant released her and stepped away. He yanked his gloves off and threw them on the bed. "He has used the resemblance for too long."

Slowly, he offered his hand to her. When she accepted, he led her gently to the chair and sat down, pulling her onto his lap. "Cherish, you have to tell me everything you saw and heard last night. Daniel is mixed up and I'm not sure how to help him."

"But if I do . . ." She hesitated. Now the firelight shone on Brant's face. She could see his warm chestnut eyes, not Daniel's cold ones. "Are you going to turn him in?"

Brant laughed. "That would be a real joke. I could just see how the sheriff would laugh if Brant Coulter tried to turn in Father Daniel for a murder. No, I could never let the law have him. Daniel would die in a prison. Even when we were children he could never pass through the tunnel without a light. I promised him years ago that I'd put a bullet in his brain before I'd ever allow anyone to chain him up in some dark place."

"You care about him."

"I owe him more than once for my life. He's the closest I've ever had to family."

"But he uses you. He has killed and allowed you to take the blame."

Touching her hair, Brant answered, "I really didn't care before I met you. I figured I would have died years ago if he hadn't saved my life, so I kind of owed him one. Plus, I guess I've done enough wrong to be hanged without Daniel's help. He couldn't have used my reputation if I hadn't started it in the first place."

Cherish shook her head in disbelief. "No, not you. I'll not believe ill of you. You brought Grayson back. He told me he would have died if you hadn't helped him. You risked your life to help and you didn't even know who he was."

Brant shrugged. "I had my reasons."

Cherish rubbed her cheek against his jaw. "You did it because you are good and kind. You're the kindest man

I've ever met and I love you dearly, Brant Coulter."

Brant shook his head. He'd given up trying to convince her otherwise. She saw only good in him and somehow her sight changed him within. She was not a child but a woman who'd seen years of pain and war. He was no saint, but it did no good to argue with this lady. Her trust might be almost childlike, but there was nothing childlike about the body that leaned against his.

"I missed you," she whispered as her bottom lip slid over his cheek. His face was smooth from a recent shave and he smelled of springwater and soap. "I've felt as though half of me was missing since you've been gone."

He folded her into his arms. "I'm beginning to think I'm addle-brained. All I've thought of this past month is you. I'm going to show you just how much I thought of you."

"By doing what?" she murmured as her lips traced the outline of his ear.

He pulled her against him. "By loving you all night long."

Cherish laughed. "And if I scream?"

"Oh, you'll scream, my love, with pleasure." He lifted the curtain of her hair and kissed her neck lightly.

"No," she cried as she pulled his mouth to her lips. She loved the feel of his mouth against her flesh almost as much as she loved his kiss. Tonight, she planned to have a banquet of both.

He stood with her in his arms and crossed the room. He dropped her onto the bed, then fell beside her. Her laughter made him smile, for he knew she'd had little to laugh about in the past few years. Now he could give her one more joy at least for a moment, if not for a lifetime. And pure joy was in his plan for the night.

He pushed her hair from her face and studied her, loving

the way she looked up at him with such trust. "Don't ever be afraid of me," he whispered.

She pulled him close above her until her breath brushed his ear. "If you don't keep your promise, you'll have reason to fear me." Her lips moved along the tender area below his ear.

"What promise, my love?" he whispered into her hair, already drunk on her nearness.

Cherish giggled and nipped at his earlobe. "To make me scream with pleasure."

There were no more words then, for the only language either could hear was in the pounding of their hearts. At first his actions were rough with desire, but as he touched her willing body, his fingers grew gentle and his kisses deep and loving. She had a way about her that made him always want to be a little more than he was.

He suddenly wanted to please her, to give her a touch of the heaven that she'd given him. His fingers moved over her body, sliding into every curve, and gently molding passion's sculpture. He loved the way she moved to his touch and cried softly from her very heart when he'd truly pleased her. The wonder that filled his head more than any liquor was the fact that she wanted him. They were a blending, not only of flesh, but of dreams and need. She took each feeling he gave her as if it were a wonderful gift she'd never known existed before, and in return she held back nothing. Her love made up for all the love he'd never known in his life. Her love made him whole.

When he entered her, her body reached to enfold him and he touched heaven as he had before in her arms. He pushed deep into her and felt her arch to meet him, her breasts flattening into the hardness of his chest. He held her to him, loving the feel of her softness and the smell of her flesh. With each thrust, he heard her mindlessly whispering the same word again and again. When he turned her head so that he could hear the word, her voice shattered all the barriers he'd built around his heart. For she whispered his name.

He caught her cry of pleasure in his mouth and kissed her gently as she floated back to earth. Their bodies were damp with sweat and hot from a fire they'd built of passion and need, but they didn't pull apart. They held one another through the night as if there would be no tomorrow.

When light turned the room from black to gray, Brant stood and pulled on his clothing. He stopped, watching her sleep and wondering how God could make such a woman. He'd always thought everyone had both a little good and a little bad in them, but Cherish was perfection in every form.

She stretched and reached for him. When her fingers didn't find him, she opened sleepy eyes. " 'Morning, my love," she whispered, unaware of how beautiful she was and of how the sight of her warmed his blood.

"I'd better go," he answered as he leaned toward her and lightly kissed her passion-swollen lips. "It will be light soon."

"Will you come back tonight?" She stretched and the covers fell below the curve of her neckline.

He'd meant to tell her no. There were a million places he'd be safer than here. But looking at her now he could only answer, "If I'm alive, I'll come back to you."

Cherish slid from the bed and pulled her wrapper around her as he pulled on his boots and shirt. "I've been thinking," she said casually, as if their future were as easy as every couple's to plan, "we could go to Colorado and live. I've heard men say that there's work in the silver mines up there. No one would know us. We could start a new life."

Brant slipped his finger from her chin to between her breasts, pulling the material aside until he could see the swell of her mounds. He didn't want to take the hope from her eyes, even though he knew that there was nowhere he could go that would be far enough to outrun his past. Someone would find him if it took a year, or even five. There was too much money riding on his head to allow him to slip away.

"You'd go with me?" he asked as his fingers explored beneath the material of her wrapper and lightly brushed one breast.

Cherish closed her eyes with pleasure. "Yes," she whispered.

She would have closed the distance between them, but he held her away as he spread his palm over her softness and ran his hand along the velvet beneath her wrapper. His voice was low and filled with desire. "Tell me that you love me."

"I love you," she answered as he pulled the wrapper free.

Again she would have advanced, but his hand held her away. His fingers took great pleasure in moving over the curves of her body. "And you'd go anywhere with me?"

"Anywhere," she answered with her usual clear decisiveness. She raised her arms out to him.

Brant could not hold her back any longer. He moved into her embrace with all the passion of a lifetime of need. "Then go with me to heaven now, for there is no place where I could be happier than here with you in my arms."

Suddenly, she was against him, as loving and wild as he'd ever dreamed she'd be. She was a feast to his senses and he'd been starving for her all his life.

He lifted her off the floor and carried her back to bed, knowing he should be miles away by now, but willing to risk his life for one more hour with her.

28

Grayson sat back against the headboard of the bed and relaxed. He'd just spent the past hour getting dressed and the simple chore exhausted him. But he wanted to be standing when Maggie came back from settling Westley's affairs. It had been a week since he'd arrived on her porch and he was sick of the inactivity. Maggie was worse than a mother hen with one chick. It was no wonder Hattie lost her mind after being bedridden for months. He was about to lose his after only seven days. His only goal today was to make it to the chair on the front porch so he could see them coming up the hill, then to stand as she walked up the steps.

Only two guests had come to the house during his recovery. One had been the lawyer to ask Maggie to drop by his office. The other, Holliday, to tell them how happy she was to hear about Westley's demise. She'd even stopped in to visit with Hattie for a few minutes, but the old woman no longer acknowledged anyone in the room. The disease in Hattie's body had closed her mind and it would only be a matter of hours before it stopped her heart as well.

Holliday cried when she saw Hattie, then blotted her eyes carefully so she wouldn't smear her face paint. Like most of the ladies of the evening, she'd gotten her start at Hattie's Parlor back before the war.

Holliday had stayed for tea, which Maggie served right on the front porch for everyone to see.

Grayson had watched them from the slits in the boarded-up window. He swore he could see Holliday putting on more airs by the minute. Maggie had a way of making those around her change, even without saying a word. By the time they'd finished tea, the old girl of the streets was strutting like she was the mayor's wife.

The only conversational topic of interest to Grayson was Holliday's mentioning of how the drunks still talked of a treasure hidden in the house, but she'd said fewer and fewer believed the tale. Westley had believed the lie and lies don't die as easily as men.

Grayson lowered himself into the porch chair and smiled as he wondered if Maggie would offer him tea today. He'd made it outside and was quite proud of himself.

His glory was short-lived however, for when Maggie saw him sitting on the porch, he could hear her yelling from the bottom of the hill.

When she stepped into the yard her anger was full-blown. She marched toward him. "How dare you get out of bed before you're told! You could have done a great deal of damage."

Grayson laughed. He'd learned to love her outbursts almost as dearly as he loved the way she kissed him good night each night with promises of what would come when he was well. "Stop yelling at me, woman. You're always trying to keep me in bed."

His good mood only fired her anger. "I liked you much better before you started talking, Yankee," she answered. "At least then I didn't think you were an idiot who tried to kill yourself by getting out of bed before you should."

Bar came through the door absorbed in the piece of pie he'd just stolen from the kitchen. He glanced up and noticed they'd squared off at one another again. With the ease of a dust devil, he twirled around and vanished back into the house. He could hear all the argument he wanted to from any location half a mile around; he didn't have to stay within throwing distance of Maggie.

Neither noticed the boy as blue-gray eyes clashed with indigo. She stood in front of his chair, tall and slender in her new navy dress. She was daring him to argue; he could taste it in the air between them.

Grayson raised one eyebrow. "You win. I'll go back to bed, but you'll have to help me."

Maggie hesitated a moment, knowing it was unlikely he'd give up so easily. Slowly, she helped him to his feet. His powerful arm covered her shoulder as he allowed her to take only part of the weight from his wounded leg. When they passed through the door frame, he stopped, raising his hands to catch the frame, and blocked her on both sides.

They stood for a moment, touching. He could feel her pressed against him from shoulder to knee and there wasn't a place where she didn't feel wonderful. "Maggie," he whispered as he leaned even closer, "I'm strong enough."

She didn't pretend not to understand his meaning. Her arm still circled his waist and he felt like an oak beside her. There was nothing soft or weak in this man. Not even his injuries had made him less virile in her eyes.

When she didn't answer, he leaned against her, pressing her back against the door frame. Even through their clothes she could feel the heat of his body. "Come to me tonight with your hair down, my Maggie."

"No," she answered, lifting her chin. "I'm not the kind of woman who crawls into a man's bed in the middle of the night."

"Then marry me," he answered, and his words shocked him almost as much as they did her.

"Certainly not. I only buried a husband this week. I can hardly marry again so soon."

"You buried him four years ago. He only finally died this week." Grayson's hand moved over her shoulder, caressing her slender arm.

Maggie's brow wrinkled in confusion. "Also, I'm not sure I could marry a Yankee after spending the past years mending the men the North shot."

Grayson slid his hand from her arm to her fingers. "The war's over. Let it end between us."

She looked up at his wonderful eyes that blended the colors of the North and the South. The war had never been against the North for her. It had only been against pain and death. She could lay it aside, but could he? He might want her, but she knew part of the reason he'd remained by her side was because he hunted the southern outlaws who were somehow tied to this house.

"I'm not sure," she whispered, and for the first time he saw how very much she needed him—almost as much as he needed her.

His knuckles brushed the side of her face. "Marry me." He breathed the words against her cheek. "Marry me and live with me the rest of our days on this earth. It doesn't matter if we live in the North or the South as long as we are together."

Just before his lips reached hers, Cherish called from Hattie's room. The moment snapped between them and was lost. She wanted to pull him back until there was only the world of the two of them, but she knew she had responsibilities. Maggie quickly helped him to his bed. As she turned to rush to see what was wrong with Hattie, Maggie heard him mutter that he wished they were alone again on the trail. For a moment she closed her eyes and would have given her house for an hour alone with him.

Grayson lay back and watched as the women came and went from the old woman's room. He didn't have to ask to know Hattie's time had come. As the hours passed he knew she was fighting death, even though she no longer had the mind to ask why.

Finally, just before sundown, Grayson pulled his way along the hallway to her door. There he saw Cherish and Maggie sitting on either side of Hattie's bed, doing what little they could to help. Bar was asleep in a chair in the corner.

After several moments of silence, Hattie mumbled, "Is my daughter here yet? Is my daughter here?"

Cherish and Maggie exchanged glances before Cherish took the old woman's hand. Maggie nodded as Cherish whispered, "I'm here. I've come to take you home with me."

Hattie smiled and took a deep breath. When she let the air escape, she let go of life. Everyone waited for several minutes before moving. Then the living stood and did what the living must do.

Grayson walked out on the porch. He had never even spoken to the old woman, but somehow her passing saddened him, bringing back all the memories of loved ones' deaths. He looked at the night sky and tried to remember what his wife had looked like, but the years and the miles he'd traveled blurred her face. He'd thought he'd never feel anything again, until he met Maggie.

Bar ran down the hill to order the second coffin in a week. Cherish helped prepare the body, then vanished into her room.

It was well after midnight when Maggie sat on the edge of Grayson's bed to say good night. "Are you asleep?" she whispered, and her voice sounded tired.

"No," he answered, covering her hand with his. She was only a shadow, but he could feel a trembling of need in her touch, a need all have to hold the living when Death walks too near.

She was silent for a long while, feeling the warmth of his hand covering hers. "I don't want to die alone, childless and among strangers." She bit her lip to fight back the tears, but she knew the only way she'd find strength was to admit her weakness. "Sometimes, I'm so afraid. It seems like everyone I care about leaves me. I get so tired of always feeling so alone."

Grayson silently pulled her down beside him and held her against his heart. He wanted to tell her all the words that he'd been thinking of while waiting for her, but none would come. It had been ten years since he'd talked of love and lifetimes together.

Slowly, he brought her hand up and kissed her palm. Then he spread her fingers over his heart and whispered, "Go to sleep now, Maggie. I'm with you."

She cuddled against his shoulder and did as she was told for the first time since he'd met her. He held her gently all night, wondering how he'd ever found such a woman. Somehow, he knew it was going to be far more difficult to whisper words of love than yell words of anger at her. But he'd best be practicing both, for she would always give as much as she demanded of love.

"Maggie," he whispered into her hair, "I'm not leaving you, for you belong right where you are at this moment. I never thought a woman like you lived, and now I've found you I can't think what it would be like to live without you. As long as there is breath in me you'll never be lonely again."

He moved his hand over her sleeping body and felt her move toward his touch.

*   *   *

Cherish closed her door and ran to the lamp. Quickly she opened the letter she'd carried in her pocket all day waiting for a chance to read it.

Brant's words were simple. He'd gone to find Daniel and would be back as soon as he could. He ended with, "Look for me at dusk tomorrow. I'll come through the tunnel."

There were no words of love. He hadn't even signed his name, but he was coming to her and that was all that really mattered.

Cherish's joy was short-lived, for the next day dawned amid a downpour. The rain hung like a damp curtain over the air as clouds hid the sun and thunder rumbled through the house.

Around noon, the carpenter brought the coffin and Hattie was placed inside. Her thin body needed only half the space, so Maggie surrounded her with the quilt that always lay over her in life. Cherish gently put the box of letters on one side and Bar placed her ancient gun on the other.

It was well into the afternoon before the mourners started to gather in the living room. Grayson's bed was moved to the corner and every chair in the house circled the room to make the visitors comfortable. As the rain slowed, their numbers grew until the house was full of a few grievers and numerous curious townspeople.

Grayson ached all over, but he wasn't about to go to bed with all these folks looking at him, and he wasn't sure he could climb the stairs. He sought refuge on the back porch and it wasn't long before Bar joined him.

The boy propped himself up on the damp porch railing and watched the last bit of rain dribble off the roof. "Where do you think all those folks come from?" he asked. "Except for the doc and Holliday, I ain't never seen them in this house."

Folding himself slowly into an old wicker chair, Grayson replied, "Folks like to come around when someone dies. Some are grieving and need to touch the living, but some just want to watch and talk. I reckon most of these are the latter. Hattie had quite a reputation in this town and them that wouldn't visit her alive will come to look now she's dead."

"I was thinkin' that on a day like this, there ain't much to do. But I'd have to be real hard up to go visit a dead person."

Agreeing, Grayson pulled a thin cigar from his pocket and lit it.

Bar shrugged his bony shoulders. "Hattie wouldn't have wanted them here. She threatened to shoot almost everyone who walked in her room with that old gun of hers. She told me once that she had enough powder in it to destroy half the men in town, but when I looked at it once I found it stuffed with rolled-up paper."

Grayson stood and moved closer to Bar. Keeping his voice calm, he asked, "What was on the paper, son?"

"Just a bunch of names."

Grayson slowly lowered himself to the first step and allowed the damp air to clear his head. He tossed the cigar into the mud. From inside he could hear the tapping sound of the nails being hammered into the lid of Hattie's coffin, but he didn't move to stop them.

Taking a deep breath, he listened to the sound of the hammer, knowing that it was forever closing inside the coffin the only list ever made of the Knights of the Golden Circle. All he had to do was go inside and demand the box be opened and he'd have the list he'd been looking for since the war ended. But if he found the list, would the war end? He'd probably find the names of a few men, like Wallman, who were up to causing trouble, but most of the men had probably gone on with their lives or died in the war. What good would it do exposing them now? He'd demanded that Maggie let the conflict die. He could ask no less of himself.

Let the conflict and the secret die and be buried with Hattie, forever concealing the list, forever ending the bloodshed. She could keep the list safe in death as she had in life.

As the hammering continued, Grayson stared into the gray clouds and buried his hatred. This rainy afternoon almost a year after Lee's surrender was the day the war ended for him in his heart. Pain had torn wounds on both sides, but it was time to let them heal. Now he could look to the future and not the past.

Now he could talk to Maggie of dreams . . . of forever.

29

Grayson watched the mourners straggle down the hill toward the cemetery at the other end of town. They were a pathetic group of aging whores and old drunkards who all had stories to tell about Hattie in her younger days. Grayson was glad he'd remained behind, for he wasn't sure he could have made the long walk through the mud. A few in the procession took torches, knowing it would be after dark before they returned. As they moved away, their bodies blinked in and out of Grayson's sight in the twilight.

He stood tall and strong until he was sure Maggie could no longer see him, then he slumped and allowed the pain of his wounds to twist his body. Using his last bit of energy to pull himself to his bed, Grayson collapsed, too tired even to make an attempt at removing his clothing. Within a breath's length he was asleep.

The world seemed quiet only a moment before noise began to invade his sleep. At first he thought the sounds he heard were part of a dream or that the thunder had returned. But the sudden shattering of glass cleared his foggy brain and the sounds became real.

Grayson forced his eyes open. The sounds were coming from Hattie's room. He could hear furniture being overturned or shoved aside. A low lamp burned in the hallway near the door, but most of the light came from Hattie's doorway near the kitchen. There should have been no one in the house, so whoever was in her room was unwanted company.

Lifting himself slowly, Grayson headed toward the noise. As he neared the stairs, he noticed a long brown robe, like Father Daniel wore, hanging over a chair. The light from Hattie's room shone more clearly now. Someone kept crossing back and forth across the room, making the lamplight flicker on the hallway wall.

The logic that had kept Grayson alive snapped into action and dulled the pain that was throbbing through his leg. If Daniel was in Hattie's room, Grayson knew he'd better face the priest armed. He believed Cherish's story of Daniel killing Westley. Pulling his Colt from its peg in the hallway, Grayson checked the bullets. Thank God Cherish had left the thing fully loaded.

A sudden crash rattled through the house as sharp as the old woman's screams had always been. Judging from the sound, whoever was in the room had just turned over Hattie's bed.

Grayson moved to her doorway, his frame blocking all escape. The room was in shambles, with a lifetime of now worthless keepsakes shattered and broken. Daniel was kneeling over the bed with a long knife in his hand. Just before the priest slashed the feather mattress, Grayson said calmly, "Looking for something, Father?"

Daniel froze for a moment, then turned slowly to face the doorway.

Grayson saw it then, the touch of insanity in Daniel's eyes. Somehow, he'd known it had been there all the time, hidden behind a veil of priestly virtue. Grayson had seen the same look before, in a few men he'd trapped. The look told him that Daniel valued no life, not even his own. That one fact made him more dangerous than any bloodthirsty outlaw. He would kill himself as well as Grayson if he were cornered.

With great effort, the priest molded his face from an angry grimace into a passive mask. "Hattie had something that belonged to me. I've searched everywhere, but I can't find it."

Grayson guessed, "A list of the Knights of the Golden Circle?"

Daniel's eyes twitched just enough to let Grayson know that he'd hit the mark. "Have you seen such a list?" He lowered the knife into its sheath inside his boot, but his knuckles were white as he gripped the handle.

"No," Grayson answered. "I'm afraid the secret of that list is buried with Hattie." He braced himself against the door frame for support. "Tell me, Father, are you looking for the list to blackmail those on it . . . or because you were a member? Brant told me once that he was too young to be a member, but you were two years older. Could it be that you signed your name to orders that sent a boatload of innocent people to their deaths?"

The twitch of his eyes again told Grayson he'd made another direct hit. The priest turned to face the destroyed room. "No one must ever find that list. I've made all those responsible pay."

"Except yourself," Grayson baited. "You were one of those first Knights who were sworn to kill."

Daniel's eyes were wide with panic. "I was too young to know what I was joining. No one must ever find the list. It's here somewhere; Hattie always told me it was. She always reminded me; that way I'd bring her opium. She loved making my life a hell by telling me I'd never have the list."

"Hattie's dead." Grayson could see his words weren't

getting through to Daniel. "They're putting her in her grave about now. Shouldn't you be there to say a few words, 'Priest'?"

"No one must have the list!" he screamed. "I have to destroy it. I have to forever burn my name from it!"

With a sudden jerk of his hand, Daniel knocked the lamp onto the mattress. The smell of kerosene filled the room for a moment before it caught fire in one mighty blaze.

Grayson turned toward the kitchen to find something, anything, to put out the fire. He'd only taken two steps when something hit him from behind, slamming into his head and enfolding him in darkness.

Daniel walked calmly from the room. Firelight danced across his face but his eyes were the dead cold of the ocean depths. He stood for a moment above Grayson, watching the fire as though it were no more than a prairie campfire. He lifted Grayson's head, exposing the Yankee's neck, and pulled the knife from his boot.

"No!" someone screamed from the other end of the hall-way.

Daniel looked up at the one woman he'd ever admired: the woman with the Blessed Virgin's eyes. "Cherish," he whispered as he lowered the knife.

Cherish's need to help Grayson was far greater than her fear. She ran toward him as Daniel backed a step away.

"Don't kill him!" she cried. "Please, Daniel, don't kill him!"

"I have to." Daniel's eyes grew wild as they reflected the fire inside Hattie's room. "He knows too much. No one must ever know that I was one of the Knights."

"And me." Cherish slid the gun from Grayson's side. "Are you going to kill me, too?"

Panic struck Daniel. "No!" he screamed to himself. "I could never kill you. I'd be no better than . . ."

"Than the men who set fire to a boatload of women and children." Cherish searched the darkness of the thin shadow of the man who'd spoken.

Daniel's eyes were liquid with pain.

Brant moved into the light. "If you kill Grayson and Cherish, you're no better than they were that night, Daniel. You've lived your life swearing vengeance, but you'd be the same."

"No!" Daniel screamed.

Brant moved closer. Cherish watched the two men who looked so much alike. They were both in black, and with the smoke that was starting to fill the hallway it was hard to tell them apart.

"I can't let them take me, Brant! I can never be chained up again." Daniel's voice was wild with fear. "Stay with me. I stayed with you on the boat. I told them I wouldn't go without you, but there was no room for you. That's why they chained us both. We'll burn together now as we should have done on the boat."

"No!" Brant was inching his way to Grayson and Cherish. "I have to get them out. They can't die for no reason. I didn't stop you before, because I guess I figured those men deserved to die, but I'm stopping you now."

The room was heating up until Cherish felt like her flesh was being sunburned. The air was thick with a dark gray smoke. She couldn't tell if her eyes were stinging from the heat or with tears.

"No!" Daniel crossed the hall and slammed the hallway lantern into the front door. "They have to stay!"

Cherish screamed as their escape exit suddenly burst into flames.

"No one must know of the sins I committed as a youth. No one! You're the only family I've ever had, Brant. Stay with me now."

Brant suddenly jerked Daniel toward him. "Do you think if we all burn you'll be clean, Daniel? Let's get out while there's still time. We can run. I'll hide out with you. I'll show you how not to get caught. You'll never be locked in some dark cell. You have my word."

"No, not this time!" Daniel backed away. He looked into Cherish's frightened eyes for a moment and reality cleared his vision. "Take the others out the basement tunnel, but I stay."

Brant hesitated. He didn't want to leave Daniel, but he had to save Cherish.

"Go!" Daniel shouted. "There's no time left. Leave me, Brant."

Their hands grasped. The scars on their wrists were the same, scars Daniel earned by pulling Brant mile after mile through the water. Suddenly it was years ago and they were together again on the flaming ship with people screaming all around them.

Brant answered from his heart. "I can't leave you, Daniel. You didn't leave me then and I can't leave you now. Help me get Cherish and Grayson to the tunnel. I'll stay with you to the end."

"Closer than brothers," Daniel whispered.

"Closer than brothers," Brant answered.

Cherish screamed, "No, Brant. No! I won't go without you."

The wall of Hattie's room was engulfed in flames. In only a matter of moments, the house would be an oven. Cherish tried to pull Grayson toward the basement door, but he was too heavy for her to move more than a few inches at a time.

"Brant, I'll die without you. Come with me or I'll stay with you." She was shouting now, to be heard above the noise. "I love you!"

Brant held fast. "Not unless Daniel comes also. I can't leave him."

Daniel looked at Cherish and saw all the love she had for Brant in her eyes—a total kind of love Daniel had never known. As he glanced at Brant, Daniel realized he'd burn in hell forever if he crushed such a love. This outlaw and this woman had found the one thing they'd searched their whole lives for and he couldn't destroy it by demanding payment of a debt made when they were boys.

"All right!" Daniel shouted as he silently prayed Cherish would stop crying. "I'll go with you. We'll get them out, then we'll talk."

Brant hesitated, but Daniel pushed him forward. "We'll talk on the outside. You get the Yankee and I'll make sure Cherish gets down the stairs."

Shouldering Grayson, Brant headed toward the basement door. The handle burned his hand as he touched it, but he forced his fingers to grip the metal and twist. Smoke was so thick he couldn't see more than a foot behind him as he hurried down the stairs.

"Cherish," he yelled when he reached the opening to the tunnel.

"I'm right behind you."

Daniel's voice screamed above the fire. "Here, cover your head with my robe." They moved across the basement where the air was not as thick or as hot as it had been upstairs.

When Daniel threw the robe over her face, he pulled her against him, violently knocking the scream from Cherish's lungs. "Take care of Brant," he whispered. "Tell him I can't allow myself to be chained again. Tell him I died in the light."

Then, with a shove that almost knocked her off her feet, he was gone. She moved into the tunnel as she heard him take the stairs up. She wanted to stop him, but she knew they would all die in only moments if she called Brant back.

"Cherish?" Brant yelled in the blackness. "Are you following?"

"Yes," she cried as she fought back a scream. Her silence was letting Brant live just as it had months ago on the train. And once again Father Daniel was helping him escape.

Smoke bellowed into the passage as they crawled onto the wet grass behind the barn. Brant lowered Grayson none too gently and the huge man groaned.

"I told you, Yank, I'd never save your mean hide again and damn if I didn't go and make a liar out of myself." Brant laughed at the black soot that covered them both. "I can't figure out how you boys managed to win the war with folks like you fighting."

The house caught flame like a huge bonfire, lighting the sky as bright as the sun.

Brant looked around as Cherish crawled from the tunnel. He pulled the robe from her face and flung it over his shoulder. "Are you all right, baby?"

Cherish folded herself into his arms, crying uncontrollably. She was covered with smoke, dust, and dirt, but she felt wonderful in his arms.

"Where's Daniel?" Brant watched the opening and Cherish could feel his body tighten.

"He's not coming." Cherish bit her lip until it bled so that she could deliver Daniel's message clearly. "He said to tell you he wanted to die in the light."

"No!" Brant screamed and started toward the tunnel.

Cherish held him tight. "Stop! It's too late. I heard him go back into the house." He dragged her back toward the tunnel as she fought to hold him. "It's too late!"

Brant stopped suddenly as the house rattled in its last breath of life and crumbled into fiery rubble. Bright flames shot toward heaven, leaving a white light glowing for a moment where they'd been.

People were everywhere, running, shouting.

Grayson stood slowly and grabbed Brant's arm. "Put on the robe," he demanded.

Brant shook his head, still staring at the fire. He could see no sign of Daniel, but he could feel the loss of him burning into his gut.

Grayson grabbed the robe and shoved it over Brant. "Maybe it's my turn to save your hide, reb."

With Grayson on one side of the "priest" and Cherish on the other, they moved toward the house.

Cherish could see people running and shouting, but their voices didn't reach her ears. All she could hear was Father Daniel's last words as he ran back toward the fire.

Maggie saw the flames from the cemetery. She'd been busy thanking everyone for coming and had hardly noticed when Cherish slipped away with the excuse that she was going ahead to check on Grayson.

Now, Maggie felt like her heart was exploding. She lifted her skirts and ran up the hill, knocking folks out of her way without giving any thought to her improper behavior. She didn't care that her only-ever home was on fire. It didn't matter that everything she had in the world was in the fire. All that mattered was that somehow Cherish and Grayson had gotten out safely.

When she saw the front door ablaze, she prayed they'd gone out the back. She ran around the house, not caring that the flames were licking dangerously close to her skirts. Vaguely, she heard someone yell that they saw Brant Coulter in one of the upstairs windows. Maggie didn't care about anything or anyone but Cherish and Grayson.

As she reached the backyard, smoke was billowing from

the downstairs while flames lit the upper floor like a crown of fire.

"Grayson!" she screamed again and again, furious with dread that there was no answer.

Maggie dropped to her knees in the center of the yard. All her life all she'd ever dreamed of was having her own house and now it didn't matter at all that the house was afire. All she wanted was those she loved. "Grayson! Cherish!"

"Stop your screaming, Maggie," Grayson yelled from behind her. "I'm moving toward you as fast as I can."

Maggie jumped to her feet and ran toward the three shadows moving from the barn. She hugged Cherish wildly, then turned to Grayson. All at once she was crying, something she'd never allowed herself to do in front of others.

"Maggie." Grayson's strong arm crushed her against him. "It's all right. We're all fine, just a little smoke-cooked."

"But I heard someone yell that a man named Brant Coulter died in the fire."

Grayson looked at the priest. "Brant Coulter did die in the fire, cheating a hangman's noose. Half the lawmen in Texas can stop their searching tonight."

Bar ran around the corner of the house. He saw them all safe and let out a hoot that could have been heard all the way to Dallas. He didn't know the words to tell them how much they meant to him, so he danced around them, smiling his joy.

Grayson pulled Maggie close. "Cherish, why don't you help the father to the mission. He may need you to look at that hand of his."

As the young couple turned away, Bar moved to Grayson's side. "But that ain't Father. . ."

Grayson slapped his hand across the boy's mouth so hard he felt his teeth give a fraction. Grayson's words were low and deadly serious. "Now, son, don't go talking about the father. Especially since he's going to be leaving in the morning for a long mission trip."

Bar might only be a boy, but he wasn't stupid. He nodded slowly and was thankful that when Grayson removed his hand his teeth were still rooted in his mouth.

The huge man leaned his hand on Bar's shoulder and allowed the boy to take some of his weight off his wounded leg. "If the two of you will help me, we might be able to get a room down at the hotel tonight. I think my bed downstairs in the parlor may be a little warm for my liking. Come morning, we'll figure out what to do."

"But shouldn't we wait for Cherish?"

Grayson smiled. "Someone's taking very good care of Cherish. She'll be fine at the mission."

30

Brant led Cherish along the back path until they reached the simple quarters behind the mission that had been Father Daniel's. The walls were thick and whitewashed. High, tiny arched windows ran near the roof line. A single candle burned low on the room's only table. Everything in the room was simple and plain, as though the man who lived there had nothing to hide.

They stepped into the soft light. Brant hesitated by the doorway. His warm eyes studied her closely as though he'd been deprived of the sight of her for far too long. "You'll be safe here," Brant whispered as he pulled his hat low to hide the emotion she'd already heard in his voice. "I have something I have to do."

Cherish fought the urge to run after him. She didn't want to be alone. She needed his presence beside her, but she trusted him, so she only nodded and watched him go.

After he'd closed the door, Cherish allowed her brave stance to crumble. She curled onto the tiny bed and let the tears flow. Above the horrible memory of the fire, she kept thinking, what if I'd lost Brant? She'd seen wives fall apart when told their man was dead, but she'd never understood until now what the depth of that pain must be like. Brant's love had unlocked her heart. With the joy of love came the feelings of fear that she might lose him. When she'd first held him, she'd thought she would just experience his loving and walk away. But there was no turning away, and a million nights in his arms wouldn't be enough to satisfy her longing.

Suddenly, she had to be with him. She didn't want to spend another moment of her life without him. She ran to the door and out into the wide hallway. A light shone from the mission chapel, beckoning her near with a warm yellow glow. She ran toward it.

As she entered the tiny church, she didn't see anyone for a moment. Several candles were burning from different corners of the room, brightening a small circle of space around each, but leaving most of the chapel in shadows. A lone man in black knelt at the altar. For a moment Cherish saw Daniel, not Brant, and the air left her lungs.

Brant moved, bending slightly as he pulled something from just beneath the altar. She saw his face and the nightmare of Daniel vanished. As she moved closer, she saw that he was pulling out weapons.

"Brant?" she whispered, not wanting to startle him.

Turning toward her, he smiled, a smile somehow laced with sadness. He sat on the step where he'd been kneeling and motioned for her to join him. The moment she was close enough to touch, his arm pulled her against him.

Cherish felt suddenly nervous. "I didn't want to be alone." He was silent, so she added, "I didn't want to be without you." She felt as though she'd broken into his privacy and wished she'd waited in the room.

His hand was reassuring as he brushed her hair off her shoulder. "I know," he whispered. "I feel the same, but I had to get rid of these before someone found them. I guess I feel I have to help Daniel keep his secret forever now.

These guns might link him to the murders."

Cherish looked at the pile of weapons lying on a blanket beside the altar. "Those were Daniel's?"

Brant closed his fingers around a rifle in almost a farewell embrace and nodded. After a moment he said, "I've known for a long time that he'd have to die. He couldn't go on murdering, even people he thought needed killing. But he saved my life and we were like brothers. Until I met you I didn't really care that I was taking the blame for most of his actions."

Tears welled in his eyes, but he wouldn't allow any to fall. "I know what he did wasn't right, but I couldn't betray the friend I'd made in him years ago. I owed him too much. Even now, no one but Grayson, you, and me will ever know the truth about what happened during the fire."

The tiny muscle along his jaw twitched and Cherish knew he was fighting his emotions as he continued. "In the end, he gave me back my life and I'll give him his respectability even in death."

Cherish moved up a step above him and pulled his head against her heart. For a long moment she just held him close, rocking slightly back and forth. She brushed his hair lightly with her fingertips and whispered, "In the end, you proved your friendship by offering to die with him and he proved his by not allowing you to. When we pick our friends, we have to take the good with the bad, but if they're with us until the end, I guess that's what matters."

Brant raised his head until their eyes were level. His eyes were the color of autumn's browns and rusts. "And you, Cherish, are you that kind of friend?"

"And more," she answered.

Brant stared at her for a long moment, looking into her very soul for the answers he needed. Finally, he smiled and kissed her forehead. "Go back to the room while I get rid of these guns. I'll only be a few moments."

Cherish followed his order and he was true to his word. When they were safe behind the locked door, Brant pulled her tightly against him as if he could no longer live without her in his arms. The horror of the evening danced in both their minds as their need to be close mounted. She'd declared her love and her loyalty and they'd both been tested by fire. No doubt lingered in his heart: he knew he was as vital to her as she was to him.

His kiss was hard and demanding as he washed the night away with the taste of her. Her mouth was warm with need and hungry for his lips.

She matched his longing with her own as she pressed her body against him and met his advances with surrender. Her hands threaded through his hair and knotted into fists, pulling his head even closer. A need for him started deep in the pit of her stomach and spread like liquid fire through her veins.

Her mouth opened, her body yielded, and he could no longer control his longing for her. He passed his hand beneath her cape and ripped her blouse open with one mighty jerk.

"I'm sorry," he mumbled as his warm fingers slid across her cool flesh. But he showed no sign of remorse and she made no protest. *Be gentle*, he reminded himself, but he couldn't dam the flood of his love for her. She'd wrapped her way around his heart and soul until the smell and taste of her were staples in his life.

He shoved her cape from her shoulders so that his eyes could see all that his hands longed to touch. Each time he looked at her she was more beautiful than even the pictures his memory had painted during the long days without her. As her fingers moved along his chest in light, feathery strokes, he became drunk with a delight that warmed with a passion that needed no stoking.

"Your clothes smell of smoke," she teased, shoving his shirt open and pulling it from his belt with impatient tugs. As he stood watching her, she slowly moved her fingers over his hard chest, examining his flesh like a sculptor examines a finished work. His body was slim, tight, and strong like a whip.

Her fingers played with the hair in the center of his chest and followed its thin line down below his belt. He remained like stone as she moved her palm over his ribs, pausing over his heart to feel its pounding. When she leaned forward to taste his skin, he felt his knees buckle and he almost stumbled forward. She only laughed and repeated her action.

Looking up at him, her green eyes alive with passion, she pleaded, "Make love to me, please." Somehow, the fear they'd felt earlier now sharpened all their senses.

She was in his arms and halfway across the room in a heartbeat. He tossed her onto the bed and fell on top of her. "You'll never have to ask twice, my love," he answered.

Cherish held him tightly and laughed. "I love you, my outlaw."

He made love to her then, wild and hurried as young lovers always do. Their clothes flew from the bed and cluttered the room. Each time he would have slowed down, she pushed him farther, for after almost dying, she wanted to feel him inside her. She wanted to know that she was wholly alive, the kind of alive only he could make her feel.

When they finally collapsed, sweaty and exhausted, they held to one another as if there were no world except the one they found within each other's arms.

"I thought I was going to lose you," he whispered as he pushed the wet hair from her face and looked down at the only woman he'd ever loved. "For the first time in my life I was about to lose something important to me, someone worth living for."

Cherish hugged him to her, loving how he felt so right in her arms. "I know," she answered. "Now that Daniel's gone, you wouldn't be betraying him by telling me about him."

"Are you sure you want to know?" He seemed hypnotized by the way her hair lay across the pillow.

"Yes," she answered, gently stroking his back. Her action was absentminded, but the tenderness of it touched him deeply. "I want to know all about your past."

Brant lay beside her for a long time before he was able to talk, and when the words came they tumbled out on top of one another. "At first Daniel only killed the men who had murdered a shipload of slaves. But then the killings didn't slow down. I knew someday I'd have to stop him and I figured it would be the end of both our lives. He couldn't stop killing and he couldn't wash the blood from his hands with the good he did as a priest. He thought if he destroyed the list of the Knights no one would ever know that he'd once been one of them."

"Were you one?" Cherish had to ask.

"No, I was too young. Daniel, being two years older, was signed into the organization; but I was only about fifteen, so I was just used to run errands. We were left on board a burning ship full of slaves once and he pulled me safely into the water. We swam for hours, chained by the wrists. Finally, we reached shore, then walked several days to arrive at a settlement. It took us almost six months to get back to Fort Worth. The chains left permanent scars on our wrists . . . and on our souls. By that time the war had broken out. I went to Hattie and begged her to give us the list so we could destroy it, but she thought she needed it for protection. Finally, I gave up and joined up to fight for Texas, but Daniel took over the duties of a young priest who hadn't made it past the Indians into town. We'd grown up around the mission so the old priest accepted him without question. That way he could keep an eye on Hattie and hopefully find the list."

Brant held her tightly. "Daniel tried everything from drugging her to threatening her life, but the old girl wouldn't give up the list. I think he would have killed her if her days weren't already so numbered. Every time he killed, he'd do months of work here at the mission, trying to somehow wash the crime away."

"What about the children he keeps here?"

"The sisters will take care of them. They'll send for another priest."

She was silent for a long time before she asked, "Can we stay here all night?"

"If you like. I've spent many a night here, wondering where Daniel was and what harm he was doing." Brant smiled down at her, thankful that the nightmare was finally over. "There's water in the pitcher. Why don't you wash the smoke off and I'll be back in a little while." When he pulled away, she clung to him and he added, "Don't worry. Nothing on the earth could stop me from coming back to you."

He dressed and left her alone for half an hour while she washed. When he returned, his hair was wet from the stream and he carried a box of medicines under one arm.

"I think there's some cream here that will help your face. It looks a little burned." Brant tried not to notice how wonderful she looked with her hair combed free. She was wearing one of Daniel's long white shirts and for a moment she looked twelve and not twenty. He thought surely God would miss one of his angels any minute and pull her back to heaven.

Cherish suddenly remembered how he'd burned his hand opening the door to the cellar. "What about your hand?"

"It's fine." Brant pulled his fingers away from her grasp.

"No, let me see it. I could wrap the burn."

Brant slowly turned his palm up. The skin was red, but not blistered. "I didn't want my hand wrapped. I didn't want anything to come between us when I touched you."

Cherish smiled. "You'll have a lifetime to touch me, Daniel."

The name shocked Brant. He tried to pull his hand away, but her stubborn fingers held tight. For a flash he thought she'd accidentally called him by another lover's name, but her face was too angelic and her touch too loving.

Cherish brushed his chestnut hair away from his eyes. "Brant Coulter died in the fire, but Dan Coulter will show up in Denver in about a month with a new beard and a new wife. No one will think the married man is really an outlaw."

Brant laughed. "You've got it all figured. Who do you think is going to be this Dan Coulter's wife?"

"I am," Cherish answered. "Even if I have to kidnap him and take him to the preacher at knife-point. He's going to marry me."

Brant smiled, a rare smile that reached his eyes and warmed her heart. "I may have it wrong, but I thought the man was supposed to do the asking."

"You're right," Cherish answered. "You do have it wrong. The woman says yes and then the man asks. Well, I'm saying yes."

Kneeling on one knee, he folded her hand in his and said, "Well, I guess I'm asking. Will you marry me?"

Cherish looked around the room, anywhere except his handsome face. "I'll think about it while your beard grows." She walked away from him as if he were only one of many men who'd asked her the same question that day.

"And where are we going to stay while my beard grows?" Brant stood and followed her.

"In a cabin I know." She played with the bottles of creams in the box he'd brought. "You'll have nothing to do but eat and sleep and let that scratchy dark stubble turn into a beard."

"I can think of a few other things that might keep me busy." Now his smile was widening and looked like it might settle in to stay for a while.

"Come here, wife, and let me give you an idea of what we might pass the time doing." He lifted Cherish into his arms and carried her back to the small bed.

Her arms reached up for him as he lowered her. He slid atop her, letting her breasts flatten against his chest. "I love you, Cherish," he whispered while his mind could still form thoughts. "I want to spend the rest of my life loving you."

She pulled his mouth over hers and there was no more time for words, for he was taking her to the ecstasy of feeling where only he knew the way. She gave herself fully to the journey.

The buttons on her borrowed shirt popped and he mumbled, "I'm sorry," against her lips, but, for the second time that night, there was no remorse in his words and no sign of protest in her response.

31

Grayson was so exhausted he hardly had the energy to remove his clothes and wash the smoke from his face and hands before he fell into the cramped little hotel bed. Sleep blanketed him the moment his head settled onto the pillow and this time not even an earthquake and a fire could have awakened him. He rested in dreamless sleep as the night passed and the fire of Hattie's Parlor cooled.

It was full morning when he awoke. Every bone in his body felt as if it had been rearranged and needed to be snapped back into place. Slowly stretching, he turned toward the window to gauge the time by the sun.

A thin black shadow materialized on the open windowsill, as Grayson squinted and blinked away sleep.

" 'Mornin' Yank."

Grayson's good mood vanished. "I thought I announced your death last night after the fire. Just my luck, you pick me to haunt."

Brant swung his long legs from the window and stepped inside as if he'd been invited. "Don't bother to thank me for carrying you out of the flames last night. If it hadn't been for me they'd have dragged two bodies from the ashes this morning. Everyone in town is up the hill looking at the charred remains of Brant Coulter. Wart positively identified my body over an hour ago. Talk is he's going to take the reward money and ask Miss Holliday to marry him."

"She'll spend his money and leave him." Grayson laughed.

"Yeah, but he'll have the time of his life for a while. And who knows, maybe it'll work out for them. I know that fate has certainly dealt us two winning hands." Brant pointed with his head toward the Yankee's leg. "How's the wound?"

"Only sore, and not fried, thanks to someone carrying me out. I won't bother to thank you. You're dead, remember? I don't want to get caught being grateful to a ghost who, by the way, should have already disappeared."

"About that disappearing part"—Brant looked directly at Grayson—"we got a few things to settle before I go. First, I guess you already figured, I'm taking Cherish with me."

Grayson stared at the younger man, his eyebrow raising as he adopted the role of Cherish's guardian. "You'll marry her?"

Brant nodded. "I asked her on bended knee last night." He couldn't help but smile as he remembered the way she looked.

"And what did she say?"

Brant laughed. "She said she'd let me know when my beard grew."

Grayson joined in the laughter. "She's as stubborn as her aunt."

"About her aunt?" Brant began, but Grayson silenced him with a raised hand.

"I don't mind telling you I care for that woman. I plan on making her a Kirkland as soon as I can drag her, probably screaming and fighting, to the church."

Nodding, Brant moved toward the window. "That's all I needed to know." He paused as he sat on the sill. "There's a cabin an easy day's ride east of here. Follow the stream that comes down from a horseshoe ridge. You'll see it; I'll leave a trail even a Yank could follow. Cherish and I will be there for a month or so, waiting while my beard grows. You're both welcome."

Grayson nodded. "If I know Maggie, she'll want to see Cherish and there'd be hell to pay if I didn't take her. I should be able to ride within a week. Look for us then."

Brant tipped his hat. "So long, Yank. Try not to get killed while I'm on my honeymoon."

"So long, stranger." Grayson smiled, adding, "I'll see you in a week. Meanwhile, I'm going to try not to get killed during *my* honeymoon."

The thin black shadow vanished as quickly as it had appeared. Grayson was still smiling when Maggie pounded on his door moments later.

"Come in," he growled.

Maggie opened the door and hurried in like a martyr with a mission. "I've come to check your bandages," she announced, crossing the room and throwing his covers aside.

"Wait." Grayson pulled at the covers.

"Don't tell me you're getting modest after all the times I've seen your body."

Grayson laughed. "I thought you were doctoring, not looking."

Maggie raised her proper little chin. "I was doing both. It's not often a nurse gets to see such a mass of scars and wounds."

Grayson surrendered and leaned back to allow her to work. His bandages smelled of smoke, but there was no longer any blood seeping from the wounds. The damage was healing nicely.

"How did you sleep last night, my Maggie?" Lord, she looked inviting this morning. All tied up in her proper dress with lace around the collar and cuffs—like a present just waiting to be opened.

"Stop calling me your Maggie." She continued to wrap a clean dressing on his leg as if he were no more than a patient to her.

"You are my Maggie." Grayson's hand rested lightly on her knee. "What do I have to do to convince you that you belong to me and have since the first time I touched you? Marry me, woman, and let me give you a real only-ever home on a farm in Ohio. I've got more land than Bar and I could ever work and a house with more rooms than we need to rattle around in."

Maggie raised her proud chin. "I can't." She shoved his hand from her knee.

Grayson bellowed like an angry bull. "If it's because I'm from the North . . ."

Maggie stood and turned her back to him. "It isn't because you're a Yankee. That's a handicap I could learn to live with."

"Hell, woman, you say the word Yankee like it was ranked somewhere between a rattler and a skunk in your vocabulary. I think it's generous of me never to mention that you're from the South."

She glared at him with a stare that would have driven most men to drink. "It's not where we were born that has anything to do with it."

"Then what?" She was doing it again, he thought. This woman would try the patience of God Almighty. If Job had had her as a wife, he never would have made it into the Bible.

"Maybe it's because I've never heard the words," she shouted back, "but I want a husband who loves me, not one who thinks I belong to him like some cow! I'll live alone, thank you, before I'll live without a loving man."

Grayson's sudden swing off the bed cost him dearly, but he was by her side before she had time to move away. "Is that what this is all about?" His words were still angry but his blue-gray eyes were tender. "I thought you knew I loved you. Hell, I've damn near got myself killed loving you."

He pulled her against him. "I've never wanted anyone in my life the way I want you. Don't you understand that you not only belong to me, but I belong to you? Hell, woman, I don't just love you; I am part of you just as you're a big hunk of me."

Maggie pressed her lips together. "Stop yelling at me and stop swearing. I'll not have a husband that yells and swears."

Grayson smiled. "And I'll not have any wife but you." He kissed her gently. "I love you, Maggie. I've loved you since that first day we met and you fit so right at my side. I know that you were made for me. I feel it. God took a rib that protected my heart and made you. In doing so, he left my heart wide open. I want you with me for the rest of our lives. I want to eat every meal looking at your beautiful face across the table and sleep every night with you in the same bed."

Maggie laughed. "You short-sighted Yankee, I'm not beautiful. You're the only man, North or South, who ever said such a thing to me."

"Then I'm the only man not blind," Grayson whispered in her ear. "Marry me, Maggie."

"Are you sure you want to settle down with a family?"

"I want to settle down with you and Bar," he answered. "I'll raise Bar just as if he were our own son. It's time I went back to working the land like my people always have."

"And what if there are more?"

"More what?" He loved the way she always whispered into his ear. When she wasn't yelling at him, she had a way of giving him great pleasure.

"More children."

"If God blessed us with children I'd be delighted, but, Maggie, it's all right if he doesn't." He remembered Westley complaining about how Maggie couldn't get pregnant.

She moved closer into his arms. "He already has," she whispered. "So I guess I'd better marry you if I want to make you a respectable father."

The joy that pierced through the huge man almost rocked him from his feet. He forgot all about his wounds as he pulled her into his powerful arms. Kissing her soundly, he tasted the passion he loved so dearly in this woman. She was the only one he'd ever met who could stand as an equal at his side and he planned to hold her forever. When he'd made both their hearts pound, he finally let her wiggle free.

"So we're going to have a baby." Grayson felt like his heart might explode with joy.

"Not just one. I plan on filling that house of yours in Ohio. And I'm a woman who gets what I set my mind to. So you can wipe that smug smile off your face."

But Grayson didn't stop smiling all day. He was still grinning that night when he watched Mrs. Grayson Kirkland remove her prim and proper dress and come to his bed.

She might see her only-ever home within the walls of a house, but his was sleeping right there in his arms.

Epilogue

Cherish bit the thread free from her needle and handed Brant's trousers to him. "If you keep eating like you have this week, we'll have to stop in Dallas for clothes."

Brant winked at her. "It's your cooking. I can't remember ever sitting down to three meals a day. If we stay here another ten days, I may not fit through the door."

Looking up at his handsome face, now framed with a dark, short beard, Cherish smiled. "I wouldn't mind." She moved into his arms easily and held him to her, wondering if she'd ever grow tired of feeling his heart against her own.

Life had become whole during these quiet days at the dugout . . . a time of healing the wounds . . . a calm after the storm. Daniel's death and the Knights of the Golden Circle had left deep scars on Brant that only time would erase. But the fire of past events had forged a love too great for words, a love that would heal the longing in both their hearts.

There were times in the quiet stillness of predawn when Cherish lay beside Brant knowing that his life had become more precious to her than her very own. Forever did not hold enough hours to express her feelings. And now, as he looked down at her with his gentle eyes, she realized that she'd have to try and make him understand how much a part of her already belonged to him.

Brant tenderly kissed the top of her head. "I can't believe you're here with me."

She snuggled closer. "I plan to be here always. Right here in your arms."

"That's a long time," he whispered into her ear, loving the way she turned toward him.

Her lips were feather-light against his cheek. "Don't worry, my outlaw. I'll think of something to make the time pass."

Brant laughed and lifted her off the floor.

He was almost to the bed when he heard the sound of horses in the distance. His muscles tightened around her as the old fear of losing her gripped his heart.

Cherish sensed his fear even before she heard the horses. "Finally, Maggie and Grayson have come." She whispered the words as a prayer.

Brant lowered her legs and reached for his guns. "Too many horses," he answered. "When I leave, lock the door and if there is any shooting, don't open it no matter what." His words were cold and hard, but his gaze was warm with love.

"There is no need for guns," she answered as she laid her hand on his. "Trust me, Brant. People, even strangers, don't always mean danger."

Brant searched Cherish's eyes for the trust he needed and slowly removed his hands from the weapons. If they were to start a new life together, a life without the shadow of his past, it was time to set his old fears aside.

They stepped from the dugout into the evening air, his hand almost crushing hers as he waited. Horses were splashing across the stream and any minute they'd break into the clearing. The old nightmare that she might yet see him die began to pollute the peace in his mind. If she were wrong, there would be time to dive for his guns. If she were right, he'd just taken his first step into the future.

A sharp yelp sounded as a boy emerged from the trees. "I won!" he shouted as he rode full force toward the house. His lack of skill was outweighed by his youthful enthusiasm.

For a moment Brant and Cherish remained frozen as Barfield galloped toward them. The boy was laughing and waving his hat in greeting, while his mount showed no sign of slowing. Brant stepped in front of Cherish without a thought for his own safety. His quick action startled the horse and the confused animal stomped to a halt.

Bar jumped from his horse so fast that Brant dropped to a knee in an attempt to break the boy's fall. Bar nearly disappeared into a cloud of dust but straightened quickly, pulling away from Brant's helping hands. "I'm a great rider, but I have a little trouble gettin' down."

Brant dusted off the boy. "It looked like a fine dismount to me."

Bar looked up into the outlaw's face. "Good to see you again, sir . . . I mean, stranger." The boy smiled at his lie. "I don't believe we've ever met."

Brant laughed. "No, we haven't. My name's Dan, Dan Coulter."

As they shook hands, Maggie and Grayson emerged from the trees. Grayson led several horses behind him as he rode beside his mate. Within moments they were even with Brant, Cherish, and Bar.

"Tie the horses, son," Grayson ordered as he pitched the rope to Bar.

The huge man lowered himself to the ground gingerly and turned to swing Maggie from her saddle. He seemed to pay no heed to her as she ordered him to be careful of his leg and to slow his pace. Still, Brant didn't miss the way

he leaned on her every other step, counting on her strength
to keep him from limping.

Maggie and Cherish ran toward one another, laughing
and crying at the same time.

"Welcome." Brant moved to greet them, suddenly won-
dering when he'd ever used that word before. "I'm Dan
Coulter and I've been waiting to meet Cherish's Aunt
Margaret. I've heard a great deal about you."

Maggie pulled herself away from Cherish and lifted her
head to stare at the young man before her. "Well, I haven't
heard near enough about you, young man." It would take
quite a man to measure up to what she thought Cherish would
need for a husband and she planned to inspect this one closely. "So," she began without a smile, "you're Dan Coulter.
Not any kin to that outlaw Brant Coulter, are you?"

Brant forced his features to remain sober, which was more
than Grayson was doing as he stood just out of Maggie's
line of vision. "No, ma'am," Brant answered calmly. "I've
heard of him though."

Maggie walked nearer. "My husband tells me he thinks
Father Daniel married the two of you the morning after the
fire. Is that true?"

Brant darted a glance at the Yank and found him enjoying
the interrogation far too much. The outlaw squared his shoulders. "Father Daniel tied us together and blessed our union."

Cherish came to Brant's aid. "This is the man I love,
Aunt Margaret. The man I plan to spend the rest of my
life loving, so stop trying to frighten him off."

"She couldn't," Brant answered. "I know she's only looking out for you, just as I plan to do from now on."

Margaret relaxed and shifted her gaze to Cherish. "Well,
being with this Coulter man certainly agrees with you. I've
never seen you looking so happy." Maggie turned back to
Brant. "I've only a few more . . ."

"Ah . . . Dan," Grayson interrupted. "Will you help me with the horses? Maggie has some news to tell Cherish and I'm sure she doesn't want to wait any longer."

"News?" Maggie touched her stomach and frowned, knowing it was too soon to tell anyone, even Cherish, about the baby. A respectable woman didn't announce her pregnancy until she had to, and certainly not if the baby was ordered before the marriage.

Grayson winked. "About our wedding."

His wife gave a sharp nod as if she'd been set back on track. She linked arms with Cherish and headed into the house, already filling her niece in on every detail since they'd parted.

Bar followed behind the two men as they moved off to water the horses. They hadn't gone more than a few feet when Grayson reached back and pulled him up even with them. "My son walks with the men and not behind them." His love for the boy sparkled in his every word.

When the trio reached the stream, Bar busied himself tending the herd. His pride in being called Grayson's son lifted the boy a step closer to being a man.

As Grayson watched Bar moving the horses downstream, he pulled a tiny pack of brown paper from his vest pocket, unfolding the plain package carefully. "Listen, reb," he began when he figured the boy was out of hearing range. "I figure I owe you one, so I bought Cherish a ring when I picked out Maggie's. It may not be what you want, but it'll last until the two of you are settled somewhere."

Brant stared at the ring, wishing he'd thought of it. He made no effort to accept the gold band. No one had ever given him anything without wanting something in return. "What's the price?"

Grayson poked his hat back with his thumb and narrowed his eyes. He'd not insult the outlaw by just giving the ring to him. "I'm afraid there is a great favor that comes with it. If you accept the ring, you have to make me a promise to take care of Bar and Maggie if anything ever happens to me. Not that I think it ever will now that I've got Maggie to keep an eye on me, but you're the nearest to family I have, next to a cousin in Philadelphia."

For an instant the last rays of the sun caught the gold of the ring in Grayson's hand. Brant knew what the promise meant. He'd have obligations. He'd have family.

"Done." Brant took the ring, unable to say more. He straightened and stood a little taller, realizing the responsibility and trust that went with such a bargain.

As the men walked back to the house, Cherish rushed toward them. She ran into Brant's open arms as she always had, silently declaring her love.

The outlaw swung her around. When her feet finally touched ground, she turned to Grayson. "Maggie said she needs to check your bandages and see if the ride did any damage." She winked at Brant. "We'll wait out here until she's finished."

Grayson grumbled. "That woman is going to bandage me to death." He turned toward the cabin, continuing to grumble to himself, but he was already smiling at the thought of being alone with Maggie for a few minutes.

Brant pulled Cherish back toward the trees. "I need to talk to you." They walked arm in arm the short distance toward the shady quiet area beyond the cabin.

"I plan to correct a lie I just told your aunt. That woman is not someone I want to look straight in the face and tell any more lies than I have to."

They were in the tall grass by the stream before he slowed. He knelt down by the spot where they'd first made love and pulled her beside him.

"Marry me," he said.

Cherish giggled. "What, here?"

"Yes, right here, right now."

He faced her as he captured her hands in his. "Marry me, Cherish."

She saw the need in his dark eyes and nodded slowly.

He bent and kissed her hands as if in prayer, then raised his gaze to hers. "I take you this day for my wife," he started, trying to remember words he'd heard somewhere long ago. "If I owned the world, you'd be all I treasured. I promise to love and protect you for as long as I live."

The beauty of his commitment melted over her and she couldn't have felt his words deeper if they'd been said in the finest church in the world. "And I promise to love you for as long as I live. I take you this day and all the days of my life to be my husband."

Brant pulled the gold band from his pocket and slid it on her finger. A current of emotion and surprise at the sight of the ring surged through Cherish's body.

"Forever, Mrs. Coulter," he whispered.

"Forever," she answered.

Several feet away, Maggie stood and lifted the bucket she'd been filling. "Amen," she whispered as a tear trickled down her cheek.

An hour later at dinner, Maggie was silent. When the dishes were done, Cherish and Brant picked up their bedrolls to join an already sleeping Barfield in the barn.

"Good night," Cherish whispered as she kissed Maggie's cheek.

Suddenly Maggie was holding her like a frightened child. Grayson raised an eyebrow in question, but Cherish understood. She dropped the bedding and held onto Maggie, hugging her best friend for perhaps the last time, holding her tightly, as she'd held Maggie all her life, knowing that her aunt would need this hug to last a long, long time.

"I'll miss you," Maggie whispered in a voice that had suddenly lost all its hardness and direction.

"I know," Cherish answered. "But remember, ties of love stretch but never break. I'll be there in your heart, whenever you need me. Just as you will always be with me. My love will walk beside you, even though your place is with Grayson."

Maggie raised her chin as her strength returned. "And you belong with this Coulter man."

Then, to everyone's surprise, Maggie turned and hugged Brant Coulter. The outlaw blushed for the first time in his life, while Grayson's laughter filled the tiny cabin.

Praise for Colleen Quinn's <u>Wild Is the Night</u>:
*"One of those rare books that will make you
laugh and cry and feel good about yourself!"*
—*Constance O'Day Flannery, author of <u>A Time for Love</u>*

——————— COLLEEN QUINN ———————

DEFIANT ROSE

*Across the new frontier, Rose Carney ran her circus
with an unsinkable spirit that was part of her show-
business heritage. The world of fun-loving performers was her home, and no one could take that away
from her—not even the arrogant stranger who was
determined to run the show. Michael Wharton's
high-society family had financed the troupe. He'd
come west to close down this unprofitable business.
But he never dreamed he would fall for this stubborn
Irish beauty.*

___ 1-55773-672-3/$4.99

For Visa, MasterCard and American Express orders ($10 minimum) call: 1-800-631-8571

FOR MAIL ORDERS: CHECK BOOK(S). FILL
OUT COUPON. SEND TO:

BERKLEY PUBLISHING GROUP
390 Murray Hill Pkwy., Dept. B
East Rutherford, NJ 07073

NAME_____

ADDRESS_____

CITY_____

STATE_____ZIP_____

PLEASE ALLOW 6 WEEKS FOR DELIVERY.
PRICES ARE SUBJECT TO CHANGE WITHOUT NOTICE.

POSTAGE AND HANDLING:
$1.50 for one book, 50¢ for each ad-
ditional. Do not exceed $4.50.

BOOK TOTAL $ _____

POSTAGE & HANDLING $ _____

APPLICABLE SALES TAX $ _____
(CA, NJ, NY, PA)

TOTAL AMOUNT DUE $ _____

PAYABLE IN US FUNDS.
(No cash orders accepted.)

389

A CAPTIVATING NOVEL OF SUSPENSE IN THE TRADITION OF MARY HIGGINS CLARK

From the bestselling author of
If Thoughts Could Kill

CRY, BABY, CRY

G.F. Bale

She left her daughter alone for only a minute . . .
Two-year-old Jessica is missing—snatched from her
baby swing nine months ago. And now her mother,
Gwyn Martin, must live with the torment of strange
dreams and visions . . . visions of a psychopath with
a hunger for revenge.

Gwyn Martin is the chosen player.
Her baby is the prize.
The game begins.

___1-55773-643-X/$4.99

For Visa, MasterCard and American Express orders ($10 minimum) call: 1-800-631-8571

FOR MAIL ORDERS: CHECK BOOK(S). FILL
OUT COUPON. SEND TO:

BERKLEY PUBLISHING GROUP
390 Murray Hill Pkwy., Dept. B
East Rutherford, NJ 07073

NAME_____

ADDRESS _____

CITY_____

STATE_____ZIP_____

PLEASE ALLOW 6 WEEKS FOR DELIVERY.
PRICES ARE SUBJECT TO CHANGE WITHOUT NOTICE.

POSTAGE AND HANDLING:
$1.50 for one book, 50¢ for each ad-
ditional. Do not exceed $4.50.

BOOK TOTAL	$ ____
POSTAGE & HANDLING	$ ____
APPLICABLE SALES TAX (CA, NJ, NY, PA)	$ ____
TOTAL AMOUNT DUE	$ ____

PAYABLE IN US FUNDS.
(No cash orders accepted.)

381